Praise for the novels of *USA TODAY* bestselling author Delores Fossen

"The plot delivers just the right amount of emotional punch and happily ever after."
—*Publishers Weekly* on *Lone Star Christmas*

"Delores Fossen takes you on a wild Texas ride with a hot cowboy."
—*New York Times* bestselling author B.J. Daniels

"Clear off space on your keeper shelf, Fossen has arrived."
—*New York Times* bestselling author Lori Wilde

"This is classic Delores Fossen and a great read."
—*Harlequin Junkie* on *His Brand of Justice*

"This book is a great start to the series. Looks like there's plenty of good reading ahead."
—*Harlequin Junkie* on *Tangled Up in Texas*

"An amazing, breathtaking and vastly entertaining family saga, filled with twists and unexpected turns. Cowboy fiction at its best."
—*Books & Spoons* on *The Last Rodeo*

DELORES FOSSEN

SPRING AT SADDLE RUN

HQN

ISBN-13: 978-1-335-54957-0

Spring at Saddle Run

Recycling programs
for this product may
not exist in your area.

HQN
22 Adelaide St. West, 40th Floor
Toronto, Ontario M5H 4E3, Canada
www.Harlequin.com

Printed in Spain

SPRING AT SADDLE RUN

CHAPTER ONE

MILLIE PARKMAN DAYTON muttered a single word of profanity when she looked at the name on the sliver of paper that she'd just drawn from the bowl.

A really bad word.

One that would have gotten her mouth washed out with soap had she still been a kid. Because it'd been a while since anyone had crammed a bar of Dial Antibacterial into her mouth, Millie steeled herself for a mouth washing of a whole different kind.

Sitting in the front row in the town hall of Last Ride, Texas, Millie's mother, Laurie Jean Parkman, gasped and then lost nearly every drop of color in her face. No easy feat, considering she was wearing her usual full coverage makeup. After the color drained, her mom pulled out the mountain-size emotional guns.

Tears filled her eyes.

Narrowed eyes that had also gotten the full makeup treatment. Laurie Jean's now hot baby blues warned Millie she'd better think fast and figure out a way to erase everyone's memory of what she'd just said.

Making waves brings shame—that was Laurie Jean's motto. It wasn't exactly needlepointed on pillows around the Parkman house, but it'd been served up verbally and often enough with morning oatmeal and the occasional mouthful of Dial Antibacterial.

Shocked chatter rippled through the town hall. There'd be gossip. Then, pity and forgiveness. Millie knew the folks of her hometown of Last Ride would cut her enough slack to overlook the f-bomb. More slack than she would ever deserve.

Because she was a twenty-nine-year-old widow.

And because everyone in the room knew why she'd cursed. With the name she'd just drawn, life had just given Millie a big f-bomb poke in the eye.

Twenty Minutes Earlier

THE GLASS BOWLS filled with names sat like giant judging eyeballs on the table in front of the Last Ride town hall. Someone on the Last Ride Society Committee—obviously, someone with an inappropriate sense of humor—had put labels on them.

"Bowl o' Names" on the left.

Not to be confused with bag o' salad or Bowl o' Tombstones on the judgy glass "eyeball" on the right.

Millie's stomach fluttered because she knew her name was in the left bowl, a place it'd been for eight and a half years since her twenty-first birthday. She was in good, and also bad, company since the name of every living adult Parkman relative in Last Ride was in that mix with her.

At last count there were about three hundred and eighty, and names were added as her cousins, nieces, nephews, etc. came of age. Names were subtracted when cousins, nieces, nephews, Parkman spouses, etc. passed. Or fulfilled their assignments.

The right bowl was jammed with folded slivers of paper with names, as well. No more coming of age for these folks though. These were names taken from the tombstones in all the local cemeteries. Millie didn't find it comforting that the Bowl o' Tombstones was stuffed to the brim.

And that her husband's name was in there.

It had been for twenty-two months since Royce had been killed, and his name had been crammed in the mix shortly thereafter. Millie hoped it stayed there until she was part of the whole "ashes to ashes/dust to dust" deal. Then, some unlucky Parkman kin could have a go at doing their duty and do the research that would almost certainly stir up more gossip than it already had.

The memories came. Of Royce's fatal car wreck. Of the fact that Millie could no longer remember his taste. His scent. Or the last time Royce had told her he loved her. But there was something she could recall in perfect detail.

That what she'd had with Royce had been a big fat lie.

Millie felt the memories and the lies roll into a hot ball, one that would surely spiral her into a panic attack if she didn't stop it. She needed fresh air, but bolting now would cause every eye in the room to turn and look at her.

To pity her.

To whisper about her behind her back.

Millie didn't want the pity any more than the gossip or the memories so she started silently repeating the mantra that she'd latched on to shortly after the panic attacks had started.

Beyond this place, there be dragons.

It was something she'd seen written on an antique map, a way to warn travelers of dangers ahead. A beautiful map of golden land and teal green waters. The image of it soothed her and sometimes—*sometimes*—it reminded her not to go beyond the gold and teal. That if she crossed over into the dragon pit of grief, she might never come back.

Beyond this place, there be dragons.

The back door opened, bringing in yet more heat and a spear of the May sun that would warm things up even more before it set in a couple of hours. The trio of overhead fans whirled, scattering the heat, some dust motes and the clashing scents of perfumes that the majority of attendees had splashed on.

"I volunteer as tribute," the newcomer called out.

The newcomer, Frankie McCann, was decked out in a full *Hunger Games*/Katniss Everdeen costume, the cool leather one from the scenes in the last movie. She'd even braided her hair, but unlike Katniss, Frankie's locks were a blend of pink, peach and canary yellow.

Frankie's announcement caused a few giggles, including a hoot, holler and a knee slap from Alma Parkman, the president of the Last Ride Society. There were also some scowls as the "eyes" turned toward the back of the hall. Millie tried to poker up her face and show nothing. Because pretty much any kind of reaction from her would spur more of that pity and gossip. Millie also kept that blank face when Frankie sank down beside her.

Even if Frankie hadn't come decked out as Katniss, her presence would have stirred up talk, but Frankie had a right to be here. Seven years earlier, when Frankie had been barely twenty-one, she'd married Tanner Parkman, Millie's brother, and even though they'd divorced only a year later, Frankie had given birth to Tanner Junior. Or Little T as people called him. Since there hadn't been a provision in the Last Ride Society to remove divorcées or those who'd given birth to Parkmans, Frankie had remained in the Bowl o' Names. Much to the disapproval of those, well, who disapproved of a lot of things.

"Hey, this is a good turnout," Frankie remarked. Her voice was like a perky dose of sunshine. Not the kind to give you heatstroke but the extra sunny kind that felt good after a long winter.

"It is," Millie agreed. Though it was the usual turnout as far as she could tell.

There were about eighty people who fell into one of three categories. Those who truly wanted to honor their founder and ancestor, Hezzie Parkman. Those with too much time on their hands who came for Alma's homemade snickerdoodles and any gossip they might have missed. And the final group was those who made time and came only out of a sense of duty.

Millie was in that last batch.

Since Hezzie had been her great-great grandmother, Millie had come every year since her twenty-first birthday to represent her father and brother who always had an excuse not to be here. Like tonight, her mother was always in the front row, in the aisle seat. Doing her duty while looking perfect. Laurie Jean wouldn't be having a snickerdoodle, and she'd been one of the scowlers when Frankie had come in and announced herself as tribute.

As for Frankie, she was all about honoring the founder, eating the snickerdoodles and apparently having fun while doing it. Then again, having fun pretty much defined Frankie's attitude about life.

Millie envied that attitude. That warm sunshine voice. Heck, she envied Frankie. But admitting that would only put her and her mom and dad under more scrutiny. Her folks didn't need any scrutiny—as Laurie Jean so often told her.

Plenty of times her mom dressed down Tanner. And Frankie. That's because Tanner had a habit of doing whatever the heck pleased him and no longer feared Dial Antibacterial threats. Frankie owned a costume and party supply shop and also did tats and piercings on the side.

While she was good at her chosen profession, it wasn't a profession that met with Laurie Jean's approval. Also, Frankie wasn't a Parkman, or a Dayton like Royce, so DNA and career choices counted against her. In Laurie Jean's mind, a lot of things counted against a lot of people.

"Heard about what happened at the gallery," Frankie muttered to Millie.

Millie suspected—no, she *knew*—everyone in Last Ride had heard about what had gone on at Once Upon a Time, the antiques and art gallery that Millie's grandmother had left her.

"What a mess, huh?" Frankie remarked.

"Yes," Millie agreed. "*Mess* is definitely the right word for it."

Two very large macaws, Dorothy and Toto, had escaped from the pet store and had flown into Once Upon a Time when someone opened the door. Along with spilling Millie's megaslurp of coffee and scattering her stash of cherry Jolly Ranchers on the floor, the birds had toppled tables, knocked down paintings from easels and pooped on a Victorian silver nut spoon before being caught.

All the while babbling *Ding-dong the witch is dead*.

After the pet store owner had finally gotten them out, it'd taken Millie and her two employees hours to right everything and get rid of the stench.

The old clock in the front corner of the town hall finally clanged six times, and it got Alma Parkman scurrying up from her front-row seat to the podium. Yes, she scurried. Alma might be past the eighty mark, but she was spry, happy and didn't care squat if people gossiped about her. That was probably why Alma had recently announced that she was retiring as the town's librarian and pursuing a career as a stand-up comic.

"How-dee," Alma greeted. She wore a pink top and capris and had her silver-colored hair pulled up in a way that resembled a mini palm tree on top of her head. "Welcome, Parkmans. And Katniss." She winked at Frankie.

No wink for Millie though when Alma's attention landed on her. The pity practically gushed right out of Alma, causing Millie to dole out her customary response. A polite smile followed by the poker face. Millie had gotten good at plastering it on.

"All righty, then." Alma put on her thick reading glasses before picking up the gavel. "I'm calling to order this meeting of the Last Ride Society." She banged the gavel three times. "We'll start with a reading of the rules." Alma looked down at the paper she'd brought to the podium with her and gave an exaggerated frown. "Hey, who scribbled that the first rule of Last Ride Society is there are no rules?"

Frankie and Alma giggled like loons, but many just looked confused. Probably because they didn't get the *Fight Club* reference. Others because they didn't approve of having a lick of fun.

"I confess, I'm the scribbler," Alma continued, still snickering. "Just trying out some of my new routine. But here I go for real." Her expression grew serious. "Our illustrious town founder, Hezzie Parkman, created the Last Ride Society shortly before her death in 1950, and each and every one of you honor Hezzie by being here this evening. Honor, tradition, family. Those are the cornerstones that make Last Ride our home."

Even though it was a short speech that Alma gave every quarter, Millie saw a few people dab tears from their eyes.

Alma held up one finger to indicate the first rule. "A drawing will take place quarterly on the first day of February, May, August and November in the Last Ride town hall. The winner of the previous quarter will draw the name of his or her successor."

Nearly everyone glanced at Ruby Chaney, last quarter's winner. She definitely fell into the category of gobbling up this particular duty. She gave everyone a wave, obviously enjoying the last couple of minutes of her "celebrity" status.

"Second rule," Alma said, lifting another finger. "The winner must research the person whose tombstone he or she draws. A handout will be given to the winner to better spell out what needs to be done, but research should be conducted at least once weekly as to compile a thorough report on the deceased. The report will be added to the Last Ride Society Library."

Since the library occupied the large back room of Once Upon a Time, Millie often caught glimpses of the reports that had started more than half a century ago. Some had been bound professionally and were several inches thick. Others were handwritten and obviously hastily done. Ruby's recent addition was over five hundred pages on a spinster who'd died back in the late 1800s.

"Final rule," Alma went on. "On the completion of the research by the winner, five thousand dollars from the Hezzie Parkman trust will be donated to the winner's chosen town charity."

"I'm hoping it's me this year," Frankie muttered. "The baseball field needs fixing up."

Millie was hoping it was Frankie, too. Not only because the woman wanted it but because Frankie was right about the baseball field needing a face-lift. Millie made a mental note to set up a donation drive for just that.

"And now to the drawing." Alma used the gavel to drum out her obvious excitement. "Ruby, come on up to the Bowl o' Names and get to drawing."

Ruby waved again and smiled at the applause. What she didn't do was hurry. Not one little bit. Still obviously trying to hang on to her moment, Ruby crept to the table and hovered her hand over the bowl. Probably to boost excitement. Many probably hoped she'd just hurry so they could spoil their dinners with those snickerdoodles.

Ruby finally reached into the bowl, swirling around the slivers of paper, paused, swirled some more. Only when people started to groan and grumble did she finally pluck one.

Ruby beamed and looked directly at her. "Millie Parkman," the woman announced.

Oh, man. What kind of crap-ery was this? Suddenly all eyes were on her. Exactly where Millie didn't want them to be.

"Congrats, Millie," Alma muttered.

There were no congrats whatsoever in Alma's tone or expression. No doubt because she, and everyone else in the room, were considering that Millie digging into that Bowl o' Tombstones would maybe bring back the memories and grief over losing Royce. But Millie didn't have to dig into a bowl to recall that memory. Everything brought it back. *Everything.*

Millie forced herself to stand, and she got moving toward the front. She silently cursed the macaws because she could have used both the caffeine and sugar fix to get her through this. Unlike Ruby, she didn't dawdle, didn't make a production of it. Millie simply went to the Bowl o' Tombstones and snagged the first one her fingers touched. She unfolded the paper.

Her heart went to her knees.

And she blurted out the really bad word.

"The name is Ella McCann," Millie managed to say when she got her mouth unfrozen.

The room went tombstone-silent, but Millie figured there was already some mental gossip going on.

Frankie jumped to her feet. "I volunteer as tribute," she repeated.

Millie considered taking her up on the offer. Considered shirking the duty that had been drummed into her since childhood. Parkman duty. Parkman pride. But it was more than that. It was spine. It would probably come as a surprise to many, but she did indeed have one. And Millie was about to prove that.

To them.

To herself.

Even if Ella McCann deserved each and every f-bomb that Millie would ever mutter, she'd do this. She'd research the "other" woman. She'd dig into the life of the woman who'd died in the arms of Millie's husband.

CHAPTER TWO

SAYING A WORD that would require him to put a dollar in the swear jar, Joe McCann sat back on the barn floor and frowned at the calf he'd just pulled from the still-grunting cow. The cow, a registered Red Angus with some pretty impressive bloodlines, turned her head and aimed a bovine eye at her newest offspring.

A white bull calf.

White.

A big one, too. Joe figured it'd tip the scales at a hundred pounds which was why the cow had needed Joe's help with the delivery.

"Got something you want to tell me?" Joe asked the cow. According to her ear tag, she was number eighty-four, but Joe called her Cowlick because of the way bits of her hair stuck up on her head.

Mentally thumbing back to the breeding spreadsheet he kept, Cowlick had been in the back east pasture with bull number three, who was also a registered Red Angus with an equally impressive bloodline.

Joe figured it was projecting on his part, but Cowlick seemed to look somewhat embarrassed about the lack of red coloring for her bouncing baby boy. Then again, maybe she was just blushing over the recollection of being covered by two bulls in the span of just a couple of days. Both the number three Red Angus and a white Charolais bull that had almost certainly broken fence from a neighbor's pasture.

Clearly, the white Charolais with a questionable lineage had won out in this particular gene pool battle, and his victory would play hell to havoc with the ranch's reputation. Saddle Run Ranch might be small, but the whole notion of being one hundred percent Red Angus registered meant something to him.

Then again, plenty of things that'd once meant something no longer did.

And, cursing, that was all the pity party he was going to allow himself today.

Joe's phone dinged with a text again. Which he ignored, again. His hands were covered with afterbirth that he didn't want on his phone. Besides, the only person he'd actually want to take a text from—his thirteen-year-old daughter, Dara—was in the house. If she needed to talk to him, she could walk the twenty yards or so to the barn or call out from the porch.

When Cowlick started cleaning her baby boy, Joe got up from the barn floor. He would have lingered a few moments, watching cow and calf get to know each other, but he heard something else that had him frowning. Not a ding from a text but the sound of an approaching vehicle.

Hell.

He checked his watch. It was a little after seven, not a time for unexpected visitors. Figuring it was one of the teenage boys who'd been sniffing around Dara, Joe didn't bother cleaning up. However, he did grab an axe from the tack room. He might be fairly new at the whole "father of a teenage daughter" thing, but axes tended to send a solid message.

And that message was—I'll chop off your dick if you try to dick around with my child.

Of course, he wouldn't actually resort to that sort of thing. Probably not, anyway. But it didn't hurt for the boys to believe he would.

Propping the axe on his shoulder, Joe walked to the front of the house just as his visitor was getting out of his truck. Not a teenage boy though, but rather Tanner Parkman.

There'd been a time, say about seven years ago, when Joe had wanted to do some dick chopping on the bad boy Tanner. That'd been about the time Tanner had knocked up Joe's kid sister, Frankie. But Tanner and Frankie had ended up getting married. For a short time, anyway. And they'd had a kid, Joe's one and only nephew.

While Tanner still had some of his bad boy ways, he was also doing the dad thing well enough, along with running the town's only motorcycle repair shop. Of course, a business like that didn't live up to the silver-spoon standards for Tanner's family, but it seemed to make Tanner happy enough.

Little T, aka Tanner Larkin Parkman Jr., got out from the other side of the truck, slamming the door behind him and making a beeline for Joe.

"You got an axe," Little T announced with all the enthusiasm of a six-year-old on a sugar high. Little T was as blond as the moon, had a spattering of freckles over his nose and jumped and wiggled when he talked. "Can I have it?"

"Yeah," Joe said, "when you're thirty and eleven feet tall. Are you thirty and eleven feet tall?"

Little T considered that a moment and gave Joe a sheepish look similar to the one the cow had. "I soon will be."

"Then, you can come back for the axe," Joe assured him, and he turned his attention to Tanner. "You can't have the axe, either, but I'm guessing you're here to ask Dara to babysit. If so, she's inside."

"Thanks, but I came about something else." Tanner looked at him as if waiting for that *something else* to magically appear, and then he glanced at Joe's shirt and jeans. "Did you just pull a calf?"

"Yeah." Which meant he probably stank if Tanner could pick up on what he'd been doing. "Sore subject though so don't ask to see it."

That seemed to intrigue Tanner a little, but then he shook his head. "Nobody's got in touch with you yet?"

"About what?" Joe thought about the text dings he'd heard, and he got a bad feeling.

"Son of a monkey," Tanner grumbled. A dad substitute for what Tanner frequently used to say. Still did say it sometimes when he forgot. "Tonight was the quarterly meeting of the Last Ride Society…"

His words trailed off as a car turned into Joe's driveway. He shifted the axe in case this was a teenage boy, but he soon saw it wasn't. Tanner's sister, Millie, was behind the wheel, and she brought the pricey but conservative-looking gray Lexus to a slow stop behind her brother's truck.

And some puzzle pieces fell into place for Joe.

Hell's Texas bells.

He hoped this was a really bad joke.

Even though Millie and he lived in the same small town, it'd been months since Joe had laid eyes on her. Of course, he'd dodged a couple of potential encounters by simply turning around and going home when he'd seen her. Added to that, he never went within two blocks of her shop. Joe bet she'd done her own share of dodging him, too.

Millie stepped out of her car and gave Joe a tentative smile. She had the moon-blond hair deal, too, and the Parkman blue eyes like Little T's. Ditto for the spattering of freckles, but she covered hers up with makeup.

"Aunt Millie!" Little T squealed, and he bolted toward her. "Uncle Joe says I can have the axe when I'm tall and old. He might give it to you though so you can give it to me."

"Are you saying I'm old and tall?" she asked, giving the kid an exaggerated beady eye.

Little T's forehead bunched up, and he was obviously trying to come up with the right answer. "Sort of," he settled for saying. Joe figured in Little T's mind Millie's five-eight height was indeed tallish, and since she wasn't a kid, she'd fall into his definition of old.

Millie shrugged. "Fair enough, but dream on, kid. I'm not getting the axe for you."

But she leaned down and gave him a noisy kiss on the top of his head. Then, she followed it with a hug that was warm, long and filled with love. Love that definitely wasn't in her eyes when they turned back in Joe's direction.

"Tanner told you?" she asked.

"No—" Tanner started.

Joe interrupted him. "I'm guessing you drew Ella's name at the Last Ride Society."

Millie nodded. No love in those blue eyes now. Just a bone-deep sadness that Joe totally got. Of course, there was always sadness on those rare occasions when they saw each other. Sadness. A squirming unease.

And questions.

Always questions.

Joe was reasonably sure that Millie didn't have any more answers than he did as to why her husband had been in the fatal car wreck with his wife.

"Heard you cussed in front of the Last Ride Society,"

Tanner said to her, maybe to break the squirming uneasiness. Or the sadness. "Is that true?"

Dragging in a deep breath, Millie seemed to steel herself. "True. It rhymes with *duck*."

Joe nearly cursed in surprise. As her nickname Millie Vanilla indicated, she wasn't the cursing-in-public sort. She was as quiet and concealed as her freckles. He figured some of his unread texts would be about the drawing. Some would be about the duck-rhyming curse word.

"Did birds really poop on your spoon?" Little T asked her, tugging at the sleeve of her pale blue shirt.

She took another of those breaths. "Not mine exactly but *a* spoon in the shop. And they trashed my stash of Jolly Ranchers. They cracked them with their beaks and spit them out."

Little T shook his head in disgust. "Son of a monkey. That's not right," he exclaimed. Like father, like son. But Joe hoped that in about ten years or so, his nephew wouldn't continue the traditions of his daddy's bad boy ways.

The three adults volleyed glances at each other. Awkward ones. Tanner obviously picked up on it and scooped up Little T. "Let's head home and start getting you ready for bed."

That went over about as well as Joe knew it would. Little T did lots of groaning and protesting as he made his goodbyes and got back in the truck with his dad.

Joe and Millie waved. Waited for the truck to pull out of the driveway. Then, waited some more. And yeah, this awkwardness kicked up a whole bunch of notches.

"Are you auditioning for a role in a horror movie?" she asked, breaking the silence. She tipped her head toward his shoulder, then his torso. "Axe. Covered with gunk."

"It's a deterrent for any boy who might come to visit Dara."

She nodded. "It could work."

And with small talk apparently exhausted, the silence came again. For a couple of seconds, the only sounds were a buzzing of a mosquito and Millie slapping at it. Where there was one mosquito, more would certainly follow, so Joe hoped she'd put a quick end to this visit.

She reached in her pocket, pulled out a folded paper and handed it to him. "That's the handout to explain what I'm supposed to do for the tombstone research. I stopped by my office and made you a copy."

Joe groaned, wadded it into a ball and stuck it in his pocket. It'd go in the trash first chance he got.

"You could say no," he told Millie. "You could tell the Last Ride Society to *duck* it."

The corners of her mouth lifted in a smile that didn't make it to her eyes. "I could, but it'd be easier if I just got it done."

He groaned and set down the axe so he could prop his hand on the handle. "It'd be easier if you just didn't do it at all. Why the hell would you want to do it?" he added in a snarl.

She sighed, kicked the axe blade. "Haven't you heard? I'm the good girl. The one who always does what she's supposed to do. I'm Millie Vanilla."

"You cursed in front of the Last Ride Society," he pointed out.

"Well, I slip every now and then. Trust me, I'll pay for it," she muttered.

Yeah, she probably would. Her mother was hell on wheels when it came to being a proper Parkman. Laurie Jean would definitely prefer Millie Vanilla to her only daughter cursing in the town hall.

"If I don't do it, someone else will," Millie said. "Probably Frankie since she volunteered."

Joe cursed, not going with the duck version, either, which meant he now needed to put two dollars in the swear jar.

"Don't blame Frankie," Millie added. "She knew how hard this would be and wanted to spare me. But she can't spare me. If I pass this on to someone else, then there'll still be talk because everyone will know it was too hard for me to do. That I'm just as wounded and hurt as I was twenty-two months ago."

"Aren't you just as wounded and hurt?" And he immediately wished he hadn't asked. Because he already knew the answer.

This was why he avoided Millie. Why he avoided talking about Ella, period.

"Yes," Millie softly admitted. She whirled around, looking at the barn instead of at him. "I'll always be hurt. Always be wounded. But the poor-pitiful-Millie looks and mutters of 'Bless your heart' will be worse than me just getting it done."

Joe wasn't so sure of that at all. Then again, his scowl usually took care of any pitying looks. "You'll trade mutters of 'Bless your heart' for back pats of 'Brave little soldier.'"

Her sigh was long, deep and acknowledged that he was right. "I'm not going to dig deep in certain areas," Millie went on. "Nothing about the last twenty-four hours of her life. Ella's life," she emphasized, and she'd said his wife's name as if it were a hunk of jagged glass stuck in her throat.

Joe would probably experience the same sensation if he

ever said her husband's name aloud. But he had no plans for that. No plans to drag all of this muck out into the open again.

"If you're here to ask for my help with the research, my answer is no," Joe spelled out.

Her nod was quick as if that was the exact response she'd expected. "I understand. I just didn't want you or your daughter to be blindsided by the talk this will stir up."

It was the mention of Dara that stopped him cold. Millie hadn't said it in the same hunk-of-glass tone but with a Texas-sized amount of concern. Shit. Dara would indeed hear about the drawing, and it'd bring it all to the surface for her. And Millie was right—that would happen whether or not she did the research. This particular son of a monkey was already out of the bag.

"I'll talk to Dara," he said, and he let that stand as a goodbye. Joe turned to head back to the barn to ditch the axe.

Just as Cowlick and the bull calf came moseying out.

The sun might be close to setting, but there was still plenty of light for him, and Millie, to see the pair. The colors were an even starker contrast now that Cowlick had cleaned her boy up a bit.

"Bet there's a story behind that," she murmured.

Joe stood there and waited until he heard Millie go back to her car. Until she drove away. Then, he cursed twenty dollars' worth, counting off each of the words that only the mosquitos could hear. He gave himself a moment before he herded Cowlick and the calf back inside the barn. He put the axe back in the tack room, and this time, he remembered to shut the barn door.

If only he could fix his life as easily.

He glanced at the lights in the house. Dara was still in

her bedroom, probably doing her homework or watching TV. They'd had an early dinner and already cleaned up the dishes because of Cowlick's labor so there was nothing left to do in the kitchen. Deciding his gunked-up clothes could wait, too, he headed to his man-shed.

When Joe had bought the ranch ten years earlier, it'd been just that. A shed. But he'd added insulation, flooring, even heat and AC so Ella could use the space to play around with her hobby—painting. Since he didn't have any hobbies, Joe used the shed for, well, thinking and brooding. Probably not a wise use, but it was what it was. He didn't want to brood inside the house where Dara might see him. She had enough of her own pain and grief without adding his to the mix.

Some of the pictures that Ella had painted were hanging unframed on the walls. So was the sign she'd hung over her easel. La La Land. Not a complete joke since she was oblivious to everything around her when she got caught up in a painting.

Normally, Joe would look at the artwork and try to remember that his life hadn't always been about dealing with the aftermath of her death.

He didn't do that tonight.

First, he scrubbed his hands in the small half bath and pulled a twenty and two ones from his wallet. He shoved them into the swear jar on the worktable. Then, he snagged a beer from the dorm-sized fridge and sank down into the recliner he'd moved in a couple of months earlier. It was ratty, stained and worn which made it an appropriate chair for a man-shed, and he sat there to study a different picture. Not on the wall but rather the one in his head.

The one of Ella and him on their wedding day thirteen and a half years ago.

No church wedding but rather vows exchanged at a justice of the peace. Mercy, they'd been young. Ella barely twenty-one and him twenty-three. Ella had worn a yellow dress that was only a few shades darker than her hair, and she'd been happy. Her smile in that mental photo was a mile wide, and there had practically been little cartoon hearts coming from her eyes when she looked at him. She'd been in love and thrilled to the bone that she was already three months pregnant with their "love child" as she'd called Dara.

There were times, like now, that Joe wished the image in his head wasn't there. That he could erase it and latch on to another one—like six months later when Ella was cradling a newborn Dara at the hospital. But that particular picture stayed firmly in Dara's baby book, not in his head.

Cursing another five dollars' worth, he lifted open the arm storage on the recliner. A spot meant for a TV remote, but that's where Joe kept the receipt from a grocery store in nearby San Antonio. The one Ella had used to scribble out the note she'd left for him.

Or rather scribble out the lie.

"Leaving for my spa day. Be back tonight. Love you, E."

After the car wreck that'd killed her, the cops had checked. There'd been no spa appointment. No appointment of any kind they could find for either Ella or Millie's husband. There'd also been no luggage in the vehicle so the pair probably hadn't been running away for good. Just maybe slipping off together. To do things that Joe didn't want to think about.

The ink was fading on the receipt, but he could still read the purchases that Ella had made the day she'd died. A gallon of two percent milk, Wheat Thins crackers, an Almond Joy candy bar.

And a One-Step Pregnancy Test.

Joe closed his eyes to shut out the words on both the front and the back of the receipt, and he let the grief—fresh and raw—wash over him.

CHAPTER THREE

THE NEXT DAY, Millie read the first thing on her research to-do list, and she sighed. *Take a current picture of the tombstone of the person you're researching.*

That's when the reality of what she was doing gave her another hard smack upside the head.

To get that picture, she'd have to go to Ella McCann's grave. She'd no doubt have to see the date of the woman's death that would be carved into marble or some other kind of stone. And that date was going to bring on the mother lode of memories for her since it was Royce's death date, too.

Of course, Millie didn't actually need to see anything like headstones or death dates to take jabs at those memories. Too much of that fateful day was still plenty fresh in her mind.

Too much of what she didn't know was fresh, as well.

She hadn't read the medical examiner's report, but she'd heard things about it. One of those things was that the crash had critically injured both Ella and Royce, but neither had died right away. In fact Ella had had the time to unhook her seat belt and had used her last breath and final bit of energy to move over onto Royce, putting her head on his shoulder. Royce had used his last breath and energy to wrap his arms around Ella.

Since Millie had heard the "wrap his arms" and "on his

shoulder" parts from one of the cops who'd been a first responder on the scene, she figured it was true. The only thing that could have added more sting to that image was for Ella to have had some recent hickeys. Or for Royce to have had a pocketful of condoms. But there'd been none of that, only the comforting gestures that were far more intimate than hickeys or condoms.

In those last moments of their lives, they'd sought, and found, each other.

"Hey, Millie," she heard someone call out. It was Monte Klein, one of the sales associates at Once Upon a Time. With his hand over the mouthpiece of the old-fashioned cordless landline phone they used at the checkout desk, he stuck his head in the doorway of her office. "Mr. Lawrence wants to talk to you about buying some of his art."

Millie frowned because the sculptures of Mr. Lawrence— aka Lawrence Parkman—weren't art. More like art attempts. They were replicas of famous landmarks—the Alamo, the Statue of Liberty, etc.—but the pieces often just resembled blobs of clay.

Normally, Millie wouldn't have welcomed such a distraction, but she was sinking fast into the pit of "arms, a shoulder and intimacy" so she didn't give an automatic dismissal to Monte. She checked her watch, calculated that it would take her less than a half hour to get out to the cemetery, take the photo and get back. Then, she could tick off the first item on her checklist.

"Tell Mr. Lawrence he can meet me in my office in an hour," Millie said, getting to her feet.

Monte's right eyebrow, which was pierced with three dime-sized gold hoops, winged up, causing those hoops to jiggle. "Mr. Lawrence," he repeated as if she'd recently been robbed of hearing and all common sense.

"One hour," Millie verified. "I probably won't buy anything, but I can at least show him some respect by meeting with him."

Monte frowned and gave her a level-eyed look. "He was at the town hall when you dropped the f-stinker?"

"He was," Millie admitted. As usual, Mr. Lawrence had been seated directly behind her mother which meant he'd been in very good hearing range. But this wasn't a case of smoothing over feathers ruffled by bad words.

Well, maybe it wasn't.

She'd followed the vanilla straight line for so long that she wasn't sure she knew why she did the things she did.

Millie grabbed her purse and what was left of her to-go cup of coffee and headed out of her office. She was only halfway to the shop's front door when it opened, and she saw someone else with ruffled feathers.

Her mother.

Correction: *her pissed-off mother.*

Coming straight toward Millie, Laurie Jean ignored Monte's cheery greeting which was more sarcasm than cheeriness, and her mother maneuvered Millie away from Monte and into the nook that contained a collection of Edwardian boudoir pieces. Her mother didn't even take the time to gather her breath, or turn up her nose at what she always considered "junk," before she dived right into her tirade.

"I've been on the phone all morning, trying to smooth over the disaster you created for your family." Laurie Jean snapped out the words while still managing to whisper. "But you've got to do some damage control of your own."

"Damage control?" Millie questioned.

Laurie Jean's nod was fast and crisp. "You need to write an apology to each and every member of the Last Ride

Society. Explain that you're still grieving for your husband and that you had a temporary breakdown when you drew that trashy woman's name."

Normally, hearing her mother say "that trashy woman" wouldn't have gotten a rise from Millie. In fact, Millie had actually thought plenty worse about Ella. But this morning, the rise came, and it rose and rose until a response bubbled out of Millie's mouth.

"Should I use the actual word I said in the apology?" Millie coolly asked. "You know, just to jog their memories."

The look that her mother gave her could have taken the scalding heat out of an erupting volcano, and Millie groaned. Yes, she'd gotten some immediate satisfaction in tossing that at her mom, but it could ignite a thousand gallons of retaliation from Laurie Jean.

"I'm sorry," Millie quickly added before her mother could unclench her jaw enough to let loose. "I'm still grieving, and all of this is getting to me." And she just kept on talking while Laurie Jean's heated eyes drilled into her. "I'll write the apologies, and I'll finish the Last Ride Society research ASAP. In fact, that's where I was heading now, to take care of the first thing on the to-do list."

Laurie Jean opened her mouth, no doubt to ramp up her blasting, so Millie knew she had to move faster than her mother's words. She didn't succeed though.

"I heard someone mention my parents." Laurie Jean's bottom lip trembled. "Both my mother and father used language like that, and some people think that sort of thing passes down through the bloodline. *My parents*," she repeated with the tremble and hurt in her voice.

That was the big guns for her mom. Laurie Jean rarely brought up anything about her parents. They'd died when

Laurie Jean had been a teenager so the only thing Millie knew about them was from gossip.

If the sources were anywhere near reliable, and that was questionable, Millie's maternal grandparents had been dirt poor scum from West Texas. Possibly criminals, depending on who was doling out the gossip. They'd possibly been murdered, or killed each other, again depending on who was telling the tale.

Laurie Jean no doubt considered their passing a blessing since she'd then been sent to Last Ride to live with her mother's cousin, Freida, who'd married into the Granger family. The Grangers had as much money and prestige as the Parkmans and Daytons and had raised Laurie Jean as one of their own. In turn, Laurie Jean had spent most of her adult life trying to shake off the bone-deep scars from her "unacceptable" roots, especially after marrying Millie's father, a Parkman. Hearing her parents' names being bandied about would no doubt take a poke at Laurie Jean's scars again.

"I'm sorry," Millie told her, and she meant it.

She couldn't understand why those roots would bring her such misery, but then Millie hadn't done the metaphorical walk in her mother's shoes. That's why she would write those apologies and do whatever was necessary to shift the gossip away from her mother and back onto her.

"I'll take care of it," Millie assured her, and she dropped a kiss on her mother's cheek. "Sorry, but I have to go now so I can get back in time for an appointment."

"She does have an appointment," Monte called out to confirm.

Of course, he'd been listening and would gripe to Millie later about how she should have stood up to her mother.

In turn, Millie would gripe to him about eavesdropping. Neither gripe would amount to anything.

Millie hurried to her car in the back parking lot of the shop and she sped off. She used the drive to curse her mother's crappy childhood, the name she'd drawn from the Bowl o' Tombstones. She even cursed her ancestor Hezzie for setting all of this in motion.

Millie totally got Hezzie's reasons for wanting to preserve the history of the area since Hezzie had been the creator of that early history. Hezzie had been a young widow, just twenty years old, when she'd founded Last Ride, and she'd used the money her late husband had left her to do that.

There were enough history books and recollection of Hezzie for Millie to know that the woman had started the town by building a church, a grocer and a guesthouse on what would become Main Street. Hezzie had personally run all three for several years before marrying her second husband, a rich rancher, who'd added, added and added to what would become his wife's legacy. After he'd passed, Hezzie's third and last husband had added even more.

Life had basically doled out lemons to Hezzie by making her a young widow, and the woman had made a whole lot of lemonade. It made Millie feel like a failure. She owned a business that she'd inherited and hadn't moved out of the grief rut after losing Royce.

Sighing, wallowing some in self-pity and wishing she'd brought some Jolly Ranchers with her, she drove by Parkman's Passed, the large cemetery that some called Hoity-Toity Hill. She kept driving, thankful that she wouldn't have to go past Still Waters, the Dayton family cemetery where Royce was buried.

Where his parents were, too.

They'd been in their forties when Royce had been born and had moved to Last Ride when he'd been a baby so his father could be closer to his own aging parents. Royce had lost those grandparents when he'd been in elementary school. Then, both his parents had passed away a few years before their only son's car accident. His father, from colon cancer. His mother, an aneurysm. Not exactly peaceful ways to die, but at least they hadn't had to deal with losing their son. Especially losing him the way he'd died.

Still Waters was on the other side of town, and she avoided it when she could. Before today, Millie had done the same to Hilltop, a nonfamily, nondenominational cemetery where Ella was buried. But today, she made the turn onto the rock and gravel road that coiled up the sprawling hill that had obviously given the place its name.

It didn't take her long to spot the headstones. Dozens of them on the front side of the hill, with probably dozens more on the back, and it occurred to her that she didn't have a clue where to look for Ella's grave. Since it would likely be one of the more recent ones, she might be able to spot the *newness* of it. Taking a hit of coffee, she got out and started the hunt.

When she'd dressed for work that day in one of her usual skirts and tops, she hadn't taken into account that she'd be walking on gravel and grass, so Millie did plenty of wobbling in her heeled sandals. Moving as fast as she could, she scanned the names on the tombstones. No Ella. And none of the white tombstones showed either age or lack thereof.

Her ankles were hurting, she was huffing a little and she'd worked up an uncomfortable sticky sweat by the time she reached the top of the hill. And her heart skittered a couple of too-fast beats when she practically came face-to-face with the girl. A teenager with thick brown hair. She was wearing shorts, a red top and flip-flops, and she was standing next to Ella's grave.

"Hey," the girl said.

Even though Millie had never met her, she instantly knew who this was. Dara, Joe and Ella's daughter. She'd been eleven when her mother had died so that meant she was thirteen now, and she'd definitely gotten her looks from her father.

"Hey," Millie managed.

Dara didn't smile, but there was something welcoming and pleasant enough about her expression that didn't send Millie running. However, Millie did start to ease away so she could give the girl privacy for this visit with her mom.

"Dad's over there." Dara tipped her head toward the bottom of the hill.

Millie shifted in that direction. With his arms folded over his chest, boots crossed at the ankles, a gray Stetson tipped low over his face, Joe was leaning against his truck that was parked beneath a sprawling live oak. Because of the Stetson and the shade from the tree, Millie couldn't see his face, but she was betting there was nothing pleasant or welcoming about it. When she'd gone to tell him about the drawing, he'd made it clear enough that he didn't want her digging into Ella's life.

"Dad doesn't like coming here so he hangs back," Dara went on. "But he drives me here at least once a week so I can bring Mom flowers. She loved daisies."

That drew Millie's attention back to the grave. And yes, there was a bouquet of daisies lying just beneath the headstone.

"They're pretty," Millie remarked. Her voice was clogged as if she was catching a cold, and she fluttered her fingers in the direction of her car. "I'm sorry I interrupted you. I'll just be going."

However, Millie barely made it a step before Dara's question stopped her in her tracks.

"Do you hate my mom?" the girl asked, and she didn't give Millie a chance to respond. "I hear what people say when they're whispering about her and your husband."

Those blasted whispers. Millie certainly hadn't thought she was the only recipient of them, but it would have put some good karma in the world if this young girl had been excluded from such things.

"No. I don't hate her," Millie said.

That wasn't anywhere close to the truth. Of course, there was hate. This was the woman who'd probably been Royce's lover. Maybe even a longtime one.

Dara stared at her as if trying to decide if she believed her or not. "Good," the girl finally concluded. "Because my mom was nice. Pretty, too."

Millie wondered which of those traits had attracted Royce. Maybe both. Or maybe he'd been attracted to her simply because she hadn't been anything like his wife.

"People talk about her because she got pregnant with me before she married my dad," Dara continued. "But Mom said let 'em talk, that she got the best deal ever by having me and she wouldn't have changed that for the world."

This seemed like TMI and personal, but Millie couldn't figure out a way to stop this flood of information that she didn't want. The girl was grieving for her mother. Missing her. And Dara hadn't been responsible for anything that'd happened between Ella and Royce.

"I understand," Millie muttered because she honestly didn't have a clue what else to say.

Dara shrugged. "Mom wanted more kids, but it didn't

happen. She said that made her sad for a long time but then she accepted that I'd be her one and only beautiful butterfly. She loved butterflies, too," the girl added.

Millie knew all about that. Wanting a baby and not having it happen. She'd never used birth control when Royce and she had been married, and she hadn't gotten pregnant in the entire five years.

No beautiful butterflies for her.

When she'd pressed Royce about them seeing a fertility specialist, he'd nixed the idea. At the time, Millie had thought it was because he hadn't been ready to be a father, but now she wondered if it had more to do with Ella McCann. It probably wouldn't do to knock up your wife while banging your mistress.

Millie shook her head, hoping that last thought would fly right out of it.

"I know you drew my mom's name at the society deal in the town hall. I'll help you with the research if you want," Dara said, yanking Millie's attention back to her.

Three responses came to mind. *Huh?* was Millie's first reaction. Followed by a mentally stuttered *What?* and *Why?*

"I want to help you," Dara amended, "so you won't just write up what other people are saying about her. I knew her better than all those nosy gossips."

Possibly. But Millie doubted Ella had shared any details about a lover with her young daughter.

"It's a generous offer," Millie finally answered, and she tried to choose her words carefully. "But I don't want to bring up any painful memories for you."

"It won't," Dara quickly assured her. She tapped her head. "It's all there, anyway. Just want to make sure you get things right about her. But there's a catch," the girl added. "I'd want you to help me with something."

Millie said that stuttered "H-huh?" aloud this time.

"I'd want you to help do some...things," Dara said.

Oh, Millie didn't like the girl's hesitation before that last word. "Define 'things.'"

Dara looked her straight in the eyes. "My bucket list."

Of all the responses Millie had considered Dara might say, that wasn't one of them. Not even close. "Uh, do thirteen-year-old girls have a bucket list?" she asked.

"I do," Dara assured her.

Okay. Maybe everyone had a list of stuff they wanted to experience. She personally didn't, but then it'd been a while since she'd thought of something she might like to do in the future. Most days, she was still just doing the minute-to-minute deal.

"Wait," Millie said when a thought occurred to her. A bad thought. "You're not like sick or anything, are you?"

"Nope. Healthy as a horse. Whatever that means. I mean, all horses can't be healthy." She waved that off before Millie could say she'd wondered the same thing about that particular idiom. "There are just some things I want to do while I'm still thirteen."

Millie's imagination started to run wild. "Does your bucket list involve anything, uh, illegal?" she pressed.

Dara's forehead bunched up. "Probably not. No," the girl amended when Millie just stared at her.

So, that meant it probably had some questionable things on it. Definitely not something Millie would jump into headfirst.

"Tell you what," Millie offered. "You write up the list, and once I've looked it over, I'll let you know." After Millie had talked to Joe, that is. For now, she took out her phone. "I can give you my number."

"I'll drop it by your shop after I've figured out everything I want to put on it." Dara turned back to her mother's headstone. "Now, I gotta go over some things with Mom. And yes, I know she's not here but I'd rather talk to her when I can see her name spelled out."

It was a polite way of asking for Millie to leave, and she did turn to do that. But not before she gave a longing look at the headstone. Apparently, she wouldn't be snapping that picture today.

"I'll just have a quick word with your father before I go," Millie muttered, heading in Joe's direction.

He lifted his head, easing off his Stetson and following her shaky walk down the hill toward him. The closer she got, the more she saw of him.

Oh, mercy. He looked tall and tasty standing there with his long, lean body and rumpled dark brown hair. Her body didn't let her forget the tasty part, either, and she went warm in places that the sun hadn't touched.

The wrong places.

This was the textbook definition of *inappropriate*. She was getting a lust kick from a man who was at the cemetery where his wife was buried. And Millie didn't even want to get started on the inappropriateness of that particular man's wife being her husband's lover.

Beyond this place, there be dragons.

That applied here, too. Joe wasn't a red-scaled creature lurking beneath the teal waters and perched on the edge of golden-colored land, but he could give her grief of a whole different kind.

And pleasure, the wrong place of her body quickly added.

But she couldn't afford the kind of grief she'd get in exchange for that pleasure. Which she was certain would be, well, very pleasurable.

"I'm sorry," she said. "I didn't know you'd be here."

He grunted.

And heaven help her, even that sounded like a testosterone-doused invitation. She was sure her own grunt of response was more like a whimper.

Joe kept his eyes—which were an *OMG, drown in me* dreamy gray—on her before his gaze dropped to her mouth. It lingered there a moment, and then he looked away. Cursed. "It'd be safer to play with fire, skate on thin ice and wake up a sleeping dog or two."

Millie wasn't sure if that advice was meant for her. Or himself. Nor did she especially want him to spell that out. She just made a slow sound of agreement and turned to head back to her car.

Yep, beyond this place, there were dragons all right. A whole flaming bunch with Joe McCann's name written all over them

CHAPTER FOUR

JOE YAWNED AND hoped that he had the energy to wash up before he fell face-first on his bed. The washing up was a necessity because he'd just pulled not one but two calves.

Both white.

Both obviously fathered by a very virile Charolais bull with escape skills that would rival Houdini's. Joe had yet to find the break in the fence where the virile shit was getting through. But that was something he'd have to deal with the sonofabitching frustration of later.

Hours later.

The shut-eye wasn't optional because he'd been up with first one cow and then the other for going on thirteen hours, since midnight, and he wasn't entirely sure he could stay awake on the walk from the barn to the house much less call his rancher neighbor, Elmer Tasker, and bitch about the trouble his Charolais was causing with Joe's breed stock.

He cursed though when he spotted an obstacle to his nap. Frankie pulled her powder-blue Jeep to a stop.

"I'm tired and going to bed," he snapped when his sister got out. "Why aren't you at work?" At this hour, Frankie should have been piercing, tattooing or selling the oddball costumes, jewelry, stationery, books and party supplies she stocked at her shop, Ink, Etc.

Joe was certain he gave her one of his better scowls. Which Frankie ignored. "I'm the boss so I gave myself the afternoon off. I come bearing gifts." She lifted a large bag of something that was already causing grease spots on the white paper. "Loaded bacon cheeseburgers for you. Veggie burger for me. There's also chili fries and root beer floats, all from O'Riley's." She waggled a tray with the two drinks.

Knowing he'd have to put yet more money in the swear jar, he cursed her again, anyway. Frankie knew that food combination was his favorite, and that O'Riley's Café was his go-to place. That meant she'd come here to either butter him up and ask him to do something for her or because she was worried about him.

It was the latter, he decided, when he caught the way she was eyeing him.

"Bacon cheeseburger, chili fries," she repeated. "Root beer floats."

Surrendering to what would no doubt hike up his cholesterol and give him the sugar crash from hell, he sighed and motioned for her to come in the house.

Joe didn't wait for her. He went in ahead of her, going straight to the kitchen so he could wash up. He also shucked off his shirt, tossing it into the basket in the adjacent laundry room, and he snagged a clean T from the pile of clothes on the dryer that he never seemed to get around to folding and putting away. By the time he made it back into the kitchen, Frankie was already taking out the food.

"I started to get Dara her favorite nachos," Frankie said, "but I figured they wouldn't heat up that well in the microwave. Maybe you can swing by later and get some for her."

Dara wouldn't be home from school for another two hours or so, but since she was an O'Riley's fan, too, she'd appreciate a quick trip there. It would also save them from having to come up with something for dinner.

Joe sat down and dug in. "Since I'm well past needing

some sleep," he started, "go ahead and spill the real reason you're here."

She shrugged and crammed some fries in her mouth. "Just checking on you. You've been kind of scarce around town."

There was no "kind of" to it. He hadn't gone into town in the five days since the drawing of the Last Ride Society. And it wasn't only the looks and the gossip he was trying to avoid.

Millie was also in the avoidance column.

Not because he didn't want to see her. But because he did.

Hellfire and damnation, what was it with her? Better yet, what was it with him? His dick had been pretty much dormant since Ella had died, but now the idiot part of him had taken an interest in a woman he should have no interest in whatsoever.

"You're irritated," Frankie pointed out. "Is it because I dropped by, or does this have something to do with the white calf you pulled a couple of nights ago?"

Joe didn't know who'd blabbed about the calf, maybe Tanner, but he hadn't expected for it to stay a secret. The calf was damn noticeable in a pasture of Red Angus. Then again, the calf would soon have some company.

"The white calf," he verified which was more or less the truth. However, his dick's interest in Millie was causing him an extra helping of irritation. "White *calves*," he corrected. "I sure as heck can't sell them for breed stock." Which was what he was known for raising. Prime breed stock with solid bloodlines.

Frankie shrugged. "Maybe you can donate them to the petting zoo over by the preschool. They're always looking for cute animals."

Well, the calves wouldn't stay cute and pettable for long. Soon, they'd be fully grown bulls, and besides, Joe wasn't sure he wanted to advertise the ranching problem he was having. Not when his personal problems, i.e. Ella and her death, were still garnering way too much talk and attention.

Joe guzzled down enough of the root beer float to give himself brain freeze, and he looked across the table at his sister. Specifically, he looked at his sister's neck.

"You've got a hickey," he snarled.

She shrugged, and even though she got very interested in picking out her next French fry, he didn't miss the little smile. "Maybe it's a new tat."

His scowl returned. "It's a hickey."

Frankie selected the fry, bit it and met his gaze. "Do you really want to discuss my sex life?"

Actually, he did want to know who had sucked on her neck enough to leave that mark. It was a knee-jerk reaction. A big brother/kid sister kind of deal.

"I'll tell you how I got this," she said, tapping her neck, "if you'll agree to let me set you up with one of my friends."

Joe was glaring and shaking his brain-frozen head before she even finished. "No. I'm not going out with one of your friends."

If he was going to break his run of celibacy, he could think of a far more interesting way to do it. A more complicated one, too. Because the face that flashed in his mind was Millie's.

"Millie," Frankie said, and for one gut-tightening moment, he thought he'd said her name aloud. "Did you decide to help her with the research?"

This was another fast and easy "No." He paused. "But Dara told Millie she would help." Joe wasn't sure what had become of that, and he hadn't wanted to press Dara on it.

"Really?" Frankie drew out the word. "Well, good for her. It'd be good for you, too, to help. Maybe you could think of the research as a purging. A sort of last goodbye before you get on with your life."

"I have gotten on with my life," he assured her and took a bite of his burger.

Frankie raised an eyebrow. "Really?" she repeated. "I've seen no proof whatsoever of that."

"Maybe I get hickeys in places where they won't be seen by siblings and others," he grumbled.

Frankie laughed and laughed and laughed. It was pure sarcasm. Then, she sobered, patted his arm. "Life gave you a kick in the balls. Millie, too. Well, maybe not in the balls in her case, but she got the same kind of kick. I think it's a good step forward that she's going through with the research on Ella."

No one would ever convince him that the last part was true. However, it was true about the kick. Millie had gotten it, too.

"I think it some ways all of this was even harder on Millie than on you," Frankie threw out there.

Joe turned to her so fast that his neck popped. "Yeah, must be hard being born with a trust fund and having everybody in town treat you like a princess."

"Yeah, must be hard having a mother like Laurie Jean," Frankie countered.

His sister had him there. Laurie Jean was a "hell on society wheels" kind of woman.

"Tanner told me that Laurie Jean handpicked Royce for Millie," Frankie went on. "She arranged dates for them when they were in high school and practically browbeat Royce into proposing."

Joe didn't want to hear any of this. But he couldn't shut it out. And now he had to wonder if this was why Royce had gone after Ella. Or maybe Ella had done the going after. Royce had those society wheels that Joe didn't.

"Laurie Jean didn't force Millie to marry Royce or vice versa," Joe said, hoping it would put an end to the conversation.

It didn't.

"No, but think of it like brainwashing," Frankie argued. "We were raised to believe we were nothing. We got neglected on good days, and on bad days we got smacked around."

They had indeed. Their father, Hardy, had been a mean drunk and hadn't held back on using his family as punching bags. It'd continued until Joe had gotten big enough to kick the old man's ass. Joe had mistakenly thought once he'd done that, their mother, Charlotte, would thank him for protecting Frankie and her and give her abusive husband his walking papers.

She hadn't.

Instead, the following day she'd left Last Ride with Hardy, and Frankie and Joe had ended up in foster care for two years. That'd lasted until Joe had turned eighteen and had gotten custody of Frankie.

"Millie was raised to believe she had to walk a very straight, fine line and do exactly what her parents told her," Frankie added. "That's brainwashing."

Maybe. *Probably*, he silently decided, but he'd had enough of this talk about a woman he was trying his damnedest to forget. He got down the last bites of the burger and stood.

"Thanks for the lunch," he told Frankie. "Now, quit meddling in my life, or I'll start asking around about that hickey. Then, I'll set you up on a date with one of my friends."

"Right," she said in a "never gonna happen" way. And she was right. The best way to clue someone in on your private life was to not keep it private.

He walked her to the door, and because of those old painful memories she'd stirred up, Joe kissed the top of her head. He'd already turned to get started on that nap when he saw a big silver truck approaching the house.

"You expecting company?" Frankie asked.

"No." And this wasn't company. Joe hadn't recognized the truck, but he sure as heck recognized the man who stepped out.

Asher Parkman, Millie's father.

The man was also Frankie's former father-in-law and Little T's grandfather though neither Laurie Jean nor Asher had a lot to do with the boy. The last Joe had heard, the couple had monthly visits, lasting only an hour or two, with their one and only grandson. Asher and Laurie Jean saw Tanner even less than that.

Apparently, Tanner had missed the brainwashing that his folks had heaped on Millie. And that meant it might not be the grandparents' choice about how much time they spent with their one and only grandson. Tanner might be doing buffer duty to make sure his kid didn't end up beaten down like his sister.

"You want me to stay?" Frankie asked Joe in a whisper.

"No." There was no reason to put his sister through a visit from Asher. Especially since the man had likely come about Millie.

"Frankie," Asher greeted, tipping the brim of his pearl-white cowboy hat. He did the same to Joe as he made his way up the porch steps.

He was a beefy man with wide shoulders and gray hair that was identical in color to his suit jacket. However, the gray hair and wrinkles that fanned out from his eyes didn't make him look old, but rather formidable. The kind of face and body that spoke of money, battles won and charm.

Yep, charm.

His term as a former state congressman and his longtime role as head of the top law firm in Last Ride had probably honed that charm. A law firm where Millie's husband had worked.

Asher had none of the nervy expressions and movements of his wife. Nope. He was very much a polished good ol' boy with enough confidence for a hundred people.

"Call me if you change your mind about my offer," Frankie said, winking at Joe. She no doubt meant the date deal.

"Call me if you change your mind about *my* offer," he countered, and she no doubt knew he meant the hickey inquiry.

Joe gave Frankie the "brother" look. The one that let her know he loved her without his having to say it, but every trace of that look was gone by the time he turned back to Asher.

"I was hoping we could have a talk," Asher said as Frankie went back to her Jeep. The man shifted as if he expected Joe to get out of the doorway and invite him in, but Joe figured this was going to be a very short conversation.

"A talk about Millie doing the research for the Last Ride Society," Joe spelled out.

Looking a little nonplussed at Joe's bluntness, Asher nodded. "I can't imagine you'd want the gossips to rehash all the talk about your wife."

"Or the talk about your son-in-law," Joe quickly countered.

The charm stayed in place when Asher gave an aw-shucks nod and shrug. "That, too. This is a no-win situation for both our families. Your little girl doesn't need to hear what's being said. Neither does my wife."

Joe would bet the entire contents of his swear jar that Laurie Jean was the one who'd prompted this visit.

"Bottom-line this," Joe insisted. "What is it that you think I can do about Millie drawing my wife's name?"

Asher looked him straight in the eyes. "It's okay if Millie does her duty and scratches the surface of this so-called research, but it won't do for her to be seen with you at your wife's grave."

So, that's what this was about. Joe hadn't seen anyone else at the cemetery, but someone had probably spotted Millie's car and his truck coming and going.

Asher leaned in, and there wasn't a trace of that charm now. "You need to keep away from my daughter."

The man might as well have tossed a tub of gasoline on an equally big tub of fire. Joe usually did a decent job of reining in his temper, but he didn't even reach for those reins right now.

"Your daughter is an adult," Joe pointed out once he got his jaw unclenched. "She can make her own decisions about where she goes and who she sees."

Clearly, Asher didn't do any reining in, either. With his own jaw going to iron, he jabbed his finger at Joe. "Now, listen here. Your sister's already slung enough shit on my family by going after my son and turning him against me. I won't let you do the same with Millie."

Oh, that was so not the right thing to say.

The temper came, rolling over him like that huge gasoline fire. "You're too late," Joe said, and he hoped he managed to look smug and arrogant instead of just pissed off. "Millie was over here just a couple of nights ago, and I can promise you, she wants to see me again."

Asher's eyes widened, and instead of temper, there was a hefty dose of shock. And with the shock deepening, Asher turned, walking down the porch steps and heading to his truck.

That's when Joe had an "oh, shit" moment.

What the hell had he just done?

CHAPTER FIVE

MILLIE DREAMED. Of Joe.

His mouth came to hers, and it was just as hot as the rest of him. His hands were on her, too. And his strong hard body was pressing against hers in all the right, warm places. Mercy, he was good at this.

She shifted, adding even more of that delicious pressure while he flicked his tongue over her earlobe and murmured to her.

"Did you know when you moan you sound just like a baby dinosaur in *Jurassic Park*?"

That cooled the fire in her loins, and Millie jolted awake. She jackknifed to a sitting position and nearly toppled off the sofa when she saw the face looming over her. Definitely not Joe and his magic mouth.

"It's nearly dinnertime," her great-aunt Freida said. "It's a little late for you to be napping, dear." She pressed the back of her hand to Millie's forehead. "No fever, but you're looking all rosy and flushed. Aren't you feeling well?"

Millie had been feeling a heck of a lot better when she'd been getting kissed and touched, but she'd keep that to herself. "I moved some of the displays around in the shop, and I was tired when I got home."

The woman looked at her with sympathy and love. Millie always appreciated the last part because it wasn't a look that she got often, but Great-Aunt Freida was always willing to dole out some love.

Freida wasn't actually her aunt, great or otherwise, but rather her cousin. However, since Freida had been the one to take in Laurie Jean after her parents' deaths forty years earlier, Millie didn't mind calling Freida by the honorary title she'd given herself.

"Well, at least you didn't sleep at the shop," Freida said. "I'm glad you stopped doing that."

Millie hadn't stopped, but she didn't mention that to Freida. There were six bedrooms on the second floor of Once Upon a Time, and while five were crammed with stock, Millie had kept one bedroom intact. Meaning, it had a real bed with an attached if not outdated bath. Actually, the entire suite was seriously outdated with its century-old wallpaper and scarred hardwood floor, but for reasons Millie had never wanted to explore, that room had felt more like home than this house. Still, she tried not to stay there too often since word of it usually made it to the gossip pool and therefore got back to Laurie Jean.

"I knocked on your front door, but you must not have heard me so I used my key to let myself in. I also put the three-bean casserole and cucumber salad in your fridge," Freida went on, sitting in the chair across from her while she tugged off her white gloves.

Yes, gloves. It didn't matter if it was hotter than Hades or an everyday Thursday afternoon, Freida wore gloves and tiny pillbox hats with netting that hung over her forehead.

Millie blinked and shook her head when she processed what Freida had said. "What bean casserole and salad?"

"The ones that were in a cooler on your porch." The look she leveled at Millie now was sympathy. "The note on the outside of the cooler said it was from the Last Ride Society."

Millie nearly blurted out a word that would have gotten her a scolding, but she caught herself at the last second. "Lord, love a duck," she muttered instead.

It was what she'd dubbed "grieving grub." The Last Ride Society had done that after Royce had died, and while Millie had appreciated the sentiment behind the meals, they'd only served as a reminder that people were pitying her. Each meal had also brought memories of Royce right straight to the surface. No way could she eat or even look at grieving grub and not remember why said grub had been made for her in the first place.

She'd been thankful when the deliveries had finally stopped a couple of months after Royce's death. Apparently, the society thought it was warranted again—though Millie couldn't see beans or salad being much of an indulgent meal to ease grieving.

Millie got up and stretched to get out the kinks from her nap, and then it occurred to her that Freida had de-gloved and was sitting there watching her. Obviously waiting. Which meant this hadn't been just a checking-on-you/catch-up visit.

"Would you like some tea or something?" Millie asked to get that out of the way.

"No, thank you. I can't stay long," Freida said, and she waited some more.

"Are you here to try to talk me out of doing the research on Ella McCann?" Millie came out and asked.

"No. Though I'm sure it's something your mother would have wanted me to bring up had she not been so upset about other things." Freida paused, took in a long, slow breath through her mouth. "Your mother heard talk you were seeing Joe McCann, that you'd been to his house."

Millie picked through that and settled on one word. "Seeing?"

"Diddling him," Freida quickly provided in her prim voice. She idly ran her fingers on the bronze stained-glass lamp on the table next to her.

"Oh, for Pete's sake." Millie groaned. "Who told her that?"

"Apparently, it came from Joe himself."

Millie dismissed that with the wave of her hand. "Not a chance."

"From Joe himself," Freida repeated. "He told your father just a couple of hours ago when Asher went out to talk to him about the research Laurie Jean doesn't want you to do."

Millie groaned again. She didn't want either of her parents involved in this and especially didn't want them going to Joe and bugging him. "My father misunderstood what Joe said."

"Maybe," Freida conceded, not sounding convinced of that at all. "Anyway, it's upset your mother."

Millie was sure she'd hear all about that from Laurie Jean herself, but it did speak volumes that her mother had sent Freida to do her bidding.

"How upset?" Millie asked, and she flashed back to the memory of walking in on her mother when she'd been staring at a bottle of sleeping pills.

Maybe Laurie Jean had just been searching for an end to insomnia, but it had given Millie a bad feeling. Like maybe her mother had been searching for an end, period. Then again, with her mother's personality, she probably wasn't the sort to consider ending her life. Still…

"Upset," Freida verified. She paused again. "This has brought up talk about her parents."

"Yes, she mentioned that when she came by the shop." Millie hadn't meant for her tone to dismiss her mother's concern, but it must have seemed that way to Freida because the woman reached out, took hold of Millie's hand and gave it a gentle squeeze.

"Your mother has always felt she had to be doubly good to live up to the Parkman name," Freida said.

Millie was well aware of that, too. "Some people call the Parkman Cemetery Hoity Toity Hill. So, not everyone in Last Ride believes the Parkmans have a name worthy of being lived up to."

Freida gave an elegant lift of her shoulder. "Some call us Greedy Grangers, and of course, there's the ever-popular Damn Daytons. It doesn't bother us because we know every family is like an apple. There's the sweet juicy part, the core, and yes, the occasional worm. But there's more sweet juicy part than the rest."

Millie frowned at that analogy. "Mom thinks gossip is a worm. I just wish she wouldn't care so much about what other people think." She heard herself and wasn't sure whether to laugh or groan. So, Millie did both. "I wish *I* didn't care what other people think," she tacked on to that.

"I know." She squeezed Millie's hand again. "Your mother simply doesn't want to do anything that would embarrass your father. She loves him and would do anything for him."

That was something Millie couldn't dispute. Laurie Jean did indeed do the whole ground-worshipping thing when it came to Asher. And there was genuine love, maybe even the heat of attraction in her mother's eyes when she looked at her husband. Pretty amazing, considering they'd been married for thirty-three years.

Or rather thirty-three and a half years as Laurie Jean would emphasize.

Since Tanner was thirty-two, her mother always wanted

to make sure that folks knew that he hadn't been conceived before Asher and she had married. That kind of speculation just wouldn't do.

"I recall when your parents first started dating," Freida went on. "They were inseparable."

Millie had heard all of this before. The grand love story and the inseparable part. They had started dating in college when Asher had been in law school and Laurie Jean had been studying interior design. Their only time apart was when her mother had studied abroad in Italy one summer, and even then Asher had flown to see her. It was hard for Millie to see her "by the book" father and her "stickler for appearances" mother being that hot for each other.

"I'm not sure I ever once had that kind of heat or attraction with Royce," Millie muttered. Of course, the moment the words left her mouth, she wished she'd choked on them and hadn't spoken.

"Well," Freida said, easing to her feet. She kissed Millie's cheek. "Every marriage is like an apple. Sweet and juicy. A core and sometimes a worm. It's likely you had all three with Royce."

And with that clever observation, Freida said her goodbye and made her way to the front door. Millie stood there, suddenly steeped in memories she didn't want. The trouble was she hadn't known there'd been anything but the sweet and juicy with Royce. Maybe it hadn't been the absolute sweetest apple in the orchard, but they'd been happy.

Maybe.

She went toward the kitchen, threading her way through the living room where she'd been napping and into the hall that led to the back of the house. The route took her past the closed door to Royce's home office.

Where she hadn't been since his death.

Well, she had opened the door once, on the first anniversary of his death, and with her eyes shut tight, she had tossed her wedding rings inside. They'd been yet something else she hadn't wanted to have to see. Reminders of Royce, of his betrayal. She'd shut the door without getting so much of a glimpse of what might be in there. However, she considered reaching for the knob now.

But Millie dismissed it just as fast.

She'd managed to pack up and donate all of Royce's clothes from the master bedroom closet, but going through the things in his office could be like opening a can of those worms that'd eaten into her apple of a marriage. There could be something about Ella in there. Pictures, maybe. Love letters or emails.

Nope, she wouldn't be going in there tonight. Maybe not ever.

Fighting back the blasted tears that burned her eyes, Millie wished she had the magical powers to burn down that specific room. Heck. Maybe burn down the whole house and start fresh in another place. But Millie Vanilla couldn't do that. This house was a Dayton legacy, one left to Royce by his grandparents, and a Dayton had lived in it since it'd been built over a hundred years ago.

She forced her feet to get going, and she stepped into the kitchen. One of the few rooms in the house that Royce and she had remodeled. It was all cool and polished. A lot like Royce himself, but looking at all the stainless and quartz now just left her cold. So did the idea of eating bean casserole and salad. Or anything else she could scrounge up from her fridge.

Millie tugged on her shoes, grabbed her purse and headed toward Main Street. Which wasn't far. She could have walked there in about ten minutes, but she would have run into people who'd want to stop and chat. She definitely wasn't in the mood for conversation.

There were plenty of places in Last Ride to get a meal that didn't take into account things like health, grief or such, but she headed to O'Riley's. She could get some nachos to go and eat in her car. Depending on how much gloom and doom she was feeling after that, she might be able to go to the cemetery and get a picture of Ella's tombstone.

O'Riley's was a 1950s-style café with a wall of windows on the front and outdoor seating on the sides. What it didn't have was a drive-through, but she parked in the back next to a half dozen other vehicles and, hurrying, Millie rounded the corner of the building toward the window to order.

And she practically ran right into Joe and Dara.

Millie froze. Joe froze. And Millie could have sworn every single person in the vicinity of O'Riley's froze, too, holding their breaths. Her theory of every frozen person quickly got shot down though when Dara made a slurping sound with the straw in what appeared to be a mango smoothie.

"Want some nachos?" Dara asked her. "Dad had a big lunch and isn't hungry. There's no way I can eat all of these by myself."

The girl was indeed holding a platter-sized paper bowl that'd been piled high with O'Riley's Treasures and Trash nachos which were topped with pretty much everything that tasted like heaven on tortilla chips.

"Uh, I was just going to get something to go," Millie said, fumbling with her words.

"No need. This is way more than I can eat," Dara insisted, but she wasn't looking at Millie. She had her attention on a group of kids around her age who came walking up. "Here." She practically thrust the nachos into Millie's hands. "I'll be right back."

Millie fully expected Joe to snag the food and tell her that she didn't have to accept his daughter's "dinner" invitation. Or words to that effect. But he was looking at the kids, too. And frowning.

"That's Rico Donnelly's kid," Joe practically growled.

Millie remembered the night she'd gone to his house to tell him about the drawing, Joe had had an axe. A deterrent, he'd called it. For any boy visiting Dara. Millie guessed Rico Donnelly's kid was one of those boys.

Since Joe looked ready to bolt over and threaten the boy, Millie tipped her head to one of the empty outside tables. "Why don't we sit down so I can have some of these nachos?"

It was still too hot to eat outside, but she doubted she could convince Joe to let Dara out of his sight. Her own father hadn't been so protective of her, but Millie had had enough embarrassing incidents with Laurie Jean practically dragging her away from whom she'd deemed as unacceptable friends.

Millie set the nachos on the table. "Let me get a Coke—"

"I'll get it," Joe said, maybe to be polite. Maybe because it would put him closer to his daughter.

Without taking his eyes, and his scowl, off the group of teens, Joe went to the order window, and less than a minute later, he came back with her Coke. He sat across from her and kept watching Dara.

Since merely sitting with Joe would no doubt stir up gossip, Millie figured the damage had already been done so she helped herself to the nachos. Mercy, they were good.

"Did you know my parents have gotten the wacky notion that you and I are having sex?" Millie asked him.

That got his attention off Dara, and he frowned instead of scowled. "Yeah. I started that rumor. I'm really sorry about that."

Millie nearly got choked on the Coke, and she shook her head, certain that she'd misheard him. "You started a rumor that we were lovers?"

His frown deepened, and he finally turned away from his daughter to face her. "Yeah," he repeated. "Asher paid me a visit, and everything he said just hit the wrong buttons. I blurted it out before I thought it through."

Millie groaned and didn't have to ask the specifics of what her father had said to Joe. Asher had no doubt played the "you're not good enough for Millie" card.

"I'm sorry," Joe and she said in unison. "I hope you won't catch any grief about that," he added.

She would have forced herself to eat bean casserole for a lifetime before she would admit to him that it'd already caused her grief. And would continue to do so.

"I can try to make things right with Asher," Joe continued. "I can tell him nothing's going on between us."

At that exact moment, his gaze lowered to her mouth. A longing kind of look that made her think something was indeed going on between them.

He motioned toward her mouth. "Cheese," he said. "There." He tapped the corner of his own bottom lip.

So, maybe not a longing look after all. Millie used her tongue to go after the cheese dribble. When that failed, she licked the other side of her lip. And she saw yet another of those looks from Joe.

Definitely longing.

Which, of course, was just another way of saying lust.

It was probably reasonable in an unreasonable sort of way. A forbidden fruit kind of thing. Then again, the lust was perhaps only on her part because the guy was panty-dropping gorgeous.

"I dreamed about you," Millie commented.

Crap, crap, crap. Why had she confessed that? Once again, she wished she could time travel and keep that little tidbit to herself.

His eyebrow winged up, and he opened his mouth as if ready to ask "What kind of dream?" But then, he stopped. Cursed and scrubbed his hand over his face. "It's because we were thrown together over this research," he said.

"Probably," she muttered, but Millie would have at least partially agreed to any reasonable explanation about the scalding dream she'd had about him.

And the thoughts.

Thoughts, like now. Oh, mercy. She was in trouble here, and she likely would have blurted out yet something else she'd regret, but Joe spoke before the blurting and blathering could continue.

"I dreamed about you, too," he said. He stopped, and the muscles in his jaw flexed and tensed. "I don't want to dream about you."

Joe hadn't said that last part in anger. More like frustration. Millie totally got that.

Groaning, Joe made a quick glance back at Dara. She was still laughing and talking with her friends. However, the Donnelly boy had moved a little closer to her, and he gave Dara a little hip bump.

"I'll be back," Joe snarled.

Millie didn't try to stop him. She needed a moment to kick-start her breathing. Needed another moment to tamp down the fantasies that'd started to traipse through her head. Fantasies about a man who would muck up her life in so many ways. However, she did feel sorry for Dara and hoped the girl wasn't going to be embarrassed by what her father was about to do.

But Joe didn't get a chance to do any embarrassing.

He was halfway between Millie and Dara when he got intercepted by a man who came out of the café. Elmer Tasker, who owned the ranch next to Joe's. Elmer immediately took Joe by the arm and started talking just as Dara waved goodbye to her friends and hurried past her dad and back to the table. She dropped down and started gobbling up some of the nachos.

Dara looked back at her dad much as he'd done to her. "It's about that white calf," she said. "It's cute and all, but it messes up the bloodline stuff." She watched them a moment longer, maybe to see if the chat was going to get heated. It didn't. So, Dara turned back to her dinner.

"I'm still working on my bucket list," Dara said in between bites.

"I wondered about that. I thought maybe you'd changed your mind about helping me."

Actually, Millie had been *hoping* that Dara would change her mind. She hated to outright refuse the girl's help. It might hurt her feelings. But Millie also hadn't wanted Dara to have to relive painful memories.

"Nope," Dara assured her. "I'm still on board for it." She checked her dad again, but this time Millie thought it was because Dara was making sure he wasn't nearby. He wasn't. Dara leaned in and lowered her voice. "In fact, I'll do all the research for you and even write up the report."

Stunned, Millie stared at her. And stared. Part of her wanted to dump this on Dara, but she couldn't. This wasn't about duty, either. This was about not wanting Dara to have to deal with any truth she might learn.

"But there's a catch," Dara continued. "I have something else I want you to do. Not for me. For him," she said, glancing at her father.

Millie just kept on staring.

"I see the way he looks at you," Dara said. "He likes you, and he hasn't looked at any other woman like that since Mom."

Millie finally quit staring and started shaking her head. "Your dad doesn't like me," she argued.

Except there was that whole *I don't want to dream about you*. Good grief. Were Joe and she giving off some kind of sex vibe that even his young daughter had picked up on?

"He does," Dara insisted. "I think he likes you a whole lot. So, here's the deal." She leaned in. "Make him better. Try to make my dad happy again."

CHAPTER SIX

JOE HAD NEARLY made it to his truck when he saw the car turn into his driveway. Well, it was sort of a car.

The vintage VW had been painted to resemble a turtle. A goofy cartoon one that was no doubt meant to be funny. Like the car's owner, Alma Parkman, the current president of the Last Ride Society. Since Alma had recently started performing as a stand up comic, Joe supposed this was her way of advertising her quirky sense of humor.

Grinning and carrying a small cooler, Alma got out and walked to him. "Fried chicken," she said, tipping her head to the cooler. "Mac and cheese. And there are even some double fudge brownies in there."

Joe didn't groan, something he wanted to do because he knew the sentiment behind this delivery. Alma was trying to soothe the grieving widower. It was especially uncomfortable since Alma's maiden name was Dayton, and she was Royce's paternal aunt. Of course, it was next to impossible not to run into a Dayton, Granger or Parkman in or around Last Ride.

"Thanks," Joe said, taking the cooler from her. "It'll save Dara and me from cooking."

Alma was all sympathy when she combed her faded blue eyes over him. "I'm glad to help in any way." She looked at the keys he had in his hand. "I guess you're heading somewhere?"

"I've got some errands to do in town." And he was already running late. Dara would be out of school soon, and even though she had a ride, Joe wanted to be home when she got there.

Alma nodded. "I won't keep you, then. I just wanted to apologize for what happened with the drawing. I didn't come out sooner because…well, because I wanted to give you a little time to get over the initial shock."

It'd been nearly two weeks since the drawing so the *initial* was definitely gone. The shock, not so much. It wasn't just the shock, either, of Millie drawing Ella's name but the fact that this Last Ride deal had inserted Millie into his mind and dreams. Before the drawing, he had tried not to think about her and her husband and had mostly succeeded.

Mostly.

But now it definitely wasn't her husband's face in Joe's thoughts. It was Millie's, and those thoughts didn't have squat to do with the drawing. Nope. This was all about the kick in the gut stirrings he was getting for Millie. That's why Joe had put off going into town. He hadn't wanted to run into her again the way they had at O'Riley's.

He was glad, too, that Dara had backed off on helping Millie with the research. At least Joe thought she had. Dara hadn't said anything to him about it, and he hadn't brought it up. This was definitely a situation of letting sleeping dogs lie.

"I wanted you to know that I've proposed a change to the drawing," Alma went on. "I don't think we should add anyone recently deceased to the drawing. Maybe wait five years before their name goes in the bowl."

Joe was reasonably sure five years wasn't going to fix what he was feeling. Every mention and every memory of Ella had the potential to tap into his grief. But it also had the equal potential of tapping into the image of that receipt he kept in the recliner in his man-shed. A pregnancy test. Yeah, that wasn't going away anytime soon. Neither was the fact that Ella had died pressed against another man.

"I'm not sure the society will approve the changes," Alma continued a moment later, "but it might help people who find themselves in your position."

Joe doubted his situation would be duplicated, but you never knew. "Thanks," he said, figuring that was a blanket answer to everything Alma had just said.

She nodded, hesitated, and it seemed as if the woman changed her mind as to what she'd been about to say. Alma turned toward her turtle car but then changed her mind about that, too.

"Look," she said, the dread and apology all over her face, "I know this drawing has upset a lot of people. You, Millie, Laurie Jean, Asher…" Her voice trailed off. "That's why I called Millie and told her I'd do the research. She thanked me but said no, that she could manage. She can manage because she feels it's the right thing to do, but I'm worried about her."

Joe suspected a lot of people were worried about Millie, but this seemed to go a little deeper than the usual concern. "Is she okay?" he wondered.

"I was going to ask you the same thing. I mean because I know you two have been, uh, talking lately."

Hell. This was about what he'd said to Asher. Joe hoped this taught him a lesson about losing his temper and talking. "Millie and I aren't *talking*," he assured her, adding some inflection to that last word. "But if the opportunity comes up, I'll make sure she's okay." He purposely checked his watch. "I'm sorry, but I have to go."

"Of course." There was still some hesitation in Alma's voice, but she hurried away.

Joe called out another thanks for the food, and he put the cooler on the floorboard of his truck. The food would keep, and he didn't want to take the time to go back inside and put it away.

He took the long way to Main Street so he could avoid going by Millie's shop. It wasn't complete BS when he'd told Alma he'd make sure Millie was all right if the opportunity presented itself. But he didn't intend to multiply the chances of that happening by being anywhere near where he thought Millie might be. That included Once Upon a Time, O'Riley's or the cemetery where Royce was buried.

Joe went by the post office to mail a contract to a buyer he had for some of his stock. Not the white calves. He was still figuring out how to handle that, but he was riding fence every day now to make sure none of the Charolais bulls had broken through. After Joe's conversation with his neighbor, Elmer was doing the same. Short of rigging his bulls with condoms, Joe didn't think there was much else he could do.

He hit the feedstore next and then the town's only florist, Petal Pusher, to grab some flowers that Dara would want to put on Ella's grave. Daisies. Joe wasn't sure if Petal Pusher's owner, Tommy Ellison, kept them in stock because they were cheap or if it was because Joe kept buying them.

Joe was heading back to his truck when he spotted the woman coming toward the florist. Not Millie. But this was someone else he hadn't expected, and didn't especially want, to see. Janice Barth.

Ella's mother.

Janice didn't just walk on past him, but he suspected that's what she wanted to do. It didn't matter that Joe had fathered Janice's one and only grandchild and had married her one and only child. Janice had never approved of him, his bloodlines or his choice of career. Which was fine. Joe had never approved of Janice and her snobby ways. Ways that she thankfully hadn't even tried to pass on to her daughter or to Dara. Probably because the woman knew Joe wouldn't have tolerated it.

"Joe," she greeted in that ice-queen tone of hers.

As usual, there wasn't a strand of her short gray hair out of place. Ditto for her dress, which was also gray. It looked expensive and modest. Like the woman wearing it.

It occurred to Joe that Janice had a lot in common with Laurie Jean. Old money and appearances. However, where Laurie Jean was a bundle of emotion and simmering temper, Janice had none of that. She didn't send flaming eyeball arrows at someone who offended her sensibilities. Janice froze them with those gunmetal eyes that were both cold and flat.

"I didn't know you were coming into town today," he said.

Nothing unusual about that. Janice rarely informed Dara or him when she'd be in Last Ride, but he knew from talk that the woman made the drive from her home in San Antonio at least once a month.

"It was a spur-of-the-moment thing," Janice explained. "There were some things I needed to tell Ella." Her voice quivered a little, but he saw Janice steel herself. "I was going to take some flowers to her grave. I'm guessing those are for her?"

He nodded and left it at that. No need to spell out that he wasn't the one who actually took the flowers to Ella. But Janice probably already knew that. The woman seemed to know plenty about grieving and remembering the dead, and she did have the occasional phone conversations with Dara.

"Good," Janice concluded. "Ella will love them." Her eyes stayed level and flat as she glanced around as if checking to make sure no one was trying to nose in on their conversation. There were a couple of people milling about, which might have been why Janice lowered her voice. "I don't think it's a good idea for Dara to visit Millie Dayton."

Of course, Janice knew who Millie was. Or rather knew her name. Knew that Millie's husband had died in the car with Ella. Janice had never once offered an opinion on why she thought the pair had been together. It was possible she knew though. Ella and Janice hadn't been close, but maybe Ella had confided in her. If that had indeed happened, Joe figured Janice would carry that confidence to the grave.

Joe sighed when he remembered that Janice was obviously still waiting for him to respond to her comment. "Dara's not visiting Millie. We ran into Millie at O'Riley's—"

"I just saw Dara go into Once Upon a Time, and I know Millie owns it," Janice interrupted. "Unless the girl's taken an interest in antiques or local art, then why else would she go in there?"

Joe did a mental double take, but he tried not to show any of that surprise on his face. No need to let Janice see that he didn't approve of Dara visiting Millie since it would only lead to one of Janice's cool lectures about keeping better tabs on the girl. And she'd used the words *tabs* and *the girl*. Sometimes, Joe wanted to tell the woman to shove her icy comments, but she was still Dara's grandmother so he would cut her some slack.

Plenty of slack.

However, it was time that he did try to sort some things out with Dara, and that started with finding out why she'd gone to see Millie. Because Janice was right—he doubted his daughter was in Once Upon a Time for anything the store might have for sale. Plus, now that school was out, she was supposed to be on her way home.

Joe said his goodbye to Janice, put the flowers in his truck and walked up the block to Millie's shop. True to its name, Once Upon a Time had a history. It was one of the original Victorian homes built in Last Ride. A fussy two-story design with a steep multifaceted roof and lots of white trim on the yellow exterior. There were even two towers, one round and another an octagon shape, and in the center perched a fairly large gargoyle. It was covered in a light green patina and reading a book. Apparently, the person who'd put it there had been aiming for scary whimsy.

He stopped outside the large bay window to peer in and try to spot Dara, but Joe immediately stepped back when he came face-to-face with someone peering back at him. Someone lifting a huge statue of a black bird. It wasn't Millie. This was a guy with a bunch of piercings in his eyebrow. One of Millie's customers or employees, no doubt.

The pierced guy gave Joe a cheery grin and set down the bird in the window display that he was decorating. Or redecorating. Judging from the stuff on the floor behind him, he was replacing an Edgar Allan Poe display with a spring picnic. All done with antiques and such.

"Come on in," the guy said. "We're open."

They were indeed. When Joe looked past the man, he saw at least a half dozen customers milling around. The cashier was ringing up a sale.

A bell jingled when he opened the stained-glass door and stepped in. Not an ordinary bell sound but more like a wind-chime sound that had come from a bronze fairy with tiny dangling stars.

Joe had never been inside but wondered if Ella had. Probably. He immediately saw several things she would have liked. A glass ball paperweight that caught the light and sent out a rainbow of colors and the tiny porcelain bluebird beside it. The room with the paintings and sculptures from local artists would have drawn her right in, too.

Joe didn't go into the art room though. He moved through the main part of the shop, looking for Millie or Dara. He didn't see either of them, but he did hear someone talking toward the back so he headed there.

"If there's anything I can help you with, just let me know," the clerk behind the checkout counter called out to him.

Joe grunted in response and kept walking. He finally spotted Dara. She was in an office. Well, it was sort of an office, anyway. It looked more like something from a movie set.

Harry Potter, he realized.

There was a desk with ornate carvings in the center of the room, and it was flanked by dark wood bookcases and stairs that curved up to the higher shelves. An arched window stretched out floor to ceiling in the center of those stairs and bookcases. The glass had a dark golden tint to it, probably to keep out the blistering light that would no doubt come pouring through in the morning.

Dara was standing in front of that desk with her back to him, and even though he couldn't see Millie because of Dara, he heard her voice.

"You want a makeover at the mall in San Antonio," Millie said.

What the heck? This wasn't about tombstone research. Confused, Joe moved closer and to the side so he would have a better view of both of them. Millie was reading from a piece of paper.

"A free makeover," Dara qualified. "Because I'm not

sure I want to spend my babysitting money on makeup. I just want to know what I'd look like when it's done the right way."

Millie looked up at her. "I could tell you that you don't need makeup, that you're very pretty without it, but I remember being told that when I was your age, and I didn't want to hear it. I wanted shiny pink lip gloss, smears of blue eyeliner and hair like Britney Spears."

"Did you get it?" Dara asked.

"No," Millie said on a sigh.

"You could get all those things now," his daughter pointed out.

Millie smiled a little, shook her head. "I missed the window for that particular opportunity." Her attention went back to the paper, and it occurred to Joe that he shouldn't be eavesdropping. He should let Dara and Millie know he was there.

But his feet sort of froze in place when Millie continued. Ditto for his mouth. Joe definitely didn't speak up.

"You want some new bras," Millie said, obviously voicing what she'd just read. "A pretty one with maybe some lace and panties to match. You want to shop for those things at a store in the mall called Sassy Silk."

Well, shit. He just kept on listening.

"Yes," Dara confirmed. Her voice had some shyness in it now. "I ordered the one I'm wearing online, but it doesn't fit right. I need to try one on to get the right size, and I don't want to buy it around here. People might get the wrong idea."

Joe mentally repeated another *shit*. His baby girl was thirteen, nowhere near the age where she should be interested in lace bras and panties.

Was she?

He definitely didn't want to think about that. But he should. Crap on crutches. Dara was barely a teenager but she must have needed a bra. Damn sure not a lacy one with matching panties, but some kind of support, and she likely hadn't wanted to go to him for that.

"Bra and panties," Millie confirmed, making a ticking mark in the air, while continuing to read. "And you want to eat lunch at Taco Cabana in San Antonio?"

Dara nodded. "It was my mom's and my favorite place. I don't want to have to take Dad there because it might make him think of her, and he'll get all down and stuff."

The punch he got from that felt like a dozen sacks of bricks smacking into him. Because it was true.

Judging from Millie's next sigh, she knew all about such places getting her *all down and stuff.* "Are you sure you want to do these things with me?" she asked. "Wouldn't you rather do them with your aunt Frankie?"

"I love Aunt Frankie, but you're like neutral. You wouldn't get too wild with the shopping or the makeup. And you wouldn't think of my mom while eating fajitas and then be all down. If Aunt Frankie gets down, my dad will know right away."

Millie swallowed hard, making Joe believe that she would indeed be thinking about Ella. Then again, maybe she'd do that with or without fajitas.

"All right," Millie finally said. "I could do all of this with you, but you'd first have to get your dad's permission. Sorry, that's not negotiable," she added when Dara groaned. "You don't have to tell him about Taco Cabana. Or that you want new underwear. But he would need to give his permission for me to take you on a shopping trip."

Dara groaned again. Huffed. Groaned again. "Okay.

I'll figure out a way to ask him, but he'll probably want to talk to you."

"That's fine," Millie assured her, but the look on her face said that it was anything but fine. "Get his permission, and I can take you this weekend."

That perked Dara right up. Unlike Millie, he couldn't see Dara's expression, but she made a little happy squeal. "Great." She handed Millie two more sheets of paper. "That's the first of the stories about Mom that you can use for your research. I'll do others. This is just to get you started."

That jabbed into him even harder than the lace bra deal. Stories about Ella. That Millie would read and then write up for everyone to read. He had to stop this now. There'd be no shopping trip. He'd figure out another way for Dara to do those things on her list.

Joe got moving toward the office, but he stopped in his tracks again when Dara added, "Now to the part about you doing something to fix my dad." She put her hands on her hips. "I think you're going to have to kiss him."

He was reasonably sure he couldn't have spoken a word had there been a loaded gun at his head. *Dumbfounded*, that was the right word for what was happening to him. Why the heck would Dara believe Millie would need to kiss him? Why had this subject even come up?

"Sir," someone said. It was the clerk. The same one with the pierced eyebrow who'd greeted Joe earlier. "Would you like for me to let Millie know you're waiting to see her?"

While Joe was still trying to get his mouth to work, he glanced in the office. At Dara who had turned and was looking at him. At Millie, who was also looking at him. Except they weren't just looking. They were all staring at each other with wide eyes and mouths agape, and it was pretty clear they had already figured out that he'd heard way too much of their private conversation.

"DAD?" DARA BLURTED out at the same moment that Millie got to her feet and said, "Joe?"

It was a toss-up as to who was more surprised at that moment, but Millie thought Joe might win that particular prize. He looked both gobsmacked and guilty, and Millie figured that's because he'd followed his daughter into the shop and overheard, well, plenty.

Monte, who was nobody's fool, must have decided he didn't want to be in the middle of this so he gave Millie a little wave, muttered that he had something to do, and he made a fast exit. There was a chance he'd try to eavesdrop. Nobody's fool didn't mean he wasn't nosy, but Monte would probably keep any gossip he unearthed to himself.

"Dad," Dara repeated. She was looking gobsmacked, too, but also embarrassed. She was probably wondering how much of the lacy bra comments her father had heard. Again, Millie was betting *plenty*.

Millie had to hand it to Joe though. He shed the stunned reaction fairly fast, and he didn't jump straight into trying to defend himself. "I saw your grandmother, and she mentioned you'd come here to the shop. I was worried about you since you usually go home right after school."

He might have fudged the truth with the worried bit, but Millie suspected there was some of that going on inside him. Along with curiosity and yes, some anger that his daughter was here to help with the research—and the bucket list stuff, too. Millie wasn't certain how Joe was dealing with his daughter wanting to exclude him from all of this, but he might be hurt that Dara hadn't trusted him enough to bare her teenage soul to him.

"I want to help her," Dara said. Not in defiance. This was more like a plea. "I want the stories about Mom to be right." She paused, lowered her head. "And I don't want you to take me shopping at Sassy Silk."

Millie winced. Joe might have backed off of not wanting the research. Might have. But saying Sassy Silk to the father of a teenager was probably akin to waving a red flag in front of a bull. A very protective bull.

"The shop doesn't just sell risqué underwear," Millie quickly pointed out. Well, she'd responded *quickly* after she'd come up with alternative words to *sexy* and *screw wear*. "I've bought some things there for myself."

In hindsight, she should have taken a moment to come up with an alternative way of saying that, too. But hopefully Joe would believe that she'd bought panties and bras there that were suitable for her Millie Vanilla name.

"Please," was all Dara said, and Millie realized that was the most effective argument of all.

Joe sighed. Then, he nodded. He didn't add any conditions. No concerns about how all of this would play out. Just the nod that caused Dara to squeal with delight. She ran to him, and Joe caught her in a bear hug.

"You ready to go?" he asked, adding a kiss to the top of her head.

Dara pulled back. "I'm meeting Bella at the library so we can work on our science project, remember? Her mom is giving me a ride to Aunt Frankie's afterwards because you said I could spend the night."

He nodded as if just recalling that, and Dara must have taken that nod as her cue to go. She rattled off a thanks to both Millie and her dad before she headed out.

Leaving Joe and Millie alone.

"Don't worry," she said, stepping out of her office to

join him. "I'll steer Dara toward the more conservative section in Sassy Silk."

"Can you steer her away from boys while you're at it?" he grumbled. "Or maybe find a section in Sassy Silk that sells chastity belts?"

Millie nearly laughed. She hadn't remembered her own dad balking about this, but then, she had rarely given her folks any balking material.

"I think Dara's sensible," Millie tried to assure him. She followed his gaze to the papers Dara had given her. Info about Ella. "And determined."

"Yeah." Dragging in a long breath, he turned and swept his gaze over the nearby shelves. "I don't want you to feel pressured into taking Dara shopping. Or for that matter, doing anything else with her. Frankie would be glad to help."

"I know she would, but I don't mind taking her."

Did she? It was so rote for Millie to go with the polite "don't make waves" approach that sometimes she wasn't sure how she truly felt. There was the worry of stirred up memories. A big worry. But there was no way she would back out of taking Dara, not when she'd told her she would.

Joe took another glance at the papers, perhaps debating if he wanted to do some memory stirring of his own, but then he turned toward the table that was only a few feet from her office door.

"It's one of the True or False displays," she explained. "My sales assistants, Haylee and Monte, choose items from storage, write a description and then let the shoppers decide if it's true or false. We won't ever run out of items because most of the top floor is filled with stuff. My grandmother loved to buy things for the shop."

For this particular display, Monte and Haylee had chosen one of her favorites. A small leather black case that contained several small vials with dried herbs, a dog-eared Bible and a simple cross necklace. Haylee had written, "A set given to a Victorian nun on the day she took her vows to her order. True or false?"

Joe looked at her. "True?"

"False." Millie smiled. She turned over the card to show him the answer. "It's actually a nineteenth-century kit to ward off vampires."

He eyed the items again, shook his head. "Too bad you don't have one to ward off that Ian Donnelly boy from Dara."

Her smile widened, and she went to give him a reassuring, "you'll get through this" pat on the arm, but she nearly patted him with the papers instead. She had no idea how much two pages actually weighed, but they suddenly felt like a ton in her hand. Without looking at anything Dara had written, she offered them to him.

"I wouldn't put anything in the research report that you wouldn't want to be there," she said.

Joe took his time, studying her, then the papers before he took a step back. "Just go through it and give me a summary."

She understood. For him, this would be like her going into Royce's office. She wasn't ready for that. Might never be. And Joe wasn't ready to go over details of the woman he'd married.

Millie cleared her throat and started skimming the first two paragraphs. It was a bio, complete with Ella's date and place of birth. San Antonio. Her father had been a doctor there, and he'd come from a well-off family. He'd died when Ella was eleven. Ella had moved to Last Ride after Joe and she had gotten married.

"It's just background stuff," Millie told him, moving on to the next paragraph.

Her skimming slowed a little because it was an account of the first time Ella had gone out with Joe. It'd been a blind date, set up by Joe's friends who'd met Ella at a party in San Antonio. They'd gone to O'Riley's for burgers and fries and then had split off from the other couple so they could drive around, just talking. If Dara's account was accurate, they'd done that for hours, until Joe's truck had run out of gas and they'd had to walk back to the party.

Ella and Joe had also had their first kiss that night. At Rocky Point. It was another spot that Millie knew. It was on the edge of the other side of town near Wildflower Vineyard. Rocky Point was a series of clear water springs that threaded through limestone boulders. It was a favorite local picnic spot. And one for making out. Not that Millie had any firsthand knowledge of that, but she was betting Joe did.

She looked at him. At that face and body that had recently inspired the pulls and tugs within her.

Yes, he had firsthand knowledge of a lot of things.

"Well?" he said, sounding both impatient and uneasy. That was uneasy times a thousand, of course.

"Your first date with Ella," Millie provided. "Your first kiss."

His jaw tightened. "Leave that out," he said.

She didn't even have to think about her answer. "Will do."

Bracing herself and wishing she could brace Joe, too, Millie went on to the next page, and picked up the pace of her skimming. She also silently cursed.

"It's about how Ella defied her mother to be with you," Millie managed to say. "About how much Ella and you loved each other. Really loved each other," she added in a murmur. "Dara underlined that. She also underlined that you and her mother would just sit and stare into each other's eyes." She paused. "Leave that out?"

"Yeah," he confirmed.

Oh, mercy. This was doing exactly what she was afraid it would do. Bringing all of those memories to the surface. It wasn't always the bad memories that ate away at you. The good ones took an even bigger bite.

"I'm not sure I ever had that with Royce," Millie admitted. "That's the worst part of this. Not knowing if what I had with him was true or false."

She looked up at Joe at the same moment he looked down at her. Their gazes met. Held. "Yeah," he repeated, and there was a world of emotion and grief in that one word.

That grief and emotion swirled between them. Survivors. But it felt like more than that. It felt as if they were on the same side. Friends, maybe.

Maybe more.

"You heard the part about Dara telling me I should kiss you?" Millie asked him.

She saw the answer in his eyes before he even confirmed it with a nod. "Dara wants you to fix me," he said with oh so much skepticism. "By kissing me." And the skepticism snowballed into an avalanche.

Millie nodded, as well. "Dara thinks you might…like me."

Silence. No nod this time. Their gazes continued to hold even when the fairy on the front door jangled. Even when Mr. Lawrence called out to her.

"Millie, I brought by that sculpture I wanted to show you," the man said.

Joe turned, obviously ready to go, but Millie took hold

of his arm. "You're attracted to me? True or false?" she added when he didn't say anything.

He continued not to say anything for several moments. Long enough for Millie to hear Mr. Lawrence's approaching footsteps.

"True," Joe finally said.

And he walked out.

CHAPTER SEVEN

TRUE.

Instead of admitting he was attracted to Millie, he should have just found a big rock and knocked himself on the head. That would have had a better outcome than spilling that his body was acting like a sex-crazed teenager.

Joe took a beer from the fridge, put it back and eyed the food that Alma had brought over in the cooler. The chicken looked good, but he wasn't hungry. What he was was restless, edgy.

And apparently in need of sex.

He closed the fridge, heading outside to his man-shed and wishing that Dara was home. Even though she would have almost certainly been in her room, it steadied him to have her nearby. No way could he give in to the gloom and doom when she might come out and see it on his face. The last thing he wanted was for his little girl to be worried about him.

But she was.

What Dara had told Millie proved that. *Now to the part about you doing something to fix my dad. I think you're going to have to kiss him.*

Yeah, she was worried all right, along with being flat-out wrong. There was no way Millie could fix him. Not with a kiss. Not with sex. Getting past what had happened was squarely on his own shoulders.

Joe stopped outside the door of his man-shed, dreading that damn receipt with the note that he knew he wouldn't be able to resist looking at again. Ella's last words to him. They were like a magnet, always pulling him right to that last day. To a past that couldn't change. Couldn't get better. And it sure as hell couldn't improve by going over those words and purchases again.

He went to his truck instead, got in and started driving. He knew where he was going even before he pulled away from his house. It was to a place that wouldn't change or improve things, but he headed there, anyway. To Hilltop Cemetery.

Where Ella was buried.

He drove across town and took the turn on the gravel road. Since it was going on 9:00 p.m., the odds were there wouldn't be anyone else visiting their loved ones. That was the good news. The bad was that he'd be there, and seeing her tombstone even from a distance wasn't going to fix this storm of emotions going on inside him. The old feelings he had for the woman who'd been his wife.

And the new feelings he had for Millie.

There was no comparing the two. Not really. He'd been in love with Ella, and she was the mother of his child. Millie was, well, a flame that was going to burn his ass if he didn't keep his distance. Keep her out of his mind. He was trying to convince himself how to do that when he nearly ran into her.

With the deer in the headlights look on her face, Millie froze. She was standing by her car, which was parked on the side of the road. Joe skidded to a stop. Then cursed before he threw open the door and got out.

"I'm sorry," she said before he could speak. His headlights lit her up as if she were on a stage. "I came to get the picture of the headstone." She motioned to the phone she was holding. "I didn't know you'd be here."

Ten minutes ago, neither had he.

"Did you get the picture?" Joe snapped. He winced and then reined in all the mess that was in his head right now. No need to dump that on Millie, not when she was likely dealing with a mess of her own. "Sorry," he muttered, changing his tone, and he repeated the question.

She nodded, and he thought she was confirming both the apology and that she'd gotten the shot of Ella's tombstone. She still had on her work clothes. A slim pale blue skirt and sleeveless top that moved like silk, but she'd ditched the heels she'd had on earlier and was wearing old cowboy boots. Scuffed and worn, like the kind people wore when they were working the yard.

"There's uneven ground up there," she said, following his gaze to her footwear. "And I didn't think anyone would be here to see me." She fluttered her fingers toward the hill. "I'll leave so you can go to her grave."

But she didn't budge. Millie stayed put and stared at him. It was a moment like the one earlier in the day where they seemed to have one of those unspoken conversations that only people close to each other should have. Millie and he weren't close, but they sure as hell had a lot in common.

Well, some things in common, anyway.

"You're having a bad night," she murmured. "Been there, done that." She lifted her shoulder. "In fact, I'm there and doing it right now. Sometimes, things just close in, you know."

Yeah, he knew. And their common ground and the bone-deep feeling of sadness that he'd never admitted to anyone else.

"You said you didn't know if what you had with your

husband was real. Whether it was true or false. I don't know, either. Parts of it had to be real. Had to be," he emphasized as the memory steamrolled over him. "But I don't know when it became something else."

Millie made a soft sound of agreement and then swallowed hard. The silence that followed should have been awkward enough to spur both of them to say a hasty goodbye and get the heck out of there.

It didn't.

"Hey, would you like to have a drink?" she asked. "Not at Three Sheets," she quickly added. "No need to stir up gossip that we're drowning our sorrows together. Best not to go to my place, either. *Neighbors*."

He didn't have any of those. Not any who could have eyes on his house, anyway, but there was no way he would invite her there. Even for that brainless part of him behind the zipper of his jeans, that crossed lines he wasn't anywhere ready to cross. Might never be.

"We could go in through the back of Once Upon a Time," Millie went on. "My grandmother had a bar built into the office, and it's stocked. We wouldn't have to talk. I could show you some of the oddball items in the shop. Or we could talk," she amended. "We could go over any ground rules you have about my shopping trip with Dara."

Joe didn't especially want a drink. Especially not one with Millie. And he didn't want to see anything oddball. But he wasn't sure he could face going back home right now, and it might be good to spell out those ground rules even if he wasn't sure exactly what they were.

"Sure," he heard himself saying. "One drink."

She smiled and, man, was that something to see. It lit up her face. Okay, the headlights probably helped with that, but seeing her smile lifted his mood just a little. Right now, he'd take *a little* to stop himself from going over that dark slope. He'd been over that slope, and it was damn hard to get back up it.

"I'll meet you at the shop in about twenty minutes," he said.

Millie would probably think that was because he wanted to go to Ella's grave. He didn't. But the twenty minutes would give him time to find an out-of-the-way parking spot so he could walk to Once Upon a Time. Because Millie was right about stirring up gossip if they were seen together. Joe really didn't want to deal with the questions, and the hope, that he was finally *moving on with his life.*

Joe waited until she'd driven away before he got back in his truck. Then, he just sat there, trying to talk himself out of doing this. He didn't have Millie's number so he couldn't text her and say that he'd come to his senses and needed to cancel.

Besides, Millie had looked as if she needed "a drink" even more than he did.

And that's why Joe finally started toward town. He decided to leave his truck in the parking lot of Three Sheets to the Wind. Or Three Sheets as everyone called it, and it had the "honor" of being the first saloon built in Last Ride. Hezzie Parkman had suggested calling it The Silver Spur, so there'd be less focus on getting drunk, but her suggestion hadn't been taken.

Joe walked the four blocks to the shop and tapped on the back door. Millie opened it before he could even pull back his hand.

"I thought you'd cancel," she said, the words rushing out with her breath. "I didn't want you to, but I thought you would."

Well, it'd been fifty-fifty for a while there as to what he would do, but here he was. "If you'd rather not—"

"No. Come in." She stepped to the side, waving him inside.

Joe did go in, and he followed her through the maze of rooms. She'd ditched the boots and was now barefoot. What she hadn't done was touch up her makeup or fix her hair. At least it didn't appear that she had. He liked that because even though they had already admitted they were attracted to each other, her lack of fuss made it feel less like a secret rendezvous.

Or so he was telling himself.

Millie led him toward her office, the only fully lit room in the place, and she immediately opened one of the bookshelves to reveal the bar behind it. "My grandmother fell in love with the Harry Potter books and decorated her office to match Dumbledore's," she said when she saw him studying the decor.

Her tone wasn't exactly conversational. There were tight nerves in her voice. "Before I forget, here's my cell number." She wrote it down on a note and handed it to him. "That way, if you want to check on Dara during the shopping trip, you can call me." She paused. "So, what would you like?"

It sounded like a really hot invitation to his overly aroused body, but Joe figured she hadn't meant it like that. Nope. The flush on her cheeks, however, told him that she knew how the question had sounded—and might or might not have meant it as an invitation. And might or might not want him to take her up on something more than a drink.

Obviously, both of them were doing a lot of emotional waffling tonight.

He had plenty of options for that drink offer. Millie had

been right about the bar being stocked. Every type of liquor was there only with small bottles of mixers. There was even an ice maker and a wine cooler.

Joe spotted a nearly full bottle of Jameson. "That." He pointed to it. "Two fingers, straight up."

Millie poured the whiskey into a cut crystal glass and helped herself to a Baileys over ice. Once Joe had his drink in hand, she clinked her glass to his. And accidentally brushed her fingers over his. "To better times ahead," she finished after a long pause. "We can stroll around the shop while we talk or stay in here."

Since Millie was so close right now that he could reach out and touch her, Joe opted for the strolling. It was better than face-to-face. Or finger to finger.

"Dara wants to do a makeover at one of those department store cosmetic places," she said as they started out of her office. Apparently, Millie wasn't going to waste any time launching into the main reason Joe had agreed to this drink. "Are you okay with that?"

Joe nodded. It was the least of his concerns for this bucket list trip. "Just make sure it's not something that'll hurt her skin or cause her to break out."

"Will do." She took a sip of her Baileys and stopped to make an adjustment to a display of antique fortune-telling stuff. Crystal balls, tarot cards, several bowls of crystals, a small poster advertising palm reading, tea leaves and a small tattered book titled, *Practical Guide to Husband Divination*.

Joe picked up the book, frowned.

"Apparently, it was the precursor to dating sites," Millie joked. "It's about how to find your perfect match. It's been in the shop for years with no buyers, but I'm pretty sure several women have snapped pictures of the pages."

Heaven help him, he smiled. Even more, the smile felt real and not one of those he plastered on to try to make people believe he was okay.

Joe pushed the "real" aside. The smile, too. And focused on Dara. "I've decided I don't want to know about the underwear shopping." He paused. "But if the subject comes up about any boy who might see said underwear, maybe you could—" He stopped and waved that off.

What the hell was he thinking? The idea was to put some distance between Millie and them, not suggest that Millie warn Dara about the dangers of boys.

"I haven't had the talk with Dara," he admitted. "But I will."

Millie's forehead bunched up, and they started walking again. "Uh, the talk might be better coming from Frankie. For girls, it's not just about safe sex. Other things come into play. I can work in some of it in a general kind of way, and Frankie should fill in the details."

"Shit," he grumbled.

This was about periods, and he really didn't want to be talking about this now. Not ever. Joe made a mental note to call Frankie and dump this on her. Frankie wouldn't mind doing it, though Joe would have to insist that his sometimes flighty, hickey-sporting sister tell Dara that she should wait to have sex until she was in love.

Or thirty.

Yeah, thirty was better.

Millie stopped again, this time at a True or False display, and she muttered a curse word. "This shouldn't be here."

Joe looked at the, well, whatever the heck it was. It resembled an old-fashioned eggbeater with a rotary crank, but instead of a whisk, there was a wood cylinder the size of a hot dog.

"True or False," he said, reading from the card. "This is a nineteenth-century butter maker. I'm guessing false." He turned the card over. Blank.

"False," she verified. Millie took the gadget and tucked it under her arms. "It's a Victorian vibrator, and it's going back upstairs in storage with the other vibrators and such that my grandmother found among some items she'd bought at an estate sale."

Joe suddenly wanted a better look at it—and the "such" in the upstairs storage—but he didn't need to give it any thought to know that was a really bad idea. Best not to discuss or view sexual aids even if they were intriguing.

"That leaves eating at Taco Cabana," Millie said, obviously continuing their discussion about Dara. "She says it won't bring up bad memories for her but will it?"

To hell if he knew. It would for him, but maybe Dara was in a different mental place than he was. "I'm not sure. But keep an eye on her just in case." He stopped again, cursed. "I shouldn't be putting any of this on you, and I should be asking if it'll bring up bad memories for you."

Millie shrugged, but the next sip she had of her Baileys was more than a sip. More like the kind of gulp a person needed when trying to steel themselves.

"I don't know. Maybe," she admitted. "It's funny. Not 'ha ha' funny," she quickly added, "but so many things trigger the bad stuff. A smell. Some random thing that someone says. Dreams." She paused. "Not you though. I thought you would, but you don't."

Yeah. Joe was right there on the same page with her. Not the normal bad stuff. But this simmering heat was posing a problem or two. That problem went up a couple of rungs on the lust ladder when he looked at her. Now that they were in the light, he could see some freckles peeking through the makeup. He didn't know why he found that "kick in the gut" hot, but he did. Then again, he was finding a lot of things hot about Millie.

She stared at him, licked the Baileys off her bottom lip. Sighed. And then started walking. Not easily. Joe could tell she'd had to force herself to do it.

"Let me give you a tour of my favorite part of the shop," she said, sounding businesslike now. Mostly businesslike, anyway. There was still some heat in her voice, and her breathing was a little rushed.

Leading the way, she took him into the local artist room. It was a lot bigger than he'd expected and figured the space had been configured by tearing down plenty of other walls. What walls remained were filled with framed paintings, photographs and even some sculptures. More sculptures had been positioned throughout the room. Ditto for even more paintings on easels.

"My grandmother started this," she explained. "Most are artists or photographers from Last Ride or from the county, but she made a few exceptions." She pointed to a pair of watercolors in the corner. "Like those. They're from an artist in Dallas who visited here back in the sixties. And I'm not sure about those." She pointed to another grouping of three canvas paintings, all on easels. "But they're my favorites."

Joe turned to look at them. And got another slam in the gut. Not from heat this time. No. But from the shock of seeing those too-familiar paintings.

"I don't know who the artist is," Millie continued. "They're unsigned, but since the paintings are all of scenes from the area, I suspect the artist is local."

They were indeed scenes from in and around Last Ride. The Fairy Pond that had gotten its name from the colorful rocks and the wild ferns. The painting wasn't of the pond itself but rather had been done on a bluff above it with the pond in the background. The second was of a remote section of the Wildflower Vineyard. The third was an old gray windmill about ten miles away from town. What remained of the crumbling windmill blades were being battered by a storm from a bruise-colored sky.

Hell's Texas bells. He remembered Ella painting these scenes. Portions of them, anyway. He'd walked into her she-shed a couple of times and had seen them. But he hadn't had a clue that she'd sold them.

Obviously, it was another of Ella's secrets.

"How'd you get the paintings if you don't know who the artist is?" Joe managed to ask, after he'd had a huge gulp of his whiskey.

"The internet," she answered with her attention thankfully on the paintings and not him. "I found a social media page called La La Land, and the artist had posted pictures of the paintings. I emailed him or her and made an offer. After some negotiations, the artist agreed but said the sale had to be anonymous. I paid through PayPal, and the paintings were left wrapped by the back door."

Joe had no idea what Ella had done with the money. Maybe she'd used it to buy things for her lover. A thought that had him tossing back the rest of his whiskey.

Millie turned to him, obviously noticing the quick finish he'd made of his drink. "Are you okay?" she asked.

No. He wasn't. And she clearly picked up on that.

"Joe," Millie whispered. Not a question but rather a soft reassurance.

She set her Baileys on a table next to some small porcelain turtles and took hold of his arm. Joe could have sworn he felt her warmth through his shirtsleeve, and he sure as heck saw that warmth on her face.

"I'm sorry," she muttered. Along with the warmth, she was obviously about to mentally beat herself up. "I shouldn't have pressed you to come here. I shouldn't—"

Joe kissed her.

He had one thought. To put a stop to that mental beating up. She'd been nothing but kind to Dara and him, and she didn't deserve to feel any guilt because of him.

But his one thought quickly shifted to something else.

Millie's mouth froze beneath his. For a second, anyway. Then, the sigh she made was long, slow and filled with what he thought might be relief. She didn't throw her arms around him, but he could feel the need. It was as real as the heat from her hand that was still on his biceps.

Even with just the lightest touch of his lips on hers, he could still taste her. Not just the Baileys but Millie herself. There was warmth here, too, and the hint of something that he knew would be pretty damn amazing.

Joe didn't deepen the kiss though, mercy, that's exactly what he wanted to do. He ached to haul her to him and explore that sweet mouth of hers. And more. Much more. He ached to explore the rest of her, too.

But he stopped. Forced his mouth from hers.

"I should go," he said.

Millie blinked like a woman dazed. "Uh, do you want to go?" There it was. An invitation that he couldn't accept.

"No," he admitted. "And that's why I should."

Joe set his glass next to hers and headed for the door.

CHAPTER EIGHT

MILLIE PUT HER coffee cup, the plate that'd held her English muffin and juice glass in the sink, streaked some dish soap over them and started washing. Hurrying a little because it was Sunday and nearly time for Dara to come over so they could go on their bucket list trip.

She had a dishwasher, but the problem with eating solo was that it took a week or more to fill it up. Plus, there was something mindlessly numbing about having her hands in the sudsy warm water.

But the mindlessness didn't stay with her.

When she washed the glass and put it on the drying rack, she got a full jolt memory of another glass. The one Joe had used to drink his Jameson when he'd been at the shop. The one he'd set aside when he'd kissed her.

Millie got a full jolt of that kiss, too, and the jolt went all the way to her freshly polished toenails. The man was a walking, talking definition of the things she should avoid.

But she didn't want to avoid him.

She wanted to kiss him again. To hold him and, yes, even just talk with him while the attraction sizzled and snapped between them. It'd been so long since she'd felt anything close to that, and Millie wanted to feel it again.

Obviously, Joe didn't feel the same. He'd walked out after issuing his *That's why I should*, and she hadn't seen or heard from him in the six days since that'd happened.

But she might see him soon when he dropped off Dara. Of course, it was likely the drop-off would be fast and that he wouldn't come inside.

That last thought barely had time to go through her mind when her doorbell rang. Dara wasn't supposed to be there for another fifteen minutes, but maybe she was eager to get started on the trip. Since Millie didn't want to risk not being able to at least give Joe a wave, she hurried to answer the door.

Millie tried not to appear disappointed when she saw that it was Frankie and Dara on the porch. Joe wasn't anywhere in sight.

"Sorry about being early," Dara immediately said. "Little T spent the night at my house, and when Frankie came to get him, I decided to get a ride with her."

"That's fine," Millie assured her, hoping she kept the disappointment out of her voice, as well. She glanced around the porch. "Where's Little T?"

"With Tanner," Frankie provided. "It's his day with him."

"Aunt Frankie isn't going into work today," Dara added, her gaze nailed to Millie. The girl lifted her eyebrow. "I was thinking about seeing if she could go with us."

Considering that Dara had already nixed having Frankie take her on this adventure, Millie shifted her attention to her former sister-in-law and saw that Frankie wasn't her usual perky self. No out-there clothes or hair. In fact, she looked sad.

"Is everything okay?" Millie asked her, motioning for them to come inside.

Frankie nodded and looked on the verge of exclaiming that she was just fine, but the tentative smile faded. "Tanner's taking Little T on his picnic date with Skylar Arnold. That'll be Tanner's third date with her this week."

There was no need for Frankie to add more. Skylar was beautiful, rich and on the prowl for a husband. Everyone in town knew that. Knew, too, that Skylar had a thing for bad boys. Tanner would be right in the woman's wheelhouse.

Despite her penchant for bad boys, Skylar was supersmart, practically a genius when it came to computers, and she'd built her own company from the ground up as a business analyst. Millie wasn't exactly sure what Skylar's job entailed, but she'd heard the woman worked with some powerhouse companies all over the state.

"I'm sorry," Millie told her. And she was. It didn't matter that Tanner and Frankie had been divorced for years, Millie believed that Frankie still had feelings for him. Maybe not love feelings, but it probably stung that her ex might be getting seriously involved with someone. Especially someone with Skylar's nonbimbo brain, looks and pedigree.

"It's okay," Frankie muttered. "I don't want to horn in on your trip. You two should go and have fun."

Millie glanced at Dara, got a nod. "You're not horning in. You should come with us. Maybe get a makeover and some new underwear."

Frankie's face brightened a little. So did Dara's, and that told Millie a lot about the girl. She hadn't wanted to do this trip with her aunt, but Dara had been willing to adjust her plans so that Frankie wouldn't be spending the day alone.

"You're sure?" Frankie asked.

"Positive," Millie assured her, locking the front door. "Let me grab my purse, and we can go."

"I've got some more stories for the research on Mom," Dara volunteered as they made their way from the foyer to the garage. She handed Millie the papers. "You can read them later, but I can tell you about them on the drive."

Millie started mentally armoring herself for that, and she wondered if hearing the stories would be better or worse now that she'd kissed Ella's husband. Then again, Ella had almost certainly kissed hers so maybe the hot feelings for Joe wouldn't play into anything Dara had to tell her.

"Uh, how is the research going?" Frankie asked. This time it was she and Millie who exchanged a glance, and Millie saw the unspoken question there. *Are you okay with all of this?*

"The research is going well," Millie assured her. "I got the picture of the headstone, and Dara's already given me lots of info I can put in the report."

"And I have lots more," Dara said with plenty of enthusiasm. "About the day Mom found out she was pregnant with me and how she told Dad. About their wedding. I even know the vows they wrote each other."

Millie took a deep breath. Something she'd no doubt be doing a lot because there probably wasn't enough mental armor in the universe to get her through the oh-so-joyful stories about the *other* woman.

But two hours later, Millie realized she'd been wrong.

Dara had sped right through the research stories, and then had asked them if they wanted to hear her latest playlist. Frankie and Millie had jumped right on that, and it'd gotten them through the drive to San Antonio. Once they were in the mall, it was easier to push aside thoughts of Ella and Royce. Hard to stay focused on the past when confronted with a "buy one, get one free" bra and panty sale at Sassy Silk.

With their shopping bags filled with lace and, yes, even

some sassy silk, they headed to the makeover counter called the Face Place. The decor reminded Millie of her kitchen. White and stainless with some pops of red thrown in. It was the kind of place she usually avoided since it was jammed with girls and women who were obviously far more adventurous than she was.

Dara had called ahead and reserved some spots so the clerk wearing a short leather black dress led them to the white acrylic counters that stretched across the entire sides and back walls. Nearly every station had a customer getting made over while a companion or two looked on and oohed, aww'ed or giggled.

The area where they'd been escorted had not one but two cosmeticians, both of whom looked pretty scary, what with their overly done faces. Ironically, one did indeed look like an aging Britney Spears with lip gloss shiny enough to trigger a seizure. Millie gladly let Frankie go ahead of her while the other, younger clerk got started on Dara.

Millie settled into one of the high counter stools to peruse the before and after pictures plastered all around. The before shots showed every blemish, the uneven coloring and the flat-mouthed expressions. The afters had little arrows pointing to the areas that'd been made over along with the names of the products that had been used to achieve such cosmetic miracles. The after customers had happy smiles and bright eyes with all flaws covered.

And covered. And covered.

She was certain that was some metaphor for her own life, but she didn't want to get into it. For one day, maybe even just one hour, she wanted to put her sulky mood aside, curse Royce and get on with normal things. Well, normal-ish. Sitting at a makeup counter while Frankie was getting pale green goop smeared on her face wasn't something Millie had on her daily to-do list.

Her phone rang, and she got another non-normal sensation when she saw the number that she was certain was Joe's. Good grief. It was like being back in high school again, and she felt the giddiness in her stomach when she hit the answer button.

"Just wondering how the shopping trip is going?" Joe asked.

Millie smiled at the sound of his voice. "Great." She got off the stool and moved away from the others to a small sitting area with a love seat and chairs. "Dara's silk purchase stayed in the mildly sassy category. Oh, and Frankie came with us so she might be able to work in some of The Talk today."

"Frankie's with you? How'd that happen?"

Millie nearly blurted out that Frankie had needed some cheering up, but that might be something Frankie wanted to keep from her brother. "She had the day off since Little T's with Tanner, and Dara wanted her to come."

If Joe had overheard all of her conversation with Dara at the shop, and she was pretty certain that he had, then he knew that his daughter had originally nixed the idea of Frankie doing the shopping trip. He was probably now wondering just what was really going on. However, he didn't push. He only made a sound that could have meant anything.

"How about the makeover?" Joe continued a moment later. "How'd that go?"

"It's still going." Millie spared a quick glance at Dara and Frankie. "Did you know that pink eye is a trend?"

"Excuse me?" he asked.

"Not the kind of pink eye that nobody wants to get. This is pink eyeshadow that goes above, below and in the corners of the eye. Dara's trying that out now. Don't worry," she quickly added, chuckling, "they sell makeup remover."

Joe groaned, but there didn't seem to be too much real objection in his tone. Then, he paused. A very long time. Then, even longer. "Look, about the other night, about that kiss…"

Millie had dropped her guard and wasn't prepared for a chat about that. "It's okay," she tried to assure him.

"No, it's not." Joe paused again, and this time there did indeed seem to be some *objection*. "I shouldn't have done that. You invited me to your shop to talk about Dara—"

"In part," she interrupted. "A big part, but I'm not going to lie and say I didn't want a kiss to happen. Even when I know kissing could complicate things."

"It could, and did," he readily admitted. "I just wanted you to know that it won't happen again." He stopped, cursed. And this time, the emotion was heavy. "I'll try not to let it happen again," he amended.

"All right," Millie said after he didn't add anything else. "But I don't think I'm going to try."

"Excuse me?" he repeated.

She watched as Frankie and Dara shared a laugh over their pink eyes and green goop. Millie wanted to be in on that laugh. She wanted to feel the joy and humor all the way to her stomach. In fact, she wanted to feel a lot of things that hadn't been on her feeling agenda for the past two years.

Including more kisses from Joe.

"Joe, there aren't enough cold showers in Texas to make me stop wanting you. It's not convenient. Heck, it's not even smart. It just is. So, I'm not going to even try to prevent a kiss from happening again. In fact, I might just kiss you. Gotta go," she tacked on to that and ended the call.

Millie figured that was the worst timing for a hang-up in the history of bad hang-ups, but Frankie, complete with a generous slathering of turtle green goop on her face, was making her way toward her.

"I have to sit for fifteen minutes," Frankie said. "Apparently, I have pores the size of moon craters, and this will help. It's supposed to harden to the consistency of a brick which means I soon won't be able to use the muscles in my face, but when I'm done, I'll glow like the sun."

"Good to know. And what about Dara?" Millie asked. "Why does she have that white denture looking thing over her mouth?"

"It's a hydrating lip mask. Apparently, she's drier than the moon in that particular area. The techs really need to come up with comparisons that aren't celestial," Frankie added in a mutter. "Anyway, Dara isn't supposed to talk, and I didn't want to cause her to slip so I came over here. They'll test out foundation and nail colors on her while she's temporarily mute." She tipped her head to the counter. "You can go ahead and get started with your makeover if you want."

Millie shook her head. "I think I'll sit this one out." Though she did wonder just how bad, or different, she'd look in the lip gloss that one of the after photos had touted as Berry My Treasure. Maybe that lavender eyeshadow, too, that had the unfortunate name of Raunchy Rose.

When she heard Frankie sigh, Millie looked at her and sighed, too. It was going to be a little hard to have a serious conversation with the pore reducer, but Millie wanted to try. "So, you want to talk about your blue mood or your green face? And it's okay if you tell me to mind my own business."

Frankie took a deep breath. "You always mind your own business. Sometimes, I wish you wouldn't."

Millie lifted an eyebrow and waited for Frankie to finish that.

"You never once told me I was an idiot for getting involved with your brother," Frankie finally said. "You must have known we weren't right for each other, and you withheld judgment."

"Oh, I judged Tanner, believe me," Millie argued.

"Sibling stuff," Frankie argued back. "You wanted him to be more responsible about Little T, and he is." She hesitated, and Millie thought she tried to nibble on her bottom lip, but apparently the goo had cemented her mouth in place. "Is Tanner serious about Skylar?" she asked.

At least that's what Millie thought she'd said. It was hard to understand Frankie since she was speaking with her jaw set and her teeth clamped together.

"Not that he's said." But she didn't want to steer Frankie in the wrong direction. "Tanner doesn't volunteer much about his private life to me," Millie admitted. She stared at Frankie, trying to suss out her expression, but it was impossible. "Are you still in love with him?"

Another shrug. Followed by a mousy-sounding sigh that was no doubt mousy because now it was getting harder for Frankie to use any portion of her face. "Maybe, a little. He's hot, and I've always had a thing for him. That doesn't just go away, you know."

Millie did know. She was going through this with Joe. But when she thought of Royce, there was no heat. And what was worse was she was worried the heat she once felt for her husband didn't measure up to what she now felt for Joe.

That was just downright depressing.

"You never settled," Millie muttered. "You wanted Tanner and despite all the wrong things about being with him, you didn't turn away and choose someone or something else."

"The har duhunt ork dat way," Frankie said.

It took Millie a moment to do the translation. *The heart doesn't work that way.* Wise words coming from a woman who some would say had made a proper mess of her life.

"I'm tired of grieving," Millie went on. Since she'd started opening this particular can of worms, she just continued. "But I feel stuck, like one of those hamsters on a wheel."

"Den, do ommting to git unstk," Frankie advised.

This translation took Millie a little longer, but when she got it, she sighed and nodded. *Then, do something to get unstuck.*

More wise words. But unsticking was easier said than done. "I just need to move on," Millie said aloud to herself.

Except she didn't say it to only herself. She looked up to see Dara. The lip mask was gone, and one cheek had one color foundation. The other cheek, another. But the big important point here was the girl was plenty close enough to have heard Millie's whining.

"I'm sorry," Millie and Dara said at the same time.

Millie just stared at her. She wasn't sure what had prompted Dara's apology, but Dara quickly filled her in. "You're getting depressed because the research is opening up old wounds and memories about your husband."

"No," Millie jumped to say. She didn't want to put any of this on Dara's teenage shoulders. She got to her feet so

she'd be face-to-face with the girl. "It's not the research."
That was a good start, but Millie wasn't sure how to finish
that. How to make sure Dara didn't feel one fleck of guilt
over what was going on. "I'm okay. What I'm feeling are
things I need to deal with."

Dara didn't look the least bit convinced of that. "We'll
stop the research," she concluded. "We can finish our make-
overs and go home. We'll skip going out to eat."

The girl was such a sweetheart, and before Millie could
stop herself, she brushed a kiss on her cheek. In hindsight
though, she should have checked for a non-made-over spot
because she ended up kissing the tawny colored foundation. It tasted a little like coconut.

"I want to finish the research and go to Taco Cabana,"
Millie insisted. "And I want to do some other things, too,"
she added when it popped into her head. "My thirtieth is in
a couple of months, and I want to do my own bucket list."

"Ucket ist?" Frankie asked, getting to her feet.

Millie confirmed that with a nod, and the ideas just kept
on popping. "I want to visit every site in the paintings that
are in the local artists' gallery of the shop. And revisit the
ones I've already seen like the old drive-in theater. I love
that place." Inspired, she added, "I also want to learn to
ride a horse."

Dara practically beamed. "I can help with that. We have
four horses." And like Millie's popping up thoughts, Dara's
beaming continued. "I can teach you to ride, and that way,
you'll get to spend time with Dad. You could get a chance
to try to make him happy. You could end up making yourself happy, too."

From the mouths of babes.

Well, the mouth of a teenager, anyway.

"I'd love that," Millie said, causing a seriously gleeful moment with Dara squealing and Frankie attempting some kind of joyful noise. "And you know what," Millie added. "I'm going to get started making myself happy right now."

She marched to the counter and the waiting stash of Berry My Treasure and Raunchy Rose.

CHAPTER NINE

JOE TRIED TO focus on repairing the corral fence, but his mind kept wandering in the direction of the front pasture.

Where his daughter was giving Millie a riding lesson.

Hard not to notice that Millie wasn't a natural rider. Equally hard not to notice that all the moving around on the back of the bay mare caused her body to move around, too. That part seemed very natural, and it was damn eye-catching.

Joe still wasn't sure how this lesson had come about, but when Dara had returned from her shopping/makeover/Taco Cabana trip five days ago, she'd announced that she would be helping Millie with some things, and one of the things would apparently cause Millie to spend a lot of time at the ranch. Time needed because it was going to take a butt-load of hours for her to learn even basic horseback riding skills. Still, she and Dara seemed to be having fun with it.

Their giggling was ear-catching.

He was glad Dara was having some fun. Since this was a teacher's training day and she was off from school, she likely would have just ended up in her room, talking on the phone or reading. It was good to see her out enjoying herself even if the enjoying was with Millie.

Part of him didn't want this newfound camaraderie between them. He was worried about Dara getting hurt if and when Millie decided she'd had enough of the gossip it would create just being around his daughter. But he had other worries, too.

What if Millie blew off the gossip and stayed around long after the research and riding lessons were done?

She'd already used nearly a month of her research time which meant in two months, she would do the report. She'd put Ella aside. But if she didn't put Dara aside, too, then—

The ringing sound shot through the questions he shouldn't be having, anyway, and he looked in the direction of the back porch where Millie had left her purse. Her phone was right beside it. She'd left it there after telling him she didn't want to break it if the mare threw her and she landed on her butt.

The phone finally stopped ringing, only to start up again just seconds later.

"Can you see who that is, please?" Millie called out to him.

Joe had nothing better to do since he obviously sucked at fence repairs today. He went to the porch and glanced at the screen. "It's Monte."

"Crud," Millie muttered. "Could you answer it? There might be a problem at the shop."

Apparently, there was a camaraderie between Millie and him, as well. Then again, the kiss at her shop had jetted them past that stage and had now moved on to him being obsessed with the way her butt looked in her jeans and answering her phone.

"It's Joe McCann," he said right off. "Millie asked me to take the call."

"Oh." Monte stretched that out a few syllables, and Joe didn't think the man's imagination was stretching, too. Millie's clerk obviously thought there was some hanky-panky going on between Joe and her.

"The message is kind of urgent," Monte said, "in a business urgent kind of way. For the past couple of months, Millie's been in negotiations to buy a pair of small mantel clocks that were made by Hezzie Parkman's first husband. Anyway, the owner just called and said she could have them for six grand if she'll pick them up this afternoon."

"Six grand," Joe muttered, shaking his head. A lot of money.

"I got the feeling the seller needed the money fast so that means Millie needs to get over there ASAP," Monte added. "There are a couple of Hezzie's heirs who are interested in buying them, and he says he'll call them if Millie doesn't show."

"All right. I'll tell her right away. Does she have the seller's name and contact info?"

"It's Lou Stinson, and she's got his number and address. He lives out on Old Sawmill Trail."

Yeah, Joe knew where he lived, and just hearing the name gave him one of those jolts down memory lane. A bad memory lane.

"Any idea if Millie would plan to go out there by herself?" Joe asked.

"Probably. I'm here in the shop until closing, and it's been a steady stream of customers for that shipment of fairy balls we got in."

Even though Joe had plenty of concerns about the trip to get the clock, he couldn't help but latch on to what Monte had just said. "Fairies have balls?"

"Not those kinds of balls." Monte chuckled. "They're the blown glass kind that people hang in their houses. Sort of like suncatchers. Anyway, it's Haylee's day off so that's why she can't go get the clocks." He paused. "Have you got some concerns about Millie going out there?"

"Some," he admitted. But he wasn't going to spell them out to Monte. "I'll ride out there with her." It wouldn't be an especially fun trip for Joe, but no way was he going to let Millie walk into that alone.

He ended the call and turned to relay the news to Millie, but she was already off the mare. Dara was leading the horse back to the barn, no doubt to brush her down, and Millie was heading toward him.

And she was smiling.

That particular expression always had a way of reminding him that she was attractive. And that he was a man who was attracted to her.

"Your daughter's a great teacher," Millie exclaimed, still beaming.

Of course, some of the beam was probably the fine mist of sweat on her face. It wasn't blistering hot today, thanks to plenty of thick gray clouds, but it was still in the low eighties. The heat and humidity had done a number on her makeup, and he could see the freckles popping through. For some damn reason, he found that attractive, as well. At this point though, pretty much everything about her was going to interest pretty much every part of him.

Joe handed her the phone. "Monte said Lou Stinson is willing to sell you the clocks for 6K if you get out to his place fast."

That upped her beaming even more, and she clapped her hands in victory. She apparently wasn't experiencing any sticker shock about the price. "I've been negotiating with that old goat for months."

Old goat was a kind name for the man. Joe thought that *old sonofabitching bastard* suited him better.

"Good thing I have a checkbook for the shop with me so

I can go out there right now before he changes his mind," she added.

"You've been out to his place before?" Joe asked.

She shook her head, pulling off the cowboy hat she'd worn to stave off the sun. "We've only talked over the phone. I've never met him." Millie stopped, combed her gaze over him. "Have you?"

"Yeah." And Joe left it at that. "I'll ride out there with you."

"Oh, but I'm sure you have work to do. It's not necessary "

"It is," Joe insisted, leaving her a little dumbfounded when he went closer to the barn and called out to Dara. "Millie and I have got to do a quick errand. Will you be okay for about an hour?"

As he'd expected, that got Dara sticking her head out of the barn. Once she got past a little shock, she gave a sly smile. Hell. Dara probably thought he was taking Millie away for a make-out session.

"Sure. I've got some homework to do," Dara said, still smiling. "So, I'll be busy."

That was code for *Take your time, do something stupid. With Millie.* His daughter had turned into a matchmaker.

Joe just sighed. "If you get hungry before we get back, the Last Ride Society dropped off more food, and I put it in the fridge."

Dara brightened even more. "Fried chicken?"

He nodded. "Along with a couple of twice baked potatoes and some chocolate chip cookies."

Dara made a yum sound and went back into the barn.

"You get fried chicken and cookies?" Millie protested. "I get low calorie dishes with salads."

Joe frowned at her menu. Apparently, Alma and the

other society members had decided not to focus on comfort food choices when it came to Millie.

"You're welcome to eat some of the latest delivery," he said without really thinking it through. He was inviting her to dinner, and if she was smart, she would say a fast no.

She didn't.

"Thanks," she said. "I'd like that."

Hell. He'd like it, too. So would Dara. That didn't mean it was the right thing to do.

"Could I use your bathroom to freshen up, and then we can go get the clocks?" she asked, picking up her purse.

Joe nodded and led her into the house. Which was spotless. Dara had done a more than thorough cleaning job before Millie had arrived for her riding lesson.

"We should use my truck," he said, showing her to the hall powder room. "It's going to rain, and Lou lives on a dirt road. Your car could get stuck in the mud." Joe didn't want to do anything to prolong this drive, and he especially didn't want to do anything to prolong their being at Lou's place.

Millie thanked him before she went into the powder room. Joe headed to the master suite to do his own cleaning up. He washed up and opened the old-style medicine cabinet for his deodorant.

And he saw the box of condoms.

Ones left over from when Ella had still been alive. Great. It was a visual cue he sure as hell didn't need, and he closed the cabinet door but not before he caught a glimpse of the expiration date on the box. They still had another year on them. Yet something else he didn't need to know.

He grabbed a clean T-shirt as he headed to the door, and he was still in the process of putting it on when he stepped into the hall.

And saw Millie.

She had just come out of the powder room and froze when she looked at him. Except her eyes didn't freeze. Her gaze slid, slowly, from his face, which no doubt had a startled guilty-of-something expression, to his chest. That particular part of him was bare since he'd only managed to get the shirt over his head.

Joe went still, too. Something that often happened when he was around Millie. But he had no trouble following the little trip her eyes were making from his chest. To his stomach. To the zipper of his jeans where there was indeed some stirring going on.

She fluttered her fingers toward nothing in particular and made a sound, also of nothing in particular. She was obviously trying to blow this off as nothing, just a hallway encounter between two people who didn't have the hots for each other.

"Son of a monkey," she finally grumbled, and the slight smile she managed was laced with frustration and need. Not a good combination.

Joe got his arms working, and he yanked down the shirt to cover himself.

"There," Millie said, lifting her shirt to reveal her bare stomach. "We're even."

No, hell no, they weren't. This tit for tat was nowhere near even. He caught a glimpse of the bottom of her bra. Peach lace. The glimpsing didn't stop there, either. Nope. Because her jeans rode low on her hips, he had no trouble seeing her navel.

And the little gold hoop she had there.

The surprise and curiosity must have shown in his eyes because her gaze flew down to her stomach. "Oh." She pulled her shirt back in place. "Frankie did that for me. To cheer me up. Long story," she added, dismissing it with a wave of her hand.

"We've got about a fifteen-minute drive to Lou's," he pointed out. "Is that time enough for a long story?"

Obviously, he needed a good knock on the head. No way should he be pushing for that kind of information. No way should he be smiling, either, but that's sure as hell what he was doing.

Millie smiled, too, and hers was a lot more potent than his. "I feel like we just played doctor," she muttered as they headed for the front door.

Yeah, he did, too. Doctor with a side dose of need that made him want to tongue kiss her navel and that little ring. Actually, there were a lot of places on her he wouldn't mind tongue kissing. Including her mouth.

"A little less than a year ago," Millie started after they'd gotten in his truck, "I went by Frankie's shop to pick up Little T so he could have a sleepover at my house. Tanner was dropping him off there, but he was running late. It was a tough day for me. The anniversary," she added in a mumble.

Joe was so sorry he'd brought this up because he knew exactly what she meant. It'd been the one-year anniversary of the car wreck. He was betting it'd been a whole lot more than just a tough day.

"I shouldn't have brought this up," Joe said, cursing himself as he pulled out of his driveway.

"No, it's okay," Millie assured him. "It has sort of a happy ending. Frankie was blue, too, because it was the anniversary of her divorce so we did an impulsive thing and both got our belly buttons pierced. It hurt," she emphasized. "But the pain and the wine chaser we had to numb the pain got our minds off the other stuff."

Frankie had never mentioned any of this. Not even the part about her being down over her divorce from Tanner.

"I should have done more stuff like that with Frankie," Millie went on, looking out the window. It was basically pastures with livestock, woods and the occasional creek or pond, but it all came together for some great scenery. "I've always liked her."

He heard the undercurrents in that. "You like Frankie, but you didn't want to have to deal with the blowback from Laurie Jean."

"Yes," she readily admitted. Her sigh was long and weary, and he hated he'd broken her light mood. "A lot of things I've done in my life have been to avoid blowback. I'm thinking that should change though. I'm not ready to dance naked in the streets, but I want to make some changes."

Joe couldn't stop himself from smiling again. His mouth was apparently being as stupid as his dick. "You're sure you shouldn't start with dancing naked in the streets? Or maybe just in that peach lace bra you're wearing."

She smiled, too. "I hadn't meant to hike up my top that high. And I don't usually wear stuff like that. It's something I bought when I was shopping with Dara."

Well, that cooled him down, and he hoped his daughter wouldn't give any boy a peek of her Sassy Silk purchase.

"Wait, stop," Millie called out.

That got his attention off Dara, bras and Millie's naked dancing, and Joe hit the brakes. Considering her reaction, he expected to see a dead animal, someone hurt or, heck, even a UFO. But when he followed her pointing finger, he saw the old drive-in theater. Well, what was left of it, anyway. The huge white screen was torn in places, but it was still standing. Ditto for the speaker poles and the concession stands, but the tall fence that had once been around it was long gone. Not a surprise since the place had shut down when he'd been a teenager.

"This is from the painting," Millie said, and she reached to open the door.

"Hold on a second," he told her, and he pulled the truck onto the shoulder. Thankfully, there weren't likely to be any other vehicles on the road. "What painting?"

"The one on the La La Land site I told you about." Millie barreled out of the truck so she didn't hear Joe's muttered profanity. He dragged in a hard breath and got out.

"I didn't see a painting like this in your shop," he pointed out.

"No. It was on the website, but I didn't get a chance to buy it. I did screenshots of the paintings before the site went away, and I remember this one. It was one of my favorites."

His, too. And yeah, he remembered it all right. It was one Ella had given to Dara so she could hang it in her bedroom.

"This looks just like the painting," she said, clicking a picture of it with her phone. She was smiling again, obviously taking it all in, and she walked closer to metal posts where some speakers still dangled from coils. "I really hope I can find the artist one day."

Joe followed her, focusing on her voice, that smile and the sound of the wind whistling through the holes in the screen. But there was another sound, too. The low rumbling of thunder.

"We should probably go," he said.

"Yes. Just give me a minute." It was as if she was drinking it all in.

It probably wasn't the perfect moment to spill the truth about Ella's paintings, but that's exactly what Joe was about to do when Millie turned to him. Their eyes met, and he caught just a glimpse of the heat. Suddenly she was moving toward him, and using both her hands, she took hold of his face, pulling him down to her.

Kissing him.

This wasn't some "testing the waters" kiss, either. It was the full-blown variety. Hunger and hot. She was drinking him in just as she'd done to the scenery. Except this time she was touching. She kept her hands in place, anchoring him as if she wanted to make sure he wouldn't pull away. But Joe couldn't have done that even if he'd wanted to. Nope. He was staying put, along with kissing her right back.

He got to live out some of his recent fantasies about Millie when he used his tongue on her mouth. She responded with a throaty sound of pleasure that gave him an instant erection. Man, he wanted her, and the kiss had just unlocked the restraint he'd been fighting to keep in place.

His restraint got another test when her breasts pressed against his chest. He thought of the peach lace bra. Of that little gold ring on her navel. And the heat for her turned into an insistent, aching need.

Joe hooked his arm around her, dragging her even harder against him. More pressure. More contact. And with it, he upped the need. This sure wasn't doing anything to cool him down.

But something did.

Joe felt the cool splats on his head and face, and even with the rumble of thunder, it took him a moment to realize it was raining. Pouring, actually. The sky unzipped, and Mother Nature hosed them down.

Obviously becoming aware they were being drenched, Millie pulled back and looked up at him. She blinked. Then laughed. She took hold of his hand and started running back to his truck. Joe wasn't laughing. Because of his erection, he was having a tough time keeping up with her.

With Millie still laughing, they practically dived into his truck, and she leaned over and kissed him again. Nothing deep this time that involved open mouths. It seemed to be a period at the end of this particular sentence.

He looked at her. No choice to do otherwise. At the way the raindrops were sliding down her face. At her damp hair. And clothes. Her shirt was clinging to her now, and he could see the outline of her erect nipples. Apparently, lace didn't do a good job concealing such things.

"Don't regret that, please," she said. Her voice was a breathy whisper, and in her eyes now was a plea for him not to feel the guilt that he was already starting to feel.

Hell's bells.

He wasn't married. He wasn't cheating on Ella. He had a right to kiss a willing woman who wanted to kiss him back. But still the guilt came. Worse, he didn't know what to say to Millie. He couldn't muster up any reassurance that they'd done the right thing by acting on the heat. Couldn't console her though he thought she might be on the guilt train right along with him.

"I don't have a towel, but there are some tissues in the glove compartment," he finally said, starting up the truck.

She stared at him. Long, quiet moments. And Joe thought she might take a poke at the barrier he'd just put up between them. She didn't though. Millie opened the glove compartment, pulled out a box of tissues.

And the wedding rings.

They slid out with the box, landing on the inside of the glove box door. His plain gold one and Ella's engagement diamond solitaire and her wedding band.

"Oh, sorry," she muttered. Millie didn't touch them. She just left them lying where they were.

"I put them there a while back," Joe explained.

But he felt he owed her more of an explanation than that. And he blamed that "owing her" feeling on the kiss. Oh, yeah. It'd knocked a crater-sized hole in his own personal wall.

"About six months after the car wreck, I had sort of a meltdown," he said. "I'd been carrying Ella's rings in my jeans pocket, and I hit the brakes when a deer ran out in front of me. The diamond cut into my leg, and when I took it out—" He stopped. Had to. Because the emotion of that day was swallowing him again. "Anyway, I took off my ring and put both it and hers in the glove compartment. I figured one day I'd take them out and give them to Dara."

He sure as hell hadn't forgotten about them. The rings were like the memories of Ella. And Royce. They just stuck and stuck and stuck.

"I threw mine in Royce's office. *Threw them*," Millie emphasized. "As in I opened the door and tossed them in. I have no idea where they landed." She paused. "I understand meltdowns."

Yeah, she did. It was that common ground again. Of course, the biggest common ground was that he wanted to throat punch the guilt and haul Millie off to bed.

She took out a few tissues, handed a couple to him. Then, as if the glove compartment door was as fragile as a soap bubble, Millie eased it closed.

"And FYI, that whole 'out of sight, out of mind' thing is total horseshit," she added.

Hearing her curse made him smile. "Horseshit, huh? That's not very Millie Vanilla of you."

"Horseshit," she repeated, and she dropped a quick, playful kiss on his mouth.

Joe liked this moment almost as much as he had the real kiss in the rain. Almost. But it wasn't wise to push things between them. Both of them could be broken—again—so he needed to take this slow. Maybe his idiot body would let him do just that.

While Millie used the tissues to dry herself, Joe drove to Old Sawmill Trail. As expected, the rain had made the dirt surface slippery, but he plowed through it about a half mile before the old house came into view.

Emphasis on *old*.

Joe had to pick back through his memory, but he recalled this had once been Lou's grandfather's house, and Lou had inherited it about thirty years ago. Joe was betting the man hadn't done many repairs or much upkeep in those three decades.

There were scabs of white paint on the exterior, and the metal roof had wide streaks of rust. Weeds, some hip high, sprouted over the yard that might or might not have had grass or flower beds. Nothing about the place, including the owner, was anywhere close to being welcoming.

"How the heck did Lou come to own clocks made by Hezzie's husband?" Joe asked.

"Apparently, he found them in the attic last year, and he called me, asking if I wanted to buy them. I'm not a clock expert so I hired someone from San Antonio to come out and take a look at them. He said they were the real deal."

Millie searched through the pictures on her phone and came up with a shot of two clocks. They were plain looking but in far better shape than the house.

"Will you resell them in your shop?"

"No, I'll donate them to the Last Ride Society. They already have a stash of Hezzie's things, but Alma's been salivating for the clocks since she first heard about them." She paused, looked at him. "And yes, it is a lot of money, but you probably already know I have a trust fund. I don't spend any of that for my personal expenses. I live off the profits from the shop, and I use the trust fund for things like this."

He nearly said "admirable," but it would have possibly come out sounding snarky. Which he didn't mean. It was admirable, and it shot to hell the original image he'd had of her being a pampered, sheltered rich girl. Of course, the kiss had played into shooting that image to hell, too. Millie was still rich, but he was considering a whole new list of adjectives to describe her.

Like hot.

And tasty.

Joe could have added other things. Naked things. But he was already uncomfortable enough so he pushed as much of it aside as he could.

"I'm going to go ahead and write the check and the bill of sale," she said, doing that while the rain battered the truck. "I want to be able to hand it to him when we go in so he doesn't try to jack around with the price."

Jacking around was something Lou would probably try to do. Especially since the man was probably hard up for money.

Joe rummaged around under the seat and came up with an umbrella that he handed to Millie. He didn't bother looking for one for himself since he was already wet, but Millie got out, opened the umbrella and hurried to his side to share it with him. Of course, that put them arm to arm and side to side, but Joe figured this was mild contact compared to what had gone on by the wildflowers.

The moment they stepped on the porch, the front screen door creaked open, and Lou stepped out. Joe had been a teenager the last time he'd seen the man, and like the house, the years had not been kind to Lou. His beer gut strained against the piss-colored T-shirt he was wearing, and his graying scruff had gone well past any fashionable stage.

Lou licked his cracked lips when he eyed Millie, and Joe thought he might indeed have to kick the man's ass before this visit was over and done. Lou shifted his attention to Joe. Scowled. Then, his dull dust-colored eyes went a little wide with recognition.

"Well, I'll be damned," Lou said, his words slurring more than a little, and his breath was boozy enough to kill small critters. "You're Hardy's kid. Boy, it's been a while, hasn't it?"

A while that wasn't nearly long enough. "Mrs. Dayton is here to get the clocks," Joe said to hurry this along. He kept the umbrella open but set it on the porch.

Joe's reminder caused Lou to turn back to Millie. And he licked his scabby lips again.

"We're in a hurry," Joe added to stop Lou from trying to undress Millie with his eyes.

Lou nodded, scratched his head and smiled. It wasn't a friendly smile. "I didn't know you'd taken up with the likes of *Mrs. Dayton*," Lou said. "You've come up in the world. I recall you getting the crap beat out of you plenty when Hardy was around." The smile faded. "I also recall you beating the crap out of him." He looked at Millie. "Mrs. Dayton, you're in the company of a man with a violent streak."

Joe gave the man a stare that could have frozen every level of hell, but Millie spoke before he could say anything.

She showed Lou the check. "Here's the payment. You can have it and then sign this bill of sale when you bring out the clocks and give them to me."

Lou didn't budge, but he did take a long look at the check. "I figured we could all visit first." He pointed to some broken down rocking chairs on the porch. "Joe and me can do some catching up, and you can tell me more about yourself."

"We don't have time to catch up," Joe snarled. "Just get the clocks."

Lou huffed, made a tsk-tsk sound. "It don't cost anything to be friendly." He looked at Millie again. "Did Joe tell you about kicking the shit out of his old man? Hardy was tough, but there's that whole 'honor your father' deal."

Millie must have sensed the anger building inside Joe because she angled her body between Lou's and his. "The clocks," she repeated. "I'm not here to discuss Joe or his father."

"Well, that's too bad," Lou scratched his gut, and his eyes turned mean. "Because Hardy was my friend. My best friend," he added, "and he had to leave because of his good-for-nothing son. Oh, yeah," Lou said, flicking his gaze back to Joe. "He came out here and told me all about it. His face was messed up. Bruised, cut. And your mama was in the car crying. You did that to them."

Millie made a sound that was part huff, part groan. She ripped the check into pieces and threw it up in the air. She took hold of Joe's arm and got him moving.

"Keep the clocks," she snapped to Lou.

Then, Millie finished that with the very word that had shocked the drawers off the ladies from the Last Ride Society.

CHAPTER TEN

"IS FROG POOP GREEN? And are you really kissing Uncle Joe?" Little T asked.

Millie blinked. She'd been prepared to give her nephew a final "It's your bedtime and you have to go to sleep" warning. Her eighteenth such warning of the night. But those questions sure stopped her. Especially the second one.

"I've never seen frog poop," she said. "And why do you think I'd be kissing your uncle Joe?"

"Because Daddy said you were probably kissing him," Little T answered without hesitating.

Millie opened her mouth to demand why Tanner would say something like that, but she decided this was a good time to hold her tongue. Tomorrow, she could blast her moronic brother for blabbing personal stuff about her around his son.

Even if it was true personal stuff.

Well, true-ish, anyway.

Joe and she had indeed kissed at the old drive-in, but that'd been a week ago, and he hadn't made himself available for more mouth to mouth. Just the opposite. He'd made himself scarce when Millie had gone out twice to the ranch for her riding lessons with Dara. Also, when Dara had invited him to go look at some scenery from some of the local paintings, Joe had bowed out, saying he had some work to do in the barn.

Millie had gotten the message. Joe was done with kissing her. But what she couldn't figure out was why. He'd obviously enjoyed their fooling around, and she'd felt the proof of that when he'd pressed against her. So, maybe he just wasn't ready for feeling the effects of being with her. She understood that. But Millie worried that his avoidance was also in part because of the things Lou had said.

There'd been plenty of rumors about Joe's parents, about some possible abuse, about them being dirt poor, but she had no idea what was truth and what was gossip. If she was to believe Lou, then Joe had gotten in a fight with his dad. Lou had made it sound as if Joe had been to blame for that, but she had to consider the source. Lou was a scumbag turd and Joe was a good man. So, anything the scumbag turd said was suspect.

Millie looked down at Little T and saw that he'd closed his eyes. Finally! She still waited a full five minutes, and then she tiptoed backward out of the bedroom she'd set up for him. Holding her breath, she went into the hall and eased the door shut.

She went straight to the kitchen and poured herself a big glass of wine. She loved her nephew more than words could ever say, but the kid was a pill when it came to getting him down for the night. It'd taken four stories and the promise of chocolate chip pancakes when he woke up in the morning from his sleepover.

It was only eight fifteen, but she was bone-tired. And yet somehow still wired. Not a good combination. A familiar one. She felt a bad night of memories coming on.

Sipping her wine, Millie went back through the house, picking up the books and toys scattered around. She left the train wreck though.

A literal one.

Little T had taken apart his Polar Express train set and had arranged it as a derailment scene, complete with an overturned Matchbox Corvette and a mini Harley-Davidson on its side. He'd added some dirt and leaves he'd plucked from one of her house plants so there'd be some *debris* from the wreckage. For even more *effect*, he'd duct-taped a jagged piece of a Pop-Tart to the railroad track so that it appeared the pastry had been the cause of the derailment. Little T had insisted on the tape because the Pop-Tart "had deserved it."

Millie wasn't sure if that was creative or disturbing.

She frowned when she looked at her own scattering that she'd left on the coffee table in the living room. Her laptop and the notes she'd taken for the research on Ella. She'd been going through the latest round of stories about Ella that Dara had given her, but she'd stopped when Tanner had dropped off Little T.

It'd been a month since Millie had drawn Ella's name, and that meant one third of her research time was over. She'd made progress. Step one of taking the picture of the tombstone was done, but she was stuck on step two— collecting the personal accounts. So far, the only info she'd gotten had been from Dara, and the instructions had spelled out to get them from as many sources as possible.

Those instructions, however, hadn't taken into account that she'd be researching her husband's lover.

Still, Ella had probably retained some social media pages. Most families didn't think to take those down after a loved one died. She could also search Ella's mother on the web. Even though the woman didn't live in Last Ride, it was possible she'd posted something somewhere that Millie could add to the research report.

Frowning and feeling that wired wave of memories breathing down her neck, she went to the front window and looked out. This street was a little like a Norman Rockwell painting meets Beverly Hills. The houses were large. Very large. But there was enough Victorian and Edwardian architecture to keep them from getting dubbed with the estate or cookie-cutter labels. It was one of the "in" places to live in Last Ride.

At the moment, it also felt like the loneliest.

That was one of the reasons Millie had jumped at the chance to have Little T for the night, but she couldn't expect her six-year-old nephew to help her fend off a bad mood.

She took another gulp of wine and was about to force herself to go back to the research, but she caught some movement on the sidewalk. A man walking in front of her house.

Joe.

Her heart did a little leap. Other parts of her did, too, but the leaping did a crash and burn when he walked right on past her house. She leaned closer, pressing her face right against the glass to see where he was going. He went a few yards, turned around and walked past her house again.

Millie hurried to the front door and threw it open. "Are you lost?" she called out before he got out of earshot.

Joe stopped, and thanks to a whole bunch of streetlamps, she saw him shake his head. Just when she thought she was going to have to head across the yard to him, he turned and started toward her.

"Not lost," he grumbled. "Just batshit."

Millie smiled. Yes, he probably would think of coming here as a totally stupid thing to do, but she was so glad to see him that she had to stop herself from throwing her arms around him.

"I parked up the street," he added as he made his way

to her porch. "I didn't figure you'd want your neighbors to see my truck parked in front of your place."

At the moment, she didn't give a rat about the neighbors, about the gossip, or about the fact she was still smiling at him. Joe probably thought she'd gone batshit, too.

"Come in," Millie insisted when he hesitated in the doorway. "I'm having wine, but I've got beer if you'd like one."

"You drink beer?" he asked, and it sounded more like curiosity than mere small talk.

"Every now and then, but I keep some in the fridge for Tanner. This way." She closed the front door and led him toward the kitchen. "Little T is sleeping over," Millie added when Joe spotted the train wreck. "But he's already gone to bed."

Even though she'd kept her voice low, that had sounded like a shouted invitation for Joe to have his way with her. But judging from his expression, he hadn't come here for kissing.

"Nice house," he muttered once they'd reached the kitchen. Now, that was small talk and probably something he felt he should say.

She avoided mentioning that it had been Royce's grandparents' home. Avoided, too, that she wasn't happy here. That would only lead to a discussion of why she didn't move, and Millie didn't want to get into the complications of selling a Dayton "legacy" or why the Daytons insisted that only Daytons live in them. Unfortunately, there was a Dayton who didn't already own a house they seemingly loved.

"The kitchen sort of reminds me of a morgue." She followed his gaze around the room. "I'm considering putting a gnome or something in the window just to loosen it up a bit."

Joe eyed her, then the window. "Or you could just re-decorate."

She shook her head. "I don't want to have to think that hard about colors and surfaces. A gnome is easy. I could just plop it right there." She pointed to the wide sill just above the sink. "Go ahead, you can tell me I'm probably going through some sort of early life crisis."

"Wouldn't dream of it. If a gnome makes you happy, then go with it."

She would and Millie made a mental note to order one first chance she got. For now though, she was far more interested in why her hesitant visitor was here.

"So, are we about to have the talk?" she asked. She handed him a cold Lone Star that she took from the fridge and then leaned against the kitchen island. Joe leaned against the other side, facing her. "The talk where you tell me you shouldn't have kissed me?"

He frowned, twisted off the top of his beer. "No. We both know it shouldn't have happened. I'm here to apologize for what went on at Lou's last week."

Of course Joe would feel the need to do that, but she felt the need to roll right over that apology. "You have nothing to be sorry for. It was Lou who was being a dick, not you."

The corner of his mouth lifted just a little and for only a blink. "I'm not sure why a small part of my brain thinks it's funny to hear you curse. Maybe because it doesn't go with the rest of you." His gaze dropped to her belly, specifically to her navel ring. "Well, it doesn't go with some parts of you."

He stopped, groaned and did some whispered cursing of his own in between two long sips of his beer. "Look, I just wanted to say I'm sorry that I was the reason you didn't get those clocks."

"You weren't the reason," she quickly pointed out. "Lou and only Lou is responsible because of his dickish behavior." Millie paused long enough to see if Joe would smile. He did. "Besides, all's well that ends well. Lou sold them to Clem and Sheila Parkman, and they're donating them to the Last Ride Society."

The relief relaxed the tight muscles in his jaw, and she hated that for one second he'd felt any guilt over what had happened at that horrible man's house.

"Since we're doing the apology deal," she went on, "I owe you one for putting you through that visit. I should have arranged for Monte to go with me. I didn't know your history with Lou." But then she shrugged. "Of course, then the kiss wouldn't have happened, and I haven't been able to muster up any regrets over that."

"You should muster up some." Just like that, the relief and any trace of a smile were gone. "Lou didn't lie when he said I beat the crap out of my father. It wasn't a lie, either, that my folks left because of that beating."

"And how many beatings did you take from your dad?" she fired back. "Or did the gossip mill get that wrong?"

"No. They didn't get it wrong." That was all he said for a long time, and Millie now had regrets. Not about the kiss but about poking at old wounds with this conversation. "My father was mean. He used his fists at lot."

Her heart ached for him and for the little boy who'd had to grow up with that. "Frankie never talks about it," she said.

He shook his head. "She was still pretty young when they left. Only seven. I was sixteen."

Since she knew how old Frankie was, Millie did the math. Joe was thirty-six. He'd been through a lot of grief during that time. A lot of happiness, too, she supposed since he had Dara.

Millie didn't say anything. She just stood there and let him sort out how much he wanted to tell her.

"My father had been drinking that day," Joe continued, "and I could tell he was aiming for a fight. And he got one. He punched my mother first, claiming she'd overcooked the supper. Frankie started crying, and the son of a bitch reached for her as if he was going to shove or hit her, too. That's when I stopped him."

She reached across the island and touched his hand. "It's okay. You don't have to explain it to me. I know what you did was right."

He looked up then, those amazing gray eyes meeting hers. "You have too much faith in me."

"Just the right amount."

She winked and because she wanted to see him smile again, she cursed. It worked, and it was good to see him smile. Millie considered asking him if he wanted to go into the living room so they could sit and chat, but the Ella research was in there. Besides, if Joe started walking, he might decide it was time to end this house call and leave.

"I've been thinking about inviting Dara and you to dinner," she threw out there to gauge his reaction. "Maybe making it a group thing by inviting Frankie, Tanner and Little T."

He stared at her. A long time. "The gossips will have a field day with that."

"Possibly." *Absolutely*, she silently amended. "But I'd like to have you and Dara here. I'd like to spend some time with you. When you're around, the edges don't seem so sharp or dark."

He'd already opened his mouth, probably to tell her that

just wasn't a good idea, but he seemed to change his mind after hearing the last part.

"I know about edges," he said, and he slipped his thumb through the moisture on his beer bottle. "Dara would like coming for dinner. So would I. Actually, I'd like to do a lot of things with you."

Well, that sounded hopeful. However, the hope didn't mesh with his expression. Joe looked very, very down.

"I shouldn't have come," he continued. "I know I shouldn't, but I'm here so I'll man up and say that I don't want to hurt you." He looked at her now, his gaze drilling into her.

"Is that something sexual?" she asked to try to lighten up his mood a little.

"No. No," he repeated after he scrubbed his hand over his face.

So, the mood lightening had failed, and Millie decided to go ahead and spell it out for him. "You don't want to hurt me because you can't give me any promises, any commitments."

There was a small storm brewing in his eyes now. "I might not even be able to give you tomorrow."

Millie matched that staring storm with her own gaze as she walked around to his side of the island. "Tomorrows are overrated, Joe. I've learned the hard way that you have to make it through the night just to get to tomorrow." She put her hand on his shoulder. "So, let's focus on now, on this moment."

He frowned at her. "I'm not sure that's good advice."

"Oh, it's not," she agreed with a chuckle. "It's fueled by your amazing eyes and your equally amazing mouth. You're on my bucket list."

He continued to frown, but the edges of his mouth were softening a bit. "Is that sexual?" he asked.

Millie laughed. "It has the potential for sexual. You're one hot guy, Joe. No denying that. But I don't want to hurt you, either. That's why we'll take this slow. One moment at a time."

He set his beer aside and in the same motion slipped his arm around her waist. "A lot can happen in a single moment."

It could.

And it did.

She had a moment all right, a mind-blowing one, when he leaned in and kissed her. Oh, mercy. He could heat her up with just a single touch of his lips to hers. But she soon learned she didn't have to settle for a single touch. Nope. Joe gave her the full monty of kisses. Deep, long and French.

Millie fumbled around to get rid of her wineglass, and once she'd managed that, she went with her own version of a clothed full monty. She put her arms around him and melted into the kiss. He tasted like something she had craved all her life but had been denied. Well, he wasn't denying her now.

The need shot through the roof when he turned her, moving her back against the island, and Joe pressed himself against her. All in all, it was a very favorable arrangement, and her breasts especially appreciated it. When he gave her a well-placed bump with his groin, other parts also appreciated it.

Too much.

"Little T's in the house," she managed to say to remind him, and herself.

As hot as the kiss was, Joe and she could end up naked on the floor, and she didn't want her nephew walking in on that.

With her breath gusting and her body burning, Millie

stepped back and looked at him. Her mind was a hot haze right now. Just like the rest of her. And that made it hard to think.

"Duct tape," she finally said.

Joe's "Huh?" let her know that her solution probably wasn't a good one. Or one that he readily understood.

"Duct tape," Millie repeated, and she hurried to Little T's train wreck to retrieve the roll he'd left on the floor.

Joe followed her, maybe thinking she'd either lost her mind or else was planning some sort of kinky sex game. It was neither of those things.

"Think of it like a chastity belt," she said. "We can't have sex if we're not naked in the right places. We can wind this around our jeans so we can't get unzipped."

"Trust me," he said. "Tape wouldn't stop me."

Except he didn't just say it. It came out as a smoky drawl. One that made her want to French-kiss him. Of course, at the moment pretty much anything he did or said would make her want to do that.

He went to her, sliding his hand around the back of her neck and kissing her. Talk about a cure for dark places, bad moods and equally bad ideas about duct tape. When he pulled back this time, Millie had no doubts, none, that she'd just been kissed by a man who was fully aware of every erogenous zone in her body.

"We're not going to have sex," he said. He drawled that, too, and Millie was hanging on to his words as if they were gold.

Or orgasms.

"We're not?" she asked. Even with the lusty haze clouding her, she could still feel seriously disappointed. But she was also skeptical. That's why she kissed him again, hoping the hot tide would take Joe under and convince him to change his mind.

"No. I want to," he quickly added. Cursing, her took her hand and dragged it down to the front of his jeans so she could feel that proof. "I want to," he repeated while he gritted his teeth. "But neither of us is ready for that."

Oh, she wanted to argue with him. She was ready all right. But Millie knew exactly what he meant. If he had regretted kissing her, then sex would send those regrets all the way to Pluto. It might do the same for her. Not guilt for herself and what she d had with Royce but because she didn't want to add any more grief to whatever Joe was feeling. She cared too much about him for that.

"A month," she muttered. "That's how long it's been since all of this started. You need time. I probably need time, too, but it's hard to think with this between us."

Since her hand was still over his erection, she gave it a little squeeze and had the pleasure of hearing Joe growl out some very bad words. Words that had her smiling, and her smile, or maybe it was the squeeze, caused Joe's mouth to come to hers again. There was still plenty of need in the kiss.

Plenty.

But he gently moved her hand from his zipper region and caught her shoulders. No doubt to anchor her in place. So that they couldn't do the body-to-body thing while they were doing the mouth to mouth.

Even though it was frustrating not to be able to touch him, Millie sank right in, taking everything that Joe and his amazing mouth were offering. And while he wasn't offering sex, he was doling out some huge quantities of pleasure.

"Frog poop must be green. It has to be," she heard someone say.

Little T.

Millie jumped back from Joe as if he'd scalded her, and she whirled around to see her nephew walking out of the hall and toward them. His little bare feet barely made a sound on the floor, which was probably why Millie hadn't heard him before he'd managed to get so close.

But maybe he hadn't seen Joe and her—

"Daddy was right. You are kissing Uncle Joe," Little T said, dashing her hopes of what he might or might not have seen. He yawned and scratched his pajama-covered butt. "If you're done kissing, can you make pancakes now?"

CHAPTER ELEVEN

JOE STOOD IN front of his closet and cursed. He'd been staring at his so-called wardrobe for nearly ten minutes. That was proof he was losing it.

No way should he be obsessing about what to wear to Millie's for dinner. Heck, no way should he be going to Millie's for dinner, period. But here he was in the middle of doing the first and within a half hour of doing the second.

Still cursing, he snatched a blue shirt from the hanger, purposely not choosing anything that Ella had ever bought him. That eliminated about ninety percent of anything on hangers since the only things Joe ever bought himself were jeans, Ts and boots. Still, he hadn't wanted to wear anything that would remind him of his late wife to a dinner with the woman he wanted to be his lover.

Yeah, he was losing it all right.

He yanked on the shirt, jeans and his good boots, and he "fixed" his hair by running his hands through it. He'd be damned if he would check it in the mirror. That would make this feel even more like a date than it already did. Thankfully though, this date wouldn't be Millie and him solo. Dara, Little T, Tanner, Frankie and maybe their dates would also be there.

Joe frowned at the thought of his nephew. Little T had probably blabbed about seeing Millie and him kiss, but Joe held out hope that the kid had forgotten. After all, it'd been four days since that kiss, and Joe hadn't gotten a single text, call or visit from Frankie about it. If Frankie had been filled in on that particular tidbit of his so-called love life, she would have grilled Joe like a well-grilled trout.

He went across the hall to see if Dara was ready, and he found her at her desk, typing on her laptop. Whatever she was writing had her complete attention.

"We can cancel this dinner if you're busy," Joe offered.

"No. I want to go." She stopped typing and looked back at him. "I'm just finishing the story about Mom that I want to give Millie. It's the one about when Mom fell in the creek when she was trying to get the little toy boat you'd made for me. She accidentally knocked you in the water, too. I like that one because she laughed a lot."

Ella had indeed laughed. Joe, not so much. But the memory of it made him smile now.

"I also want to loan Millie my baby book so she can go through it," Dara continued. She hit Print, and while the printer was chugging out the single sheet of paper, Dara took the book from her desk drawer. It was basically a photo album, and Ella had added handwritten notes to some of the pictures.

Joe quit smiling. "You're sure Millie will want to see that?"

Dara made a perky uh-huh sound. "The book is mostly about me, but there are some fun stories in it, too. Millie can maybe use it in the research." She gathered up the book, the paper and her phone. Then, she looked at him. "Millie doesn't hate Mom. She said so. Do you hate Millie's husband?"

Joe considered some answers. Dismissed them and decided it was a good thing that he wouldn't have to do any research on Royce Dayton. The Last Ride Society wouldn't care much for one of their silver spoon deceased to be called a cheating sack of shit. Joe wouldn't care much for it, either, since the label would also apply to Ella. And he wasn't ready to go there just yet.

"What if there was a different reason they were together in the wreck?" Dara asked when Joe didn't answer her other question. Maybe she'd picked up on something in his expression, something to do with that lying sack label.

Joe had tried to figure out the same damn thing. Like maybe Ella had had car trouble, and Royce had been just giving her a ride. But that theory got shot down when he'd found Ella's car in the grocery store parking lot. It was running just fine so obviously she'd left it there and then Royce had picked her up.

"What reason?" Joe asked her.

Dara shrugged. "Maybe they were doing something like undercover work. You know, for the CIA or the Texas Rangers."

Obviously, his daughter had an active imagination. Or maybe Dara was just trying to hang on to anything that made sense. Anything that would allow her to keep that laughing, falling-in-the-creek image of her mother.

"They could have maybe heard about a crime," Dara went on, "and they were making themselves bait to draw out the criminal."

That was a good one, and if it gave his daughter any peace, then Joe hoped she'd hold on to it.

Dara gave another shrug. "Or maybe Millie's husband was going to buy some of Mom's paintings so they were meeting to talk about that."

Joe went still. "What do you know about your mom's paintings?"

"I know that she sold some," Dara readily admitted.

"I saw her packaging them up and she said someone had bought them. There were three of them."

Probably the three in Once Upon a Time. "When was this?"

Dara's forehead bunched up while she was obviously giving that some thought. "I'm not sure, maybe a couple of months before she died." Dara stopped, and her eyes went wide. "I wasn't supposed to tell you. I was supposed to keep it a secret."

The stillness inside him vanished and in came the storm. Another damn secret. "Why weren't you supposed to tell me?"

"Because it was going to be a surprise." Dara's tone had taken on a dismissive "no big deal" edge, but she was clearly seeing how this was affecting him. It wasn't a good kind of effect because Joe was sure he was scowling.

"Mom was putting the money in an account, and once she got enough, she was going to tell you about it," Dara continued. "I think she wanted to use it for a big vacation or something."

She'd added that last bit for his sake. To try to take away the sting of hearing that Ella had kept yet something else from him.

"Anyway, you can probably find the account on her laptop," Dara added. "I think it's still in your man-shed." She checked her phone. "But you'll have to wait because it's time for us to go. You should look at it though when we get back."

Oh, he would indeed do that. And if he found out it was Ella's slush fund that she was using to buy stuff for her lover, then it'd finally be time for him to give her that label. It'd finally be time for him to move the hell on with his life.

MILLIE WAS NOW sorry that she'd been in such a hurry to move on with her life. Or rather she was sorry she'd chosen to do that moving on by hosting her first dinner since Royce's death.

In hindsight, she should have opted for something less hazardous. Maybe like juggling flaming balls or alligator wrestling.

Actually, this dinner had some similarities to both of those things. Instead of juggling and wrestling though, she was trying to keep the very tense dinner conversation going. Little T was helping. In his own Little T way.

"Elephant poop is gray. It has to be 'cause elephants are gray," he declared while poking at the herbed potatoes on his plate. He'd already gone through the other colors of various animal waste despite Frankie's warning for him to change the subject.

Tanner was doling out some warnings, too. Nonverbal ones to Frankie who was shooting eye daggers at the stunning Skylar, who Tanner had bought as his dinner date. Skylar was either oblivious to Frankie's bristling toward her or else she didn't want to cause a scene by saying anything.

That left Joe and Dara, who were seated directly across the table from Millie. Joe had seemingly hit his own personal mute button, but Dara was doing a good job of giving exaggerated eye rolls for Little T's commentary. Also doing a good job at dinner conversation, too. She hadn't mentioned her mother, something that Millie truly appreciated, but had instead gone on about how much fun they'd had on their shopping trip to San Antonio.

"Millie bought this lipstick called Raunchy Rose," Dara added with a chuckle.

"Oh, I love that color," Skylar exclaimed, and that was

enough to cause Frankie to shoot the woman a glare. "I'll bet it looks good on you, Millie."

"I haven't tried it yet." In fact, Millie had forgotten about it, but she added a smile to her comment for Skylar to off-set Frankie's reaction.

Even though Millie didn't think Skylar was anywhere in or near the right wheelhouse for her brother, she wasn't going to be unfriendly to the woman. Unlike the unfriendli-ness Millie was aiming at Tanner. For him, Millie wouldn't spare his feelings.

Her brother had known that Frankie would be at this din-ner, and he shouldn't have brought a date. Especially a date that he should have realized would rile his ex. Of course, just about any date would do that because Millie was dead certain Frankie was still in love with the man who'd already crushed her heart six ways to Sunday.

"Dara's giving me horseback riding lessons," Millie an-nounced when the conversation lagged again.

"How fun." That from Skylar. "You're doing that at Joe's ranch?"

The woman eyed her over the rim of her water glass but probably wasn't fishing for details about whether Millie was doing more at the ranch than mere riding. Then again, Little T had likely blabbed about the kissing he'd seen Joe and her do. Tanner, in turn, might have re-blabbed to Sky-lar.

"Yes, at Joe's," Millie confirmed.

"I love the name of his ranch," Skylar went on. "Saddle Run. Though it sounds more like a name for a horse ranch than one for cattle."

"I came up with it," Dara spoke up. "I was really little, maybe four or five, and Mom said I should think of a name and she could paint a sign to put out in front by the mailbox. I was just learning to ride, but I guess I wanted to go faster so I told her Saddle Run."

Millie smiled and looked at Joe to see if he intended to add anything to that.

He did.

"Ella did the trio of paintings that you have in your shop," he said in a voice as flat and calm as a lake.

Millie definitely hadn't expected him to add *that*, and she felt her mouth drop open. "The landscapes from La La Land?"

He nodded, crammed a forkful of broccoli with cheese into his mouth and chewed as if he'd declared war on the vegetable.

"Mom's paintings are in Once Upon a Time?" Dara asked. Her eyes lit up. "I want to see them. She'd be so happy that you've hung them in the shop."

Millie sure as heck wasn't happy. She was confused and shocked, and she was pretty sure Joe was feeling some of those things, too. "You didn't say anything about Ella when I showed them to you," Millie reminded him.

He swallowed first, then drank some water. "I only recently found out that she'd sold them to you."

Well, wasn't this special? Her favorite paintings in the entire shop of thousands of things had been done by her dead husband's lover. By the wife of a man she was lusting after on a minute-to-minute basis.

Millie was aware that nearly every eye at the table was on her, waiting for her reaction. Every eye except Little T's. Her nephew was using his food to build towers and construction around his smashed-in bread roll. Joe was looking at her, but it was obvious that no answer was expected.

Son of a monkey.

This had hurt him. Of course, it had. And it had likely

snowballed in that million other pounds of grief because it was yet another part of his wife's life that he hadn't known about.

Because there was nothing she could say to him that would make this better, Millie instead shifted her attention to Dara. "You're welcome to come by the shop anytime and see the paintings. In fact, I want you to have them. They were your mother's, and they should belong to you. I can bring them to the ranch tomorrow when I have my next riding lesson."

"No," Dara quickly disagreed. "They should be exactly where they are—in an art gallery." She smiled and looked giddy. "It's like a little piece of Mom is still here, and everyone will get to see that."

Oh, yes. Everyone including Millie. No way could she be petty enough to crate them up and stuff them in storage where they'd be out of sight and hopefully out of mind. No, they'd stay put, but Millie doubted she'd be going in the local artist room anytime soon.

The meal finally ended when Skylar got a call that she said she had to take, that her grandmother was sick and the call was an update about her condition. She scurried out of the dining room while Little T latched on to Dara to take her to his room that he used when he stayed over. No doubt to show Dara the latest train wreck he'd set up. Apparently, this one involved the dinosaur collection Millie had bought for him. The boy had also whispered to Dara that he knew where Millie kept her hidden supply of Jolly Ranchers suckers. Since Millie hid that supply in plain view on her desk in her home office, it wouldn't be hard to find.

"I need to make a call, too," Tanner said to no one in particular, and he headed toward the back porch.

Her brother had gotten several texts while they'd been

eating. Texts that he hadn't answered, but it was as obvious as the nose on his face that he was ducking out now because he didn't want to be with Frankie so she could take snipes at him. However, his leaving turned out to be unnecessary. Frankie immediately excused herself to go to the powder room, muttering that she'd be back in a couple of minutes to help Millie clear the table.

And then there were two.

Joe and her.

"I'm sorry," they said at the same time.

She couldn't help it. She smiled. "Simultaneous apologies seem to be a habit of ours. Anyway, I'm sorry you didn't know about the paintings."

"And I'm sorry you now own something you probably want to burn to ash."

Millie lifted her shoulder and started gathering up the dishes. "I'd go with the crating up option if I needed them out of the shop. But I want Dara to be able to see them, to be able to show them to others. She's proud of her mother."

He cursed softly, shook his head. "You're good to my daughter. Thank you for that."

"No thanks needed. She's a good kid, and she's helping me. I wouldn't own a peach lace bra or have Raunchy Rose lipstick if it weren't for her."

As she'd hoped, that made Joe smile. It didn't last, but it was something. A moment that wasn't fate taking another painful poke at them.

She took some of the dishes into the kitchen, and when she came back to get the rest, Joe was gathering up the plates and glasses. Millie snagged the rest, and they went into the kitchen together.

"I probably should have waited until we were alone before I told you about the paintings," he said, putting the dishes on the counter by the sink and the dishwasher.

"It's okay. I knew something was bothering you. Good to know that it wasn't me."

"You bother me," he admitted. Their eyes met. Held. "But in a whole different kind of way." The corner of his mouth lifted, and she didn't have to ask if that was a sexual way.

It was.

"I think we have a 'kiss and run' thing going on," she pointed out, keeping her voice at a whisper in case the others returned. A throaty whisper because, hey, this was Joe, and he had a way of making her tingle. "We kiss, and then I don't see or hear from you for days. Is that because of me or because of you?"

"Me," he readily admitted. He whispered as well, but his was a thousand times sexier than hers. "Sometimes I want you more than my next breath. Other times, I'm not sure I'll make it to my next breath."

And just like that, she went from sex thoughts to worry. Millie ran her hand down the length of his arm and then linked their fingers together. "I won't push you for more than you can give me. No tomorrows. No tonight. Just this very minute."

"I know." He said that like the profanity he often muttered. Then, he leaned down and pressed his forehead against hers. "But I can't keep jacking you around like this. It's not fair. You deserve better."

At the moment she couldn't think of anything better than Joe. She ached to kiss him. To hold him. But the truth was, he deserved better, too. She might be attempting to move on with her life, but she was still mentally a mess. Too bad she couldn't just shove all that aside and haul him off to bed. She thought it might do both of them some good.

Well, maybe.

Sex with Royce hadn't been anything to rock her world. That meant she likely hadn't rocked him, either. And that was a whole different guilt trip on Regret Road that she needed to avoid for now.

Joe moved away from her when Skylar came walking in. "Good news," she announced. "My grandmother's doing better. She'll be getting out of the hospital in the morning."

"That is good news," Millie said with Joe repeating something similar.

There was no need though for them to make small talk with Skylar because Tanner came in from the back porch. "I tracked down the parts I need to fix your Harley," her brother immediately said to Joe. "I can get started on the repairs in a day or two."

This was the first Millie was hearing about Joe having a motorcycle, but she had vague memories of him riding it around town way back when. Maybe before Dara had even been born.

When Joe and her brother started talking about those repairs, Millie excused herself to go find Frankie. Her trip to the powder room had likely been BS, and Frankie was probably holed up in there, seething about Skylar and waiting for Tanner and the woman to leave. However, before she even made it to the hall, Tanner caught up with her.

"Are you sleeping with Joe?" her brother came out and asked.

Millie put on the best shocked, annoyed, "none of your business" face that she could manage. "Why would you ask that?"

"Little T," Tanner answered.

Millie added a huff and folded her arms over her chest. "Little T said I was sleeping with Joe?"

"No, he said you were kissing him, but I figure if you're kissing, you're doing other things."

"Then, you figured wrong." She dropped the attitude and sighed. "You figured wrong," she repeated in a much softer voice, "but since you're poking your nose into my personal business, I'll do some poking into yours. Why would you bring Skylar here tonight? You must have known it would bother Frankie."

He sighed, too, and groaning he leaned back against the wall. "I didn't want to bring her, but Skylar was down about her grandmother. She's nice, Millie. Too nice," he added.

"You're sleeping with her, of course." It definitely wasn't a question.

"Of course," he verified. He opened his mouth as if he might elaborate on that, but then he stopped and stared at her. "Have you talked to Mom or Dad lately?"

Millie certainly hadn't seen that question coming, and her first thought was that this was some kind of deflection because he didn't want her pushing him about his relationship with Skylar.

"I haven't talked to either of them in the last week or so. Why?" Millie countered.

"Something's going on," Tanner said.

That was certainly cryptic. Then again, something was usually going on with their mother.

Millie made a circling motion with her finger for him to continue when his pause dragged on for way too long. "What's going on?"

The muscles flickered and tightened in Tanner's jaw. "I think Mom's having an affair."

Millie couldn't stop the laugh from practically bursting out of her. A laugh that went on, and on.

"It's not a joke," Tanner snarled.

"It has to be." And she just kept on laughing.

"It's not a joke," Tanner repeated, and this time, he got right in her face. He definitely wasn't sporting a "ha ha" expression. He could play pranks and wasn't above doling out some BS, but he wasn't doing either of those now. "I think Mom's having an affair," he repeated.

This time, the words sank in. Slowly. And they didn't sink in well.

Wow. Just wow. The news of the paintings had stunned her, but this had made her knees dissolve. Well, they dissolved until Millie actually considered it. Then, dismissed it. Laurie Jean was too worried about appearances to risk cheating on her husband.

"Why would you possibly think that?" Millie demanded.

Tanner didn't hesitate. "Because last night, I saw her sneaking out of the back of Once Upon a Time. It was late, close to midnight, and Skylar and I were walking from Three Sheets to my place."

Millie couldn't think of a single reason why Laurie Jean would have been at the shop at that hour, but her mother did have a key to the place. Both of her parents did.

"I think she was fooling around with somebody in that upstairs bedroom where you sometimes sleep," Tanner added.

She shook her head and just kept shaking. "You don't know that—"

"The light was on in that bedroom, and I saw her kiss a man who was just inside the doorway," he interrupted. "I only got a glimpse of him and it was dark, but it sure as hell wasn't Asher. This guy sort of looked like Elvis. Black hair, a white suit and he was carrying a shoulder bag. She kissed him," Tanner emphasized.

It took Millie a moment to gather her breath and swallow the lump in her throat. "Yeah, I heard that part. I don't suppose you asked her about it?"

"No way in hell. I got Skylar out of there."

"Skylar saw this?" Millie pressed.

Tanner nodded. "It'd been hard for her to miss it since it happened right in front of us. There's more," he said while she was still reeling from trying to process all of this. "Those texts I got at dinner were from Aunt Freida. She says this afternoon Mom asked Freida to lend her some money."

That was laughable. But Millie didn't even snicker this time. "Mom doesn't need to borrow money. Dad will give her any amount that she wants."

"Think it through. Mom didn't ask Asher because she didn't want him to know." He stopped, cursed and shook his head. "Aunt Freida said Mom was upset and that she needed the money right away."

Some bad thoughts started to go through Millie's mind. "You don't think Mom is going to run off with this man she was kissing?"

Tanner leveled his gaze on her. "No, but based on what Aunt Freida said, I think someone's blackmailing her."

CHAPTER TWELVE

IT WASN'T A common occurrence for Millie to want to talk to her mom, but this was one of those times. And, of course, Laurie Jean hadn't returned her call. Ditto for not being home when Millie had dropped by to see her before she'd gone into work at the shop.

She wanted to think her mother was just busy and wasn't avoiding her, but since Aunt Freida hadn't returned her call, either, Millie figured everything Tanner had told her the night before was true.

But how could it be?

No matter how Millie tried to play all of this out, she just couldn't wrap her head around the possibility of Laurie Jean doing something sordid like this. Then again, she didn't want to imagine her mother having sex. Especially sex with a guy who looked like Elvis.

After her dinner party guests had left, Millie had walked over to Once Upon a Time and had gone upstairs to the bedroom. The light wasn't on, but she had noticed that some things were out of place. The trio of throw pillows on the bed weren't in the usual order, and the antique Turkish rug was slightly askew.

Millie had ruled out Monte and Haylee having made the "adjustments" by subtly asking them if they'd been upstairs, maybe to look for something stored there. But neither had, leaving her with the unsettling, strong possibility that Tanner had indeed been right.

Damn.

He could be right.

Millie fired off a text to Sherry Parnell, owner of the cleaning service she used for the shop and her house, and asked Sherry to add the room to the next scheduled service. Hopefully, during that cleaning, they wouldn't find anything that'd be an obvious pointing of the finger at Laurie Jean.

She didn't want to speculate how her mother's affair could play out. Or who would know about the affair and blackmail Laurie Jean. Those were things she could try to suss out later if anyone in her gene pool actually returned her flippin' calls. And she was extending that gene pool to Frankie, who was dodging her, as well. Millie needed to find out what was eating the woman. For now though, she changed into her jeans and boots and drove to Joe's for her riding lesson.

She steeled herself for this visit, something she didn't usually have to do because she looked forward to the lessons and seeing Joe and Dara. She still wanted to see them— mercy, did she—but she was worried about Joe, about how down he'd been about Ella's paintings.

It had taken all of her willpower not to drive to his house and check on him after she'd made the visit to her shop. But Millie had decided Joe might need time to try to come to terms with it. So did she. It put a nasty, tight ball in her stomach over the possibility that Ella might have sold her those paintings while having an affair with Royce. Millie hadn't known the identity of the artist, but Ella had certainly known she was the buyer since the paintings had been delivered to the shop.

Millie drove to the ranch, and when she got out of her car, she started toward the house to let Dara know she was there. But before she made it to the porch, Joe called out to her.

"Dara's running late," Joe said. He was in the doorway of the barn. "She's having a study group at the library, and they have a couple more chapters to get through. If you're in a hurry, I can give you the lesson."

Millie heard what he said, every word of it, but those words sort of floated in her head because just the sight of him brought on another round of brain fuzz.

And heat.

Oh, my.

He was naked. Well, his upper body was, anyway, and she got a long, lusty look at all those manly delights. She seriously doubted that Joe had stepped foot in a gym since high school, but he was toned, tanned and tempting. Very, very tempting.

"I just washed up," he said. "Had to pull a calf."

Joe reached out and took something from a stall door. A T-shirt, she realized, when he put it on and ended the dirty little fantasy she was having about him.

She felt like a woman in a trance when she walked to him. One slow step ahead of the other. Her gaze, probably hot and hungry, fixed on him. Once he had his head and arms through the shirt, he did some gaze fixing, as well.

And he smiled.

"You look...interested," he said as if carefully choosing how to finish that.

It was the right finish, and the right conclusion. Millie went to him, slipped her arm around his neck and drew him to her. He smelled good, not like someone who'd just pulled a calf. She caught the scent of his deodorant and the detergent from his clean shirt.

Millie couldn't resist. She pulled Joe down to her for a kiss. She didn't make it nearly as long and deep as she wanted. If she had, she likely would have jumped him right then, right there, and while she was certain that would be very enjoyable, she needed to make sure he was okay.

"How are you?" she asked, easing back from him. She couldn't stop herself from running her tongue over her bottom lip so she could hang on to the taste of him a little longer.

"Better." He used his thumb, sliding it over her mouth, retracing the path her tongue had just taken. "I've decided to put off thinking about the paintings or what Ella did with the money from the sale of them. How about you? Are you all right? You seemed a little shaken after dinner last night."

That was a whole lot for her to consider. Going in the order of the things he'd just brought up, she could tell him how much she'd paid for the painting, but putting all of that aside was the way to go. However, she wasn't sure she wanted to put the reason for her being "shaken" aside.

There was zero doubt in her mind that her mother wouldn't have wanted her to discuss this with anyone, but Millie needed a sounding board. And Joe was a good one. Then, afterward, she could kiss him again.

Joe was good for that, too.

Millie laid it all out there for him, giving him the condensed version. "Tanner thinks my mother is having an affair and that she's being blackmailed."

Joe still had his fingers under her chin, and she felt them go still. "What?" he asked.

His surprise was probably in the same range as hers had been the night before. "Tanner says he saw Laurie Jean kissing another man in the back doorway of my shop. He didn't get a good enough look at the man to know who he was."

"It was probably your father," Joe quickly pointed out. "They might have been at the shop for a new hanky-panky venue."

While that was a good guess—and an intriguing one about new-venue hanky-panky—she had to shake her head. "The guy had black hair. And I've spent a good chunk of the day coming up with the names of the black-haired men in Last Ride who'd consider my mother fling material."

Of course, it might be more than a fling, but Millie just couldn't go there yet. She was still dealing with the idea of the prim and proper Laurie Jean doing anything like what Millie had fantasized about doing with Joe.

Joe's forehead bunched up. "What about the blackmail?"

Millie gathered her breath. "Apparently, my aunt Freida believes that because my mother wanted to borrow some money from her. I've spent a good chunk of my day trying to figure out a reason for that. A reason that doesn't involve blackmail," she added.

Joe stayed quiet a moment, obviously processing that. "Is it possible that Tanner got all of this wrong and that your mother simply wants to borrow money to buy Asher a gift or something?"

"From your lips to God's ears." She sighed and wiped the quickly forming perspiration from her head.

Joe must have noticed her sweating, and since the sun was beating down on them, he took hold of her and moved her into the barn. It was a heck of a lot cooler inside, and she immediately spotted the cow and the calf.

"Oh, how cute." She started to go closer to the wobbly legged calf but stopped when the cow lowered her head and made a low throaty moo that didn't sound the least bit friendly.

"Best to stay back," Joe advised. "She tolerated me helping with the delivery, but she's being protective about her new baby."

Millie didn't need a child of her own to understand that. "He...she's not white like the other calf I saw."

"She," Joe supplied. "I got a look under her tail. No testicles. And you're right about the white. She's the color she's supposed to be. The Charolais bull must have tapped out his potency or else didn't make it to the part of the pasture where Elsie was."

"Elsie?" Millie smiled. "I thought she'd have a number instead of a name."

"Oh, she does. But every now and then, a name sticks."

Millie thought that maybe a lot of names stuck with Joe. "Softy," she accused.

It felt so good just to feel good and joke around with him like this. Joe was one of the few people who could remind her that happiness was a strong possibility for the day. And that had nothing to do with kissing him. That said, kissing him could certainly give her a happy boost.

Judging from the gleam in his incredible eyes, Joe was having a similar thought.

"I can give you that riding lesson," he offered again. He hooked his fingers in the empty belt loop of her jeans and eased her closer. "Might be a good time for you to get used to riding in the saddle with someone."

Now, that sounded interesting. "Would that someone be you?"

He nodded. For such a simple gesture, it packed a wallop. Probably because his expression took on that sexy slant.

Which it often did. It happened when he smiled. When he was breathing.

Millie didn't resist when he tugged on her loop to move her toward him. "Does that mean we would be pressed very close together in such a way that I could accidentally cop a feel?"

"Copped feels are optional," he drawled, lowering his head to touch his mouth to hers. "But if we're going to ride, we'll have to leave this barn and saddle up."

Neither of those things held as much promise, or heat, as staying put did. Especially staying put when Joe kissed her again.

Her whole body sighed. Then, possibly whimpered because he could do things to her so fast. Like take her from heated to scalding. From wanting to needing. And he made those particular journeys oh so very interesting.

He was a good six inches taller than her so Millie had to come up on her toes to get the full deal of pressing her mouth to his. Even though she made an urgent little sound of need, he didn't speed up. He just kissed and kissed. And kissed. Before he moved his incredibly talented tongue past her lips and into her mouth.

More heat spiked, and it occurred to her that she hadn't felt this much heat even with sex. Maybe not ever. Joe was doing a thorough job of seducing her just with his mouth.

Still moving as if they had all the time in the world, he shifted their positions, so that her back was against a thick wooden pole. It turned out that he had a darn good reason for that. It was so they wouldn't topple over when he pressed his body to hers.

Which he did.

Oh, they fit all right. Her nipples got especially excited about being against all those muscles. Ditto for the hot spots on her neck since that's where he dropped the next round of kisses. But the winner of her excited parts was the center of her body. Between her thighs. Where Joe managed to add some pressure that made her want to rip off his clothes. Her clothes, too.

They were in a barn, she reminded herself, and the cow and calf were right there, maybe watching them. It was hot and not the best smelling place to fool around. But even with those drawback reminders, Millie didn't move. Well, other than to slide her hands from Joe's back to his butt.

Like the rest of him, that particular part of his anatomy was toned, too, and she got a really clear mental image of clamping on to his superior buns while he plunged into her.

"Someone's coming," he said, tearing his mouth from her neck.

Because her heartbeat was thundering in her ears, Millie didn't get what he'd said until he repeated it. And until he moved back from her.

Blinking hard to clear her vision, Millie looked past him and out the barn door. She saw the car pull to a stop next to hers.

And she cursed.

"That's my mother," she managed to say.

"Yeah. I know," Joe verified. "She's never been to my place so I'm guessing she's here to see you."

Millie cursed again, and she thought of the "Call me back now" message she'd left for Laurie Jean. Millie had added in that message that she'd be taking a riding lesson from four to five so her mother had probably figured out where that ride would be. Especially since it was almost certainly a topic of gossip.

"Millicent Marie Parkman!" her mother called out.

Great. She'd used her whole name, the way she had in

the Dial Antibacterial days. So, either she was pissed or she thought there'd be more than one Millie around and wanted to specify which one she was there to see.

Millie had to hand it to Joe. Most men would have simply stayed back rather than risk facing an irate Laurie Jean, but Joe went to the barn door. "Good afternoon, Mrs. Parkman."

That only made her mother's face go even harder. "I want to talk to my daughter."

"I'm here," Millie said, stepping to Joe's side. She looked up at him and realized he looked as if he'd been thoroughly kissed.

Which meant she did, too.

This was going to be a fun conversation with her mother. Especially considering that Millie was going to have to bring up the other stuff that Tanner had told her.

"Pray for me," Millie muttered to Joe.

"You want me to kiss you or make a show of holding your hand?" he said, and she didn't think it was a complete joke.

Even if it was, Millie turned the tables on him and gave him a quick peck on the mouth. The kind of kiss that screamed of familiarity and possibly previous occurrences of sex and more sex.

Millie started toward her mother with the "dead man walking" mantra going through her head. The kiss, however, had seemingly robbed Laurie Jean of her fuming temper tantrum, and her mother stood there, wide-eyed and shocked.

"You kissed him," Laurie Jean said. "You kissed *that man*."

Millie was certain that any and every curse word she'd

ever used wasn't as filthy sounding as her mother's "that man."

"Joe," Millie provided, and because she'd seen his full name in some of the research she'd done, she added, "Joe Cooper McCann."

Of course, Millie instantly regretted her snark, and it backfired at it usually did. She could see her mother gearing up for one of her classic explosions. One that Millie normally would have just endured and weathered on any other day.

But today was not that day.

"Is everything okay between Dad and you?" Millie threw out there.

If there'd been a picture of a big sail suddenly losing the wind, it would have been the exact metaphor to describe her mother's expression. The anger vanished. Wide eyes returned. And she appeared to be trying to use laser vision to see inside Millie's head.

"Why do you ask?" There was plenty of caution, and concern, in her mother's tone now.

Millie sorted through some possible answers and went with, "I've heard some things."

Laurie Jean gasped. It was a deep cut, and Millie was pretty sure she was going to have to do some bloodletting to get to the truth.

"Are people gossiping about me?" Her mother flattened her hand on her chest, and her fingers were trembling. So was her mouth.

And dang it, Millie wasn't immune to those reactions. That's why she tamped down some of the bile. Something she always ended up doing around her mother, but this time, it felt as if the tamping was the right thing to do.

"Mom, what's wrong?" Millie pleaded. "Are you in some kind of trouble? Just tell me," she added when her mother didn't say anything.

Laurie Jean stood there for several long stewing moments. Perspiration glistened on her face. She turned a little red, and Millie was ready to catch on to her arm and try to force her to sit down. But Laurie Jean must have realized Millie's "nefarious" plan because she stepped back and gave Millie a hard stare.

"Is that man, Joe, the one who's doing this to me?" Laurie Jean spat out, and the venom was back.

Millie stared back at her. "What are you talking about?"

"Is he the one trying to ruin my life?" she said as if the answer were obvious. "Is he the one who wants money?"

It took Millie a moment to realize her mother had likely just confirmed there was a blackmailer. And that Laurie Jean thought that blackmailer was Joe.

"Joe isn't doing anything to you," Millie said, trying to make herself sound like the voice of reason—something her mother clearly wasn't. "But someone obviously is. Why is someone trying to blackmail you?"

Millie figured this could go two ways. Her mother could start crying and collapse into her arms or she could have one of her tirades. Laurie Jean went with door number two.

"You stay out of it," Laurie Jean warned her.

Millie ignored that warning and went with an offer that she figured Laurie Jean wouldn't appreciate. "Mom, tell me what's wrong, and I'll do whatever I can to help you."

Nope. She didn't appreciate it one bit. The anger flared in her eyes.

"You can help. By never seeing that man again." Laurie Jean flung her index finger toward the barn and started for her car. She said the rest of her rant with her back turned to Millie. "Joe Cooper McCann and his sister are trying to ruin our family, and you're letting them do it."

CHAPTER THIRTEEN

JOE PULLED INTO the parking lot of the motorcycle repair shop that sat at the very end of Main Street. Unlike some of the other businesses in Last Ride, it didn't have a catchy name like Three Sheets, Once Upon a Time, Ink, Etc. or Petal Pusher. In fact, the shop didn't have a name at all.

When Tanner had bought the place about eight years ago, he'd had the previous name, Ace Repairs, painted over and hadn't added anything other than a second coat of flat white paint. Members of the Last Ride Society were always trying to remedy that by suggesting names and some kind of exterior adornments that would add "class." In fact, the last suggestion he'd heard was Zen and the Art of Motorcycle Maintenance. Alma had tacked on the idea of Tanner making a wine and reading room in the corner of the large repair bay.

The shop was still white, still had no name and it definitely didn't have a wine/reading room. Joe was sure that suited Tanner just fine. He had painted over his upper-class upbringing the way he had Ace Repairs.

Joe drove to the back of the repair bay where there was a large vertical sliding door that would allow him to pull in his truck to get the motorcycle when it was ready. The door was closed now, so ducking from the drizzle that had just started, Joe went back around front to go in the main entrance. The sign on the door was turned to Closed since it was already past five, but Tanner had called Joe and told him to come on by, that he'd be working until he'd finished changing out the parts on the Harley.

Joe stepped inside the small waiting area and spotted one of Tanner's mechanics, Rico Donnelly, coming out of the repair bay. Joe didn't bother to clamp down on the scowl, his usual reaction to Rico who'd been the bad boy of Last Ride long before Tanner had played around with that particular title.

Tanner had settled down, some, but from everything Joe had heard, Rico was still going strong in his own bad boy sort of way. Three ex-wives, a son from each of them, and a string of women who seemed to favor those bad boy looks. The tight white T-shirt, low riding jeans and the assortment of tats and piercings that showed off his interests and personality. A dirt bike complete with flying mud on his right bicep. A roaring tiger on his left.

And a tat of Rico's own face, sporting his usual cocky smile, on his forearm.

Since Rico was one of Frankie's frequent customers, Joe knew the man had ass tats with the names of women who'd likely grabbed on to said ass at one time or another. Rico had even had Frankie ink some blank hearts that could be filled in later. Obviously, Rico's lovers didn't consider it tacky to have such reminders of the women who'd come, and gone, before them.

"Joe," Rico greeted. He grinned around the cigarette that was dangling from his mouth. "Tanner's back there." He hitched his thumb toward the repair bay. "Hey, I heard my boy's been hanging out with your girl."

Yeah, and that was the reason Joe was scowling.

"Dara's only thirteen," Joe snarled. "She's not allowed to date."

Rico gave a careless shrug. "He can see her without dating her."

Joe stared at the idiot. "Not if I have a say in it, he won't."

Rico chuckled, and it was just as casual as the shrug had been. He came out from behind the counter and hefted up a toolbox from the floor. "Now, now. It won't do any good to shelter the girl. Kids grow up. Gotta go," Rico quickly added, maybe because he sensed he might be on the verge of getting his heart-tatted ass kicked. "I'm doing another repair job for Millie's mom."

That got Joe's attention, and Rico must have taken Joe's intense stare as a cue that he wanted more into

"Laurie Jean wanted me to have a look at her car because it's been sputtering sometimes when she starts it up," Rico said. His tone was bragging now. "She's always coming up with sideline repair jobs for me." He chuckled, and that sounded like a brag, too. "And, hey, speaking of Laurie Jean, I've heard you're messing around with Millie. Good for you."

Rico reached out as if he might give Joe a friendly, celebratory slap on the back, but the look Joe gave him had Rico taking a step back. "All right, man," Rico said. "Catch you later."

Joe kept his glare in place until the man was out the door, and he made a mental note to talk to Dara about the dangers of bad-boy assholes. It was possible Rico's son hadn't inherited his father's dickish ways, but Joe wanted to warn her just in case.

He went past the counter and into the large repair bay. It was crammed with motorcycles, a golf cart and even a mobility scooter, telling Joe that Tanner likely had plenty of business. There were parts lying around on the smooth concrete floor. Parts on worktables, too. The place smelled of motor oil, sweat and the spring storm that was moving in.

He spotted Tanner working on the Harley that Joe had brought over the morning after the dinner deal at Millie's. Millie was very much on Joe's mind.

Both then and now.

Of course, after the kissing and touching that'd gone on in the barn, it was impossible not to think of her. Impossible not to want her, too. Soon, very soon, he was going to have to make a decision about where all of this kissing and such was going with her. The sensible thing was to stop seeing her, so that neither of them would end up getting hurt. But Joe doubted he had enough sense to manage that.

"I'm just about done," Tanner called out to him. "Give me another ten minutes or so. Once it's fixed, I'll open the bay door and help you load the Harley."

Joe would give him that ten minutes and more because he needed to have a talk with Tanner. A talk that was best done in person which was why he hadn't called Tanner after Millie's visit to his ranch, and his barn, three days ago.

"Trouble?" Tanner asked after eyeing Joe's face.

"Maybe." And it occurred to Joe that it was trouble that really wasn't his business. Except it affected Millie. And until he'd made that "sensible" decision as to what to do with her, he was making her trouble his business. Plus, Laurie Jean had reined him into this family problem by pointing the finger at Frankie and him.

"A couple of days ago, Millie was at the ranch for a riding lesson," he started. "She told me what you'd said about Laurie Jean, a possible affair and blackmail."

Joe watched Tanner for any clue that Millie had already spilled about their conversation, but Tanner's blank stare told Joe that she hadn't. Tanner finally sighed. "When Millie gets off from work, she's planning on going over to talk to Laurie Jean, to try to get to the bottom of what's going on."

Joe checked the time. It was just after six which meant Millie was either already at her mother's or on the way there now. He hoped like the devil that Millie stood her ground and got the truth.

"While Millie was still at my place, Laurie Jean showed up," Joe continued. "She didn't confirm the affair but she did more or less confirm she was being blackmailed. She seemed to believe I'm responsible for that. Maybe Frankie, too. Why would she think that?"

Tanner groaned, cursed and pushed himself away from the Harley. He sat on the floor, looking up at Joe. "The woman's batshit. *Mean* batshit at that. As for why she'd say something like that, it's probably just to try to put a wedge between Millie and you. I'm sure dear ol' batshit Mom has heard you two have been seeing each other, and she wants to put a stop to it."

Joe couldn't believe he hadn't thought of that, but yeah, that was something Laurie Jean would do. He frowned though over the "has heard" part. Frowned, too, that he hadn't remembered there would indeed be talk, especially after he'd gone to Millie's house for dinner.

"I'm sorry Laurie Jean said that about Frankie and you," Tanner added. "And if you're looking for a 'misery loving company' deal, I can give you that. Laurie Jean, in the full she-bitch mode, went over to Skylar's parents' house a couple of days ago to try to convince them to force Skylar to stop seeing me. Laurie Jean likes that Skylar's family has money and such, but apparently, our dating is causing gossip because folks think I'll ruin Skylar's reputation. Laurie Jean gave them this whole whine and spiel about why Skylar and I should break up."

"How'd Skylar take that?" Joe asked.

"Not well. She's pissed, and trust me, it takes a lot to piss her off. She told Laurie Jean to shove it, in a more polite kind of way. Skylar rarely loses her temper, but Laurie Jean can push buttons you don't even know you have. I swear, Skylar's mad enough that I wouldn't be surprised if she's the one who's doing the blackmail."

Joe could see that happening if enough of those buttons had been pushed. But blackmail seemed extreme. A reaction to something worse than a "dump the bad boy" chat with the parents. If the blackmail wasn't being done for just the money angle, then it could be payback for Laurie Jean's bitchiness.

And that led him to Frankie.

"I haven't brought any of this up to Frankie," Joe explained. "I wanted to run everything past you first, but do you really think there's a chance Frankie is behind the blackmail?"

Tanner rested his forearms on his knees. "Maybe. Frankie could have seen Laurie Jean with this other man, and after the way Laurie Jean mistreated her when we were married, Frankie might be wanting some payback." But then he stopped, shook his head. "But even with all Laurie Jean's dumped on her, I can't see Frankie doing it."

"Neither could I, but I know she doesn't always tell me what's going on in her life." Joe recalled the hickey he'd seen on her neck. That'd been about six weeks ago when she'd come over to check on him after Millie had drawn Ella's name at the Last Ride Society. "Does Frankie ever talk to you about, uh, her personal life?"

Joe groaned and shook his head to wave that off. "No need to answer that." Because he recalled something else. The "freeze in hell" glances that Frankie had shot Tanner and Skylar from across Millie's dinner table.

"Her personal life," Tanner repeated. Not a question. Judging from his tone, he was giving that some thought. "I haven't heard if she's seeing anybody. Have you?"

"No," Joe admitted. "And that's the problem. Usually when Frankie's dating someone, she's eager to tell me all about it. Even if I don't want to hear it." Which was most of the time. "But I think she saw someone..." Hell, he was tired of beating around the bush. "She had a hickey and dodged giving me any info about who gave it to her. That makes me think she's gotten involved with someone she knows I won't approve of."

"Yeah, it does," Tanner muttered.

Joe couldn't be sure, but he thought that what he was hearing and seeing from Tanner was regret. Or heck, maybe even jealousy.

"I just don't want Frankie to jump into anything stupid," Joe added.

Of course, that was more than a little like the pot calling the kettle black since he was thinking about doing something stupid with Millie.

Muttering some profanity, Tanner moved back to the Harley repair. "There's cold beer in the fridge in my office," Tanner said. "Why don't you grab two, and once I'm finished here, we can sit down and talk about anything but my mother, Frankie or Skylar."

Even with the limits Tanner had put on conversation, Joe still wanted the beer so he headed out the back of the repair bay and into the narrow hall that led him past a storage room, a small bath and finally to Tanner's office. It definitely had a man-shed feel to it with its outdated furniture, but the papers on the desk were stacked in neat piles and everything was clean.

Joe grabbed two beers, opened his and had a long pull before he headed back to the bay. However, he stopped when he heard Millie's voice.

"She accused you of blackmailing her," Millie said. "And when I told her that was BS, she said I was probably behind it."

Joe sighed. He didn't have to see Millie's face to know she was upset. Angry, too. But he could also hear something else. The hurt. Laurie Jean still knew how to take jabs at her.

"I hope you didn't just stand there and let her talk to you that way," Tanner responded.

Millie's silence told Joe that's exactly what she'd done. Joe had another sip of the beer and decided it was time for him to try to repair some of the damage Laurie Jean had obviously done. Once again though, he stopped.

"Laurie Jean demanded I stop seeing Joe," Millie went on. "She had the nerve to say I was being disrespectful to Royce by seeing Joe. *Disrespectful*," she repeated in a near shout. "Can you believe she said that?"

"Yeah, because she's batshit," Tanner replied.

"I'll tell you what disrespectful is," Millie snarled, obviously not ready to end her rant, and Joe couldn't blame her. "It's having an affair with a married woman. And that's just the tip of the iceberg as far as I'm concerned. Despite what everyone thinks, Royce wasn't Mr. Perfect. There, I've said it."

Ah, hell. He shouldn't be hearing any of this, but it squeezed at his heart to hear the broken sob that tore from Millie's mouth. He also heard some moving around and figured that Tanner was getting up to comfort his sister.

Joe looked around for a door so he could make a quick exit, but there wasn't one. There were windows, very small ones, in the bathroom and behind Tanner's desk. Joe thought he might fit through them. Might. If he got stuck, it wasn't going to improve this situation so he just stood there and tried to block out what Millie was saying.

He failed big-time.

Joe heard her all right. Every single word.

"Royce wasn't perfect and neither was our marriage," Millie continued. "And Mom brought that up, too. She says it was my fault that my marriage wasn't all sunshine and roses. My fault that Royce cheated. Apparently, if I'd been better in bed, he wouldn't have looked for anything on the side."

Joe mentally repeated his "ah, hell." Why had Laurie Jean gone there? Of course, he'd tossed some of those same questions at himself. His own marriage hadn't been all sunshine and roses, either, but the sex had been good. Damn good. Then again, maybe that's what he wanted to believe because there sure as hell had been a reason for Ella to go off with another man.

"Better in bed!" Millie repeated in a snarl. She'd obviously worked herself up even more. Was crying, too, because she was talking through sobs.

"Millie," Tanner said, but that was all he managed to say before Millie's sob broke.

"Mom could be right." No anger now. Millie had moved on to just the hurt. "I never had an orgasm with Royce."

Joe's ah, hell turned to an "oh, shit."

"Never," she repeated. Tanner was doing some repeating, too, by saying her name in such a way that Joe was pretty sure Tanner was trying to tell her they weren't alone. Other than her name though, he didn't get a word in edgewise. "I tried, I swear. I read all the books about it, but I didn't have a single one. Well, not with him, anyway. I can manage them just fine solo—"

"Joe's here," Tanner finally blurted out.

Millie gasped, and she whirled around just as Joe stepped out of the hall. He'd been right about her crying. The tears had streaked down both cheeks. But it wasn't the grief and anger he saw on her face now.

It was pure, undiluted embarrassment.

"Oh, God," she muttered, and the blush seemed to spread over her from head to toe.

"Millie—" Joe said.

But that was all he managed before Millie turned and ran out. Fast. The door slammed shut with a loud thud behind her.

Joe and Tanner stood there a couple of seconds, both of them spewing some profanity, before Joe also bolted toward the door. But he was already too late because Millie jumped in her car and sped away.

"I'll go after her," Tanner said.

Joe shook his head. "I'll do it." After all, this was mostly his fault. If he hadn't overheard her sex confession, it would have stayed as just a venting between siblings. But having him overhear it took it to many levels beyond venting.

It was no longer merely drizzling when Joe hurried outside to his truck. It had moved on to the pouring stage, which was common during spring and early summer. Still, it cut his visibility big-time, and when he pulled out of the parking lot, he didn't see Millie's car anywhere.

He didn't bother trying to call her. He knew her well enough to know that if she answered—and that was a big if—she'd just blow it off as nothing. She'd apologize and tell him not to worry about it. And all of that would be a big pile of crap. Because she sure as hell wouldn't be blowing it off, and he sure as hell would worry about it until he saw her and had a chance to tell her...

Well, he didn't know exactly what he was going to say, but he'd figure that out once he found her.

He drove to her shop first, but her car wasn't in the parking lot. Ditto for it not being in the driveway of her house. So, Joe kept driving, kept looking for her car, and he ruled out Frankie's where Dara was spending the night. He even ruled out her parents' place and his ranch. Though he was pretty sure that was the last place she'd go, he checked it out, anyway. After he'd ruled out all of those places, he just continued to drive around.

And mentally kick himself.

He should have spoken up the moment he heard her voice. Or tried to climb through the window. No way should he have just stood there and heard such a private conversation.

I never had an orgasm with Royce.

There was no way to erase that from his mind. Even heavy blows with rocks wouldn't do the trick. Worse, he was certain he wouldn't be able to keep the shock of hearing that off his face. One look at him, and Millie would know that he...

Shit.

She'd know right from the get-go that he felt sorry for her. That he pitied her, which would send her spiraling to rock bottom. Like him, she didn't handle pity and grief very well.

Joe drove past every business and through every neighborhood before he thought of another rainstorm. Of the day she'd insisted he stop at the old drive-in. Millie had said she loved the place so that's where Joe headed next.

And that's where he found her.

Or rather where he spotted her car. It was in the very center of the parking rows, the front of her car facing the screen. Unfortunately, he couldn't tell if she was still inside, because the rain was lashing down in thick, windy waves, and it was mixed with some serious cracks of lightning and thunder.

Joe's truck bounced and bucked over the uneven ground, and he pulled to a stop beside the car. He still couldn't see Millie, but since the windows were fogged up, he had to guess she was inside.

"Millie?" he called out after lowering his window.

"Go away," was her answer.

An answer Joe wouldn't take.

Sighing and knowing he was going to get soaked to the bone, he got out and went for the passenger's side door of her car. Which was locked, of course. He jiggled, tugged and pulled while she repeated her "Go away," but Millie must have felt bad about him getting wet because he finally heard the click of the locks. He threw open the door and got inside.

She'd done more crying since she'd left her brother's shop. Her eyes were red. Her mouth, too, but he soon realized that's because she was sucking on a cherry Jolly Rancher lollipop. It probably wasn't her first of that color since the huge bag of the candy was in her lap, and she was obviously picking through it for the red ones.

Neither of them spoke. They just sat there with Millie staring at the rain sheeting down the windshield and with Joe staring at a candy-sucking Millie.

"I'm sorry," they finally said—in unison again. They had this joint-apology stuff down pat.

"I'm sorry," he repeated, "but you have nothing to apologize for. I shouldn't have been listening."

"But you did." A tear streaked down her cheek, and she sucked harder on the candy. "You know why Royce cheated on me."

Joe groaned. Of course, she would turn this around and take the blame for her husband dicking around. She'd also taken the blame for the dick not being able to get her off. Joe fixed that by kissing her.

Okay, so maybe the kiss wasn't an actual fix, but he wanted his mouth on hers, and he was positive it would help that particular craving. It would also get her mind on something else other than the dick she'd married.

Man, she tasted good. Millie mixed with the sweet cherry flavor. Even if he hadn't had a close to permanent hard-on for her, he could have dived right into the kiss.

Millie did some diving, too. She grabbed on to his wet hair and plunged her tongue into his mouth, making him believe that she might have her own female version of a close to permanent hard-on for him. She kissed him, and kissed him, and kissed him, until they might have passed out from oxygen deprivation had she finally not hit the pause button.

While dragging in some quick breaths, she looked at

him, blinked, sighed. "Are you doing this because you feel sorry for me?"

"I don't believe in pity kisses," he assured her.

She made another sigh, a very breathy one that hit against his mouth like a kiss. "I want you, but I really suck at this. Really suck at it," she emphasized. "I'm too Millie Vanilla, too—"

He kissed her again to stop her from beating herself up. She'd already done enough of that.

When he had her on the verge of needing another hit of air, he pulled back and met her eye to eye. "Good sex is a lock and key kind of deal. It's the key's job to find the right chinking and maneuvering to get the lock to open."

She stared at him a long time. "Maybe some locks aren't capable of being opened by keys."

"Bullshit. For now, this will be the key." He lifted his hand. "And maybe this." He touched his mouth with his fingers. "Because every lock's got a sweet spot. The key just has to find it."

"I have found it." She squeezed her eyes shut and groaned. "Alone. But you heard me say that already."

"Yeah, and alone is fine, but it can be a whole lot better with a partner."

Millie opened her eyes and glanced at the front of his jeans. "Better for you, too."

"Yeah," he repeated, "but this is a different kind of lock and key thing. An experiment of sorts to show you that getting off can happen with a partner. I'm going to touch you, and you're going to pretend these and these—" he touched his mouth again and wiggled his fingers "—are this." He took her hand and put it over his erection.

The corners of her mouth lifted, and the look she leveled at him could have seduced a eunuch monk. "Why can't we use the big key?" She gave him a squeeze that caused his eyes to cross.

He prayed his voice didn't break. Or his willpower. "Because I don't have a condom on me and because the experiment is a better option."

Simply put, she was going to feel some guilt over this, and it'd be far less if they hadn't actually had sex.

Joe cupped her chin and lightly touched his mouth to hers. "I maybe can't give you tomorrow, but I can sure as hell give you right now."

Because simply put, he was going to feel some guilt over this, too. Later, when his body had quit burning for her. But for now, he let the burn take over.

He flicked the candy aside and kissed her, but this time he didn't go for her mouth. Joe went after her neck, and he kept kissing, kept moving his mouth until he heard the first click of the lock.

Millie's low throaty moan when he kissed the spot just below her ear.

The moan increased big-time when he let his breath land in that general area. Now that he had some progress, he went in for more. He slid his hand over her breasts. She was wearing a thin sleeveless top the color of a ripe blueberry. Emphasis on *thin*. Her bra must have been lacking thickness, too, because he had no trouble finding her nipple and giving it a gentle pinch.

Another notch up the moan ladder.

So, he touched, fondled and then lowered his head to kiss her through her top. It took some maneuvering, and Joe thought he might have bruised his kidney when he banged it on the gearshift, but Millie's moan was worth it.

He kept that up until he was on the brink of driving them both stark raving mad.

Then, he shoved up her top, pushed down the cups of her bra and put his mouth key to good use.

Millie responded.

She called him a bad name that had his blood churning and his erection hardening even more. But Joe ignored his own pain and discomfort and continued to kiss and do dirty things with his tongue. She arched her body as much as she could, twisting and turning until she had her back against her door.

Joe did his own twisting and turning, and with his mouth and tongue still playing with her breasts, he slid up that slim skirt of hers. Inch by inch. Up her thighs and all the way to her waist.

Outside, the storm had whipped up into a frenzy. Rain, wind, lightning. Inside, there was a frenzy, too, because Millie's moans had turned to sounds of urgent yearning. With some curse words mixed in. The woman did like to talk dirty.

Joe talked dirty right back to her. It seemed to go well with the kisses he was giving her nipples and his exploring fingers that skimmed up the same path her skirt had recently taken. From knees, to thighs.

He made it to the top of her panties. Not lace but there was plenty of "kick in the gut" sexy about the plain white panties that were cut low on her hips. He slid his hand into her panties. Then, lower, he slid his fingers into her.

Mercy, she was soft and hot and wet in exactly the right place.

Joe decided to keep his mouth on her breasts, for now, anyway, but if he needed any help with her *lock*, he could double team her with some touching and some exploring kisses. For now though, he touched. Moving his fingers through all that slick heat.

Sliding, touching. In and out. He listened for her subtle cues. The hitch of her breath. The murmured profanity. The lift of her hips to deepen his strokes inside her. Other cues weren't so subtle when she caught on to his hair and pulled his face against her body. Not that she had to pull far. Joe was right there.

Trailing his tongue from her breast to where his hand was working her, he kept up the strokes but added a flick of his tongue. And yeah, he heard the click.

Heard Millie's gasp of pleasure.

As that lock of hers opened right up for him.

MILLIE JUST LEANED there against her car door. Spent but with an amazing buzz that was flickering like little gold sparks all over her body. She didn't even try to speak, because the "spent" extended to her mouth, but she did manage to slip her hand around the back of Joe's neck.

His shirt and hair were wet from the rain, making him look hot and rumpled. As if he'd just finished up shower sex. He dropped his head against her chest, silent except for his heavy breathing, but she suspected he didn't have buzzing, flickering gold sparks going on. He was probably throbbing and not in a good way since he hadn't gotten the extremely pleasurable release he'd given her.

That reminder jolted her into doing something about it. Millie slid her hand in the direction of that huge bulge in his jeans. Joe stopped her though, and worse, he moved away from her.

Crap.

He was already feeling guilty, which was yet another

reason for her to attempt a hand job. Or maybe one of the dual key deals that he'd used on her. She definitely didn't mind kissing him in places other than his mouth. In fact, it was something she very much wanted to do and she could add it to her bucket list. In fact, she could add more orgasms with Joe, too.

"Lock," she said, pointing to his erection. "Keys." She lifted her hand, wiggled her fingers and blew air at him.

He smiled. Groaned. And shook his head. "Tempting. Very tempting," he rasped, "but we need to take this slow."

Millie couldn't think of a single reason why, but then, she was fueled by that amazing orgasm and an urgent desire to get her hand in his boxers. Or briefs.

"I can do slow," she assured him. "I don't think this rain is going to stop anytime soon so we'll be here for a while."

Millie had no intentions of mentioning the half dozen or so umbrellas tucked under the seats and in the glove compartment. She also wouldn't mention that Joe had braved the rain to get into the car with her and could brave the rain to go back to his truck. She didn't want him to leave and wanted to hang on to this at least a little while longer.

"Maybe I can't give you tomorrow, but I sure as heck can give you right now," she said, paraphrasing what he'd told her minutes earlier.

He stared at her, studying her face, then laughing when she blew air at him again. "Very tempting," he repeated. "But since we're at the drive-in, why don't we watch a movie until the rain passes."

She frowned. "A movie?"

Joe made a sound of agreement. "A different kind of lock and key game." He reached out and started drawing something on the condensation on the windshield. "It's one of my favorite movies," he added, and he proceeded to draw a fish.

No, not a fish, she amended, when he added a dorsal fin. "A shark."

Another sound of agreement from him, and he added a little stick figure in front of the shark. A stick figure with boobs.

"Jaws," she blurted out.

He flashed her a smile. "Yep, and I saw it for the first time right here at this drive-in. It was a retro night special. Now you draw your favorite movie."

Millie had a ton of favorites, but the first that came to mind was *Bridesmaids* so she started drawing women on the windshield. It didn't take her long to realize she sucked at this so she went with another favorite and attempted a T. rex Apparently, she sucked at that, too, because Joe just stared at her attempts and didn't venture any guesses.

"Bridesmaids," she finally said, pointing to the group of women. Then, she pointed to the dinosaur. *"Jurassic Park."*

"That's a pretty wide range of favorites." He settled back against the seat. "So, other than Jolly Ranchers, what are you eating while we watch your T. rex duke it out with my shark as our stick people stand by and watch in horror? I'm going for popcorn, extra butter, and a root beer."

"Lock and key," she muttered, smiling now. "This is a sort of 'getting to know you' deal." And while she preferred to be fooling around with Joe in a carnal sense, this could be fun, too. "One of those big salty pretzels with mustard and a Coke. Do you wear boxers or briefs?" she asked. Because that was definitely something she wanted to know.

"Boxers," he readily supplied. "You knew my middle name," he tacked on to that. "I heard you say it to your mother."

She nodded. "I saw in some of the research." Millie nearly cringed when she heard those words leave her mouth, and it would probably spoil this amazing sex buzz that was still humming between them. "You're named for the old Western actor Gary Cooper?" she quickly added.

"The singer, Alice Cooper," he said with a smile that told her the buzzing and humming was still there. "First place you had sex?" he continued.

"A bed. I know, it's so Millie Vanilla of me. You?"

He hiked his thumb to the back seat. "A car. A Taurus to be specific. Not a comfortable, or particularly long, experience."

Millie laughed. "How old were you?"

"Fifteen. How about you? How old and where?"

She wrinkled up her nose, wincing before she even answered. "In a River Walk hotel in San Antonio on my twenty-first birthday." Which, of course, told him loads. She'd been with Royce then so he'd been her first along with her one and only.

Until now, that is.

While Joe and she hadn't actually had sex, Millie was going to count him as her second. A far better experience than her first, too. She was pretty sure her smile made him aware of that.

Millie stayed frozen, their gazes locked. The heat still sizzling. "You did give me an amazing moment," she murmured and would have reached for him, but her phone rang.

She took her cell from her purse. "Tanner," she said, looking at the screen.

"Answer it," Joe encouraged. "He's probably concerned about you."

True. After all, she'd run out of his shop humiliated and

in tears. The moment she hit the answer button, Tanner's voice raced out.

"God, Millie, I'm so sorry. I should have told you Joe was there, and I had no idea you were going to say what you did."

"That makes two of us on the last part," she said. She hadn't gone there to bare her soul and make the "no orgasm with Royce" confession. Heck, she'd confessed to solo orgasms, as well.

"I'm so sorry," Tanner repeated. "Joe went looking for you. Not sure if he found you or not, but he was worried about you. Hell, I'm worried about you. Millie, are you all right?"

Her smile returned. "I'm okay." And for the first time in two years, Millie thought that just might be true.

CHAPTER FOURTEEN

"I BROUGHT OVER two locks for you to choose from," Jimbo Bodine said to Millie.

Millie tried very hard not to laugh. Or blush. Jimbo was the town's best locksmith, and he was doing her a favor by coming in after hours to change the locks on the shop's doors, and it would only confuse the man if she broke into a giggling fit over his comment.

But, sweet heaven, it was hard not to do just that.

She thought she might never look at another lock and key again without thinking of Joe and his incredible mouth and hands. In fact, she might not make it a full minute without thinking of Joe, period. The man certainly had a way of making a lasting impression. Her body agreed, and it was begging her to have another round of lock and key experiments with him.

Jimbo cleared his throat as if to get her attention. Which had definitely strayed. And he held out one of his offerings, still encased in its plastic case.

"This one here is a jimmy-proof double dead bolt similar to what you got now. If you want something more secure, and pricier," he added, showing her the second one. It was in a box. "It's got a security cam and keyless entry. Last Ride might not be a hotbed of crime, but you can't be too careful."

Wise words, but Millie wasn't worried about thieves. She

was more concerned with keeping Laurie Jean and her lover from sneaking into the place. Since her mother wouldn't even discuss the subject with her, or acknowledge that there was a lover, Millie was going to remove the temptation of giving Laurie Jean a convenient place to diddle around.

"Even if you go with something like you already got," Jimbo went on, "you should probably consider having me put a peephole in the back door. There are plenty of windows out front so you could see who might be out there, but there aren't any windows by the back door."

He was right so Millie nodded. "Definitely go with the peephole."

Jimbo grunted his approval and held up both locks again. "So basic dead bolt lock or the fancier one?"

Because her mind was in the gutter with Joe and his magic mouth and hands, Millie thought of sex. And she quickly pushed it aside when she heard the bell jingle over the front door. The shop was closed, but she hadn't changed the open sign.

"Let's go with the first one with the peephole addition," Millie muttered, turning to see who'd just come in.

Frankie.

She glanced around the shop until she spotted Millie. "Got a minute?" Frankie asked.

Even if Millie hadn't seen the woman's dour expression, she would have heard it in her tone. Frankie definitely wasn't daydreaming about sex, or if she was, it certainly wasn't "magic mouth and hands" stuff.

"Of course," Millie told her. "You want some coffee or something to drink?" she added.

"No, thanks." Frankie headed toward Millie as Jimbo mumbled something about getting started on the lock installation.

Since it was obvious that Frankie had something on her mind, Millie motioned for her to follow her into the office. She got herself a Coke and lifted a second one to offer it to Frankie. She took it, but instead of opening it, she ran her fingers up and down the cold can.

Oh, yes, she definitely had something on her mind. Millie just propped a hip on her desk. "Where's Little T?" she asked.

"It's his night with Tanner." Frankie paused, stared at the Coke can as if it were worthy of a long stare. "So, how's the research going for the Last Ride Society?"

"Good." Millie wasn't sure if this was small talk or the reason for Frankie's visit, but she decided to go ahead and elaborate in the hopes that it would get Frankie to open up. "Dara keeps emailing me stories, and I've gotten some pictures off Ella's old social media pages."

Some of the color drained from Frankie's face. "Not any pictures of Royce and her?"

"No, not even a mention of him," Millie quickly assured her.

That would have been a serious jolt, but there had been some shots of Ella and Joe that'd given her a jolt of a different kind. Because they'd looked happy and very much in love. Of course, most people didn't post unhappy and "out of love" pictures of themselves.

"There was nothing on her social media about her paintings," Millie went on. "Did she ever say anything about her art to you?"

Frankie lifted her shoulder and finally popped the top on the Coke. "I knew she painted, and she'd mention it sometimes in a general sort of way. I think she was nervous though about showing her paintings to anyone. Maybe because she didn't think they were good enough?"

"They were good enough," Millie assured her. Very good, in fact, but Millie dealt with enough artists to understand that some were insecure and afraid of criticism. Maybe Ella had been.

"And what about the bucket list?" Frankie asked several moments later. "Any progress on it?"

Loads, but Millie wasn't going to bring up her fooling around with Joe, which had certainly been progress. The fact that the fooling around had happened at the drive-in, one of the places she'd intended to visit meant it was a double bang on the bucket list.

"Thanks to Dara, I've learned how to ride a horse." Millie paused, sighed. "Frankie, what's wrong?" she came out and asked. "Are you here because Laurie Jean accused you of blackmailing her?"

Frankie blinked, not in a shocked kind of way but as if she'd forgotten about it. So, that likely wasn't the reason for her visit.

"Over the years, Laurie Jean has accused me of a lot of things," Frankie said. "I do the 'water off a duck's back' thing when it comes to her."

Maybe, but Millie couldn't help but notice that Frankie hadn't denied the blackmail. Which only added to the puzzle of this particular mess. Aunt Freida was dodging her calls, and Laurie Jean had clammed up. Millie had zero intentions of going to her father about this so she was just going to have to put it aside until it blew up in their faces.

Something that Millie was certain was going to happen.

"I slept with Tanner." The confession just gushed right out of Frankie.

Now Millie blinked, and it was definitely from shock. "Recently?" she asked.

Frankie made a so-so wave of her hand. "Recent-ish. About six weeks ago, right before he started seeing Skylar."

All right, that explained Frankie's bristling toward the other woman, and Millie felt some bristling toward her brother. For Pete's sake, had Tanner gone from Frankie's bed straight to Skylar's?

Because Frankie looked as if she could use it, Millie went to her and pulled her into a hug. "Are you still in love with Tanner?"

Frankie pooh-poohed that with a hollow laugh, but Millie suspected it was true. Or at least leaning toward the truth. "The sex just sort of happened. Tanner had come over to read Little T a bedtime story, and after he fell asleep, Tanner and I had a beer. One thing led to another."

Millie didn't want to fill in the blanks, but that had been a big leap between "one thing" and "another." Or maybe it hadn't.

"Had you two slept together before this?" Millie pulled back to look Frankie in the eyes. "I mean, before six weeks ago but after the divorce?"

Frankie swallowed hard. Nodded. "It happens every now and then."

Millie bristled even more for Tanner. It wasn't right for him to play around with Frankie's emotions this way. Then again, Frankie might be willing to put up with the playing around for good sex. Millie was starting to see such things as having many shades of gray.

"I'm late," Frankie said in that same blurting-out tone as before.

It took Millie a moment to realize Frankie wasn't talking about an appointment. It was "the" kind of late that had put this seriously troubled expression on her face.

"I haven't taken a test yet," Frankie went on. "But I was

hoping you'd do me a huge favor and buy me a couple of the pee sticks. I don't mean here in town but maybe at the Quik Stop off the interstate. If I go in to buy them, I'll start crying. Or maybe screaming."

Frankie stopped, moved on to some mild hyperventilation, and she caught on to Millie's arms. "I can't be pregnant. I just can't be. The gossips would have a field day over me getting knocked up again. Little T would get teased about it and Tanner, well, he wouldn't be very happy over making the same mistake twice."

Since Frankie seemed to be on the verge of doing that crying or screaming right now, Millie hugged her again. "I'll be here late tonight while Jimbo redoes the locks, but I'll get the tests for you first thing in the morning."

"No," Frankie answered in a flash. "Little T's having some of his friends over for a sleepover tomorrow, and I don't want to get bad news right before that. Day after tomorrow is fine. And then maybe you can stay with me while I pee on the stick."

"Absolutely," Millie assured her. She'd never watched another woman pee, but she'd done plenty of the tests herself and knew how the waiting could mess with your mind.

And how the results could break your heart.

In her case, it'd been the negative results that'd done it. Those minus signs were little SOBs, but Frankie would have to deal with the opposite. A plus sign could mean her world being tipped on its axis.

Frankie went stiff when the bells jangled on the front door. "It's probably Jimbo," Millie murmured, and she walked out into the shop to check. Definitely not Jimbo.

"It's Joe," Millie relayed to Frankie.

Behind her, Millie was certain that Frankie was in the frantic mode of trying to gather her composure and not look as if her world was doing the axis tip thing. Millie, however, tried to put on her best "nothing's wrong/so wonderful to see you" face. The last one was actually true, and the first one was a dismal failure because Joe obviously saw right through it.

"What's wrong?" he asked.

"Just a girl deal," Frankie said, hurrying out of the office.

Frowning, Joe looked at Millie, and he was no doubt wondering if the girl deal meant that she'd told Frankie about what had gone on in her car at the drive-in. Millie quickly shook her head.

"I was upset about Laurie Jean accusing me of blackmail," Frankie added. "But Millie cheered me up." She made a quick sound of surprise when she looked at her watch. "Gotta go. Thanks, Millie. Bye."

Millie seriously doubted anyone could have gotten out of the shop faster than Frankie. It was practically a sprint.

"Is she okay?" Joe asked, watching his sister's blur of motion as she darted out of sight.

Rock meets hard place. And she had to go with that sliver of space in between that was neither a lie nor the truth. "Laurie Jean shouldn't have accused Frankie of blackmail. Then again, she shouldn't have accused you, either."

Joe made a sound that could have meant anything. "I figured Frankie was here because she was riled about Tanner seeing Skylar."

"That, too," Millie acknowledged, and because she wanted to get off the subject of his sister, she motioned toward her office. "Want a drink?"

He glanced at Jimbo, who was engrossed in installing the lock on the back door. "Sure," he said. He followed her into the office.

And he shut the door.

Millie might have turned the question around and asked him what was wrong, but she was way off base. It was more of what was right. Very right.

Joe hauled her to him and kissed her. It was one of those thorough kisses, too, that both melted and rattled her at the same time. Along with also confusing her because he pulled back almost as fast as he'd pulled her in.

"Dara will be home soon so I can't stay long," he explained.

Oh, so there would be no lock and key repeats. She tried not to feel so disappointed even though it likely wouldn't have happened, anyway, what with Jimbo in the shop.

Joe reached in his pocket, pulled out three foil-wrapped condoms and showed them to her. Three. Condoms. Three! So, maybe sex was going to happen after all?

No, she decided when she looked at him. There was some serious disappointment as well on his face, along with a dash of uncertainty. He might not officially be her lover, but she was reasonably sure that wasn't his lover expression.

"Consider them tokens," he explained, glancing down at the condoms. "Give it some thought as to what you want to do with them. You can use them. Or not."

Millie had to shake her head. "Color me confused. The only thing I'd want to do with them is use them on you, and I really don't have to give that any thought."

She ended that with a smile.

And an invitational wink.

He swallowed hard. "You need to think," he insisted. "Because this could explode all over us."

Oh, yes. She definitely had sex on the brain because that didn't sound like a bad thing to her. Then again, with Joe's kiss still whirling around her body like a hot tornado, she probably wasn't a good judge of that.

"Give it some thought," he emphasized. "And if we go for round two, I have three conditions. You'll need to give those some thought, too." He dropped one of the condoms on her desk. "If we keep seeing each other, I don't want to talk about our spouses."

Millie nodded so fast that her neck popped.

Joe laid another condom on her desk. "I don't want us to be together in the houses we shared with our spouses."

Again, she gave him a fast nod. No way did she want fresh memories of Joe mingling with those old ones of Royce. And she especially didn't want to do any memory mingling in a space that'd once been Ella's.

"We can use the room upstairs," she suggested, especially since she'd had it cleaned from top to bottom.

She picked up the two condoms again and wondered if he'd consider five seconds enough thinking time.

He dropped a third condom on the desk. "Final condition. It has to stay just sex. A moment-to-moment, maybe hour-to-hour kind of deal. Because I'm not ready—"

"I know," Millie interrupted. "I'm not ready, either."

However, she had the unsettling feeling that she was a lot closer to being in ready mode than Joe was. Or ever would be. That's why Millie mentally repeated to herself that sex was the bottom line with Joe. Still, it was far better than any other bottom line she'd had in a long time.

"I'll think about it," she said just to appease him. But she knew if she had her way, using all three of the condoms would happen. "Why don't you go ahead and pencil us in for a sex date. The shop is closed Sunday. Maybe that would work best." And the two days between then and now should be enough thinking time. "Sunday evening," she clarified since she had to buy the pregnancy test for Frankie that morning and then hang with her while she took it.

"Sunday evening," he agreed. "But only if you're absolutely certain it's what you want to do."

It all sounded very official. Formal, even. When he kissed her again though, Millie knew there was nothing formal about it. This was a basic-instinct lust kind of thing with Joe poised to come through on giving her all sorts of pleasures. Hopefully, getting pleasure from her, too.

Her heartbeat was throbbing in her ears when he pulled away from her. Actually, other parts of her were throbbing, too, which was probably why she hadn't heard the bells jingle on the front door.

"Someone just came into the shop," Joe grumbled, stepping back from her.

It took her several moments to catch her breath. "It's probably Jimbo doing the locks." She opened her office door, looked out and nearly gasped. Definitely not Jimbo.

It was Dara.

And the girl wasn't alone. She had two boys and another girl with her.

"Millie?" she called out, sounding just as cheerful as usual. "I brought some friends by to see Mom's paintings. I hope that's okay."

Millie crammed the condoms in her desk drawer, and her gaze flew to Joe's, silently asking how they should handle this. "You could stay out of sight until they leave," she whispered to him. That way, Dara wouldn't have questions about why he was there.

Joe didn't stay out of sight though. That probably had something to do with the voices that started to trickle through the shop. Boy voices. Joe stepped out of the office, his gaze zooming right to the four teenagers heading their way.

"That's Rico Donnelly's kid," Joe grumbled.

Yes, it was, and the boy had the unfortunate timing of slinging his arm carelessly over Dara's shoulder so that his fingers dangled over her right breast. Millie thought she heard Joe growl.

"Settle down, Papa Bear," Millie whispered to him. "I'll get him something else to do with his hands. Dara," she called out in the same breath.

Millie went to the girl, reaching out for a hug, but Dara was also reaching out—to move the boy's arm off her. No need to intercede. Dara had taken care of it herself.

"Dad," Dara said, shifting her attention to him.

Hard to miss those thudding footsteps of his. She opened her mouth, probably to ask why he was there, but then she closed it, smiled a little.

"Hi, Mr. McCann," the perky blonde girl said.

"Good to see you, Bella." But his scowl stayed fixed on the Donnelly boy who was withering inch by inch.

"Oh, I should make introductions," Dara said after an uncomfortable silence. "Millie, this is Bella Conroy. We've been best friends since preschool. And that's Jace Mendoza and Ian Donnelly." The dark-haired boy, Jace, gave a greeting nod to Millie, then Joe. Ian, aka Rico Donnelly's kid, continued to wither.

"Is it too late for us to see Mom's art?" Dara asked. "I mean, I know you're closed, but I saw the light on and your car in the parking lot so I figured you were here. I didn't see your truck," she added to Joe.

"I'm parked up the street." He'd done that probably to avoid gossip about him being in the shop. "I thought Bella's mom was giving you a ride home."

"Oh, she is," Dara verified. "She's at the hair salon, but she should be done soon. I told her we wouldn't be long."

"You can ride back with me," Joe said, and nope, he still hadn't taken his eyes off Ian.

"Dad," Dara said like a plea. "I really want Bella's mom to do that. And can Bella stay the night? Please?" Dara added.

Joe didn't say anything for some snail-crawling moments. "Yeah. She can stay." He finally turned to Millie, and again going with intuition, she thought he might be about to tell her goodbye, but when he cast another glance at Ian, no form of goodbye left his mouth.

"I want to see the art, too," he snarled. His tone in no way indicated that he wanted to do that. It was obvious he simply wanted to continue being Papa Bear to his daughter.

Millie led them toward the local artist display yes, a room she'd sworn to avoid. But this was Dara so she'd make an exception. She stopped though when Bella picked up an antique from a True or False display. "This is an Edwardian medical device for holding an anesthesia cloth in place over a patient's mouth," she read. "True or false?"

Bella studied the claw-looking object. It had a wooden handle at the top with a spring level between it and the five metal prongs that jutted out like a robot crab from a really bad nightmare.

"True," Jace guessed, but the girls both went with false. Ian's mumble was too indistinguishable for Millie to decipher.

"False," Bella read when she turned over the card. "It's an antique apple picker." She set it back down, looked around. "You have a lot of fun stuff in here."

Millie thanked her and took them into the room that she personally wouldn't find fun. There were plenty of paintings and art to look at, of course, but her eyes went straight to the trio of Ella's paintings. That's where Dara went, too, so rather than focusing on Ella, she watched Dara and the sheer joy the girl got from showing off her mother's artwork.

Joe stayed back, watching them as well, and Millie went to stand by him, leaving the teenagers to their chatter.

"You knew they were her paintings when you came here for a drink," she muttered. It wasn't a question.

He nodded. "I didn't know before that night, but I knew Ella called her studio La La Land so I made the connection. Plus, I recognized her work."

She thought back to that night, which seemed a lifetime ago. But she remembered the sudden change in Joe's mood. Millie had thought it was because of his grief or because he was feeling guilty because he was attracted to her, but seeing the paintings must have given him a bad jolt.

"I'm sorry," they said in unison, and Millie's quick laughter had Dara and the others glancing over at them. Millie gave them a friendly wave and waited until they turned back to the paintings.

"Okay, I'm sorry because you had to find out from me that your wife had sold me paintings," she continued. "That should have come from her. So, what are you apologizing for?"

"You loved the paintings. You told me that. And now, there's no way you can love them. That love got taken away from you through no fault of your own."

It sounded as if he was talking about more than art. Maybe their marriages? Joe and she were definitely in the same boat there. It'd been no fault of their own that their spouses had died.

Well, probably no fault.

Millie still had mixed feelings and some guilt over the fact she'd never been able to have an orgasm with Royce.

Something Royce must have known. It could have played into some feelings of inadequacy—

She stopped that thought in its tracks. She wasn't going to take the fall for this. No. This was on Royce and Ella, right where the blame belonged. And damn it, Joe was right about her loving those paintings and now hating them. Except it wasn't so much hate as it was a trio of pokes at the memories that she hadn't been enough for Royce but this talented artist had been.

Oh, well. Because she'd already seen them now, at least she could remove the scenes from the paintings off her bucket list. All the scenes but the drive-in, anyway. She'd coated over the painting memory with memories of her own. Good ones, too, with Joe and her.

The kids finally finished looking at the paintings and came back toward them. "Ian and Jace are going to walk with Bella to the salon, and then Bella's mom will pick me up here. That way, I'll have a chance to talk to Millie. About the research," Dara added to her father.

Joe's groan was very low, but Millie still heard it. "I'll wait outside," he grumbled. "Get back to me on the other stuff," he told Millie, making her blush a little. Because the other stuff involved sex and those three condoms.

"We'll talk tomorrow, Ian," Dara called out to the boy.

Ian grinned. Then, he promptly quit grinning when he saw Joe staring at him. Joe was right behind the teenagers when they left, and Dara didn't say another word until the jangled bell indicated their exit.

"Look," Dara said, turning to her, "if seeing my mom's paintings makes you sad or upset, you need to tell me. I'll figure out another place to put the paintings so you won't have to see them."

Millie was about to give a huge lying denial of being

sad or upset, but the girl deserved the truth. "It is hard to look at them," she admitted. "But your mom was a very talented artist, and unless someone opens a gallery, the paintings can stay here."

Dara stared at her as if trying to figure out if that was the truth, the whole truth and nothing but the truth. She must have believed it was because she finally nodded. "Okay. But if they get to be too much for you, just let me know."

"I will," Millie promised. She paused. "Do you have any idea why your mom didn't tell your dad about selling me the paintings?"

Dara shrugged. "Dad asked me that, too, and I told him that I thought she kept it to herself because she wanted it to be a surprise."

For the first time, Millie saw a crack in Dara's usually sunshine personality. Her bottom lip quivered a little. "I don't know why," the girl said. "I don't know why she did a lot of things, but I can't believe she was running off to be with your husband. She loved my dad. And he really loved her."

Because Dara looked close to tears, Millie pulled her into a hug. "I know he did," she murmured, and she left it at that.

Heck, maybe Ella had indeed loved Joe. Laurie Jean certainly loved Asher, Millie didn't doubt that, so maybe there were reasons other than falling out of love that would cause a spouse to stray.

Dara pulled back and looked at her. "Let's finish the research about my mom so you don't have to keep thinking about her. Can you come over on Sunday? I can give you another riding lesson, and we can go through all the other stories I have about Mom."

Millie sighed. Nodded. "Okay. I can be at the ranch early afternoon on Sunday. Does that work for you?"

"It does," Dara replied, and she brushed a kiss on Millie's cheek. "See you then," she added with a little wave before she headed for the front door.

Judging from Dara's quick smile and bounce in her step, she'd gotten back some of her perkiness. Good. Millie didn't want any of this to drag Dara down.

"Sunday," Millie repeated, sighing again.

She'd just work in the research and riding lesson in between Frankie's pregnancy tests and sex with Joe.

Easy peasy.

CHAPTER FIFTEEN

FOR DAYS JOE'S mind had kept circling around one thing. Or rather three things. Millie, sex with Millie and just how much sex with Millie could and would screw up both of their lives.

Of course, one could argue that their lives were already in the screwed-up category and that sex wouldn't do any harm. But that was dick thinking. His dick. And he knew that part of his anatomy well enough to know that it could come up with all sorts of rationalizing to get what it wanted.

And what it wanted was Millie.

Hell, Joe wanted her, too. When he was with her, the grief let up enough so he could breathe. So he could experience something other than the dark ache that'd been inside him since Ella's death. Millie made him smile again. Laugh. She made him *feel*. It was still "to be determined" whether or not that was a good thing, but Joe had decided he wasn't going to wait for that determination. Both he and his dick were going to have sex with Millie.

Tonight.

He'd already gotten his proverbial ducks in a row for their date. Dara would be staying the night with Frankie. That had meant asking Frankie for the favor without telling his sister why he wanted Dara out of the house for the night. It had also involved convincing Frankie to tell Dara the little white lie that she needed babysitting help since she had a bunch of paperwork to do for her shop.

It was entirely possible that both his daughter and sister had seen through his lined-up ducks and knew the real reason he'd wanted to make these arrangements. Still, he hadn't had to spell it out which suited him just fine.

He heard the car pull into his driveway, and he came out of the tack room to see if Millie had shown up way early for her research date with Dara. His stomach actually did a little flutter at the thought of seeing her, but the flutter vanished when he realized who his visitor was. Definitely not Millie.

Janice.

Well, hell. This couldn't be good. Janice rarely showed up at the ranch, and her sour mood would only get worse if Millie arrived while she was here. Even though Janice had probably never met Millie, his former mother-in-law would without a doubt know who she was.

Since it was only ten in the morning, Joe figured he'd have at least a couple of hours to find out what Janice wanted and send her on her way before Millie arrived. He was betting that it would take far less than those couple of hours though. Unless she was breaking her usual habit, Janice almost certainly wouldn't want to sit around and have a long-drawn-out chat with Dara or him.

Joe washed his hands and made his way out to Janice's car. Even though Dara was likely still in bed, he nearly called out to her, to tell her that her grandmother was here, but he decided against that when he saw Janice's face.

Shit.

She'd been crying.

Joe quickly picked through his memory to see if today was some kind of anniversary. Janice "celebrated" any and every date in Ella's life. It wasn't Ella's birthday or any other milestone he could think of. However, it was only a week and a half from the two-year anniversary of Ella's death.

Maybe that was the reason for Janice's tears.

Joe could sympathize with her on that. He wouldn't cry on that two-year mark, probably not, anyway, but he sure as hell wasn't looking forward to the memories it'd bring.

"Janice," he greeted. "You want to come in and have some coffee or iced tea?" Joe added when Janice just stood there next to her still-open car door. It was already too hot and too muggy to stand outside and listen to her vent about whatever it was she'd come here to vent about.

She kept a white-knuckle grip on the door. "Yesterday, I got a visit from Laurie Jean Parkman." Her eyes might be red and sad, but that was an angry set to her jaw. "You know who she is," she started.

"I know her," Joe verified. "What'd she want?" Though he was pretty sure he already knew the answer to that.

Janice's jaw tightened even more. "Laurie Jean wanted to inform me that you've been seeing her daughter, Millie."

Yep, he'd been right about that answer. Since he figured Janice was about to fill him in on what else was said during that visit, he just stayed quiet and let the woman spew in her own ice-queen kind of way.

"Laurie Jean said you even went to dinner at Millie's house and that you took Dara. *Dara*," Janice emphasized. "I couldn't believe you would put your daughter through something like that."

Okay, staying quiet was over. "Dara likes Millie, and she's been helping her with the research for the Last Ride Society. Millie drew Ella's name..." He had to pause and do the math. "About seven weeks ago."

He didn't have to ask if Janice knew what he was talking about. The fire that lit her eyes was somehow ass-burning hot and butt-freezing cold at the same time.

"You shouldn't have allowed Dara to do that," Janice snapped, her voice as sharp as a bullwhip. "That Dayton woman could be trying to manipulate Dara into telling her lies about Ella so she can put it in that so-called research report. A report she can and will use to smear Ella's name."

Joe should have felt torn between defending Millie and Ella. But this wasn't about that. This was about Janice and a crapload of faulty logic.

"I hate to remind you," he said, hanging on to his temper, barely, "but Ella's name is already smeared."

Janice gasped, pressed her hand over her heart, and she flinched as if he'd physically punched her. In her mind the truth was probably worse than a punch. And that's why Joe instantly regretted it.

Dragging in a weary breath, Joe backtracked so he could try to smooth things over. Something he always seemed to be doing when it came to Janice.

"Millie isn't going to smear Ella's name," he spelled out. "She's using stories that Dara has given her. Good, positive stories of a daughter's happy memories of a mother she loved."

"I don't believe that," Janice fired back. "Of course Millie wants to get back at Ella. She wants revenge because she mistakenly believes my Ella was having an affair with her husband. Ella wasn't doing anything of the sort. And there's nothing, absolutely nothing, that you can say that'll make me believe otherwise."

"Then, why was she in that car with Royce Dayton?" Joe snapped before he could stop himself. So much for smoothing over. He was adding some potholes and maybe even a crater to his and Janice's already rocky relationship.

Janice stayed quiet for a moment. "I don't know." She swiped away a single tear that spilled down her cheek and repeated it.

Her second "I don't know" lacked the anger of the first one. In fact, all the anger seemed to drain right out from her, and in its place came some very dark pain and grief.

On a heavy sigh, Joe walked toward her, intending to pull her into his arms and offer her what comfort he could, but Janice shook her head and stepped away from him. "Don't," she insisted. "I'm all right."

No, she wasn't. Janice was far from being all right, but Joe stayed put, figuring if she broke, it would only make things worse. No way would she want him to witness her having a full-fledged meltdown though he had to wonder if that would help in the long run. Heaven knew Janice needed something to shove her past this wall she'd built up around her.

And that's when Joe realized something.

That Millie had helped him with his own shoving. His own wall demolition. The help hadn't come as a meltdown but with the feelings he had for her. It didn't matter that he was still uncertain about those feelings, it was a start that Millie had given him. Maybe, just maybe, he'd done the same for her. If so, they just might get through this hell on earth that had been doled out to them.

"My daughter didn't cheat on you," Janice stated after she'd composed herself. "And you should be doing everything possible to find out why she was with that man when she died. You should be working to clear her good name."

Joe wanted to say that he didn't want to find out or clear anybody's name. But he did. It was another realization like the one about Millie, walls and shoving. He needed to know what had been going on with his wife that had caused her to be in that fatal car crash with Royce.

"Dara's inside if you want to see her," Joe pointed out when Janice got back in her car.

"Please tell her hello for me." The woman was back to her icy, tight tone. "I'll call her soon."

Joe didn't try to stop the woman. No sense in it. Janice had closed down again. But she'd also issued him a not-so-subtle call to action.

One that he'd take.

He went straight to his man-shed and took out Ella's laptop that he'd stored away in a box on the highest shelf above her old worktable. The battery had long since been drained, but he fished out the charger cord, plugged it in and sat in his recliner while he turned it on. He had no trouble recalling the password Ella had used for all her online accounts so it opened right away for him.

Plain and simple, this was snooping, something he'd never thought he would do, but he sure as hell did it now. In fact, it was something he should have done months ago, if for no other reason than to rule out that there was something to find that Ella hadn't wanted found.

Like proof of an affair.

He clicked on her email account and sat, and sat, and sat while the emails loaded. Apparently, the spam had just continued in the past two years, so he had to wade through ads for penis enlargements, weight loss pills and pleas to split inheritances if she provided a bank account number. There was one from a Nigerian astronaut wanting to sell bottles of air from outer space.

Joe skipped through all of those to make it to an email conversation between Ella and her high school friend from

San Antonio, Shelby Wright. In the half dozen emails, they shared and tweaked recipes for Christmas cookies. Unless "cream the butter" and "dribble in food coloring" were code for something else, Ella hadn't confided in her old pal.

There were some emails from Janice where she'd forwarded inspirational memes and such. Some back-and-forths with Frankie about preschool and pre-K recommendations for Little T. Joe kept scrolling until he got to an automated notice of a monthly statement from Liberty Bank in San Antonio.

He felt his chest tighten.

Ella and he had had a joint account for the bank in Last Ride, and he'd never heard her mention doing business with one in San Antonio. Maybe it was something Janice had set up for her way back before Ella and he had married.

But the tightening in his chest got worse.

He kept looking and saw that Ella had gotten one of the automated notice reminders every month since her death. Before her death, too. Joe finally made it to the first one. The one congratulating her on the account. She'd apparently opened it six months before she'd died.

Hell.

Why hadn't Ella told him about this?

Shoving that question aside and cursing the continued tightness in his chest, he opened the bank statement issued the month she'd died. It took him to the bank site where he figured he'd stall because it would require a password. It did, but Ella had used an automatic password saver so all Joe had to do was click.

His finger hovered over the key.

And hovered.

Before he finally pressed it.

It took only a couple of seconds for the statement to load,

and he saw that the account was in both Ella's name and La La Land. The balance was $6,687.43. Not a fortune but definitely not pocket change, either. He worked his way through it and the other statements to find the initial deposit of six grand.

The date matched up with what Millie had told him. This was no doubt payment for the three paintings. Two thousand apiece. He supposed that was good money for a new artist. But there were other deposits, too, that appeared to be from other buyers for the paintings. No purchases were as big as the one from Once Upon a Time, but there had been a fairly steady stream of income in the six months Ella had had the account before she died.

A steady stream of monthly withdrawals, too.

Two months before her death, Ella had set up payments to Easy Storage, a place just on the outskirts of Last Ride. The payments had continued, including the most recent one of just a week earlier. So, the account was still active.

He opened up the last receipt and got the number of the unit she'd rented. Joe jotted it down, along with the account info, and then he just stared at it.

And stared.

He wasn't sure he wanted to speculate about what would be in that unit, one that she hadn't told her husband about, but it was hard for him to imagine that it had something to do with an affair with Royce.

Unless that's where Ella had stored gifts he'd given her.

Royce would have had to be overly generous in the gift department though for her to need an entire storage unit. Then again, storing even small tokens from a lover would have kept Dara or him from running across them had she stashed them around the house.

He considered asking Dara if she knew about the unit.

Or the bank account for that matter, but if she didn't, then this might make her worry. It was certainly making Joe worry. Because even though there didn't seem to be a reasonable explanation as to why Ella had been with Royce, Joe wanted to hang on to the possibility that there was one.

Either way, he needed an explanation whether it was reasonable or not. Hell, whether it crushed him or not. He didn't have a bucket list like Dara and Millie, but there were plenty of things he should be doing. Like moving on with his life. He'd made a start of that with Millie, but he had a long way to go, and clearing up the past was part of that *long way*.

Joe sent a quick text to Dara to let her know he was running an errand. She tended to sleep late on Sundays, but she might be up. However, when she didn't respond right away, he figured she was still in bed or in the shower.

He got in his truck and drove the fifteen or so minutes to get to the storage facility. Thankfully, he didn't pass anyone along the way that he knew because he was positive that he had a very troubled expression right now. Anyone that saw him might think he'd finally snapped.

There was no attendant on duty at Easy Storage so he parked and walked through the rows of units until he came to number twenty-four. He'd expected there to be a standard sliding door with a padlock, but this was a temperature-controlled unit with a reinforced door and a keypad. The instructions on the keypad said to enter your four-digit pin for entry.

Joe tried Ella's birth year. The lock didn't budge, and the little light above the numbers stayed red. He tried Dara's next. Still a no-go, and it didn't open when Joe put in his own birth year.

Cursing, he hoped to hell that Ella hadn't used just some

random number. If so, it'd be a first since she always had trouble remembering passwords and such. It twisted at his gut more than a little to consider that the pin might have something to do with Royce. His birth year or, hell in a handbasket, some other numbers that lovers might hold dear.

Joe had no idea if the keypad would shut down if there were too many failed attempts to log in. He just kept going. The year Ella and he married. Janice's birth year. The lock still didn't budge. Until he typed in the year that Ella had graduated from high school.

Bingo.

The light on the keypad turned green, and the lock made a clicking sound when it disengaged. He reached out, turned the knob and opened the door just a fraction. He hated that he had to steel himself just to think about going in. Hated that the thought of what might be inside made him sick to his stomach.

Aggravated with himself and his gut reaction, he gave the door a kick with his boot, and it flew open. The cool air rushed out toward him, but he couldn't see squat because the light was off. He fumbled around on the wall next to the door, located the switch and flipped it on.

And then he just stood there and took it in.

Shit.

The room was filled with yet more secrets.

CHAPTER SIXTEEN

MILLIE GRABBED THE two pregnancy tests that she'd bought from the Quik Stop the day before and shoved into her purse.

She cursed when she checked the time. It was already ten thirty. She'd lingered way too long in her bubble bath while dreaming of Joe, and she was now running late. She had to get the tests to Frankie, deal with the aftermath of the results and then head to the ranch to deal with whatever aftermath the research with Dara would cause.

At least the end of the research was in sight. She'd take the last of the stories from Dara, write them all up into the report and add them to the info she'd gotten from her internet searches. Then, she'd try to forget about Ella.

Fat chance, her mind whispered.

Millie couldn't argue with her mind. Ella would always be there, a part of the memories that hovered like a storm cloud over her life. Still, Millie wanted to look through those clouds and see the bright side. The research had started what she now had with Joe.

Or rather what she could possibly have with him.

For that *possibly* to progress though to a strong *maybe* and then beyond, she had to get through this day so she could get moving on to the hot night she had planned with him.

She'd just made it to the door when her phone rang, and

she saw Frankie's name on the screen. Millie juggled her purse to her shoulder so she could answer it.

"I'm sorry," Millie said right off. "I'm running late, but I should be there in about five minutes."

"No need. It was a false alarm. I'm not pregnant." Frankie practically sang it, and judging from the other sounds that Millie heard, the woman was doing some jumping up and down.

Millie was jumping up and down with her in spirit, and some of the tension vising her head eased up. "Thank God," Millie muttered.

"Yes, God, Mother Nature and anybody else who had a part in getting my butt out of this particular sling. I've never been so happy to be bloated and have cramps from hell."

Millie could hear the happiness. Along with more jumping. She considered adding something about it being a good idea for Frankie to be more careful, but she had to believe Frankie had learned her lesson.

Well, maybe she had.

"Uh, you said Tanner and you still had sex every now and then," Millie reminded her. "So, maybe it'd be a good idea to keep some condoms handy."

"I do, and we use them. It's just when my period was late, I thought maybe the condom had a leak or something. They're only like 85 percent effective."

That was a "squirm in the seat" kind of reminder, considering Millie was planning on using a condom with Joe. But a second reminder came of all those times Millie had tried to get pregnant and had failed. Still, she'd check the expiration date on the condom packets Joe had given her. No way would Joe want to deal with an unplanned pregnancy with her. Still, Millie let the fantasy of her having Joe's child spin for a couple of seconds.

"Anyway, there's no reason for you to come over," Frankie continued, the sound of her voice yanking Millie out of her daydream. "But a thousand gallons of thanks for you being willing to sit with me through the test and talk me down from any possible ledges."

"Anytime," Millie assured her. And she meant it. She did want to be there for Frankie, and their new closeness was yet something else she could attribute to the research. Frankie and she had always gotten along, but Frankie's worry about the research had brought them together in a good kind of way.

"Gotta go," Frankie said. "I really need to take something for these cramps."

Millie figured that was the first time she'd smiled over a woman suffering cramps, but she ended the call and checked the time. Instead of being late, she'd be too early if she went to the ranch now so she'd have time for an early lunch. Then, she could mull over her choice of underwear for her date with Joe.

Something she'd already mulled over for hours, including the entire time of her long bubble bath. It was probably ironic that she was putting this much thought into something that she sincerely hoped Joe would shuck right off her.

She set her purse on the kitchen island and was about to head upstairs to the bedroom when her doorbell rang. For a couple of heart-fluttering, body-flaming moments, she thought it was Joe, and that's why she practically sprinted to answer it. Not Joe though.

Aunt Freida.

"I just came from church and decided to stop by so we could talk," Freida greeted.

It wasn't unusual for Freida to do that, especially since Royce's death. But since the woman had been dodging her calls for days, Millie certainly hadn't expected her to just show up.

"Are you here to finally tell me what's going on with Mom?" Millie came out and asked.

Freida made a noncommittal sound, stepped in and walked past her, heading to the kitchen. "It's too early for a glass of wine, but I think it'd be all right to have an Irish coffee."

Millie sighed. If Freida needed booze to get through this, then it was going to be *bad*.

Sighing some more and silently cursing, too, Millie followed Freida into the kitchen and started assembling the doctored coffee. It wouldn't take long since she could use the Keurig and then pour in some whiskey. A large amount of it. Freida wouldn't mind if they skipped the whipped cream.

Her aunt stood and glanced around as if seeing it for the first time. "I thought you would have redecorated by now," Freida muttered.

Millie glanced back at her and saw that Freida's forehead had bunched up and that she'd gone a little pale. Oh, yeah. This was going to be bad.

"Actually, I'd rather move," Millie threw out there even though it would only add more to the bad stuff that was no doubt about to be aired.

"The Daytons won't like that," Freida said, stating the obvious. She finally sat at the table in the breakfast nook and began to tug off her gloves.

"No, but it's possible the scandal that's about to hit will overshadow any complaints they have."

Freida made a groaning, moaning sound. What she didn't do was deny that a scandal was in the making.

She finished the coffee, set it on the table in front of

Freida and then took the seat across from her. Just as her phone dinged with a text. Millie snagged it from the counter where she'd left it and saw that it was from Dara to let her know that it was okay for her to come over anytime. Millie didn't answer and wouldn't until she figured out how long it was going to take her to pull this info out of Freida.

"I need you to spill everything," Millie insisted, sitting down again. "What do you know about Mom, an affair and blackmail?"

Freida had a not-so-prim sip of the coffee. It was more like a gulp. "What do you know about it?"

"Uh-uh. I asked first. Spill it," Millie repeated.

Freida had another gulp, dragged in a long breath and then another before she spoke. "Marriage is a complex union with its ups and downs."

Millie ducked down so that Freida could see her scowling face. "Spill it," she three-peated.

Her aunt still paused long enough to grow chin hairs. "Laurie Jean did ask me for money, five thousand dollars, and I gave it to her."

All right. That was a start. "Why did she need the money? Is someone actually blackmailing her?"

Freida nodded, gulped, breathed, gulped. At the rate she was drinking, she'd either get tipsy or need a second cup. Or a paper bag to stave off her hyperventilating. "Yes. This person apparently saw Laurie Jean in what he or she thought was a compromising situation."

"Thought?" Millie questioned. "Or was it actually a compromising situation?"

"The second one," Freida confirmed.

Even though Millie had already heard about that situation from Tanner, or rather a situation like it, Freida's admission shouldn't have made her sick to her stomach. But Millie had held out hope that her brother had been wrong.

"Laurie Jean doesn't want any of this getting back to Asher," Freida quickly added. "So, I want you to keep all of this to yourself while your mother resolves it."

Millie hoped that was possible, but it seemed to her that these kinds of payouts could go on forever. "Who's blackmailing her?" she asked.

"I don't know. I don't know," Freida repeated when Millie huffed. "Laurie Jean thinks it could be Joe McCann, his sister, your brother, Skylar Arnold or you. She's even speculated that it could be Joe's daughter."

Millie rolled her eyes. "It could be the man Laurie Jean's been seeing. Affairs are a complex union with their ups and downs," she added, paraphrasing Freida.

That earned her some steely eye from eyes that were looking a little glazed. "True," Freida admitted. Hesitantly admitted, "But I don't know who he is. I don't want to know," the woman emphasized. "I just want all of this to go away so that all of you will be happy again." She stopped, paused. "You look happy. A rosy glow. Does it have anything to do with you being with Joe at the drive-in?"

Millie was about 90 percent sure the question was a deflection, that Freida wanted to close the discussion about Laurie Jean, the affair and the blackmail. And apparently Freida wanted to accomplish that by bringing up a second possible affair. The one Millie was having with Joe.

Or rather the one that Freida thought Millie might be having with Joe.

Millie nearly asked how she'd known about Joe and the drive-in, but she could guess that someone had driven by and had seen their vehicles. The gossiper/gawker wouldn't have been able to see in the car because of the fogged-up windshield, but it wouldn't have been hard to guess what was going on—even if said gossiper/gawker had seen the stick figure drawings Joe and she had made.

"I'm not having sex with Joe," Millie offered, and she hoped she wouldn't be able to say that after tonight. "I was upset and went to the drive-in. Joe found me there and offered me some comfort."

Her lips quivered on the last word. And crud, she smiled. But it was the truth in a roundabout sort of way. The orgasm had indeed given her some comfort, along with a massive amount of pleasure.

"The drive-in," Freida said, the disapproval coating her voice.

Millie nodded. "I love it there. It's one of my favorite places. That's why I've been thinking of buying it and reopening it." Actually, she hadn't been thinking about it, but she would now. Joe and she had created some very fond memories there.

Freida stared at her, and Millie could practically feel the woman trying to use ESP on her. Millie gave her the same look, and after a standoff that lasted probably a full minute, Freida finally looked away and stood up. When she staggered a little, Millie got to her feet to take hold of her arm.

"I'm all right," Freida insisted.

"No, you're not. Come on. I'll drive you home."

"I walked to church today, and I'll walk home. It's only three blocks."

Since it was only three blocks, Millie didn't argue with her, especially since she was betting that Freida needed a little alone time to deal with her Irish coffee buzz and the worries that the woman she'd raised had screwed up her own life.

Millie walked with Freida to the front door and stood there until the woman was on the sidewalk and out of sight.

Then, she texted Dara that she was on the way to the ranch. However, Millie held out, waiting a couple of minutes so she could drive past the route Freida would have taken. She caught a glimpse of Freida going inside her front door so with some relief, she made the drive to finish the research with Dara.

It wasn't relief Millie felt when she pulled into the driveway at the ranch. It was lust. That's because she immediately spotted Joe coming out of the barn. He was shirtless again and had obviously just hosed down. The water was sliding down his body and going into places that Millie planned to do some sliding of her own.

Like the waist of his jeans.

He didn't exactly smile at her, but she hoped that's because he was having the same dirty thoughts about her as she was about him. She went to him.

And kissed him.

While she was at it, Millie trailed her fingers over his water-trickled chest and gave herself the thrill of touching his bare skin. She also got the thrill of hearing his breath hitch a little and seeing the lust creep into his eyes.

Yes, he was having dirty thoughts about her.

However, those thoughts didn't last. He glanced over her shoulder when the back door of the house opened, and Dara called out.

"I'm inside," Dara said, "but take your time."

Millie thought maybe the girl added a giggle to that, and she looked up at Joe to make sure he wasn't embarrassed that his daughter had just witnessed him being kissed. He didn't seem embarrassed, but there was definitely something on his face. Something that didn't have diddly to do with wet kisses in front of his barn.

"We'll talk tonight," he murmured, brushing his lips almost absently over hers before he turned and headed back into the barn.

Crud. That talk was likely about rules, ones that would include them not doing any more kissing in front of Dara. Millie would definitely agree to that. Agree, too, to keeping anything about their relationship solely between them. Millie hated that Dara might be pulled into this before she was ready to see her father involved with another woman.

However, Millie immediately had to revisit that last theory when she reached the porch and Dara hugged her. "I'm so glad you're with Dad."

Millie started to correct her, to say that she wasn't actually with Joe, but no way would Dara buy that since she'd obviously witnessed that kiss.

"Your dad and I will take things slow," Millie settled for saying.

Of course, there was the possibility that slow would turn to a complete stop if Joe was having second thoughts about meeting her at the shop tonight.

"Slow is still a start," Dara said with her usual glee. She caught on to Millie's hand and led her out of the kitchen and into a family room. The first thing that caught Millie's eye was an amazing wall mural of the Fairy Pond.

"Mom painted it," Dara explained. "You should see the one of the painted mermaids on the ceiling in the bathroom. When I was a little kid, I hated baths so she painted it to give me something to look at. She put this one here so Dad would have something to look at when he worked."

Following the direction of Dara's head tip, Millie saw the desk. A cluttered one with stacks of papers and folders.

"The house is small," Dara told her. "Only two bedrooms, so Dad doesn't have an office. This is his space.

Well, this and his man-shed, but I think that's mainly where he goes when he doesn't want me to see him sad."

Millie could see Joe doing just that. Could see him sitting here, too, going through invoices, breeding spreadsheets and whatever else ranchers did.

"Somewhere in that desk are the plans for a bigger house," Dara explained. "Dad wanted to build it by the pond and let Mom have this house as an art studio." She paused. "He mentions the new house every now and then, but I guess there's no hurry to get it built."

Probably not since his wife had died.

"I know you didn't want me to do the research report for you," the girl continued, "but I thought you might have changed your mind since you'd looked so sad when I came by to see Mom's paintings."

There'd definitely been plenty of sadness, but Millie hadn't wanted to put the burden of the report on Dara.

They stopped in the hall bath so Dara could show her the mermaid ceiling. Yes, that would definitely hold a fussy child's attention during bath time. Ella was obviously a good mother to even consider something like that.

When they made it to Dara's bedroom, Millie saw another painting. Of the drive-in, and despite the fact that she now knew Ella was the artist, it made her smile. Her smile faded though when Dara picked up a thick manila envelope from her desk and held it out for Millie. Judging from the thickness, she'd obviously added a lot more stories.

"If you don't want to use what's in here," Dara continued, tipping her head to the envelope, "maybe you can just go through what I've written and pick and choose what to put into your report."

On a sigh, Millie set her purse on the bed and took the envelope. It was heavy. In fact, it seemed to weigh a ton.

"Thank you. I'm sure you've done a great job and I'll read it soon."

"You don't have to hurry," Dara assured her. "The report's not due for another month." She paused. "I just don't want it to make you sad, and right now, you look sad."

Millie immediately tried to adjust her expression. It was best to change the subject, too, so she glanced around the room, and her attention landed on the mural. It was a pastoral scene of a wildflower meadow, a stream, trees and a beautiful mustang cropping at the grass.

"Your mother's work," Millie muttered. So much for changing the subject. They'd gone right back to Ella.

"Yeah. She did that for my tenth birthday." Smiling, Dara studied it a moment before turning back to Millie. "I wish you could feel happy when you look at it."

Millie studied it, as well. "I can certainly see the beauty in it. Remember, I was a fan of your mom's work. Sounds kind of dramatic, but I felt as if it spoke to my soul."

It still did. Maybe that made Ella and her kindred spirits. If Royce had sensed that about Ella, it might explain why he'd been attracted to her.

"Are you okay?" Dara asked, and she gave Millie's arm a little squeeze.

"I am." Millie shoved aside thoughts of kindred spirits, and cheating husbands, and put her attention back on Dara. Suddenly, she thought of something they could talk about that wouldn't involve Ella. Something that had been bothering Millie for a couple of days now.

"I'm glad you brought Ian and your friends to the shop," Millie said, breaking new conversational ground. "Have all of you been friends a long time?"

"Bella and I have. Jace is sort of a new friend since Bella

likes him." She paused, bit her lower lip. "And I sort of like Ian. Dad doesn't," she quickly added.

"No," Millie agreed. "Fathers of teenage girls aren't big on the teenage boys who show an interest in them. Or ones who might try to cop a feel."

Dara blushed, winced and sat down on the bed. "You saw that, huh? I moved his hand."

"I saw that, too." Millie sat next to her and hoped like the devil that she wasn't stepping over any lines here. Still, she couldn't imagine Joe wanting to discuss this with his daughter. "Has Ian done that before?"

"No," Dara insisted before another pause. "But he hasn't since then. I stopped him, but I have kissed him. I liked it. It made me feel sort of light-headed. And maybe a little confused."

Millie thought that was a very accurate description of kissing.

"Sometimes, I want him to touch me," Dara went on, "but not touch me, touch me, if you know what I mean."

"I do," Millie assured her. She gathered her breath. "It's your right to say no, to push Ian's hand away or tell him to slow down. If he doesn't, it's okay to remind him your father has an axe."

Dara laughed. "Ian's terrified of Dad."

"As he should be." Because it felt like the right thing to do, Millie kissed her cheek. "And if you ever need to talk to anybody about this, just call me. We'll get together for a post-research root beer float."

"I'd like that." The happiness in her voice and smile were the real deal. So was the hug she gave Millie.

So was the stiffness that suddenly came into Dara's arms and shoulders.

The girl pulled back, her gaze fixed on Millie's purse.

Millie looked down, and she cursed when she saw that she hadn't zipped up said purse. The kits were right on top of the rest of the stash, and it was very easy to read the label.

One-Step Pregnancy Test.

"Millie?" Dara said.

"They're not for me," Millie blurted out as fast as she could. "They're for a friend. Or rather were for a friend, but—" She stopped rambling and waved that off. "They're not for me," she repeated.

Dara didn't exactly spew out a breath of relief. Maybe because she thought Millie wasn't telling her the truth.

"My mom bought one of those," Dara said. "Right before she died, she bought one. I saw it in her shopping bag."

Millie felt her own arms and shoulders go stiff. Actually, every part of her did. "Was your mother pregnant?" Millie managed.

Dara shrugged. "I don't know. She didn't say." Dara's tone wasn't of grief or sadness from memories. It was more like somber curiosity. "But if Mom was pregnant, she must have told Dad."

Millie could think of a huge reason why Ella might not have done that. And that huge reason was one that caused Millie's heart to drop to her feet.

Ella could have been pregnant with Royce's child.

CHAPTER SEVENTEEN

JOE PARKED AT Three Sheets and started walking toward Millie's shop. There were a couple of people smoking in the parking lot, and several cars passed him as he strolled along. One of those cars belonged to Alma Parkman, and she beeped the weird-sounding horn on her equally weird-looking car and gave him a friendly wave.

It was entirely possible that every single person who saw him knew he was going to see Millie. Knew, too, that they had plans to play out the fully loaded lock and key game.

He'd already heard murmurs about someone spotting their vehicles at the drive-in. Nobody had dared question him about it though. His widower label acted like a shield against nosy questions like that.

Well, for most people, anyway.

He had no doubts that if he ran into Laurie Jean, Asher or Janice, they'd have a thing or two to say about him being with Millie. If that happened, Joe could blow it off, but he hated that Millie might be getting the third degree over him.

She didn't let things like gossip slip and slide off her the way he could. She still had a family reputation to protect. That's why he was going to give her an out about having sex with him. He would go in Once Upon a Time, tell her they had to talk—which they did—and he'd tell her what he'd found in the storage unit Ella had rented. After he got her take on it, he'd insist she rethink their sex plans for the night. It wouldn't be easy to convince his body that was the right thing to do, but it was. He was sure of that.

Almost sure, anyway.

Joe walked to the back of the shop, glanced around, and when he didn't spot anyone, he tapped on the door. It opened almost immediately, and Millie took hold of his arm, pulling him inside. At first he thought that was so he wouldn't be seen, but no. With the door still wide-open, she took his mouth in a hot, hungry kiss.

And he took her mouth right back.

Oh, man. He was toast. She tasted way too good. In fact, everything about her was way too good. She slid her arms around his neck, fit her body to his and just kept on kissing the daylights out of him.

"I missed you," she said, her voice all sin and breath when she finally pulled back from him.

"I missed you, too," he admitted.

Which, of course, was the opposite of what he should be saying to her. So much for doing the right thing and insisting she rethink this. Instead, he was rethinking his notion about her rethinking. Right now, he wanted her more than his sanity.

She grasped his hand to tug him the rest of the way inside. She finally closed the door, locked it and looked up at him. It was dark in the alcove where they were standing, and the only light came from the various displays throughout the shop. Still, he had no trouble seeing her dazzling smile.

"So, what did you want to talk to me about?" she asked.

He saw some nerves edging through the dazzle and the lust, and Joe knew he was the reason for those nerves. After their earlier kiss in the barn, he'd told her, *We'll talk tonight*, and she had probably been worrying about that all day. He should have just kept his mouth shut and waited until now to let her know that something was wrong. Except *wrong* wasn't the right word. *Confusing* was a better word for it.

"I went through Ella's laptop this morning," he started, and he watched Millie go still. "I found a bank account that she'd set up. She started it with the payment you made for the three paintings."

"You didn't know about the account," she said, her gaze combing over his face.

He shook his head. "It's not with a local bank but rather one in San Antonio." Joe would let Millie draw her own obvious conclusions about that. Ella hadn't used a bank in Last Ride because someone might have mentioned it to Joe.

Millie sighed. "I guess I'll have to check and see if Royce had a secret account, too."

He nearly said that probably wasn't necessary, but it was. This can of worms was open now, and to move on with their lives, they needed to see everything inside. Even if what was inside hurt like hell.

"There's more," Joe added a moment later. "When I looked at the bank statement, I saw that Ella had rented a storage unit. Again, not the one that would have been close to the ranch but one just outside of town. I went there this morning, and opened it."

Her breath made a wheezing sound when she sucked it in. "What did you find?" Her voice was a whisper, and she was probably imagining all sorts of worst-case scenarios.

"Paintings," Joe said.

"Paintings?" Now she sounded confused but also a little relieved.

"Fourteen of them. I remember her painting some of them. By that, I mean I'd poke my head in her studio every now and then and see bits and pieces of what she was working on, but after she died, I didn't even think about what'd happened to them." He paused. "There was also one I hadn't seen before. It was of Royce."

He could practically feel her heart sinking to the pit of her stomach.

"It was the only portrait in the room," he went on. *Just get it all out. Say it and get it over with.* "Royce, wearing a suit and sitting in an impressive-looking chair positioned in front of a window."

The man had looked like a pompous dick. But Joe admitted that maybe his feelings for Royce were playing into that.

"There were no paintings of them together?" Millie asked.

Joe shook his head. "But there were some sketchbooks in there that I didn't look at. I will, but I'd had enough for one day."

The silence hummed between them and somewhere in the shop several clocks began to chime out the nine o'clock hour.

"I'm sorry," she said, and a heartbeat later, he followed it up with his own, "I'm sorry." It was Joe who continued. "I'm apologizing because I didn't want to mess up this night for you."

Her next breath was long and weary. "Well, I'm going to have to mess up your night, too. While I was with Dara today, she mentioned that her mom had bought a pregnancy test just a couple of days before she died."

Oh, great. *This* had reared its ugly head.

"Yeah, I knew about it," he admitted. "She left the good-bye note for me on the receipt for the damn thing. According to her note, she was heading out for a spa day. We both know that wasn't her actual plan."

Millie groaned, then cursed. She turned, marched a few

steps out of the alcove. The kind of marching somebody did when trying to walk off a fit of anger. "Was she pregnant?"

"I don't know. If she was, she didn't say a word about that to me."

Of course, there were a lot of words his wife hadn't said to him. The pregnancy test, going off with a married man, the bank account, the storage unit and that sonofabitching portrait of Royce.

Millie continued to pace a couple more seconds before she turned back to him. "Maybe Ella was buying the test for someone else."

The thought had occurred to him during those times when he'd wanted to hang on to the pipe dream that his wife had loved him and hadn't cheated on him with a pompous dick.

"Maybe," he acknowledged, not sounding at all convinced of that.

But there was something about Millie's reaction. Something below the surface. Maybe because she'd bought such a test for someone.

Ah, hell.

"Dara didn't bring up the pregnancy test because she needs one, did she?" Joe snapped.

Millie laughed, and even though he didn't usually like being laughed at, it helped his insides unclench. "No," she quickly assured. "Dara has no need for something like that. She's got boy boundaries, Joe, and you don't have to worry about her."

He hoped to hell boy boundaries meant Dara would knee Donnelly's kid in the balls if he crossed the line with her.

Smiling again, she went to him and pressed her hand on his cheek. "I'm sorry all of this spoiled the mood for the night. We can still have a drink or a bite to eat. Or we can go upstairs and look at some Victorian porn."

Joe had been about to kiss her good-night and tell her to get some rest, but that last thing stopped him in his tracks.

"Victorian porn?" he asked.

She smiled, nodded. "It helps me get my mind off things. Remember that antique vibrator in the True or False display?" She didn't wait for him to respond, probably because she knew there was no way he'd forget something like that. "Well, there's a whole room of that kind of stuff. Actually, there's more than one room of it but only one for the Victorian era."

It was such a guy thing to want to see it, and Joe didn't resist one little bit when Millie took him by the hand and led him up the narrow back stairs that led to a landing with two equally narrow halls. There'd been no major renovations here, no walls removed to create the open spaces below for the shop.

They went past a bedroom, the one where Millie had no doubt planned for them to spend their evening, and he felt a pang of guilt that he was going to ask her to postpone that. A pang of heat, too, because his body didn't want to postpone anything. He wanted her now, but then, he always did whenever he was around her.

Still clutching his hand, they went by another room, this one crammed with antiques. No porn, not that he recognized as such, anyway, but he spotted spinning wheels, old farm tools and dozens of clocks. She stopped outside a door, one with a handwritten sign that read, "Nothing in here goes downstairs. Nothing! I mean it."

"The Victorian porn room," she announced, throwing open the door.

It was plenty cluttered, too, with boxes, machines and

gadgets, none of which looked very porn-like. Well, none until Millie took down one of the boxes and opened it. It was a box of dildos.

And other stuff.

"Apparently, the Victorians liked variety when it came to objects they inserted in various orifices," she explained as if describing a potato masher instead of something that'd obviously been used for sex.

She held up a two-dick dildo made of shiny leather. It even had four leather balls that dangled down from it and would have almost certainly slapped a thigh or two once it was set into motion. The second one Millie pulled from the box was made of stone and was triple the normal size of a man's dick.

"You could call this an early version of an inflatable doll," she continued. "I don't touch it because I'm not sure Victorian men cleaned up after themselves."

This time, she took out a wooden box and opened the lid to reveal a woman's mouth. The red cloth mouth was wide-open to reveal a deep, padded throat. It definitely didn't arouse Joe or give him one grain of desire to put his dick in there, but it obviously took all kinds.

She set down the box, took out another one. "Rectal dilators," she explained, showing him the assortment of butt plugs, including some with what appeared to be a rough sandpaper texture.

Yeah, all kinds.

"Where'd you get all of this?" he asked.

"My grandmother left it up here. She'd buy entire estates, sight unseen, and apparently, several of those estates had red rooms that would put Christian Greys to shame. There are pictures and devices from several historical periods, but there was so much Victorian stuff that it got its own room."

Closing the box, she pointed to a weird-looking toy horse. "That's called an action saddle."

She pulled the rope reins, and the saddle began to move, following the movements of the reins. According to what was painted on the side of the horse's neck, the action saddle was for "Inspiriting pleasure."

"Inspiriting pleasure," Millie emphasized. "They used spanking machines for that." She pointed to several. "And there were also squirting machines."

Millie motioned toward several copper hose–looking deals that poked up like striking snakes. "The idea with those was to fill up that tank." She pointed out something that looked like the skin left behind from those shedding, striking snakes. "It's some kind of animal bladder, and the pump would send the water into the hoses so you could squirt water at your genitals."

Joe shook his head, wondering just how the notion of that had come about.

Millie grinned at him. "Has this gotten your mind off your troubles?"

"Yeah," he had to admit.

"Works every time," she muttered.

He could see that. She was looking a hell of a lot happier than she had when they'd come up the stairs. "When you said porn, I thought you meant it'd be more…titillating."

"Titillating," she repeated with a wink. "Now, that's an interesting word because the Victorians were big into that, too."

She hauled down a big box that'd been stacked on top of other big boxes, and she balanced it on the Inspiriting Pleasure Action Saddle. The moment she lifted the lid, Joe saw what she meant. There were dozens of pictures, many with women's breasts as the primary focus point.

"These are the tame ones," she explained, fishing down one layer. "These are less tame," Millie added.

She came up with photos where women, and men, were spread-eagle, displaying their wares while also displaying goofy smiles that seemed more suited for a pleasant parlor game of cards rather than the game they were gearing up to play.

"These aren't anywhere in the realm of tameness," Millie warned, and when she drew out more shots, Joe could see that the "show your junk" game had turned into put cocks and other hard objects inside things. Vaginas, mouths, devices, between breasts. But there were other games in progress, too.

"They really liked whippings and spankings," Joe remarked.

Millie made a sound of agreement while continuing to fish out more and more pictures. These were penetration shots, mainly cocks into vaginas, but the participants were still sporting those goofy smiles.

"Notice there's not one of them in a missionary position," she pointed out. "That probably has something to do with not being able to get a good shot if the man and woman are smooshed together."

Joe looked up at her when he heard the slight shift in her tone. "You don't like missionary?"

She didn't smile, goofy or otherwise. Instead, her forehead bunched up as if giving that some thought. "No one's ever asked me that before, but no, I don't especially like it."

Intrigued, Joe pushed a little harder. "Any particular reason? Like claustrophobia, not being in control?"

She shook her head. "It has to do with spit."

Joe was certain he gave her a blank, confused look, and she laughed.

"I think it goes back to when I was a kid. Tanner would tackle me, hold me so I couldn't get away and spit in my hair. It got him grounded every single time he did it, but despite my joy over him being punished, I think it set me up to remember snotty spit when I'm being pinned down."

"So, no missionary when—" He stopped, remembering that he shouldn't be going there right now.

Turning fully to face him, Millie studied his expression. "Did you come here tonight to remind me that it can't be anything but just sex between us?" She paused, studying his face. "No, you came here to tell me that you'd reconsidered doing my lock and key lesson?"

He nodded. Cursed. "It's the right thing to do."

She licked her lips. Then, leaned in and licked his. "Still want to do the right thing?"

Joe didn't even have to think about this. "No."

He pulled Millie to him and started inspiriting some pleasure.

MILLIE WOULD HAVE squealed with delight had Joe's tongue not already been in her mouth. She'd hoped this trip down Victorian smut lane would get his mind off the paintings he'd found and the pregnancy test. That had been a tall order, but the porn had come through for her. He was kissing her now, and she didn't think there'd be any turning back.

However, there was some turning. There was only one bare spot on the wall, but Joe located it and put her back against it. That sandwiched them between a spanking machine and a foot-long wooden dildo affixed to a stand-up board.

"Sorry," he grumbled, and there was more turning.

He switched positions with her so that he was the one

pinned against the wall. She wanted to tell him that against the wall didn't trigger spit memories, but she would have had to stop the kiss to do that. Wasn't worth it. They could talk later.

Like a man on fire, Joe just kept on kissing her, maybe because he thought she needed to fire up, as well. But Millie was already there. She'd been there for weeks now. Wanting and lusting after Joe McCann.

Those tongue kisses migrated to her neck, to just below her ear. And the fire took off like a rocket. Until he'd kissed her there at the drive-in, she'd had no idea just what a trigger spot it was for her. Joe apparently had figured that out and was exploiting the heck out of it. Exploiting her breasts, too, because he cupped them and flicked his thumb over a nipple.

The pleasure continued to build, build, build. Until she ached for him. Until she was certain he'd drag her to the floor. But he stopped, and pulling back a fraction, he looked her straight in the eyes.

"You're sure about this?" he asked.

It was the most unnecessary question in the history of unnecessary questions. "Yes." Her breath gushed out with her answer. She went after his belt. "I'm hoping since your key is bigger than your fingers, it'll be easier to open my lock."

The corner of his mouth lifted, and he clamped his hand over hers to stop her from undoing his belt. "You'd think, but it can still be tricky." He tipped his head to the foot-long wooden dick to his right. "Even that has to hit the right spot."

With the ache going through her like a wildfire, Millie issued a challenge. "Hit the right spot, Joe."

Their gazes held a moment later, and she knew he'd

accepted the challenge when he dived back in to kiss her again. And touch her breasts. And slide her dress up her thigh so he could press the heel of his palm to the front of her panties.

She saw gold stars. Wonderful glittering, shimmering things. But she could also see that she didn't want him to finish her this way. He'd already proven to her that he could bring her to climax, and Millie wanted to advance climaxing to the next level of this particular game.

"Inside me," she managed to say.

"Working on it," Joe assured her.

He was a man of his word, and he proved it by reaching behind her, unzipping her dress and shoving it off her. It made a light thud when it landed on the floor around her feet. With her half-naked, he obviously had a lot more places to kiss on her, and he proceeded to hit as many of those spots as possible, all while ridding her of her bra.

"I want your clothes off, too," she protested.

But the protest died on her lips when he shoved down her panties and kissed her center. Oh, yeah. He would be able to find the notch in the lock again. And he would have likely found it very, very fast had Millie not latched on to his hair and pulled him back up to her.

"Clothes. Off," she repeated.

She soon found out she wasn't nearly as good as getting him naked as he'd been with her. Millie struggled, and struggled, but she finally got off his T-shirt. Finally got her hands on his bare chest. But she put her "get Joe naked" plans on hold for a second while she tongue kissed some of those glorious muscles. The man was built.

And bulging hard.

Millie discovered that when she lowered her mouth to

the front of his jeans. The kiss, and nip with her teeth, she gave him might have been done through the denim, but judging from his groan and profanity, it'd been effective.

"Clothes off," he grumbled, helping her with his jeans.

They joined her dress and underwear on the floor. He kicked off his boots, dragged off his socks and tossed them off to the side. That left him with only his boxers, and Millie wanted to just rip them off. However, she forced herself to slow down. Hard to do with him clearly so hard and ready.

The man made her mouth water.

So, she tugged down the boxers. Half inch by half inch at a time. Slowly. While she gave him a dirty little smile. When his erection sprang free, she put her watering mouth on him.

Joe cursed again, and this time it was aimed specifically at her. Grimacing, he took hold of her, maneuvering and lowering until he was sitting on the floor with his back still against the wall.

And he pulled her onto his lap.

Her mouth would have to be satisfied with kissing and licking because her new goal was to get all his long hardness inside her. She would have managed it, too, but damn it, he stopped her again.

"Condom," he growled when she cursed him.

Millie groaned because she thought she was going to have to run downstairs and get the three condoms from her desk drawer, but Joe dug out one from his jeans' pocket.

"Remember, lock and key," he said, putting on the condom. "Gotta find the right notch. If I'm not hitting it, you'll have to tell me."

Millie wasn't sure she could speak, especially after he

gripped her hips and pushed inside her. He went slow, that whole half inch by half inch deal as she'd done with his boxers. It took a while. A torturous, perfect, glittering while for him to go tip to hilt inside her.

"Tell me," he repeated. His voice was husky and all male. Like concentrated bottled testosterone. It caused places inside her to quiver and pulse.

Joe moved, one slow long stroke, again going tip to hilt. Millie went up yet another level of pleasure. Then, another. He kept doing that until the levels just kept spinning up, up, up. Until the heat just kept building.

She was somewhat aware that she'd never made it this far before, but she still wasn't sure she'd be able to reach that sexual nirvana that had evaded her for a long time. In fact, she might not be able to do this, even with Joe.

"Tell me," he insisted.

He was watching her face when he shifted them. He lifted his hips, moved hers down, and he added the lightest finger stroke to the spot that had just brushed against his erection.

It was the spot all right.

The mother lode of all pleasure. Sparkles and glitters burst like the Fourth of July, birthday candles and a billion fireflies. Thanks to Joe, the spot let go, and Millie felt her center spasm and clamp around him.

There was no need for her to "tell him" that he'd done it. Good thing, too, because all she could manage was to hang on to Joe and let the pulses, glitters and pleasure slide through every inch of her.

Moments later, Joe followed right behind her.

"Next time," she finally managed to whisper in his ear, "we'll use the Edwardian porn room."

With his eyes glazed and sated, he looked at her. "Edwardian?"

She nodded, bit his bottom lip. "Oh, yes. It's way, way hotter than this Victorian stuff."

CHAPTER EIGHTEEN

THE MOMENT JOE stepped inside Petal Pushers flower shop, the owner, Tommy Ellison, thrust out the bunch of white daisies. "I saw you parking your truck," Tommy explained, "and I got them ready."

"Thanks," Joe said, taking out his wallet as Tommy moved behind the register to ring up the purchase.

"Tell Dara I put some extra ones in the bouquet," Tommy went on, making change from the twenty Joe handed him. "Since it's the anniversary..."

The florist's words trailed off when Joe lifted his eyes and looked at him. Joe certainly hadn't forgotten it'd been two years to the day since Ella had died. It was the reason he'd come in for the flowers. Joe had figured Dara would want to mark the day. He, however, wanted no such marking. Hell, he would have preferred no reminder but that would have been like asking the sky to not be blue.

"Two years," Joe muttered. But it felt closer to two lifetimes.

"I added water tubes on the bottoms," Tommy continued, his voice a little uncertain now. "So they'd last longer in this heat."

Joe looked at the tubes—they were green plastic V-shaped vials that looked sharp enough on the bottoms to put out an eye. The stems of the daisies were inside them and anchored together with some thin wire.

"I used the spiked water tubes," Tommy explained. "That way, Dara can stand the bouquet up. It shows off better that way."

So, Tommy knew that Dara was the one who took flowers to Ella's grave. Hell, everybody in Last Ride probably knew. It was ironic that Ella had managed to keep a boatload of things to herself in a town where secrets had a very short shelf life. Sort of like the freshness of flowers in the blistering heat.

"Hope Dara's waiting until later to go out to the cemetery," Tommy said. "It's supposed to get up to ninety-eight today."

Joe made a sound of agreement, thanked Tommy again and headed out. Dara would indeed be waiting until later since she was taking final exams today and wouldn't be home for hours. He planned on driving her out to the cemetery right at sunset. Then, he could go back to his man-shed and brood about two-year anniversaries.

And Millie.

The brooding about her would no doubt lead to lustful thoughts. Thinking of Millie always did, but there was a grimy film of guilt over it. Definitely not a good combination. He'd braced himself for it, figuring it would come now that he'd had sex with Millie.

And it had.

It'd come with a vengeance.

The night with Millie had been amazing. She'd been amazing. Amazing, amazing, amazing. The word repeated through his head, making him curse. Because it was true down to the bone. And she didn't deserve a man who couldn't take that amazing stuff and give it right back to her.

But the question was—what was he going to do about it? It was too late to end things before she got hurt. She would get hurt, period. Sex only brought them closer. Or rather, it brought her closer to him. He could feel it. So, yeah, she'd get hurt.

That's why he was considering just letting this run its course. An affair that would possibly last through the summer and burn itself out. There'd still be hurt, but she'd be better ready for it.

Or so he was telling himself.

In fact, Joe was mentally repeating that when he heard Frankie call out. "Wait up," she said. She was hurrying up the sidewalk toward him and had her hand clamped around Little T's.

"Uncle Joe," the boy greeted. "You got pointy, pokey things." He reached out to touch the flower tubes, but because of that whole "looking sharp enough to put out an eye" deal, Joe moved them out of his reach. "Can I have 'em?"

"When you're thirty," Joe said, giving his automatic response, and he glanced up at his sister. His *harried*-looking sister.

"Could you watch Little T for about an hour? First graders are done for the day with their summer program, and his sitter got sick and just dropped him off at the shop. Tanner's swamped with repairs, and I'm in the middle of inking matching butt tats."

Frankie didn't have to explain that she didn't want her six-year-old son around to watch her poking at asses with needles. Plus, Little T would almost certainly get into something unless supervised, and Ink, Etc. was pretty much a danger pit for a kid looking to get into something.

"Sure, I can watch him," Joe said.

Gushing out thanks, Frankie hugged him, narrowly avoiding getting stabbed with the flower tubes. "Are you okay?" she asked Joe, and he knew that she had also remembered the anniversary deal.

"Fine," he assured her. "Go do the butt tats."

Frankie hesitated a moment, sighed and then kissed Little T. She told him to "Be good," and practically sprinted toward her shop while calling out to Joe that she'd text him later. No doubt so she could repeat her "Are you okay?" question. He could repeat his "Fine" answer, and then this crappy day that marked an even crappier day would finally end.

Little T looked up at him. "Can I have the pointy, pokey things now?"

Joe was actually thankful for the distraction. "Are you thirty and eleven feet tall?" he countered.

Little T sighed. "No." He stretched that out and added a little pout. "Why do the flowers have pointy, pokey things?"

"For poking them in the ground." Joe fished out Little T's booster that he kept behind the seat. He got in place and helped Little T strap in.

"Can we poke them in the ground?" the boy asked.

Joe nearly gave him the same pat response again, but he looked at Little T, at the flowers, and he thought of Millie. It seemed as far-fetched as Little T growing up to be eleven feet tall, but maybe he could find some peace at the cemetery on this crappy anniversary. Maybe he would take one look at Ella's grave and realize that what he was feeling for Millie, and doing with her, was okay.

"We'd have to poke the flowers in the ground at the cemetery," Joe told him.

"You mean like where the dead people live?" Little T questioned after giving it some thought.

Joe nodded and despite his sour mood, he was amused at the way the boy had put that.

"All right." Little T beamed. "Can we go out there now and do it and then stop by O'Riley's and get ice cream?"

Joe wasn't sure what would make Little T happier. The jabbing flowers into dirt or the ice cream. Either way, it was obviously the kid's idea of a fun time with his uncle.

"Yeah," Joe agreed. "Let's go."

Now worked fine because if he put it off for even a couple of minutes, he might realize just how stupid of an idea this was and turn around and go home. Of course, this meant he would need to buy more flowers so that Dara would be able to do her weekly ritual. Then again, she might be so happy that he'd made this visit that she wouldn't care that she hadn't been the one to put them on her mother's grave.

With Little T asking a ton of questions about bugs getting squished on the windshield, where belches went after they got belched and if the temperature was going to soar to a jillion, Joe drove across town to Hilltop Cemetery.

He parked in his usual spot, beneath the big tree at the bottom of the hill, but parking was the only thing usual about this visit. Normally, he just stood back and waited for Dara to put the flowers on Ella's grave and say whatever it was she said to her.

Keeping the flowers away from Little T, Joe started up the hill with the boy jumping and hopping while occasionally taking a normal step. The kid was sure bouncy. And talkative. Joe focused on that, the sound of his nephew's voice, while he stepped in front of the tombstone. He halfway expected lightning to strike him or something since he'd sworn this was something he'd never, ever do, but there wasn't a bolt of lightning anywhere in sight. The air stayed still and hot, almost as if it were waiting for something to happen.

Little T tugged on his arm. "Can we poke in the flowers now?"

"Just give me a second." He'd have to get his hands working to accomplish something like that, and right now, his hands and legs seemed to be frozen. Ditto for his eyes. They were fixed on that headstone.

"You come here to talk to Aunt Ella?" Little T asked.

Joe had to swallow hard. "Dara does."

"That's Aunt Ella's name right there on the white rock. I can read it. What's di-ed mean?" the boy tacked on to that.

At Joe's puzzled look, Tanner pointed to the word *Died*.

He had to swallow hard again. "It's *died*. It means the date of her death."

Little T bounced around again and took a sudden interest in a cricket that was hopping on top of the short cut grass between the graves. "Uncle Royce has a di-ed date on his rock, too."

Joe nodded. "It's the same as Aunt Ella's. Two years ago today." He was already frowning over that reminder, but his frown deepened when exactly what Little T had said sank in. "Your aunt Millie takes you to your uncle Royce's grave?"

"Nope. Grandma Laurie Jean did. *Grandmother* Laurie Jean," he corrected with an eye roll. "She doesn't like it when I say grandma. Says it makes me sound like a bunkin."

The kid probably meant bumpkin. Joe was betting Laurie Jean didn't like a lot of things, but it was puzzling why the woman would bring Little T there. Then again, Royce had been the boy's uncle by marriage, and he'd heard that Laurie Jean and Asher had handpicked Royce for Millie. So maybe there'd been genuine love between them. Love that hadn't been doused simply because Royce hadn't turned out to be Mr. Perfect after all.

Joe thought of another angle though. It was possible that Laurie Jean was taking the same head in the sand approach as Janice and believed that Royce and Ella could do no wrong.

"Is it time to poke in the flowers?" Little T asked, tugging at his arm again.

Clearly, the boy was looking more forward to this than Joe, so he handed Little T the bouquet. Carefully handed it to him. "Just jab the ends in the ground," Joe instructed. "Don't touch the pointy bits."

"All right," Little T said with all the enthusiasm of a kid who'd just been handed something really cool.

The boy jabbed in the flowers, not on the top of the grave but to the side of it. Without studying his "work" to see if it was the right place for the daisies, Little T took them out, jabbed them again and might have gone in for a third try if Joe hadn't stopped him.

"I think that's the right spot for them," Joe assured the boy.

Little T shrugged, stepped back and spared the flowers the briefest of brief glances before he bent down again to pick up something from the ground.

"It's a nickel," he announced with the same enthusiasm of someone who'd just found buried treasure. "Maybe it's a magic one."

Joe wasn't sure why Little T would think that, but then the boy was always coming up with something imaginative. "Could be a lucky one," Joe suggested. "There's an old saying. Find a penny, pick it up and all day long you'll have good luck. You'll probably have five times the luck since it's a nickel."

The sound the boy made was one of awe as if that buried treasure had been worth a fortune. He stared at it a long time before he slipped it in his pocket and looked up at Joe. "You can go ahead and talk to Aunt Ella before we go," Little T insisted. "I won't listen." He jabbed a finger in each ear and squeezed his eyes closed.

Joe smiled, but he didn't feel that smile in any part of his body. He was also sure there was nothing he wanted to say to his late wife.

But he was wrong.

The words just spewed out before he even knew he was going to say them. "I wish you could tell me why you were in that car," Joe whispered, stooping down so he was eye level with Ella's carved name. "I wish you could tell me a lot of things."

Of course, there was no response. No woo-woo kind of message from the grave like a rainbow or butterfly fluttering by. He hadn't expected anything like that, but that didn't stop him from continuing. This time though, it didn't gush out. Joe slowed down. Calmed down, too.

"I need to tell you something," he said to Ella's headstone. And because Little T might or might not be able to hear, Joe carefully chose his words. "I had s-e-x with M-i-l-l-i-e," he spelled out.

Despite Little T's claim that he could read, Joe seriously doubted the boy would be able to follow along with the one-sided conversation.

"I want to be with M-i-l-l-i-e again, but I can't really give myself to her, not completely. Because you're still there between us. Until I know what happened, why you were in that car, you'll always be there between us."

Again, nothing.

Joe felt the anger start to churn inside him. Anger mixed

with hurt. With betrayal. And with all the other shit feelings he'd had since the woman he'd loved had died in the arms of another man.

"Why the h-e-l-l were you with him?" Joe snarled. "Why?" he said far louder than Little T's finger earplugs would block out.

Nothing. Absolutely nothing. Just the whirl of memories. The past. And the future he wasn't sure about.

Joe looked down when Little T tugged on his arm again. "Did Aunt Ella answer your spellin' question?"

Yeah, Joe supposed she had. And it was an answer that somehow he was just going to have to learn to live with.

CHAPTER NINETEEN

MILLIE HAD LEARNED something over the past week since Joe had proven to her that his key worked wonders in her lock. What she'd learned was that she thought about sex a lot, that she wanted it a lot. That she wanted it a lot with Joe.

But a lot hadn't happened.

That's because sex turned out to be tricky. Well, working out the timing of it was tricky, anyway.

After Joe had spelled out that whole bit about this only being sex and nothing more and after Millie had spelled out her agreement to that, again, they'd had a scalding hot kissing session in the barn when Dara had been at a friend's house. If there'd been more time, Millie knew beyond a shadow of a doubt that Joe could have done a repeat performance of what no man before him had managed to do. Get her to climax while he was inside her.

Millie was counting on Joe continuing to prove it to her.

That's why she'd arranged to introduce him to the porn of the Roaring Twenties. *Tonight*. They would soon run out of smutty antique things to puzzle over and ogle, but Millie figured Joe and she could figure out how to get off without the weird visual aids.

Their date had taken some planning for Joe, too, because he hadn't wanted Dara to know that he'd be gone for a night of sex. Millie totally got that, and she suspected it wasn't something Dara would want to know about, either.

Parent sex was ick info both now and across the genera-
tions. Thankfully, it hadn't taken much for Joe to suggest
that Dara spend the night with Frankie and Little T, so that
meant Millie might have Joe all to herself.

With that in mind and with her body already tingling,
Millie closed the shop an hour early and started the walk
to her house so she could change her clothes and begin
getting ready. But she nearly ran right into Mr. Lawrence,
the sculptor who often produced bad art. He was standing
in front of the main window, apparently studying Monte's
latest display of Bram Stoker memorabilia.

"Millicent," he greeted, tipping his hat in the formal
way he always did.

Actually, most things about Mr. Lawrence were formal.
The linen suits he always paired with crisp white shirts. The
pewter gray hair. The pleasant but somewhat aloof expression. Since he was a Parkman, they were distant cousins,
and Millie recalled her father saying that Mr. Lawrence
and he shared a paternal grandfather.

She forced a smile. "I'm sorry, but I'm closing early."
And she prayed he wasn't there to try to sell her another
piece of art. There hadn't been even nibbles on the two
pieces she'd already purchased from him. Not a surprise.
There wasn't a huge market for bad blog replicas of the
Great Pyramid or the Taj Mahal.

"It's all right," he said, his voice proper and a little
prissy. "I was just passing by." He paused a heartbeat.
"Your mother mentioned the new display, and I thought
I'd have a look."

Millie automatically bristled. "My mother? I didn't know
she'd seen it."

Even the nod he gave was formal, but his eyes widened a

little, and he cleared his throat. Maybe because Laurie Jean hadn't been especially complimentary about the display.

"I should be going," he quickly added. He tipped his hat again, muttered for her to have a pleasant evening and headed in the opposite direction from where she was going.

Puzzled by his reaction, Millie stood there a moment and frowned. The display had been up for nearly a week, but to the best of her knowledge, Laurie Jean hadn't come into the shop since then. However, it was possible her mother had seen it if and when she'd tried to get back in the shop.

With her lover.

With her lover, Millie silently repeated, and her mind whirled back to all the drawings of the Last Ride Society. Where Mr. Lawrence always sat directly behind Laurie Jean.

Millie couldn't recall the two ever having anything more than a casual and polite interaction, but perhaps they were interacting in a whole different way. It was hard to imagine her mother bouncing around with a man, any man, but if Laurie Jean were to take a lover, it would almost certainly be someone like Mr. Lawrence. Rich, cultured and an artist, in a general sort of way, that is.

Still frowning over the possibility that she might have just ID'd her mother's secret man, Millie forced herself to turn away from the retreating Mr. Lawrence and get home. She was nearly halfway there and toying with the idea of fixing a picnic supper for Joe and her when she heard the hurried footsteps behind her. For a moment, she thought it might be Mr. Lawrence hurrying to spill all, but Millie looked over her shoulder and saw Skylar running toward her.

One look at the woman, and Millie knew something was horribly wrong.

Skylar's hair rarely had a strand out of place, but at the moment it was hard to see a strand *in* place. Her makeup was long past the smeared stage, and her eyes were red, no doubt from a crying jag. The proof of that jag was in her hands where Skylar held some wads of wet tissues.

"Tanner broke up with me," Skylar burst out, and she said it loud enough that Millie suspected they'd draw attention. At the moment Skylar probably didn't care about that, but she soon would once the shock of the breakup had worn out.

Millie took her by the arm and led her off the sidewalk and behind a large oak. People could still hear, but the tree would muffle at least some of the sound.

Or not, Millie amended, when Skylar let out a loud wail.

"I'm in love with him," Skylar went on. "I told him that, and he broke up with me."

Millie didn't like thinking about sibling sex any more than parent sex, but she could see how this would have played out. "You told Tanner you loved him when you were in bed?"

Skylar nodded. Sobbed some more. "We'd just made the most perfect love, and I couldn't stop myself. I just blurted it out."

Millie knew her brother well enough to know that'd go over like a lead Victorian inspiriting saddle. She debated how to go with this. No need to spell out that Tanner's relationships rarely lasted more than a month. And that his relationships were mostly about sex. Mostly meaning about 95 percent. He had a horrible track record with romance, and no woman in her right mind should just hand him her heart.

No. No need to spell all of that out.

"Tanner isn't in a good place right now to have someone in love with him," Millie settled for saying.

"It's not Tanner," Skylar argued. "It's Laurie Jean. She's the reason this happened."

Millie had to pause and give that some thought. "You mean because she went to see your parents?"

"That and because she convinced Tanner that he wasn't good enough for me." Skylar was no longer crying, and she'd obviously found her mad. "She's always trying to sling mud at him, and she finally got to him. He started to believe what she was saying and he broke up with me."

Again, Millie had to pause. "Tanner told you this?"

"No, but I know that's what happened," Skylar snapped. "Your mother's a stone-cold bitch."

Millie couldn't argue with that, but there was no chance in all the levels of hell that Tanner would listen to Laurie Jean and do what she wanted. Just the opposite. Millie was surprised her brother hadn't proposed to Skylar just to get a dig in at Laurie Jean.

"I want to find some dirt on Laurie Jean," Skylar snapped. "I want to hurt her where it'd hurt most."

Millie eyed her and was on the verge of asking her if she was behind the blackmail. But Skylar dropped a question that Millie definitely couldn't and wouldn't answer.

"Do you think Tanner's been seeing Frankie?" Skylar asked.

Millie only hoped her face didn't spill the truth. Besides, she didn't know what the truth was, anyway. Tanner had slept with Frankie and she'd thought she was pregnant. That could be all there was to it.

But Millie didn't think so.

"I don't know," Millie lied, and she justified the lie by convincing herself that it would not only save Skylar's feelings but that it could prevent the woman from having a nasty confrontation with Frankie.

Skylar stared at her a long time, maybe hoping that Millie would rat out any secrets she knew about Tanner. But she didn't. She caught on to Skylar's hand, the one without the wad of tissues, and gave it a squeeze.

"Why don't you go home and take a long, hot bubble bath," Millie suggested. "Drink some wine, pig out on ice cream and watch a movie that won't make you think of men, my brother or anything to do with romance."

After several owl-eyed moments, Skylar nodded, but she looked far from convinced that any of that would help. It would in a small way that might get her through the next couple of hours. Millie had firsthand knowledge of that since she'd spent many tearful nights because of Royce and Ella. Royce hadn't broken up with her face-to-face, but the breakup had happened.

When Skylar finally left, Millie continued the walk home. She took out her phone, intending to call Frankie to ask her about the pregnancy test that Ella had bought. But she shook her head and put the phone back in her purse. That was a question best done in person, and she'd make time to go over and see her on Sunday when both their shops would be closed.

Millie sighed when she got home and saw Alma setting a cooler on her porch. The woman beamed with her usual sunny smile, but she also gave Millie the once-over that often accompanied grief grub deliveries. Alma was obviously checking to see if Millie was having a bad day, and that meant Alma hadn't heard any gossip that Millie was seeing Joe.

Though she was certain such gossip was going around.

"Veggie stir-fry and a sugar-free, healthy version of carrot cake," Alma said, pointing to the cooler.

Millie had no idea why Royce's aunt thought she practiced a healthy diet so she just smiled and thanked the woman.

"I hope the meals help," Alma added. "Grief is a long process. Just when you think you've got it licked, another little pocket of it bubbles up and kicks you in the tushy."

Those were wise words that made Millie nod. But other pockets bubbled up, too. Like these new feelings she was having for Joe. Part of her was deeply worried about ending up like Skylar. Sobbing and crying on the sidewalk when Joe ended things with her. However, the other part of her—and no, this wasn't about her *lock*—wanted to keep going full steam ahead and hang whatever happened between them.

Joe had already told her that he couldn't give her tomorrow, but he had given her moments. Now she wanted a night from him. They could go from there, night by night, until he felt he had no choice but to back away.

Grief could indeed take a bite out of you.

"Oh, you're looking sad now," Alma said. "I'm sorry. I'm sorry, too, that I didn't come to check on you last week. You know, on the anniversary of the car crash."

There'd been no need for Alma to clarify "last week." Millie had been well aware of the red-letter day. She'd gotten thirty or so calls and texts, and probably that many visitors had dropped by the shop just to check on her. She'd appreciated their concern, but it had been a day that she wished she could have just x-ed off the calendar.

"Look, if there's any way I can help you, just let me know," Alma added.

"Fried chicken," Millie blurted out. She winced a little but figured she'd better explain. "Please don't feel you have to prepare more meals for me. Please. But if you do cook, I'd prefer fried chicken."

Alma smiled. "With mashed potatoes and buttered biscuits?"

"That sounds perfect." Millie smiled, too, and gave her a hug.

"Are you all right?" Alma asked when she pulled back and met Millie's gaze.

"I am." And while it wasn't the total truth, it wasn't anywhere close to a lie. "I'm getting better," she added.

"Good." Alma patted her cheek. "Because if anybody deserves to be out with the old and in with the new, it's you. You deserve a big ol' serving of happiness."

Millie had no idea why she'd earned such praise from Alma, but she was definitely feeling better when the woman said a cheery goodbye. Millie hauled the cooler inside, carrying it toward the kitchen.

But she stopped outside Royce's office.

"Out with the old and in with the new," she repeated.

She stared at the door. Something she'd done hundreds of times since Royce's death two years ago. And each of those times, Millie had walked away, vowing to keep it shut. Out of sight, out of mind.

However, she didn't do that this time.

Setting the cooler down, she gripped the knob, gathered her breath and opened it. She made a sweeping glance around the room. No ghosts, but everything had a fine coating of dust, and motes were drifting through the air in such a way that made her think of dandelions shedding their fluff.

Millie stepped in and spotted her rings on the floor. They'd landed right by the front of Royce's desk. Even through the dust, they still sparkled and caught the light slanting in through the bay window.

She'd forgotten how "Royce" the room was. It suited

his taste to a T because it'd been his design plan, and it mimicked the colors in the kitchen. Or rather the lack of colors. A sleek white desk with a glass top, minimal art and no rugs on the glossy wood floor. It was so unlike his office at work with all its ornate wood and rich man's furnishings. But then, Asher would have been responsible for those decorating choices since it was after all his law firm.

Millie had no idea if Royce had been happy working for her father, and that made her a little sad to know it was a conversation they'd never had. Then again, they'd apparently missed out on many talks and left way too much unsaid.

Hoping to remedy part of that "unsaid" stuff, Millie went to his desk and started looking around. There were no files remaining from his legal career. She had a vague memory of Asher sending someone over to collect anything work related. But Royce's laptop was still there, and there were several handwritten notes next to the computer. She brushed aside the dust on one and saw that it was a reminder to "make dinner reservations and order flowers."

The date he'd jotted down for the reservation was her birthday. That put a knot in her throat. Until she realized that the dinner might not have been for her but rather for something he had planned to celebrate with Ella. The knot vanished, and her determination soared.

Millie plugged in the laptop so it could charge while she started going through the drawers, tossing stuff out so she could get to what was beneath. Which was pretty much nothing out of the ordinary. No sex toys. No secret jewelry purchases for his lover. It was just the usual stuff you'd find in a man's desk. The only thing that was remotely interesting was a packet from one of the online ancestry sites.

She recalled Royce using the DNA kit because Vonnie

Diaz, the office manager at the law firm, had given them to everyone as Christmas gifts. Asher probably hadn't used his kit for fear of finding out something that might tarnish his roots, but Royce had done the test and had seemed pleased that he had a smidge of Native American blood.

Setting aside the test packet, Millie opened the laptop next and started looking through the emails and files. They'd had separate bank accounts and credit cards, but Asher had dealt with closing Royce's accounts and then transferring the assets to Millie since according to Royce's will, she'd been his sole heir. It was a will Royce had made shortly after they'd married, and he hadn't made any changes to it.

Millie didn't see anything in the files that were of a personal nature. All were related to his work, but her scrolling came to a quick halt when she came across an invoice for payment to La La Land for a painting. There were no specifics about said painting, but Royce had sent an electronic payment of two thousand dollars.

So, maybe the painting Joe had seen in the storage unit hadn't been Ella's portrait of her lover.

The portrait might have been something Royce had commissioned online after browsing through the La La Land website. Ella's paintings had certainly impressed Millie when she'd looked at them online so maybe they'd done the same to Royce. In fact, it was possible she'd even mentioned the La La Land site to him when she'd purchased the three paintings for the shop.

Still, if it was something as simple, and innocent, as that, why hadn't he mentioned it to her? And why hadn't Ella said anything about it to Joe?

Millie continued scrolling through the emails. Mercy, what was it with the penis enlargement spam? She stopped again when she saw the emails from the ancestry company that'd supplied the test. Apparently, they'd provided Royce with DNA matches, and some of those matches had reached out to him, touting their connection of being his cousin, many, many times removed. There were hundreds of them, and many weren't identified by name but rather a code number.

Hundreds.

And that got her thinking. It was an out-there theory, and maybe she was grasping at straws that fit into the many, many times removed category, but what if one of those matches had been with Ella?

It was possible.

Ella wasn't from Last Ride, but Royce and she could have had a shared ancestor. It wouldn't have spurred Royce to meet her for a family reunion, but it could explain how they'd connected. First, through the ancestry site and then maybe to get together in a friendly distant-cousin sort of way.

Millie wasn't sure why knowing that sort of thing even mattered, but it was a thread that she wanted to tie off. She took out her phone and texted Joe.

Any chance you can come over to my place or come early for our date?

For some Civil War porn? he texted back.

She sent him a laughing emoji. Maybe afterwards. First though, we need to talk. I found some things in Royce's office that I need to tell you about.

Millie wasn't surprised when it took Joe a long time to answer. He was probably thinking the worst. Dara's home, was his next response.

She'd figured that, and it was why she'd asked him to come to her place. It's nothing bad, she explained. I just have some questions, and you might be able to help.

Finally, Joe responded. I can't leave right now. I'm waiting on a delivery that I'll have to sign for. I don't want Dara to have to deal with that, but you can come over right now if you want.

I'm on my way.

Millie had just hit the send button when she heard the front door open, and she groaned when Laurie Jean called out for her. She automatically braced herself, answered with a brisk "In here." It didn't take her mother long to follow the sound of her voice to the office.

"What are you doing?" Laurie Jean asked. She didn't gasp, but it was close. "Are you going through Royce's private things?"

There was probably nothing that Laurie Jean could have said that wouldn't have caused Millie to bristle, but that accusation was very high on the list of bristle-worthy stuff.

"Royce is dead. He doesn't have any privacy," Millie flatly reminded her.

"This is his office," Laurie Jean fired back as if that were a logical argument.

"His office, my house," Millie fired back as well because that was logical. Dead men didn't need offices.

Then, Millie sighed and reined in her temper before this escalated to something that would take her a lifetime or two to undo. Millie didn't ascribe to the "making waves brings shame" theory, but making waves with Laurie Jean created a lot more trouble than another cliché of battening down the hatches and weathering the storm. She didn't have time for a long drawn-out anything with her mother because she wanted to go to the ranch.

"I was in here to see if there were any loose threads that needed to be tied off," Millie said as calmly as she could manage.

Actual alarm went through her mother's eyes. "And did you find any?"

Millie shrugged and lifted the ancestry packet. "I learned that Royce had his DNA tested."

"Those things are a hoax," Laurie Jean snapped. "The company takes your money and they make up the results. You should toss that in the trash and put it out of your mind."

Millie tucked the packet underneath her arm. "I was on my way out," she said, heading to the office door.

But Laurie Jean didn't go out of the room. With a look of horror and disbelief on her face, she hurried to the rings and picked them up.

"You should be wearing these," Laurie Jean muttered. "If not on your finger, you should wear them on a chain around your neck."

Millie rolled her eyes. "And why is that exactly?"

Her mother whipped back around to face her. "Because you should respect your marriage. The good parts of your marriage," she amended. "And don't tell me there weren't good parts because there were."

Millie sighed again. "Yes, there were good parts, but they're over. My marriage is over, and I'm trying to move on with my life."

"By seeing that cowboy." The anger relit in Laurie Jean's eyes.

Millie was oh so tired of her mother dissing Joe and using that holier-than-thou tone. "Yes, by seeing that cowboy." She certainly didn't mimic her mother's tone, but there was probably some anger in her eyes. Enough anger in the rest of her, too, that she decided to try an experiment. "Mr. Lawrence," she tossed out there.

Laurie Jean pulled back her shoulders, and while she wasn't especially throwing off any "yes, he's my lover" guilt vibes, she did look very uncomfortable. For a moment, anyway. She quickly recovered.

"You're a widow," Laurie Jean went on, obviously sliding right back into the lecture mode. "You shouldn't be seeing other men for at least five years, and even then, it shouldn't be someone like that cowboy."

Well, that relit Millie's own hot button. "Mom, I won't lecture you about your affair or blackmail if you won't lecture me about Joe."

Laurie Jean gasped. "You'd dare say that to me?"

"Yes, because I need you to hear me. Butt out of my life and focus on solving your own problems. I'm not a married woman having an affair, and I'm not being blackmailed."

"But you're a widow having *relations* with Joe McCann." Laurie Jean shouted all the words except *relations*. That one she whispered.

Millie met her gaze and spoke as clearly and calmly as she could. "Yes, I am, Mom."

And with that, Millie headed out the door to get started on another round of those very satisfying relations.

CHAPTER TWENTY

WHEN JOE HEARD the approaching vehicle, he got up from his desk so he could go outside to welcome Millie. He wanted to see her. Maybe even kiss her. But right now, he was very much interested in hearing what she'd found in Royce's office.

However, it wasn't Millie.

Tanner pulled to a stop in the driveway. Hell. Joe's first reaction was that something had happened to Millie because she should have been here by now, but he forced his worst-case scenarios to calm the heck down.

"Is everything okay?" Joe asked from the porch.

"Not really. You got a minute to talk?" Tanner started across the yard.

"Yeah, I got a minute, but Millie should be here soon."

The corner of Tanner's mouth lifted. "I'm glad you two are seeing each other."

"Well, that makes five of us. Dara, Millie, Frankie, me and you."

Though Joe wasn't sure exactly how "glad" he was that he'd turned his life upside down and was well on the way to hurting a woman who didn't deserve to be hurt.

"You want something to drink?" Joe asked. "Dara's inside," he clarified in case this wasn't a discussion Tanner wanted the teenager to hear.

Tanner waved that off, stepped onto the porch and sank down onto one of the rockers.

"Thanks for watching Little T this morning," Tanner said. "I appreciate it."

"Anytime." But Joe was a thousand percent sure that Tanner's gratitude was simply a way of easing into what would no doubt be a hard conversation. Something was definitely wrong and rather than press him on it, Joe just waited him out.

"I broke up with Skylar," Tanner finally said.

Joe just kept on waiting. No way had a breakup with a woman Tanner had only been dating a couple of months put this look of total gloom and doom on the man's face.

"I shouldn't have ever started up with her," Tanner went on. "But she was hard to resist."

Welcome to the club. He was having the same problem with Millie, but Joe kept that thought to himself.

"Anyway, I hurt her bad." Tanner sighed, cursed. "She's spitting mad right now, but it won't take long for that hurt to set in."

Welcome to the club, Joe mentally repeated. Millie might not be mad, spitting or otherwise, when things ended between them, but there'd be hurt—on both sides of this relationship coin.

Tanner paused, the seconds ticking off, and the sweat starting on every sweat-able part of their bodies. "I had to end things with her, well, because I slept with Frankie. Now, don't get out your axe," Tanner quickly added. "It happened right before I started seeing Skylar. In fact, that was one of the reasons I asked Skylar out. I just figured I needed to put some distance between Frankie and me, and that Skylar would be the fix for that."

Joe thought back to the hickey he'd seen on his sister's neck. Yeah, the timing was right for Tanner to have been the hickey maker.

"Why are you telling me this?" Joe finally came out and asked though he doubted it wasn't anything more than his former brother-in-law wanting to vent his guilty conscience over having ex-sex.

But Joe was wrong.

Tanner looked up at him. "Because I'm still in love with Frankie."

Joe couldn't have been more surprised if Tanner had just confessed to being a dancer on Broadway. On a heavy sigh, Joe took the rocker next to him.

"Bottom-line this," Joe said. "Do you want me to talk to Frankie and tell her how you feel, or would you rather I try to talk you out of being in love with her?"

Tanner groaned, and there was both determination and confusion on his face when he looked at Joe. "I want her back, and I need you to tell me why that can't happen. Go over all the times I screwed up with Little T and her. Tell me what a dick I am and what a dick my folks will continue to be to her if Frankie hooks up with me for another round. Convince me that I messed up her life once, and that there's no way in hell she should give me the chance to do that again."

Well, Tanner had definitely bottom-lined it, and all of those were valid points. "You have been a dick," Joe confirmed. "So have your parents, and they acted like dicks with Frankie." Again, all valid, but the next point was the cherry on top. "There are no guarantees whatsoever that Frankie will ever take you back."

Tanner groaned again. "I know. I have no trouble getting her into bed, but I'm not sure she'll want me ten minutes after she's gotten off."

Joe had to clamp down the urge to punch Tanner for that. Or remind Tanner that he really didn't like discussing his sister getting off. Instead, Joe went with his own bottom line as it applied to Tanner.

"You're really in love with her?" Joe asked.

"Yeah, really, really in love with her."

Joe nodded. "Then, I'm thinking you'll have to tell Frankie and try to convince her that you deserve another shot even if you're not sure you actually deserve anything. But this time," he added in a snap, "you need to stop being a dick."

Other than making a sound of agreement, Tanner didn't respond to that. Probably because they both saw and heard Millie's car turning into the driveway.

"I'll go," Tanner said, getting to his feet. "I don't want to mess up your afternoon with her."

Joe was worried it might already be messed up, with whatever she had to tell him. Even non-bad things about Royce didn't make for pleasant conversation. In fact, it might bottom out their moods so much that Millie could cancel out of their sex date.

Something that he should be hoping would happen.

He obviously wasn't capable of resisting her so it would have to be Millie who put a stop to things. If she didn't, these sex dates would run their course, the guilt would roll over them like avalanches and they'd ruin what passed for their lives.

Millie looked at him. Smiled. And once again, he was a goner. Yeah, it would have to be up to her to put a stop to this.

However, she didn't stop one bit. When she made it up the porch steps, she kissed Joe with that smile still on her mouth.

"I was just leaving," Tanner muttered.

Millie took her mouth from Joe's and stepped in front

of her brother. "So, you broke up with Skylar. I saw her in town, and she told me," Millie added when Tanner cursed and grumbled something about news traveling fast. "Are you here to ask Joe for advice?"

"Sort of." Tanner's chin came up. "I'm going to try to get back with Frankie. Got any complaints, bitches or gripes about that?"

"None whatsoever." Millie shrugged. "Frankie's in love with you."

Tanner's eyes went wide, and he grinned like an idiot. "She is?"

"She is," Millie verified. "Why, I don't know. I think you might be that one guy she just can't manage to get over."

Tanner's grin got even goofier. "Is that sort of like saying I'm the love of her life?"

"Or the dick of her life," Joe contributed, but even that didn't tone down the wattage of all that brightness Tanner seemed to be feeling.

Joe nearly reminded him about all the doubts he'd just had, about all the reasons why a reunion was a shitty idea. But apparently "Frankie's in love with you" was the cure for all doubts.

"Dick of her life," Tanner said, holding out his hands as if weighing them. "Love of her life. It's all about perspective. I need to get to work on perspective. Good timing for it, too, since Dara is babysitting Little T tonight."

Whistling and looking as if he could actually do the ballet, Tanner hurried off the porch and to his truck. Apparently, Dara's babysitting was allowing the possibility for two sex dates. Tanner and Frankie's. And Millie's and his.

"Did he come over to have you try to talk him out of getting back together with Frankie?" she asked, watching her brother drive off.

"Pretty much." Their gazes met when she turned back to him. "What'd you find in Royce's office?"

"This." Millie took out the large white envelope she'd had tucked under her arm. "It's from one of those genealogy sites. Apparently, Royce had his DNA tested shortly before he died."

Joe felt himself frown. Millie had told him this wasn't bad, but he'd thought it'd at least have a connection to the car wreck or the secrets he'd kept from her.

"Did Ella ever do a DNA test?" Millie asked.

Still drawing a blank on why Millie had made a visit to tell him this, Joe shook his head. Then, stopped shaking it when he recalled something. "Frankie gave her one of the kits for her birthday. In fact, she gave us both one. I didn't use mine, but Ella might have. Why?" he immediately tacked on to that.

She waved that off. "It was just some out-there, stupid idea I had. One that could have explained why Royce and Ella were together. I mean, an explanation other than the obvious."

"I'm listening," Joe assured her. And he was. Every bit of him was tuned in to her. Because an idea, stupid or otherwise, was more than he had now.

Millie bobbed her head from side to side, gave a nervous little laugh. "I thought maybe both had done the DNA tests and they'd learned they were related. Judging from what I found on Royce's computer, he was making at least email contact with some of his genetic cousins. If he'd found out that one of those cousins was right here in Last Ride, he might have suggested they get together. You know, like for lunch so they could go over their family trees."

Joe went through every nerve-filled, babbled word she'd just said. And he wanted to latch on to those words as gospel. He wanted this to be the answer to the "Why" he'd asked Ella.

But there was a problem with that.

Not once had Ella ever mentioned any DNA results, and if she'd found out Royce was indeed a relative, why hadn't she just told Dara and him? That wouldn't have been something she'd feel the need to keep secret.

Joe was trying to figure out the best way to break that news to Millie, but he spotted the large truck coming up the drive. "The delivery's here," he said. "Go on inside and get out of the heat. This won't take long, and we can talk this out."

"Good, because there's more I need to tell you about." With that cryptic comment, she gave him a quick kiss, took the DNA packet from him and headed indoors.

Joe needed the feed and large animal medical supplies, but he wished the driver, Donny Betterton, had come an hour earlier or later. Of course, Donny wanted to chat while he unloaded the supplies at a sloth-like pace. Joe pitched in, dragging off feed bags and dropping them into the barn before going back for more. It took nearly a half hour to get everything off the truck. Joe dashed off his signature on the invoice but then had to listen to a couple more minutes of small talk with Donny.

By the time Joe hurried back inside, he was plenty sweaty and should have headed straight for the shower, but he stopped when he heard Dara talking to Millie. He was pretty sure they were just up the hall in her bedroom.

"So, you think you and Dad will get married?" his daughter asked.

Judging from the sound he heard next, Millie had gotten choked on her own breath. Joe had the opposite problem. His breath had gotten jammed up in his lungs and he couldn't speak.

"Things aren't that serious between me and your dad," Millie finally said. "We're really just sort of seeing each other."

"You're making him happy," Dara concluded. "That seems serious to me."

No choking sound from Millie this time, but Joe figured she was mentally doing some hemming and hawing. It also occurred to him that he'd overheard more conversations in the two months since the Last Ride Society drawing than he had in his entire life.

"Your dad and I are taking things slow," Millie explained. "We could date for a while and then decide things aren't going to work out between us. I don't want you to be hurt or disappointed if that happens."

"Okay," Dara said after a long pause, and she said it in such a way that Joe was certain she would indeed be hurt or disappointed when things ended with Millie.

"And if your dad and I stop seeing each other," Millie went on, "that doesn't mean you and I will have to stop. We can still go on shopping trips and still talk if that's what you want. I'll be here for you if you ever want or need me to be."

It was the right thing to say, and it obviously pleased Dara, because when Joe stepped in the doorway of his daughter's bedroom, Millie and Dara were hugging it out while they sat on the foot of her bed. The hugging stopped though when they spotted him, and Dara practically sprang to her feet.

"I'll get that snack now," she said, obviously hurrying out to give Millie and him some alone time. Perhaps so he could propose marriage.

Or kiss her.

Actually, the kissing wasn't a bad idea. Especially now that he knew Millie fully expected *this*—whatever this was—to come to an end.

Smiling at him, Millie stood and went to him. She trailed a very provocative finger down the front of his shirt. "You're sweaty. I like that," she added when he started to step back from her.

She leaned in and kissed him.

Joe kissed her right back, and then he got that kick of heat. Both familiar now and unfamiliar, too. Familiar because it was a taste that he now knew well and had started to crave. But there was a new sensation, too. A new slide of heat that seemed to go one notch over the ache he had for her in his groin.

Joe decided not to think about that right now. Especially since Millie had those other things to tell him.

"What else did you find in Royce's office?" he asked.

The question caused her dreamy, aroused look to fade, and that caused him to curse. He made a mental note to put some money in his swear jar and hoped that Millie hadn't been trying to soft-pedal it when she'd told him earlier that what she'd found wasn't bad.

"Apparently, Royce commissioned Ella to do the portrait of him," she explained. "I'm still not sure how he knew to get in touch with her about doing that, but it could be because of the paintings I bought for the shop."

In other words, the painting wasn't proof of an affair. "Why wouldn't Ella have just told me that?"

Millie shrugged. "I was hoping you'd have a theory or two about that."

Going with the "non-affair" angle, Joe couldn't come up with much, and it felt like grabbing at straws. "Maybe

Ella thought I wouldn't approve of her painting Royce. Or people like him. You know, rich, snobby."

He winced a little because he thought Millie might be offended by that. The *rich* applied to her. Not the *snobby* though. But she only nodded.

"Yes, that could be it, and that could explain why she wouldn't have told you if she was a cousin match with Royce." She smiled, latching on to that straw as if it were a lifeline.

"And as for why Royce wouldn't have told me," Millie went on, "it probably wouldn't have occurred to him that it was something I'd want to know. In hindsight, we didn't have a lot of conversation that didn't revolve around his job, redecorating the house or us joking about the constant flow of dinner parties and such my mom was hosting."

She stopped, sighed and absently trailed her finger down the front of his shirt again. "The sweat is drying," she remarked.

"And will soon stink to high heaven. I need a shower, but I want to hear the rest of what you have to say first. There's more, right?"

Millie nodded and blew out a long breath. "Another hindsight—I don't think Royce and I had a lot of meaningful conversations. The exception, however, leads me in a roundabout way to something else I wanted to tell you. The whole time Royce and I were married, I tried to get pregnant, but it never happened."

Everything inside Joe went still. Hell, was Millie about to tell him he'd gotten her pregnant? It'd only been a little over two weeks since they'd had sex, and they'd used a condom but maybe—

"No," she said, laughing. "I'm not pregnant. God, your face. You've gone pale."

Joe ignored her laughter, her comment on his paleness, and focused on the middle part of what she'd said. "I'm not pregnant." That was such a relief that he kissed her, and the relief must have shown through in the kiss because she laughed again.

"I mentioned my fertility issues," she continued, "because I wanted you to know I bought a lot of pregnancy tests over the years. Word of that probably got back to Frankie because she asked me to buy her a test when she thought she might be pregnant. I don't think it's the first time, either. I believe she's had other scares."

Joe mentally plowed through all that information, easier to do now that the blood had stopped rushing to his head. "She thought she might be pregnant with Tanner's baby," he concluded.

Millie nodded. "And by telling you this, I've breached a very important female-to-female confidence and given you far more TMI than you've probably ever wanted about me or your sister."

Oh, yeah. The mother lode of TMI, but Joe thought he saw the little nugget of info in there that Millie was trying to pass along to him.

"You believe Frankie asked Ella to buy her a pregnancy test," Joe said.

This time, Millie's sigh had some relief in it. "I think it's a strong possibility. I haven't talked to Frankie about it, but I was thinking you might be able to work it into a conversation with her."

"A TMI conversation," he mumbled, causing her to laugh.

She smiled, patted his arm. "I have to go. I'll see you in a couple of hours," she said. "I want to see if I can work you up into another sweat."

And Millie got started on that sweating by dragging him to her for a long, promising kiss.

MILLIE FROWNED AT the Roaring Twenties porn in the upstairs room of her shop. Normally, looking at the weird contraptions and grainy naked pictures amused her. Perhaps added a smidge or two of titillation as well, but glancing through the porn offerings for the period left her with a "been there, done that" feeling.

Of course, when Joe showed up for their date in twenty minutes or so, he'd probably still get a kick out of the numerous pictures of groups of women revealing their secret places for the camera. But she wanted more than a kick. She wanted a punch, something that would make him feel as incredible as she had when they'd had sex. The problem was, she'd never actually been sexually adventurous.

But that was about to change.

Joe had made it clear what they were doing together wouldn't last, that he wanted it to be just temporary sex. She got that and was fine with it. Well, fine-ish, anyway, but he might be more inclined to stretch out the temporary sex if she kept him on his toes, sexually speaking.

Millie caught a glimpse of herself in an art deco mirror rimmed with painted erect penises. Ignoring the penises, she studied her dress. Sexy enough, she supposed. It was snug and red, and she'd planned on slipping on a pair of heels before Joe arrived, but she was pretty sure she could make a better statement.

Or a more direct one.

Millie peeled off the dress. Her underwear, too. Then, she glanced around the room for props she could use. The dominatrix-looking corset with the metal tassels would almost certainly hurt like the dickens so she went with a feather boa that she wrapped around her neck. She pulled on a pair of black garters, but switched them out when she saw these, too, had penises on them and opted for ones with sparkles. No way would she shimmy into any of the antique underwear, which all appeared to be size zero, so Millie went with letting the boa dangle from the front of her midsection.

She had another look at herself in the penis mirror and nodded. Joe definitely wouldn't be expecting this.

Millie was still at the top of the stairs when she heard the knob rattle on the back door. Naked, and nearly tripping over the boa, she hurried to the door and would have thrown it open for Joe had she not heard the voice.

Not Joe's.

But a woman's. She was whispering something while the doorknob continued to jiggle.

Millie put her eye to the recently installed peephole and saw her mother. And Laurie Jean wasn't alone. There was someone just to her right, but no matter how Millie angled her eye, she couldn't see him.

"She changed the locks," Laurie Jean snarled. "I can't believe she did that without giving me a key."

Millie nearly blurted out that the reason for the lock change was so Laurie Jean couldn't get in to do whatever she was planning on doing. Millie would have thrown open the door and confronted her mother if she hadn't been wearing only a boa and garters. Instead, she ran to the front of the shop and, staying back from the display windows where someone could spot her, she peeked out, hoping to get a glimpse of her mother and lover.

But nothing.

Laurie Jean had obviously had the good sense not to go out on the sidewalk on Main Street, which meant she'd no doubt sneaked away using the alley that ran along the backs of Once Upon a Time and the other shops on each side of it.

However, speaking of sneaking, Millie saw someone doing just that. Joe. He was on the sidewalk, but he stopped well before he got to her shop and ducked between the other buildings. Heading toward the back, so that's where Millie headed, too. She looked out the peephole again, waiting for him, and the moment he came into sight, she jerked open the door.

"Did you see them?" she blurted out. "They were just out here a couple of minutes ago."

Joe opened his mouth. Closed it. And ran his suddenly very interested gaze down her body. "Are we playing a porn game?" he asked.

Frustrated, she shook her head. "No." She took hold of his arm and pulled him inside. She locked the door, had another look out the peephole.

No one was out there.

"Then, what are we playing?" he asked, fingering the boa.

Millie huffed, but the huff wasn't for him. Especially when his finger skimmed her nipple. That had some of the annoyance about her mother melting away. The annoyance vanished completely when he moved his finger lower to her navel ring.

"Laurie Jean and her lover just tried to get into the shop," she explained. "I changed the locks so they couldn't get in and they went away."

The skimming and fingering stopped, and his eyes came to hers. "Who's her lover?"

"I didn't get a good look at him, and if he spoke, I didn't hear his voice." She paused. "But I think it might be Mr. Lawrence. I know Tanner said the guy had black hair, but

Tanner saw him from a distance in the dark. He could have mistaken Mr. Lawrence's hat for his hair."

Joe's forehead bunched up for a couple of seconds, and she expected him to laugh or ask why he'd think that, but he finally nodded. "I guess he'd be your mother's type. He's somewhat like your father, only friendlier and with that upper-crust artist vibe."

"Yes," she quickly agreed. "He does have a lot in common with my father, and that's why I'm skeptical that he's the one. I mean, why would Laurie Jean go after someone who's so similar to the man she already has?"

She waved that off before he could even attempt an answer. Millie truly didn't want to get into any discussion that could be turned around to Royce and Ella.

"It could be Rico Donnelly," Joe threw out there.

It took Millie a moment to make the leap that Joe was putting Rico in as a possibility for Laurie Jean's lover. Millie considered it, shook her head. "He's so not her type."

But considering she'd just made the argument for Mr. Lawrence being too much like her father, maybe Laurie Jean had gone for the opposite of her husband. And Rico was definitely the opposite. He was also two decades younger than her mom. Still, Rico was a player, one with black hair, and he could have tempted Laurie Jean into sampling down and dirty sex.

Something that she absolutely didn't want to think about.

"Are you okay?" he asked.

It was automatic for her to lie and say she was fine, but she wasn't. "I hate that my self-righteous mother tried to sneak into her love nest. I especially hate that the love nest is a room I love and use often—for sleeping," she clarified. She'd never be able to do that again.

"We can reschedule our date," Joe offered.

"No." She didn't have to think about that. She wanted to be with him. And she especially wanted to be with him when he did more fingering. This time, to her other nipple.

"No," she repeated, and this time there was an aroused, dreamy tone to her voice. "But I did go with a change of plans. No perusing Roaring Twenties porn. Instead, I'll be the porn."

Smiling, he hooked his index finger under the garter that was high on her thigh, and he used the grip to inch her to him. "You do the porn justice," he drawled. "But FYI, I don't need props or porn to want you."

Oh, it was so the right thing to say, and Millie felt herself melting like butter in the hot Texas sun.

"I just want to keep you interested," she managed even though he'd started to slide his very clever fingertips down her belly.

"I'm interested," he assured her in that drawl that was so much more titillating than decades and decades of porn. "So, do you have costumes for me, or will butt naked work?"

"Butt naked will always work when it comes to you."

He pulled out the big gun and smiled. Joe also used his finger hook around her garter to draw her just a little bit closer. Just enough so that her breasts brushed against his shirt.

"You have a choice of adventures tonight," she said over the little hitch in her voice. "We could go into the Tarzan memorabilia area." She fluttered her hand to the back right side of the shop. "Loincloths, ropes. Jane spilling out of whatever she's wearing. Second option. The Sherlock Holmes display." She fluttered her hand in the other direction. "There's nothing remotely raunchy in there, but it does have a comfortable settee."

"Option two," he said, and he yanked her the rest of the way to him.

Mouth met mouth and, just on meeting, Joe jumped from first base to practically a home run with the way he kissed her. It was hungry and hard. Just the way he was, she realized, when her center landed against his erection.

Since it was obvious Joe wasn't going to play around too long with the foreplay, Millie started moving them in the direction of Sherlock's lair. It was really just a cubby in the back corner, but she doubted they were going to need much room. Or time. While they kissed, walked and bumped into things, she started undoing his belt.

"I'm on fire here," she muttered against his mouth. "Let's go for a quickie and then something longer."

It was possible he made a sound of agreement. Possible, too, that he even spoke, but Millie's heart was thrumming so loud that she wouldn't hear him. The mindlessness soon followed when he kissed her neck hot spot and slipped his fingers between her legs.

Good thing he was holding on to her, because her legs buckled, and Joe had to sort of drag her along. The moment they reached the display, Millie dropped onto the settee and pulled him down with her.

Joe landed on top of her, but he quickly remedied that by sitting so they were face-to-face again. Just the way Millie wanted. Her hands were free to start getting him naked. Her mouth was in the right place to kiss him long and deeply. And her knees were free to clamp around his thighs so she could wiggle against his erection. That gave her more than a few thrills and jolts, but it was obvious that it was torture for Joe.

She helped him out of his misery by ridding him of his shirt because, hey, even a quickie didn't mean they couldn't be bare chest to breasts. Her breasts obviously approved of that because her nipples hardened and peaked. Joe did some torturing of his own when he lowered his head and kissed those peaks.

It didn't take long, mere seconds, before Millie was frantic to get at him. She went after his zipper again. Freed him from his boxers and would have had him inside her if Joe hadn't stopped her.

"Condom," he reminded her.

It seemed to take an eternity for him to get the condom from his pocket, and while he put it on, he continued to kiss her in all the right places. He nudged her in the right place, too, when she felt the tip of his erection push inside her. He went slow again. As if savoring it. And her. Before that one final, hard push into her that robbed her of every bit of her breath.

Millie couldn't stop herself from moving. From sliding into the long strokes that were definitely pushing right where they needed to push. It was as if her body, her lock, had made the adjustments, because it didn't take long before she felt herself climbing, climbing, climbing.

Joe must have felt it, too, because he moved faster. Harder. Hitting the spot that spiraled her, climbing, climbing, climbing until everything inside her gave way. The coil of tension and need snapped, filling her with the rush of pure pleasure. Wave after glorious wave.

She wanted to go limp, to collapse against him, but she wanted something more. She wanted to watch him as she pushed him over the edge.

Because she knew his spot, too.

She was already slick and ready so Millie could take him in, and in, until she felt him buck beneath her. Until the wave after glorious wave racked him, too.

There was another reason Millie enjoyed this position. With them still face-to-face, she could kiss him while they both shuddered. While their breaths gusted.

Smiling, she dropped her head onto his shoulder. His arms came around her, holding her close. Heart to heart. And yes, everything was perfect.

Millie heard herself murmuring something through the haze of pleasure. Words, but it took her a moment for those words to sink in. And they caused her heart to lose more than a couple of beats. Because those words were definitely something she should have never, ever, ever said.

"I love you, Joe."

CHAPTER TWENTY-ONE

I LOVE YOU, JOE.

Millie knew that had been the worst possible thing she'd ever babbled. He'd known it, too, because she had felt him freeze. Then, he'd cursed. What he hadn't done was ask her why she'd said it. Joe had continued holding her for a while, and then after he'd made a pit stop in the bathroom, he had told her that it was best he head home.

And he had done just that.

He had dressed, given her a peck on the mouth that was missing any and all the heat of his usual kisses. Millie had sat there, still wearing her boa and garters and had watched him walk away from her. Pull away from her, too.

Millie had dressed as well, gone home and then taken the advice she'd given Skylar. Plenty of wine and ice cream. Those items had become staples in her diet for the past couple of days, but the indulgent pity food hadn't helped. Nothing would. She had basically taken a really good thing and shot the hell out of it by blurting out "I love you."

It wasn't even true.

Well, it probably wasn't. She cared deeply for Joe. He was a good person. A good father. An amazing lover. And she'd told him things she'd never spilled to another living soul. But that couldn't mean she was actually in love with him.

Because love would ruin everything between them.

Maybe if she just played it cool, he'd eventually want another date. Perhaps even a sex date. If she got that chance again, she'd use a ball gag—there had to be one somewhere in one of the porn rooms—so she wouldn't get the chance to blurt out anything else that fell into the stupid category.

It was her day off from the shop, but Millie considered going into work just to get her mind off Joe and the research she'd been doing on Ella, but then she thought of something else that could occupy her mind. It had risks though. It might also spur her into a deeper foul mood, possibly even the dreaded pit of despair, but it was something she needed to finish.

Bringing along her lunch glass of wine, she went into Royce's office.

It was cleaner than it had been when she'd last been in here. That's when she'd walked out on her mother. Laurie Jean must have dusted and straightened up. Must have picked up her wedding rings, too, because Millie saw them on the center of the now-clean desk.

Millie had no idea why Laurie Jean was so insistent that she hang on to a marriage that no longer existed. Maybe because her mother had put her own marriage in such a precarious position? Perhaps. But it could be something as simple as Laurie Jean not wanting to deal with the talk there'd be when her widowed daughter started dating again.

Public dating, that is.

Even though plenty of people probably knew that she'd been seeing Joe—correction, that she *had* seen Joe—they hadn't gone out together as a couple. Now that might never happen.

Drinking more wine and cursing that thought, Millie dropped down into Royce's chair and laid out a search plan. No more willy-nilly prods and pokes. She wanted to go through every inch of the place, thoroughly, and then she could put the room, and maybe Royce, to rest.

She searched back through all the desk drawers again. Top to bottom. And didn't see anything she hadn't already seen. So, she went to the filing cabinet. It was white, modern, and the top drawer slid out with just a touch. There were some client files inside, but there were also gaps, probably ones that Asher had had removed and taken to the law office. According to her father, Royce had a habit of doing most of the work for clients in his home office before moving them to the law firm.

The second drawer had folders of receipts, paper credit card statements and such. Millie thumbed through those and realized that a thorough search would include her going through each statement line by line to see if Royce had made any unusual charges. She might be able to ask Frankie to help with that. They could turn it into a girls' night, and then Millie would have a shoulder to cry on if she found something that shattered her into a million more pieces.

She sat on the floor when she opened the bottom drawer and saw it was filled with photo albums. And his baby book. Thumbing through it, she could see that his parents had been diligent about taking pictures of him and keeping up with his milestones. He'd learned to walk when he'd been eleven months old.

Millie doubted that she'd need to go through the albums and baby book with the same "digging for secrets" eye that she would the credit card statements, but she would take another look.

For now though, she moved back to his laptop, turned it on and started scrolling through the genealogy emails again. If Royce and Ella were indeed related, the proof of it might be in one of those.

None of the emails mentioned Royce by name and had been sent through an email that he must have set up through the genealogy site. Royce had used a reference number for his ID, and the people who'd contacted him had mostly stuck to that, too. However, there were some from people giving multipage info dumps about their family trees when matched as Royce's third, fourth and even fifth cousin. Millie didn't recognize any of the names, and since it didn't appear Royce had responded to them, he might not have known them, either.

She continued to skim, but the skimming came to a quick halt when she saw the email from a woman named Roberta Guthrie.

"'I believe I know who you are,'" Millie read aloud from the email, "'and I've put off writing to you many times. I hope contacting you is the right thing to do. Your DNA connects to mine through my brother, Harlan Guthrie. I believe you're his biological son which would make me your aunt.'"

Millie stopped, reread that and repeated the name, Harlan Guthrie. Like the names in the other emails, she didn't recognize it, but none of those other DNA cousins had purported to be Royce's aunt. Or hinted that he hadn't been the son of David and Sarah Dayton.

"'You were put up for adoption when you were just a baby,'" Millie continued to read, "'and because of the circumstances, I was told it was best if I didn't try to contact you. I suppose that was the right thing to do, but I want you to know there hasn't been a day that I haven't thought of you, and I pray you're well. There's so much I'd love to tell you about your family. If you want to talk, let me know and I'll send you my phone number.'"

Millie couldn't move her fingers fast enough, looking for a response, but she didn't see one. However, using the search function in his emails, Millie did find one with the name Harlan Guthrie. Royce had sent that particular message to Wilbur Franklin, the PI that the law firm used. And Royce had copied Asher on it.

She sat back, trying to process that. So, Royce had taken Roberta's claim seriously enough to involve the PI. Her father, too. They must not have found anything or surely Royce or Asher would have told her, but Millie kept looking.

Until she found Wilbur's brief reply.

Report on Harlan Guthrie attached.

It, too, had been sent both to Royce and Asher. Millie clicked the attachment, wondering if she was experiencing the same kind of jitters that Royce probably had when he'd opened it. However, her jitters soon turned to shock as the words jumped out at her.

Confessed to murdering his wife in Houston. A life sentence, no possibility of parole.

She sat there, staring at the words. Then, cursing them. Well, cursing one word in particular. Her father's name. Asher had known about this. Millie took out her phone to call him, but she was going to take a page from the PI on this and go over it in person. However, she did make a quick call to Asher's assistant, Vonnie Diaz, to make sure he was in the office. He was.

Fuming, seething about being kept out of the loop on this, Millie changed out of her yoga pants, brushed the wine off her teeth and grabbed Royce's laptop in case her father had a sudden case of amnesia and claimed he didn't know what she was talking about.

However, before she left the house, she fired off an email to Roberta Guthrie, just a quick hello to tell the woman that she was Royce's wife and wanted to talk to her. It took only a few seconds after she hit the send button to get an automatic reply that the email address was no longer valid. Millie had no idea if that meant the woman was no longer alive, but she would need to do a search on her. After she confronted Asher.

She got in her car and drove straight to the law firm. It wasn't far, right in the center of town, and she would have easily walked there, or rather marched there, but she hadn't wanted to risk running into anyone. She had questions, and she wanted answers to those questions right now.

Vonnie welcomed her with a bright smile. "Your dad's in with a client right now, but he'll be finished in just a few minutes. I told him you were coming in."

Millie doubted he'd try to sneak out without seeing her, but she decided to keep watch on the parking lot just in case. She paced while she waited. And glanced up at the oil portrait of her father. It was huge, at least twelve feet tall and maybe just as wide, and the artist had captured Asher's wealth, power and cool sneer.

"It does make a statement, doesn't it," Vonnie remarked.

Yes, it did, but "flattering" wasn't one of those statements. However, it did cause her to think of something.

"Did Royce ever mention having a portrait like this done of himself?" Millie asked.

Vonnie smiled. "Why, yes he did. In fact, I'm the one who brought it up to him. I'd seen the paintings you had in Once Upon a Time. I told Royce he should hire that artist to do a painting of him." Her smile faded. "He said he emailed her, but I guess he didn't have time to go through with getting the painting done."

"When was this?" Millie asked. "When did he say he'd emailed the artist?"

Vonnie tipped her eyes to the ceiling a moment and then shook her head. "I'm not sure, but it wasn't long before the, well, before the car accident. Maybe a couple of months before," she added.

So, perhaps that's what had first brought Ella and Royce together. The start of their affair. If there was an affair, that is. For two years Millie had been certain the reason Ella and Royce had been together was because they'd been heading off for an afternoon of sex. But maybe she'd been wrong. Maybe everyone had been wrong.

The door to her father's office finally opened, and Millie saw Mr. Lawrence come out. He eased off the hat that he'd just put on and gave her his usual friendly smile. Millie attempted to smile back, but she got a flash of her mother between the sheets with him.

She exchanged a short greeting with Mr. Lawrence and went into Asher's office. He was seated behind his impressive desk, reading through some papers, and he didn't even look up when she came in.

"I'm assuming this is important," Asher said.

"It is. Why was Mr. Lawrence here?" she asked.

Now he looked up at her and frowned. "He's a client. I can't discuss him with you."

She ignored that, opened Royce's laptop to the emails from the PI and set it on the desk in front of him. "Can you discuss this with me?" And, no, didn't tone down the venom in her voice.

Her father took one short, audible breath and leaned back

in his chair. What he didn't do was look at the emails. Because he clearly already knew what they were.

"I advised Royce to delete those," Asher said. Unlike her, his tone was calm as if discussing the weather. So was his demeanor.

"Delete them?" she snapped, and she was loud enough that it prompted him to get up and shut the door. That told her that his assistant had been kept out of the loop on this, too.

"Yes," Asher verified. He was still calm, on the surface, anyway, but he went to his liquor cabinet and poured himself a shot of his favorite Oban scotch. He downed it like medicine. "I knew you'd be upset if you found out."

Apparently, this was going to be a conversation where she did a lot of repeating. "Upset." She was snarling now. "What about Royce? He had to be upset, too, when he learned his father was a killer."

"He was." Asher set his glass aside and went back to his desk to sit. He stared up at her. "Royce didn't even know he was adopted so I'm certain he hadn't expected to hear any of this because of a DNA test."

So, his parents had kept his adoption a secret. Millie wasn't sure how they'd pulled that off, but she hadn't heard even a whiff of gossip about Royce not being their biological child.

"His parents did the right thing," Asher went on. "It would have been traumatic for Royce to learn his biological father murdered the woman who gave birth to him. And what would be the point?" He outstretched his hands in a gesture that she was certain he'd used when pleading a case to a judge or jury.

"The point would have been for Royce to know the truth about who he was," Millie argued.

"And what would be the point of that?" Apparently, Asher was going to do some repeating today, too. "Royce certainly wouldn't have wanted a relationship with a killer. Telling Royce and letting the word get out would have done nothing but feed the gossips."

Millie couldn't dispute the gossip angle. Oh, yes, there would have been plenty of that, and it was probably the primary reason the Daytons hadn't told Royce. Still, Royce should have known. Too bad neither of them was alive so she could ask them exactly why they'd thought they had a right to keep such a vital piece of information from their son.

"After Royce got over the shock of what he'd learned," Asher continued, "I advised him not to tell anyone, including you."

Oh, that gave her another slap of anger. "I was his wife," she reminded him.

"Yes, and there was no reason for you to know this. It had nothing to do with you and, frankly, it was nobody's business."

Millie heard the sound of strangled outrage burble from her throat. Outrage not only for Asher and his advice but for Royce for taking that advice. But the anger that had lit so fast and so hot fizzled out as quickly as it'd come. It left her with bone-deep weariness. Along with the realization that this was yet something else she hadn't known about her husband. But Asher did. In fact, her father could have some missing pieces of a very important puzzle.

"Does Royce have any biological siblings?" she asked.

Asher blinked, frowned. "I don't know. That's the truth," he snapped when she groaned. "Royce said he wanted to do a thorough background check on Harlan Guthrie and

Harlan's sister, Roberta, but I talked him out of it. Again, what would have been the point?"

Because it could be the answer to why Ella and he were together. That was a huge point. One of the biggest in her life. But Millie didn't tell her father that.

What would be the point?

Picking up the laptop, she walked out. And she knew just where to go. Millie got in her car and drove to Joe's ranch. Only after she got there, it occurred to her that he might not be home, but she spotted him in the corral. He was climbing out of the saddle on a dapple-gray horse.

And looking pretty amazing while he did it.

Then again, Joe had "pretty amazing" down pat.

He didn't smile when he saw her, but he did come out of the corral toward her. No way was he glad to see her. Not with the walls he was trying to put up between them, but as he got closer, she thought she caught a glimmer of heat in his eyes.

"I was thinking about doing an H. G. Wells display in the shop," she said. "I could add a time machine. Then, I could take back what I said to you. I'm hoping you'll consider it post-orgasm insanity." She managed a chuckle.

No chuckle for Joe though. "Millie," he said on a rise of breath. He said it in such a way that she heard every bit of the weariness he was feeling.

He was probably about to launch into a talk about why they shouldn't see each other, but Millie decided to nix that. For now, anyway. She could give him the chance to crush her heart later.

"I've learned a whole bunch of stuff about Royce that you should know," she started, and then tossed out the million-dollar question. "What if Ella and Royce were brother and sister?"

Obviously, she should have provided some backstory first because he just gave her a long stare.

"When I went through Royce's emails, I found out he was adopted," she explained, and Millie gave Joe a brief overview of what she knew about Harlan Guthrie.

Joe stayed quiet, obviously trying to process that, and he finally took hold of her arm. "Let's get out of the heat. Dara's inside the house," he added. And that explained why he led Millie into his man-shed. He probably didn't want to spring any possibilities like this on his daughter until he had all the facts.

"Here's the report," Millie said once they were in the shed. She set the laptop on the worktable, and brought it up on the screen. "And here's the message from Royce's aunt. No mention of Royce having siblings, and her email addy is no longer valid."

Joe scanned through the email and report, and then he used the laptop to do a search on Harlan Guthrie. There wasn't as much info as Millie had expected, but then the man would have been convicted of murder over thirty years ago.

Thirty-two to be exact when Royce would have been just a baby. She saw the date of Harlan's confession on one of the pages. What she didn't find was any mention of Harlan's son or other children.

"There are archived news articles that might have the info," Joe said, scrolling through the pages. "We'll have to subscribe to a service to get them, but let me make a call first. To Ella's mom."

Of course. In her frustration over her conversation with Asher and her hurry to get here, Millie had forgotten about the one woman who could maybe give them an immediate answer. Then again, that answer wasn't going to come easy.

Joe took out his phone, and she could see him steeling himself. Still, he scrolled through his contacts and made the call. He didn't put it on speaker, but Millie had no trouble hearing the woman's voice when she answered.

"Joe, is everything okay?" she asked, and Millie didn't think she was wrong about the woman sounding surprised. Maybe Joe didn't call her that often.

"Some things have come up, and I have a question." And he didn't waste any time getting to that question, either. "Janice, was Ella adopted?"

When Millie didn't hear her response, she moved closer to the phone.

"Janice?" Joe prompted. "Was Ella adopted?"

Again, no response. Well, except for a sharp intake of breath right before Janice ended the call.

CHAPTER TWENTY-TWO

JOE FINISHED BRUSHING down the horse he'd used to ride out and do fence repairs. Repairs that had taken hours. He was tired, hungry and wanted a shower. After that, he hoped he could just fall into bed and into a deep sleep. One with no dreams.

And with no thoughts of Millie.

He figured his chances of not thinking about her were nil. For the past four days since Millie had said that *I love you*, she'd been the main thing on his mind. And that was saying something, considering all the rest of the crap that had been keeping him from getting that deep, dreamless sleep.

A lot of that crap involved Janice. She still hadn't returned any of his calls, still hadn't answered the question about Ella being adopted. If the woman kept up the silent treatment, he'd have to drive into San Antonio and confront her face-to-face. And what fun would that be?

"Not much at all," Joe grumbled under his breath as he started toward the house.

But the truth had to come out, and since he hadn't been able to find anything else on Ella's DNA test, it meant Janice might end up being his sole source to confirm or debunk the theory that could explain why Royce and Ella had been together.

He wondered if Millie was having any better luck with

getting info about whether or not Harlan Guthrie had had more than one child. Probably not. If she had, she would have contacted him. Even the awkwardness between them wouldn't have put her off from telling him something that important.

And, of course, he was now thinking about Millie again.

Cursing ten dollars' worth that he'd owe his swear jar, he opened the kitchen door and came to a halt. Dara was standing on a chair and hanging something from the drop-down light fixture.

A banner with Happy Birthday colored with rainbow glitter.

Joe did a quick mental double take to make sure he hadn't forgotten Dara's birthday, or his own. He hadn't. But there sure as heck was birthday stuff on the table. A cake complete with candles, paper plates, napkins and even little pointy party hats. Dara had even made some party food. Chex mix, little sandwiches and queso dip with tortilla chips.

"What's going on?" he asked, stepping inside. Then, he froze again when he saw the icing writing on the cake.

Happy Birthday, Millie.

Dara beamed out a big smile as if there was something to beam and smile about, and she got down from the chair. She eyed the banner, stepped a few inches back and did more eyeing. "I know Millie's birthday isn't for a few more days, but I figured she'd have plans on the actual day so I'm throwing her a surprise party tonight. I had Aunt Frankie pick up some of the things, and she dropped them off while you were working."

Joe had some vague recollection of Millie soon turning thirty, but this was the first he was hearing of a surprise party. "I don't think this is a good idea," he grumbled.

Dara shifted her attention from the banner to him. And she stopped beaming. "I get it. Things aren't good between Millie and you right now."

He scowled. "How do you know that?"

She made an "it's obvious" eye roll. "You're grouchy and moody so I figured you've started to feel bad about seeing her. Because of Mom and all. I'm staying out of that, but Millie is still my friend, and I wanted to throw her a party."

Dara checked the clock on the stove. "Frankie, Tanner and Little T will be here soon so you might want to go ahead and get your shower. As soon as Aunt Frankie's done with work, she'll pick up Little T from the sitter and head over. They're going to park behind the barn so Millie won't know they're here."

Joe's mind was stuck on the "grouchy and moody" comment so it took a couple of seconds for the rest of it to sink in. The party was bad enough, but now there'd be guests? Of course, those guests were family, with the exception of Tanner, but still...

"You should have asked me before you did all of this." And yeah, he grumbled that, too.

"When I asked you this morning if you were going out tonight, you said no, that you'd be home," she reminded him.

Yeah, he had said that, but that didn't mean he'd wanted to attend a party for anyone, especially Millie. He couldn't imagine Millie being particularly thrilled with it, either.

"How'd you convince Millie to come here?" he asked.

"I told her I had a few more research notes to give her about Mom. She's trying to finish up the report, but I fibbed and said it was stuff I knew she'd want to include." Dara checked the clock again. "She'll be here in like forty-five minutes."

Hell. He couldn't demand that Dara cancel, but he could regret that Millie had apparently become such an important part of her life that she'd throw her a surprise party.

No way would Millie have turned Dara down, either, because he suspected that Dara had become an important part of Millie's life, too. He knew they'd met for lunch at O'Riley's with Frankie and Little T. There was also another shopping trip in the works to celebrate Dara getting all As on her end-of-school-year report card. That's why Joe had given her a gift certificate to the mall. Dara would probably use it to hit that silk underwear place again and buy makeup with names that made him think of sex with Millie.

Then again, a lot of things made him think of sex with Millie.

Joe started stripping the moment he was in his bedroom, and he cursed enough that he'd have to write a check to his swear jar. There were probably enough funds in there now to sustain a small country.

He showered as if he'd declared war on life and worked out some of his mad. Not mad at Dara. Hell, not even at Millie. But at himself. He'd known if he got involved with Millie that somebody would get hurt. She had. He had no doubts about that. But he hadn't expected his own heart to get stomped on. Of course, he was responsible for the stomping since he'd been the one to back away from her, but that didn't make it hurt any less.

After he dried off, he stood in front of his closet, wondering if he should put on an actual shirt instead of a T. But then he realized the only reason for that would be to look halfway decent for Millie. Something he'd want if they were still seeing each other. Since they weren't—or they possibly weren't—he grabbed one of his everyday T-shirts, a gray one, and pulled on a pair of clean jeans. By the time he finished dressing and came out of his bedroom, he heard the unmistakable chatter from Little T.

"Can we yell 'boo' instead of 'surprise'?" the boy asked.

"No," Dara answered. "You yell out surprise for a surprise party. But remember when you're supposed to do that?"

"Yeah, after you bring her in here. It'll be dark 'cause you're going to turn off the lights, and we're gonna hide. When you bring her in the kitchen, we'll jump up and yell 'surprise.' Then, we can have cake. Can we have cake now?"

Dara was explaining why they had to wait—candles, wishes, etc.—as Joe walked in. One look at Tanner and Frankie, and he knew they'd had a fairly recent booty call. No doubt while Little T had still been with the sitter. Joe spotted the fresh hickey on his sister's neck, and Tanner was looking laid-back and satisfied.

"If you break her heart again, I'm getting out the axe," Joe muttered to him while Frankie, Dara and Little T were putting on their party hats.

"I'll try very hard not to do that. We haven't worked out everything," Tanner quickly added. "And we've decided to take things slow."

"Not so slow that you didn't have time to give her a hickey," Joe pointed out.

Tanner shrugged, with a smile that was still mostly cocky/bad boy. But there was also a bad boy version of a blush, too.

"Millie's here," Dara said when there was the sound of an approaching car. "Aunt Frankie, go ahead and light the candles." She slapped off the kitchen lights. "And, Dad, put on a party hat before you hide." She practically shoved one in his hand before she ran out of the kitchen.

Joe didn't put on the hat—he added it to Little T's instead—but he did hunker down by the fridge, mainly because that's where Little T dragged him. "Shhh. We gotta stay real quiet," the boy said in a loud voice that could possibly have been heard one county over.

He heard Dara turn on the TV, probably to drown out anything else the boy had to say. Then, moments later, Joe heard Dara open the front door and greet Millie. There was some chatter, followed by footsteps approaching the kitchen, followed by Dara switching on the lights.

"Surprise!" Dara shouted.

Tanner, Frankie and especially Little T echoed that shout, but Joe couldn't seem to get the single word out of his mouth. That's because his gaze locked on to Millie's face, and he saw the worry there. She was still pretty enough to take away his breath, but it appeared she hadn't been sleeping any better than he had.

For just a split second, he imagined being in bed with her. Falling into that much-needed deep sleep after having some much-wanted sex. But Joe shoved that image aside when Millie broke the eye contact because of the rush of hugs she was getting from Frankie and Little T.

"I can't believe you did this," Millie murmured, glancing first at Joe before hugging Dara. "Thank you."

"It was all Dara's doing," Joe volunteered, but he wished he'd kept his mouth shut. Because it sounded as if he'd wanted to make sure that Millie knew he'd had no part in it.

"And Frankie's," Dara supplied. "She did the grocery run for me."

Millie thanked them both again, and she teared up when she looked at the table. "I haven't had a birthday party since I was sixteen. This is very nice." That spurred more hugs, but Joe stayed back.

"You'd better blow out the candles before they catch the place on fire," Tanner joked, earning him a required elbow poke from his sister.

There was somewhat of a blaze going on. Frankie had lit all thirty candles, and some of them were flickering pretty high.

"Make a wish," Little T shouted, and out of excitement or perhaps because he believed they'd all become hard of hearing, he repeated it three more times.

Setting her purse on the counter, Millie nodded, closed her eyes a moment and then blew and blew and blew. She was a little winded when she finished, but she managed a laugh. The sound of it caused the tension in his chest to fade. Caused a flood of thoughts and memories about her, too, that he didn't want, but mercy, it felt good to see her happy.

"What'd you wish for?" Little T asked in the same breath as, "Can we eat cake now?"

Millie kissed the boy on the nose. "The wish is a secret."

Joe wondered if it had anything to do with him. Or sex with him. Oh, yeah. He was losing this battle over trying to stifle thinking about her.

"Presents first," Dara said, handing Millie a small wrapped box she took from the seat of one of the chairs.

Frankie whipped out one, too, from her purse, and so did Tanner. It wasn't wrapped, but he pulled a little envelope from his pocket. Then, Little T produced something from his pocket, but he kept his hand clamped around it.

Well, hell. Joe certainly hadn't gotten her anything. He hadn't even known there'd be a party until less than an hour ago. But maybe that was for the best. If he had known, he would have gotten her something.

Correction—he would have agonized over what to get her.

Something too trivial could have perhaps made her think she meant nothing to him. Something too big could cause her to believe they could go full speed ahead with that *I love you, Joe*. This way, there'd be no wrong choice of gift, only the crappy feeling that he was the only one who hadn't gotten her anything.

Obviously a little overwhelmed, Millie stood there for several moments just looking at the gifts, and Little T's hand. And she teared up again. One of those tears actually spilled when she opened the box Dara had given her and took out the necklace. It was a small etched silver heart on a silver chain.

"It's a locket, and you can put your picture in it." Dara opened it to show her. "I know you don't wear much jewelry—"

"I'll wear this one," Millie interrupted, pulling her into a hug. "Thank you," she murmured.

When she eased back from Dara, she immediately put it on. Or rather she tried. After fumbling for a couple of seconds, she turned around for help. Just as Dara went to the sink. Maybe to get something. But Joe suspected it was a ploy since he was the only one not holding anything. Silently cursing his daughter, he went to Millie.

Touched her.

No way to avoid that. The clasp was the size of a flea nostril so he ended up doing plenty of touching, some adjusting, even some bumping of her butt before he finally got the darn thing on her.

"Thank you," she said in that same warm murmured tone that she had to Dara.

"Mine next," Little T insisted. He waited until he had Millie's attention before he opened his hand to reveal the nickel. "It's a lucky one," he explained. "It's five times luckier than a penny 'cause I found it and picked it up."

Joe held his breath, waiting for the boy to blurt out that he'd picked it up by Ella's grave. That would certainly put a damper on this party, but the boy didn't add that little detail. He just handed over the coin, the very one that awed and excited him. Maybe some of that awe and excitement had worn off, but Joe was betting it was still valuable to Little T. And he'd given it to Millie.

"Thank you." She kissed the top of his head. "I'll keep it with me all the time. For luck," she added with a wink. "And because it's from you." Millie opened the locket and slipped the nickel inside.

"Me next," Frankie said, holding out the gift.

This time, Millie hugged and thanked her before she even opened it. Then, she laughed when she saw what was inside. A tiny gold fairy dangling from a loop. It took Joe a moment to realize it was a navel ring.

Frankie nudged Joe and winked at him. "Want to put this one on Millie, too?"

Tanner and Frankie had a good laugh about that, and Millie let him off the hook by putting the fairy back in the box and into her purse. "I'll try it on later."

Well, shit. That put more images in his head. More memories, too, of tongue kissing the navel ring she already wore.

Tanner handed her the little envelope, which held a gift card from O'Riley's. Not as imaginative as the ones from Little T and Frankie, but it earned him a hug.

"Sorry," Joe mumbled when the others looked at him.

"I didn't tell Dad about the party in time for him to get you a gift," Dara jumped in to explain. "Plus, I figured he'd want to wait until your actual birthday to get you something."

His daughter had just thrown down a gauntlet, one that she probably hoped would fix his bad mood by getting Millie a gift that would in turn get them back together.

"Cake now?" Little T asked, jumping up and down and clapping his hands.

Dara nodded and went to the counter to get a knife. While she was doing that, Millie stepped closer to Joe. "Nothing from Janice?" she whispered.

He shook his head. "Nothing more about Harlan Guthrie?"

She opened her mouth to answer, but Dara came back with the knife and positioned herself next to Joe. Millie clammed up while Dara cut and served the cake. There was some idle chatter as they chowed down, but the moment Millie had finished eating her piece, Joe took hold of her hand.

"I need to talk to Millie," he said. "We won't be long." And he led her out of the kitchen before anyone could say anything about that. Of course, there'd probably be plenty of speculation, but Joe could deal with that. For now, he wanted to know if Royce and Ella had been siblings.

He took her to the front porch and shut the door. He didn't have to prompt Millie though. She launched right into it.

"I read through all the archived newspaper articles on Harlan, and it appears he beat his pregnant wife, injuring her to the point of putting her in a coma. The doctors were able to deliver the child, but his wife died. All of this happened in Houston," she added.

"Was that child Royce?" he asked.

She nodded. "Had to be since the dates line up. Unfortunately, there's no mention of Harlan having other children, but that doesn't mean there wasn't a half, step or even a full-blooded sibling."

It surprised Joe that something like that had been kept out of the press. Then again, the murder had happened in one of the largest cities in the country. A domestic homicide might not have gotten much attention.

"The aunt who emailed Royce died," Millie went on, "and I haven't been able to find any other relative on the DNA links. I did ask Alma, but she says she had no idea that Royce was adopted. Apparently, before he was born, his parents went away for about a year, under the guise of helping take care of her ailing mother, and when they came back, they told everyone they'd had a child."

People must have bought that since Joe hadn't heard anything to the contrary. Just the opposite. The only talk about Royce before the car crash had been how much of a "shining star" he was in the Dayton family. Afterward, all the talk had been about the way he'd treated poor, pitiful Millie and poor, pitiful Joe McCann.

Joe was sure Millie had tried to shake off that label. He certainly had. But at the moment, they both had a little of that pitiful vibe. They'd hoped too much that learning about Harlan would fix what had happened. Nothing could fix that.

"I'm sorry," he said just as she said it, too. Their timing was perfect when it came to apologies.

It was Millie who continued. "I'm sorry I couldn't find more about Harlan Guthrie, and I'm really, really sorry about that whole stupid 'I love you' thing."

Stupid.

Joe wasn't sure why he took offense to that, but he was glad she'd said it. Well, sort of glad. They couldn't go back to that almost carefree feeling of going through antique porn and having sex, but he didn't want to feel...

He mentally stopped and repeated it. He didn't want to feel...

Again, he stopped and pushed aside suggestions his dick had for finishing that. Instead, Joe let his somewhat crushed heart fill in the blanks. He didn't want to feel as if he'd lost Millie.

Even if she wasn't his to lose.

He looked at her. No smile. Just some sadness in her eyes, and he hated seeing it there. Knowing that he'd had some part in making her feel like crap.

"So what'd you wish for when you blew out the candles?" he asked, hoping to lighten the mood.

"For you to kiss me," she said after a long pause.

Well, so much for lightening things up. He'd expected her to go with a joke, maybe like a new porn collection from the Great Depression. But he could tell from her expression that she'd told him the truth.

Joe could also tell, from the way his body was urging him on, that he was going to make that wish come true. Even if she wasn't his. Even if it was a stupid thing to do. In fact, he did so many stupid things concerning Millie that he needed to set up another jar just for that.

He leaned down and brushed his mouth over hers. Hardly a kiss. So he did better. Without putting his hand on her, he just moved in closer, pressing his lips harder against hers. Turning it into a real kiss when he slipped his tongue into her mouth.

She moaned, that pleasure sound that always gave him an instant erection. He heard himself moan, too. A needy, hungry sound of a man who was starving for this. Starving for her.

Now he touched her. Joe dragged her to him though he didn't have to put up much of an effort there since she was already heading in his direction. They landed against each other with a heavy thud and just kept on kissing. In fact, Joe thought he might be able to keep this up for days.

Or not.

He had to amend his "days" pipe dream when he heard the sound of a door slamming. For a moment he thought someone had come out of the house and onto the porch, but it had come from a car that was now in front of his house. Joe hadn't even heard it pull up, but he sure as hell saw who got out.

Janice.

And it was a million times obvious that she had seen him kissing Millie.

"Sorry to interrupt you," Janice said.

Joe studied her because there was none of the expected anger and perhaps even disgust in her voice. In fact, she looked ill, and that's why Joe hurried off the porch. Millie stayed put.

"You have company," Janice murmured.

"Millie's birthday party," he supplied, taking hold of her arm. "Dara, my sister, her son and Millie's brother are inside."

"I don't want to go in there. I don't want to be around anyone right now." Janice stopped him from taking her onto the porch. "I'll just say what I need to say and then leave."

Hell, this was bad, and he tried to brace himself for whatever she was about to spill.

"Ella was adopted," she said, her voice soft and thin. Janice stared down at the ground as she spoke. "But I gave birth to her."

Joe was certain he looked confused. "Then, why'd you say she was adopted?"

Janice swallowed hard. "Because I got pregnant with her before I got married." She looked up at him with what he thought might be apology. Maybe because she'd given Ella so much grief about getting pregnant with Dara.

"Ella's biological father couldn't, *wouldn't*," she corrected, "marry me and told me I'd just have to raise the child on my own."

All of this was still whirling around in his head, but he asked the obvious question. "Who was he?" Joe asked.

"No one you know. No one Ella knew. He was a country music singer I met when I went to one of his concerts."

Everything still kept whirling. He couldn't image Janice as a groupie—to anyone or anything.

"Anyway, I gave birth to Ella," she went on, "and I got married when she was two. Daniel adopted her." Some fire lit in her eyes now. "And he was her father in every way that mattered."

Joe nodded. He didn't doubt that one bit.

"You can tell Millie if you feel you must," Janice added. "But swear her to secrecy. I don't want Dara to ever find out, and I don't want a word about this in that research report Millie's doing."

She didn't give Joe a chance to try to assure her that this wouldn't make Dara think less of her, but Janice was already hurrying back to her car. She kept hurrying, too, when she drove away.

Joe stood there a moment, just breathing. Just thinking. Then just cursing. Because yeah, he'd tell Millie, along with asking her not to put anything about this in her report. That was a must. Then, Millie would know that Ella and Royce hadn't been siblings. That they were not both the children of a man who'd killed their mother. That they still had no explanation as to why their spouses had been together and had died with Ella's arms around Royce.

And that would put Millie and him right back on the emotional roller coaster they'd been on for two years.

CHAPTER TWENTY-THREE

MILLIE SAT AT her desk in the shop. She had her laptop positioned in front of her so that anyone who spotted her would assume she was working. She wasn't.

Couldn't.

So, she just looked out at the customers who trickled past her door and to and from various displays. It was like watching a really boring TV show. It didn't seem real with everything just moving and floating while her mind was stuck on what Janice had told Joe.

She should have been used to these fixations by now since it'd been nearly twenty-four hours since Joe had passed on to her what Janice had said. Until she'd heard him say the words, Millie hadn't realized just how badly she'd wanted it to be true that Ella and Royce had been siblings.

Such a bombshell would have restored their good names. Would have assured Joe and her that they'd had good marriages after all. It wouldn't have changed what happened, but it would have fixed some things.

Now nothing was fixed. And worse, she was caught up in a very dark place. She couldn't totally blame that on this fresh grief though. No, this was more her own fault. She'd fallen hard for Joe, knowing that he wasn't ready for a relationship. He'd spelled out for her that the best he could do was give her some moments, not even a confirmed tomorrow. Millie had known he was telling the truth, but she'd practically thrown her heart at him.

And now it was broken.

Her body was actually broken, too. Every muscle ached, and she had plenty of scrapes and even a blister. Instead of indulging her broken heart only with wine, ice cream and crying, she'd added some heavy physical labor by moving and boxing up stuff that should have been moved and boxed up months ago. She wasn't finished, but she'd made a dent in it.

"Want me to lock up?" she heard Monte say, and Millie looked up to see him standing in the doorway. "Haylee's checking out the last customer now, and it's past closing time."

Millie nodded, muttered a thanks.

Monte didn't budge. "Want to talk about it?"

"No." But she muttered another thanks.

Talking wouldn't help, but maybe packing more boxes would. Or eating some more large quantities of the little tubs of Ben and Jerry's ice cream. Millie ticked off some other possibilities, including a third call to Frankie—uh, no, correction, that would be a fourth call where Millie had already whined to Frankie in a vague sort of way since she couldn't re-spill what Janice had spilled. Frankie probably thought she was on the verge of a breakdown.

Millie nixed the ice cream, the fourth call and would probably skip more box packing, as well. She didn't want to go shopping for more B & J's. Didn't want to keep bugging Frankie. And didn't want to throw out her back by lugging around more boxes. Besides, the only thing that would be a surefire cure for her mood would be to see Joe. She so desperately wanted to see him that for a moment, she thought she had conjured him up as a mirage.

No mirage though. It was Joe in the "holy smoke!" flesh that stepped up behind Monte.

"Got some time to talk?" Joe asked.

"I'll go ahead and close the shop," Monte said, smiling a little. Probably because Millie felt some of the darkness just float off her.

She didn't quite trust her legs, they suddenly felt wobbly, so she kept her hands anchored on the desk when she stood. "Yes," she said. "I'd love to talk." Now that her cure was there, she was game for anything.

Joe just stood there, his eyes locked with hers, while she could hear Monte and Haylee scurrying—yes, scurrying— to close up. The bell jangled on the front door and Monte called out, "Bye, boss. Have a good evening," before she heard the click of the locks.

Monte probably thought their hasty exit would spur some hasty sex between Joe and her, but Millie could have told him he was wrong to think that.

Or not.

Joe went to her and pulled her into his arms. It wasn't anything close to sex, but it still felt amazing.

"Frankie's worried about you," he said, easing back to meet her eyes. "How are you holding up?"

"I'm better." And that wasn't a lie. Oh, mercy. She had it bad—and not for what had happened two years ago but for the man looking down at her with those incredible eyes. "How about you?"

"Better," he repeated. And that probably was a lie. "Janice has called me about a dozen times to warn me not to tell anyone her secret. I assured her I had no immediate plans to do that, but that down the road, I thought she should tell Dara."

Millie nodded. "She should know if for no other reason than family medical history."

He made a sound of agreement. "I doubt Dara will care one way or the other since she didn't know the man who adopted Ella. For Janice, I think it's mostly about appearances. She doesn't want anyone to know that she had a child before she was married."

"Appearances," Millie repeated. "Janice has a lot in common with my mother. Laurie Jean's number one priority in life is appearances."

"Anything new on the blackmailer?" he asked.

She shook her head. "Well, maybe there's something new. Truth is, I've been avoiding Laurie Jean. Something I won't be able to do much longer though. The poop will hit the fan when word gets out that I'm donating my house, *Royce's house*," she amended, "to the Last Ride Society."

Joe froze for a moment, then did a sort of double take. "What brought that on?"

"Basically, I hate living there, always have, so while I was..." she stopped, rethought the confession she'd been about to make regarding her ice cream consumption and brooding "...boxing up the last of Royce's stuff last night," she continued, "I had an epiphany and decided I wanted to box up my stuff, too, and didn't want to spend another night in the house."

He continued to study her for a long time. "Good for you. What will the Last Ride Society do with it?"

This had been part of the epiphany, too. "I'm going to suggest they use it as the new library for the Last Ride Society. I figure that'll please Alma to no end. She and her ilk have been wanting some place other than the back room here at the shop to store all the research reports, but the donation will rile Laurie Jean."

"Because she wants you to hang on to the house?" he asked.

"Because she wants me to hang on to being Royce's wife. I don't want to do that," Millie quickly added. She also quickly felt the anger over her mother's shitty attitude. "And you know what—I don't think Royce would want me to do that, either."

Because she'd added a punch of emotion with each word, Millie waved that off. "The epiphany came post ice cream, post wine, post crying jag, so I wasn't sure it'd make sense in the light of day, but it does. It's what I want to do."

Joe skimmed a finger down her cheek. Just a flicker of a touch. Oh, but it was a magic seal of approval. "Where will you live?"

"I'm working on that. Well, working on a short-term solution, anyway." She smiled. "Yes. It was a very long epiphany," she said, taking hold of his hand. "Let me show you." Millie led him to the back stairs.

"Are we going to one of the porn rooms?" he asked.

She smiled because it didn't sound as if he would completely object to that. "Some of the former porn rooms," she explained. "The porn and rest of the stuff up here will go into storage. But I can give you the code for the storage unit if you want to go visit it sometime." Millie winked at him.

He laughed, and it was good to hear it. Yeah, he was the cure all right.

With her anger gone and her mood improving with each passing second, Millie pointed to the long hall that was now stacked with boxes of stuff she'd moved out of the rooms.

She opened the door to the nearly empty storage room. "The house is zoned for both residential and commercial so there shouldn't be a problem with building permits. I want to have this room and the adjoining one reconfigured into a living-kitchen area."

Even though it was now just a blank canvas, she could see how it would be. A large cook's table that could be used for dining, open cabinets, soapstone countertops. She wanted color, lots of it. Cobalt blue, sea green and butter yellow. It definitely wouldn't suit everyone's palate, but Millie thought designing a space like that would make her smile.

"I can use it until I find a house I want to buy, and then I can rent this out as an apartment," she explained. "Monte's already got his name on a renter's waiting list," she added with a chuckle.

Moving down the hall, Millie opened up the next room she wanted to show him. "This and the adjoining one will become the master suite. Not a huge space, but it'll do."

"You're excited about this," he remarked.

"Definitely. I'm excited about anything that'll get me out of my current house and into something that feels more like me. Like I said, this will do so I can take my time to shop around."

She might have to close the shop a day or two while the renovations were being done, but she'd deal with that when the time came. Deal, too, with Laurie Jean.

"I'm glad what Janice told you didn't cause you to spiral down," he said.

She turned, studying his face as he'd done to her. "Is that what it caused you to do?"

"No." He dragged in a long breath and repeated it before he touched her cheek again. This time though, he slid his hand around the back of her neck. "I spiraled because I knew I'd hurt you. That I'd continue to hurt you if I kept seeing you. But here I am, anyway."

Millie figured he was about to spell out why he was there, but she didn't want to hear it. Didn't want to listen to him say that coming here was a mistake. In his mind, it was. Nothing she could do to change that.

"Let's just go back to our moment-to-moment arrangement," she said and touched her mouth to his.

A sound rumbled from his throat. "I want to say yes because I want you. But, Millie, I can't—"

He stopped, cursed and kissed her. In that order, and she wasn't sure if the f word he said was part of the cursing or if he was informing her what they were about to do.

She felt his frustration because she was feeling it herself. This inability to resist each other even when resisting was probably the way to go. But right now, she only wanted Joe, his mouth, his arms. And the rest of him. Yes, there'd be hell to pay, but at least she wouldn't have to pay until she had another dose of him.

Joe clearly wanted to get on with that dosing because he kissed her as if he might never be able to kiss another woman. A thought that might have wormed its way into her head if he hadn't put her back against the wall and started taking off her top. He was definitely a multitasker when it came to clothing removal because he just kept kissing her. Until she had no breath. No thoughts. Only a boatload of need.

Still kissing her in that man-on-fire kind of way, he pushed up her skirt to her waist, and in the same motion he shoved down her panties. And then, he touched. Mercy, did he. Joe used those clever fingers to shoot her straight up the peak. Just as Millie was about to fly right off that crest, he moved his hand and pushed his body against the part of her that was now aching and begging.

Actually, Millie was ready to beg, too, but Joe French-kissed her and put an end to anything she might say.

Mentally begging and cursing him, she went after his belt and zipper. Obviously, this was going to be a fully naked kind of thing, but she had to free him from his boxers. Easier said than done because he was huge and hard.

And he wasn't helping.

It took her a moment to realize why that was. He was having his own battle with freeing a condom from his wallet. When he finally got it out, he tossed the wallet on the floor, and nearly pushed her off that crest again while he worked his hands between them to put on the condom. His fingers bumped and nudged until Millie wasn't sure she could take any more.

But Joe gave her more. Yep, he hoisted her up, hooking her legs around his waist, and he pushed all that huge hardness inside her. It was perfect. It was intense. It made her come. And come. And come.

With her body clamping around his erection, Millie clamped her teeth over her bottom lip to make sure she didn't blurt out "I love you" again. She didn't want to risk blurting out anything. Instead, she made all those incoherent sounds of someone who'd just gotten the best lay ever.

But apparently, Joe wasn't finished with her.

Somehow, he managed to slide his hand between them and touch her again. All without dropping her. Millie started to tell him that she wasn't a two-orgasm kind of woman, but he just kept at it. The kissing, the touching, the long hard strokes in and out of her, and she felt the tension start to build again. Not the bad kind of tension, either. This was the snowballing need to have him all over again.

Since Joe was already in place, already doing exactly what he needed to do, the "all over again" happened. Millie soared to the peak and shot straight up past it. Until the tension snapped and made her feel like the most pleasured woman in the history of pleasured women.

She was smiling, all slack and slow, when Joe made his own climb and peak. He pushed into her, released, and she felt his body shudder. He stayed pressed against her, his mouth on her cheek, his hands cupping her butt while he fought to catch his breath.

Just in case all the slack and slow made her mindless, Millie caught her bottom lip in her teeth again. Because silence was definitely the way to go here. And that's why it stunned her when Joe didn't take the silent route.

"Millie, I love you," he whispered.

JOE SAT AT his desk and stared out the window. Something he'd been doing a lot of today. Not only out the window. Just staring, period. And thinking.

He'd been doing plenty of that, too.

The night before he'd had sex with Millie, again, and while that was more than enough to add to the existing complications of messing around with her heart, he'd said words he'd had no intentions whatsoever of saying.

I love you.

Where the hell that'd come from, he didn't know. Which was why he was doing a lot of staring and thinking. It had shocked him to the bone. Had done a pretty good job shocking Millie, too. He'd seen her eyes go wide, and her mouth had dropped open. However, she'd recovered faster than he had and had given him an out.

It was post-orgasmic insanity, she'd claimed.

Something she had experienced when she'd blurted out the same to him. Millie had added that she knew it wasn't true. And she'd been right. It wasn't true, but that hadn't stopped Joe from dwelling on it all damn night and now into a good chunk of the day.

Forcing his mind back on anything but Millie, he signed the contract for the sale of some bulls to a cattle broker over in Spring Hill. Not the white calves. They were too young to be weaned, but when they were, he'd find another buyer, one not looking for solid breed stock as this broker was.

This was his business, Joe reminded himself, to raise and sell prime livestock. It was how he made a living, a decent one at that, but he always felt a little pang of loss when it came time to sell the heifers and bulls that he'd seen born. Hell, some that he'd given names. But with the new calves being born every week, the cycle would start all over again.

And yeah, he'd still give some of them names.

He put the contract in the large envelope and called out to Dara that he was heading to the post office. She was on the phone with Bella and probably still would be when he got back from his errand. Sometime soon, he'd need to sit down with her and have a chat, to find out just how attached she'd gotten to Millie. Then, he'd need to explain to her, well, he didn't know what to explain yet, but he couldn't continue to jack Millie's heart and body around like this.

Joe went to the post office and ignored the behind-the-hand whispers and judgmental looks. Or maybe he was projecting about the judgmental part, but he would bet the gossip was about Millie and him.

He walked out of the post office, intending to head straight back home, but he ended up driving past Once Upon a Time. He didn't see Millie, but she was probably in there since the shop wasn't due to close for another two hours. Joe had to admire that she was taking steps to move on with her life. The upstairs renovations, giving away her house, clearing out Royce's things.

Steps that he sure hadn't taken.

He'd visited Ella's grave and donated her clothes, but those were just dents in what needed to be done. He couldn't give away his house, but he could get moving on the plans for the new place he wanted to build. A place that'd be Dara's and his home. He could also toss the receipt that he'd spent way too much time dwelling over—especially now that Ella had almost certainly bought the test for Frankie. He could also pack up the rest of her stuff in his man-shed.

And that left the storage unit.

He hadn't gone back after he'd discovered it existed, but that was something he could get started on now. *Now* though took him a couple of minutes. Joe drove around some more, stalling under the guise of mulling over how and where to move the paintings. However, it didn't take him long to get fed up with his own wishy-washy mood, and he headed for the storage unit.

Like before, he used the code to go in, and a little part of him hoped that he had imagined all of this. But, no, the paintings were still there, including the one of Royce. He forced himself to go closer to it and study it with an eye that wasn't jaded because this might have been his wife's lover.

Excellent work, he decided.

Ella had managed to capture his golden-boy looks all wrapped up in a professional package. And speaking of packages, there was a thick envelope taped to the wall beside the portrait.

Hell, not another secret.

Groaning, he peeled it off, opened it and saw a contract. It was similar to the one he'd just signed for the sale of cattle, but he cut through the legalese to realize this was a contract Royce had initiated to commission Ella to paint a portrait of him that was to be hung in his law office.

Everything was spelled out. Size, payment and completion date. A date that was a week after Ella and Royce had died. Both Royce and Ella had signed it.

So, a secret but not a bad one. Ella hadn't painted her lover's portrait because of her feelings for him. It'd been a job. But that didn't mean the feelings hadn't also been there. Even so, this portrait belonged to Millie now, and he'd need to ask her what she wanted to do with it.

Tucking the contract under his arm, Joe glanced around at the other paintings. All landscapes, and they were connected. It was sort of a sweeping view of Parkman Pass, one of the prettier spots around Last Ride. It was a valley known for its wildflowers, ribboning streams and red oaks. Ella had captured a good quarter mile of the Pass with the "snapshot" paintings.

He spotted another envelope taped to the wall next to a painted meadow of bluebonnets. Another contract from the looks of it. So, maybe Royce had commissioned these, too. Joe opened it and read through more of the legalese.

Then stopped cold.

It was a contract all right but not with Royce. This was with an art gallery, Artista, in San Antonio. Joe had heard of the gallery. In fact, Ella had taken him there once after one of their Taco Cabana outings. He knew next to nothing about art, but there had been some nice paintings in it.

He continued reading and stopped cold again. This agreement was for Ella to provide fifteen to twenty paintings for an art exhibition. Unlike the contract with Royce, this one wasn't signed, but there was a note paper-clipped to the second page of the contract. It was Ella's handwriting and was on a grocery receipt.

"Check measurements for exhibit space."

Joe reread it, looked around at the paintings and let it

all sink in. These paintings were for an art exhibition. One that she was obviously still considering since she hadn't signed it. Or rather she hadn't signed the copy here in the storage unit. He looked at the bottom of the second page and spotted the signature block for Payton Kirk, owner, Artista Gallery. He or she hadn't signed, either, but the address and phone number were there so Joe took out his phone and made the call.

He figured he'd have to leave a message or go through an assistant, but the man who answered said, "Payton Kirk. How may I help you?"

It took Joe a moment to get his tongue untwisted and to gather his thoughts. "Uh, I'm Joe McCann. Ella McCann's husband," he added.

There was a beat of silence, followed by a heavy sigh. "Mr. McCann, I heard about your wife's death on the news. I'm so sorry for your loss."

The last part was something people said all the time to him, but it sounded genuine. "You knew Ella?" he asked.

Another beat of silence. "Yes. I found her paintings online. I contacted her and asked her if she had other paintings, that I was very interested in seeing them. She came to the gallery, showed me some examples of her other work, and I offered her an exhibition." He paused. "That's a huge deal for an artist, Mr. McCann."

Joe had already figured that out. "Did you tell Ella to keep all of this a secret while you were working out the details?"

"No. Actually, she was the one who wanted to keep it quiet. She wanted to wait until everything was all set up before she brought you and her daughter in for the big reveal."

Joe couldn't get any words to come out of his mouth. They were just stuck there in his throat. Oh, God.

Oh, God.

"Ella was very nervous about all of this," Payton went on. "She thought maybe the exhibition would fall through and she didn't want to get up your hopes. She swore me to secrecy, Mr. McCann." He paused again. "After I heard about her death, I figured there was no reason to tell anyone about it."

Joe cleared his throat. "Was she coming to the gallery the day she died?"

"I'm not sure, but it was possible. Her lawyer was revising the contract, and once they had worked out all the details, they were going to bring it in to me so we could sign it together. I'd told Ella I'd be in the gallery all that week, but we didn't have a set time for an appointment."

Suddenly, everything fell into place. "And her lawyer's name?" Joe asked.

"I've got that right here." There was the sound of clicks on a keyboard, and several moments later, Payton gave Joe the answer he already knew. "Ella's lawyer was Royce Dayton."

CHAPTER TWENTY-FOUR

MILLIE LOCKED UP the shop and started the walk to her house. She smiled when she thought of the renovation plans she was making. Smiled, too, at the thought that soon her commute to work would be very short indeed. It was only yards from her office and up the back stairs to the living quarters.

Her living quarters.

Yes, it was temporary, but the house she'd eventually buy would be hers, as well. She still hadn't shared that with Laurie Jean, but she just hadn't been in the mood for a big fight. Soon though, she'd have to spill and weather whatever hurricane her mother blew at her.

Speaking of weather, it felt like she stepped out into a sauna. A storm had rolled through a couple of hours earlier and had left everything feeling sticky and humid.

"Millie?" she heard Joe call out.

She whirled around to see him making his way toward her. During the whirling, she automatically tried to bolster herself in case he'd come to apologize to her, again, about the "I love you." Or maybe he'd come to make a clean break with her. If so, he was looking forward to it because he looked relieved. Or something. Millie couldn't quite suss out his expression.

"Is everything okay?" she asked.

He didn't answer, but he did take hold of her arm and

moved her off the sidewalk and under some trees. He glanced around as if to make sure no one was close enough to listen. No one was.

"I just came from the storage unit Ella had rented to store some paintings," Joe said. He moved his hands to her shoulders and looked her straight in the eyes. "A gallery owner in San Antonio wanted to do an exhibit with her art, and Royce drew up the contract for it. Ella asked the gallery owner to keep it hush-hush until it was a done deal so she could surprise Dara and me."

Since Royce had commissioned Ella to do a portrait, that didn't shock Millie. Nor did it shock her that Ella had wanted this to be a grand surprise.

Then, it sank in.

"That's why they were together in the car?" she murmured.

Joe nodded, and she got a glimmer of what his expression was all about. He was relieved. "I talked to the gallery owner, and he said Royce and Ella planned to bring in the contract and sign it there at the gallery."

Her breath rushed out in one long swoosh, and Millie was thankful Joe was still holding on to her because the bones vanished from her legs.

"That's why they were together in the car," she repeated, but this time it wasn't a question.

Trying to gulp in air, Millie managed to step back so she could lean against one of the trees. Had her heart stopped for a couple of seconds? It certainly felt like it. In fact, it felt as if everything had stopped except for the thoughts that were racing through her head.

That's why they were together in the car.

Joe didn't ask her if she was okay, probably because he'd had the same experience she was having when he'd first discovered the truth. He knew what she was feeling, and she knew why she'd seen the relief on his face. Relief mixed with so many other emotions. Those emotions came over her in thick, hot waves, and she finally just sank down onto the ground.

Joe sat, too, beside her. Not holding her. Not trying to reassure her. Probably because this still had to be sinking in for him, too.

The minutes crawled by as they sat there. Millie was aware of people walking past them on the sidewalk. Some were probably gawking, too, and wondering what the heck was going on. Thankfully though, none of them stopped to ask if she was okay. Good thing because Millie wasn't sure she knew the answer to that.

"There was nothing in Royce's files about doing the gallery contract for Ella?" Joe asked some long moments later.

Millie shook her head. "Nothing that I found, anyway, and if there'd been something about it at the law firm, Asher would have said. He would have gladly said," she amended. "Because it would have given Royce a legit reason to be with Ella."

Squeezing her eyes shut a moment, she forced herself to go back through her conversations with Royce. "Royce didn't mention anything about doing an art gallery contract. And Asher sometimes complained that Royce sometimes did work at home before bringing it into the office."

"Plus, this might have been something Royce was doing as a favor," Joe added. Of course, he'd given this some thought. "Royce obviously liked Ella's work because he commissioned her to do his portrait. In fact, they could have worked out a deal where his legal services covered some or all the cost of the portrait."

Yes. That was possible. A business arrangement, one that

the client had asked to keep quiet so she could surprise her husband and daughter.

That's why they were together in the car.

They hadn't been sneaking off to have sex and cheat on their spouses. And that slammed hard into Millie. He hadn't tossed his marriage vows out the window. He'd loved her, just as he'd said many, many times.

Tears stung her eyes, and she felt them spill down her cheeks. Joe didn't try to wipe them away and give her any "now, now" pats. He let her cry it out. No tears for him, but mercy, she could see this giving him some hard slams, too.

All those months of doubting their spouses, of feeling the betrayal and weathering the pain of that betrayal. All of that had been false. The relief came. Then, the guilt that she'd doubted him.

Then, the grief.

A fresh wave of it that fell over her like an avalanche.

Millie continued to sit there, continued to let the emotions bash and batter against her. There were more murmured voices on the sidewalk, and while she wanted to dismiss them, it wouldn't be long before someone called Laurie Jean and told her that Millie was sitting under some trees with Joe and that something had to be wrong because she was crying. No way could she deal with her mother right now, so Millie gathered up what composure she could.

"I need some time to think about this," she muttered. "God, Joe. I have to rethink the last two years."

She dried her eyes and dug out a tissue from her purse so she could blow her nose. With Joe's help, she got to her feet. She had no idea what to say to him or how to offer any comfort, so she just wrapped her arms around him and hugged him. He hugged her right back until Millie finally eased away from him.

"I'll walk you home," he insisted. "That way, maybe no one will stop you and try to talk. Then, once you're inside, you can have that time to think."

Millie nodded, understanding that he needed that time, as well. That "I love you" was no doubt weighing on him. Just as it was on her. In fact, everything seemed to be weighing on her at the moment.

"Does Dara know?" she asked when they reached her porch.

"Not yet. I needed to settle myself down first." He followed her up the steps. "But I'll tell her today."

"Good," she murmured as they walked. The girl would be overjoyed. Then again, Dara hadn't seemed to believe that her mom had cheated on her dad. Smart girl. Millie wished she'd hung on to that same faith.

Her hands were shaking when she grabbed her key, so Joe took it from her and unlocked the door.

"I'll wait to tell my parents until after Dara knows," Millie said. She opened the door but stood there while she finished. "Because once Laurie Jean gets hold of this, it won't take long for everyone in town to hear that Ella and Royce weren't lovers, that Royce was simply doing legal work for her."

The sound of someone gasping stopped Joe in mid-nod, and both Millie and he turned toward her foyer. In the same motion, Millie switched on the light.

Joe and she definitely weren't alone.

There were at least a dozen people crowded into the foyer, and more were peering out from the living room. She spotted her parents, Alma and her husband, Frankie, Tanner, Monte, Haylee and even Aunt Freida.

"Surprise!" Little T shouted through the stunned silence.

No. Not now. Millie couldn't handle this now.

"It's another birthday party," Little T informed her. "Can we have cake now?" he asked.

No one responded. Everyone just kept their eyes on Joe and her.

"It's true?" Laurie Jean finally said. "Royce and that McCann woman weren't lovers?"

Even with the grief, Millie felt the anger over her mother's tone. "*Ella* and Royce weren't lovers. Joe found proof that Royce was doing some legal work for her."

Laurie Jean stared at Millie for a moment and then started applauding. "I knew it. I just knew it." She hurried to Millie and spun her around in a happy twirl.

It was totally out of character for her usually dignified mother, but the glee caught fire, going through the party guests, and Millie was suddenly engulfed in hugs, more twirls and lots of gushing joy.

Joe didn't get left out, either. Frankie hurried to her brother to do the same celebration with him. So did Alma.

Aunt Freida tugged off her gloves while she waited her turn for a hug. "I'm so happy for you. When I planned this party for your birthday, I had no idea we'd have so much to celebrate. Wonderful news, just wonderful."

Everyone was talking at once, the words firing like buckshot in Millie's head. She was still shaking, too, and that's probably why she didn't put up an objection when Laurie Jean took hold of her and ushered her away from the other guests and into the living room.

"It's true," Laurie Jean repeated. She was smiling, really smiling, and she let go of Millie so she could fold her arms over her chest. "This changes everything. Everything. You won't have to donate the house. You can keep living here, and you won't have to live in those horrible little rooms over the shop."

That gave Millie a mental slap, one that allowed her to shut out everything else except what her mother was saying. And Laurie Jean just kept on *saying*.

"You should put your wedding rings back on," Laurie Jean went on, "and wear black at least for a few months. I know it's been two years, but this will restart the grieving cycle."

Unfortunately, that last part rang true-blue. But that was the only thing she was in complete agreement about.

"I don't want to live here," Millie stated. She didn't need a grief cycle to know that.

That wiped the glee out of Laurie Jean's eyes. She leveled her now firm gaze on Millie. "Your husband didn't cheat on you. He was a good man just as I always knew he was. You need to respect him by mourning his death."

Millie sighed. The timing sucked for this discussion, but she wanted to get some things straight. "I have and will mourn Royce's death. I just won't do it in this house or while wearing black or my wedding rings."

As Millie had expected, her mother's level gaze slid into the "that just pissed me off" realm. Then, Laurie Jean spewed out her favorite quote. "Making waves brings shame, and you're bringing nothing but shame to yourself and your family by running around with that Joe McCann. It doesn't matter that his wife wasn't a harlot and didn't throw herself at Royce, you shouldn't be disgracing Royce's good name by seeing that man."

That was not the right thing to say. Millie was certain her own gaze jumped straight into the seriously pissed-off realm. "I care very deeply for Joe. Very deeply. Hell, I think I could be in love with him. I'm sure as hell having sex with him." Millie didn't even try to lower the volume of her voice. "But you know what, Mom? It's none of your business."

Then, Millie said the word that had stunned the drawers off the members of the Last Ride Society. Only this time, she added a "you" to it.

Other than Laurie Jean's extremely loud gasp, everyone else hushed. Dead silence. But even in her fury, Millie glanced around to see if Little T had heard her f-you blast.

"Little T's in the kitchen looking at the cake," Tanner supplied as if he'd known exactly what her concern would be. He grinned, gave Millie a thumbs-up, and then hooked his arm around Frankie to give her a tongue kiss.

That caused Laurie Jean to bubble and stew, and she would have no doubt included Tanner on her next round of bashing. But Millie slung off the grip Laurie Jean had clamped on her arm, and she went out to look for Joe. If he was still around, he would have heard her confess that she might be in love with him, and she didn't want that particular weight on his shoulders now.

Not when he was grieving for Ella.

Millie was about to step onto the porch to see if Joe was there, but Skylar nearly knocked her down. The woman looked better, appearance-wise, than she had the last time Millie had seen her, but there was an "I'm riled" look in her eyes that would have paled Laurie Jean's.

"It's all here," Skylar exclaimed, holding up a tablet. Some smugness crept into her expression. "Come on, everyone. Have a look. Trust me, this is something you'll want to see." Pressing something on the tablet, she held it up like a prized trophy.

Millie couldn't imagine that there truly was something everyone wanted to see, but then she heard Laurie Jean gasp again. No gasp for her father, but the color drained from Asher's face.

"Come on, everybody," Skylar invited, "take a look at Laurie Jean playing sex games."

Millie stopped in her tracks, and it was a stunned Tanner who pulled her forward. There, on the tablet screen, was Laurie Jean, bare-assed naked except for some pasties that were even more noticeable because she was swinging her breasts around like a stripper.

"Stop it!" Laurie Jean yelled.

Her mother ran to Skylar and tried to rip the tablet from her hands. Considering though that Skylar had a good six inches on her, she failed. Laurie Jean flailed around, jumping to reach it all while the sex tease played out on the screen.

Laurie Jean wasn't alone, either.

Millie fastened her attention to the dark-haired man, who was wearing only boxers and sporting an erection. Judging from the angles of the footage, a camera had been positioned on the Victorian pleasure action saddle that had until only recently been in one of the storage rooms above the shop.

Millie's stomach bottomed out, and her gaze flew around the room to locate her father. Surely, he'd be devasted that his wife was about to jump in bed with another man.

Asher was there, his eyes frozen on the screen, and he cursed. However, Millie didn't hear the shock and anger she'd expected to hear. No, this was embarrassment.

"It's Dad," Tanner said, drawing Millie back to the screen. "It's Dad wearing a black wig."

Millie shook her head, trying to make sense of that. Trying to see. Hard to do though with her mother still jumping up to try to get the tablet.

"Yes, it's your dad," Skylar verified. Her smile was not nice. It was definitely a mean-girl smile. "They made a sex tape. Two old people screwing each other's brains out. Not very dignified for an almighty Parkman, is it, Laurie Jean?"

No, it wasn't. In fact, it had the biggest yuck factor possible. Not because of their age or because they were having sex but because they were her parents and had filmed this.

"Why?" Millie asked, volleying the question at both her mother and father.

"That's personal business!" Laurie Jean shouted, and she punched Skylar smack-dab in the face.

The punch wasn't even enough to snap back Skylar's head, but the woman's eyes narrowed to tiny slits. Skylar balled up her fist, no doubt to return the favor, and would have succeeded had Monte and Tanner not taken hold of her. Aunt Freida and Alma had to grab Laurie Jean, who was obviously ready to turn this into a brawl.

Frankie hurried off in the direction of the kitchen, muttering that she needed to make sure Little T didn't see or hear any of this. Since Millie wasn't sure she wanted to see or hear any of it, either, she nearly went with her. Instead, she reached over and hit the pause button on the video.

"Where did you get that?" Asher asked Skylar. Except it was a demand, not a mere question.

Skylar gave an indignant wobble of her head. "I found it, and don't think about trying to break my tablet. I've uploaded the video to YouTube. Soon, everyone will see it and know just what a sick bitch your wife is."

Millie rarely found herself on her mother's side, but she didn't think it would earn her the sick bitch label. Maybe the label of a horny wife playing sex games with her husband.

Which, of course, brought on more yuck and ick.

"Laurie Jean and I just wanted to spice up things," Asher

said, sounding unapologetic and somewhat reasonable. "There's no harm in that."

Well, no harm unless you didn't take steps to keep the recording private. "Did you use a digital camera?" Tanner asked, clearly picking up on what Millie was thinking. "Or that old camera that uses discs that can be uploaded to a computer?"

"The old camera," Asher supplied, his jaw tightening now.

"You bitch!" Laurie Jean shouted, pointing her finger at Skylar.

Several people were still having to hold her back, and she was kicking so hard that it caused her dress to fly up and expose her panties. Millie figured when her mother finally looked back on this that many things, including the panty shot, would embarrass her to the bone.

"You're the one blackmailing me," Laurie Jean added to the shout.

And that, too, would add to the embarrassment.

"Not me," Skylar insisted. "I wouldn't take one penny from you, you petty old hag."

Ignoring that insult and the one that Laurie Jean fired back at the woman, Millie turned back to Skylar. "You found the disc with the sex recording?"

Skylar was still sporting plenty of mad and indignation when she turned to Millie. "Not exactly. But I found the person who had it."

The woman was obviously picking and choosing her words. Probably because she didn't want to come right out and confess to hacking. But that's almost certainly what Skylar had done. She'd put her stellar computer skills to good use and found it.

"The person who had the disc was blackmailing Laurie

Jean," Millie pointed out—which was obviously news to plenty of the people in the room. "Where did you get it?"

Skylar just kept that smug expression. Until Tanner stepped in front of her. "Where did you get it?" he repeated.

Maybe it was the sight of Tanner, but something seemed to click inside Skylar. The realization of what she'd just done. Millie doubted Skylar regretted exposing Laurie Jean, but she probably hadn't intended to do that at Millie's surprise birthday party.

"I found the emails the blackmailer sent to your mother, and the recording was attached to one of them," Skylar answered in a whisper. Yeah, definitely a hack job. "I downloaded the video and then tracked the emails to the source."

"And the source would be?" Tanner pressed when Skylar didn't say anything else.

With her head dipping down, Skylar lifted her hand. "She's the one blackmailing your mother." And then Skylar pointed to the woman next to Laurie Jean.

Aunt Freida.

CHAPTER TWENTY-FIVE

SIPPING HIS BEER, Joe sat in the dark in his man-shed and didn't even pretend to himself that he wasn't brooding. He was doing exactly that and had been for the past two weeks. Since he'd learned that Ella hadn't cheated on him.

It'd been a crappy two weeks, filled with guilt, grief, regret. And a whole lot of cursing. His swear jar was spilling over, so Joe had just started tossing twenties at it. At the rate he was going, he'd need a swear vat before this was over.

If it was ever over, that is.

I'll have to rethink the last two years, Millie had said to him, and she was right. He'd had to rethink them, too. Every last day of them.

Millie was no doubt doing the same thing except she had a crapload of other stuff to deal with. Wanting to give her that rethinking time, Joe hadn't talked to Millie other than some short texts to ask her if she was okay.

Okay-ish, she'd texted back. You?

Okay-ish, he'd replied.

When she hadn't responded with anything else, Joe had figured she was neck-deep in dealing with the fallout from what had happened at her surprise birthday party. Fallout he'd heard plenty about because Frankie had seen fit to keep him informed.

Apparently, after Joe had slipped out from the party, Skylar had burst in and shown a sex tape. Of Laurie Jean and Asher. Joe truly wasn't sorry he'd missed that particular showing. Sorry though that he hadn't been there to give Millie support. If that was possible, that is. It was more likely that his being there wouldn't have helped one bit.

According to Frankie, things had gone from bad to worse after the sex tape. Skylar had skirted around how she'd gotten the recording, but the general consensus was that hacking had been involved. Hacking that had led to Freida being ID'd as the blackmailer. Freida had then confessed to finding the disc recording in Laurie Jean's driveway where the woman had likely dropped it. Freida had watched it and had been so appalled that Laurie Jean would do such things while bashing her kids for their sexual behavior. Freida had said she wanted to teach Laurie Jean a lesson.

Joe wasn't a Laurie Jean fan, but it was a hard lesson as far as he was concerned. Ditto for the public viewing of the recording. It had likely sent Laurie Jean into a downward spiral, one that had then sent the woman and her husband on an extended trip to an undisclosed location. They probably hoped while they were gone that everyone in Last Ride would develop amnesia. It wouldn't happen, of course, but folks would move on to other gossip. He was betting that Frankie and Tanner's reunion was already sparking some talk.

Probably talk about Millie and him, too.

But that would die down if people realized there was nothing new to add to the gossip mix. Two weeks was a long time to go without any new fuel. A long time, too, for him to not talk to Millie.

A couple of days after their "Okay" exchange, he'd texted Millie again with the question, Staying sane?

Her answer had been, More or less. How about you?

If he'd told her the truth, his response would have been

"mostly less," but he hadn't wanted to worry her. Definitely hadn't wanted her to think that he was sitting around brooding so he'd answered, Staying busy with the ranch.

At least it was the truth. Summer was always a busy time on the ranch what with hay that needed to be cut and cattle that had to be moved to other pastures to prevent overcrowding and overgrazing. Joe always hired several hands to help him with that, but he didn't mind doing a chunk of the work himself. Usually, the routine settled him.

But not this time.

Nothing about him was settled right now.

The door opened, the sunlight spearing into the shed. Joe had purposely left off the lights because it better suited his mood, but Dara turned them on now. She took one look at him, sighed and then dropped something into his lap. Something in a thick envelope.

"It's the research report Millie did on Mom," Dara explained. "It's due day after tomorrow before the next drawing, and she wanted to give me a chance to read it and make any changes before she turned it in."

Joe sat up straighter in the recliner. "Millie was here?" And damn it, his heart did a little leap over that.

But Dara dashed his excitement by shaking her head. "Monte dropped it off about two hours ago when you were out in the pasture checking on the new calves. I read it," she added. "It's really good. Millie used all the stories I gave her and then added quotes from the art gallery guy about how talented he thought Mom was."

"She was talented," Joe agreed.

Dara made a sound of agreement. "Anyway, Millie thinks I should be the one to give it to the Last Ride Society. I mean, after you read it. Is that okay?"

He wasn't sure if his okay would be for his reading it or

for her handing over the report. Joe just nodded to both. Dara made a sound as if she was pleased about that, and she glanced around at the paintings he'd moved from the storage unit. There were some in here, all wrapped up like the research project and some others were in the house.

"What should we do with all of Mom's paintings?" she asked. "Do you think we should try to get her that showing at the gallery in San Antonio?"

Joe was still considering that. Considering some other options, too. "Maybe we could set up a gallery for her here in Last Ride? I could use the money from my swear jar," he added in a mumble.

Dara chuckled and went over to try to stuff some of the loose bills into the jar. "We could use the house," she suggested. "You know, after you get the new, bigger one built. We're not that far out of town, and I think people would drive out here to see it. Plus, they'd get to see the murals, too."

That was an idea, one that he'd have to give some thought.

"If we lived in the new house," Dara went on, "it might not make Millie uncomfortable to visit you."

Frowning, he looked at her. "Huh?"

"You know, because it's a house that belonged to Mom and you," Dara added in a duh tone. "Millie might want to visit more if it was just my and your house."

He thought about Millie's and his sex agreement. That they wouldn't be together in places they'd shared with their spouses. That agreement seemed like a lifetime ago, but it could still apply if Millie and he were going to be together again.

"You like her a lot, don't you?" Dara pressed, not waiting for an answer. "And I know she likes you a lot."

"It's complicated," he settled for saying.

She made a sound of agreement. "Because you're both happy that Mom and her husband didn't cheat. But you're both kind of sad, too. It probably wouldn't be easy to get past the happy or the sad even if you really like each other."

"No, it wouldn't be easy," he mumbled.

"But, hey, it's doable," Dara concluded in her perkiest perky voice. She dropped a kiss on his cheek. "Read the last line of the report," she whispered before she walked out.

Joe wasn't sure he wanted to read any of the lines. His mood was already low enough, but he set aside his beer and took out the report. It was a lot longer than he'd expected, close to a hundred pages, and he skimmed through the stories that Dara had given Millie. Accounts of how Ella and he had fallen in love. Their first date. Their wedding.

Dara hadn't left out much and had even given Millie some pictures that she'd included. Happy photos of happy times. Millie had added other accounts as well from interviews with the locals who'd known Ella. There was one from the kindergarten teacher praising Ella for the mural of cartoon characters she'd painted in the classroom. As Dara had said, Millie had talked with the gallery owner who had high praise indeed for the paintings he'd planned to exhibit.

Joe kept skimming, kept turning pages until he made it to the last one. There was a picture here, too. Not of Ella's tombstone as he'd expected. No. This was a casual family shot taken by the photographer of the town's newspaper at the Fourth of July picnic. Dara had been about eight, and the three of them were sitting on a blanket, looking up at a sky filled with fireworks. Well, Dara was looking up, anyway, but Ella and he were smiling at each other.

There was no mistaking the happiness on their faces. The love. The family. No mistaking at all.

Joe forced his attention to the bottom of the page. To the last line that Millie had written.

"A gifted artist who was loved and will always be loved by her husband and daughter, Ella McCann's memory will live on."

Joe sat there, rereading it, and he let the grief—and the happy memories—wash over him.

As IF THE bouquet were fragile and might break in her hand, Millie lay the yellow roses on Royce's grave. A first for her. She had avoided this place like the plague when she'd thought Royce had died with his lover. But now that she knew it wasn't true, it had been somewhat easy for her to come.

Somewhat.

There was sadness in place of the hurt and anger, and she wasn't sure that would go away. Still, it was something she could live with. And that was the key word. She needed to *live*. That started with making her peace with Royce.

"Sorry that I thought you were a lying, cheating scum-bag," she muttered. She'd hoped her light tone would lighten her heart.

It didn't.

"So, it turns out you were the great guy that I and every-one always knew you were all along." She paused, sank down to sit beside the tombstone. "But it turns out, I'm not the woman you married."

She stopped, gathered her breath and gave the roses an adjustment they in no way needed.

"Let's not even get into the 'I never had an orgasm with you' thing," Millie continued a moment later, "but you should know that I wasn't over-the-moon happy in our mar-riage. I was Millie Vanilla at my most vanilla. That wasn't fair to either of us. You should have had a wife who thought you were her moon and stars."

She didn't get a cosmic signal that Royce had heard that, or that he agreed or disagreed, but she just kept on talking.

"I didn't look at you the way Ella looked at Joe in that fireworks picture I put in the report," she told Royce. "I didn't look at you the way I look at him." The tears burned her eyes and fell like rain. "And I'm sorry about that. Sorry that I couldn't feel for you what I feel for him."

And wasn't that a confession to make to a dead husband? Millie figured she deserved a lightning strike or two for that.

"I've been crying a lot lately. Thinking a lot lately, too. Life's kind of messed up what with Mom and Dad's sex-tape scandal. Wonder how you would have handled that? Probably with the voice of calm and reason," Millie added, swiping at the tears. "Me, personally, I'm going to handle it by trying not to cringe whenever I remember the bits of the tape I saw. And by not throwing it in Mom's face whenever she rags on me."

She fully expected said ragging to start as soon as Asher and she had returned from their "walk of shame" trip. Laurie Jean would bounce back from this, and Asher would carry on as if he and his wife of nearly four decades didn't have the extreme hots for each other. Hots that Millie definitely hadn't had with Royce, but with Joe, well, a lot of things had been different for her with Joe.

"I'll endure some of Mom's ire and will push back on the rest. What I won't do is budge on donating the house, and I won't put my wedding rings back on or wear widow's black. Oh, and I'm not stopping the reno on my new living quarters above the shop."

Millie stopped. Smiled a little.

When she spelled it out like that, she realized she wasn't budging on anything important. Well, anything important that she could control. She couldn't control what Joe felt for her, and it might take him a lot more than two weeks to decide if he wanted to see her again.

In fact, he might never decide that.

That dismal thought caused her smile to fade, and Millie stood, touching her lips to the top of Royce's tombstone. "Have a good afterlife, Royce," she whispered. "Maybe I couldn't give you the moon and the stars, but I did love you."

She lingered a few more moments, gathering herself and wondering if she truly felt better or if she was on the verge of heatstroke. The sun was setting, but it was still sweltering.

Wiping the perspiration and the rest of the tears off her face, she went to her car, got in and cranked up the AC. She was still gathering herself when her phone dinged with a text. She could have sworn every part of her body did a little dance when she saw it was from Joe.

She expected it to be another short text to ask her how she was doing. But it wasn't. "Meet me at the drive-in?" she read aloud.

For two weeks, she'd felt as if someone had squeezed a fist around her heart, but just seeing the message caused some of that tightness to ease up.

Be there soon, Millie texted back though her hands were trembling so it took her a couple of tries to get the reply right. She hit Send and drove away from the cemetery— fast. Millie considered if she should feel guilty about racing from her late husband's grave to see a man who'd become her lover.

No guilt. All right, maybe some, but it wasn't as much

guilt as it was regret that she hadn't given Royce the one hundred percent that she wanted to give Joe. The problem was, Joe might not want that percentage. In fact, this meeting might be so he could make a clean break with her.

That caused her to slow down.

Unlike her, Joe had given his all to Ella. And vice versa. He might not ever be able to dole that much of himself out to another woman. Even if he did, that woman might not be her.

Millie was driving at a crawl by the time she reached the drive-in. The sun had already set, but she could see the interior light on in Joe's truck. She kept up the crawling pace to reach it, and she parked beside it. Gathering her breath, she got out and threw open the passenger's side door of the truck.

She'd already opened her mouth to say she was sorry, an apology that would include a multitude of things, but the words died in her mouth when she saw the interior. Joe was behind the wheel, and on the console between the seats was a tray with a platter of O'Riley's nachos, a Coke, a root beer float and a candle. The light from it flickered from the evening breeze she was letting in.

Millie looked over the candlelight to meet Joe's eyes. Oh, my. Those eyes would always slug her with some lust. Ditto for his face. And pretty much the rest of him, too.

He didn't smile at her. In fact, he kept his face blank. "I thought we could try a date, but I wasn't sure if you'd go for one in public."

No way could she keep her own face blank after that. Millie smiled. "I'd go on a date with you anywhere, anytime." She climbed into the truck seat, leaned over the tray and brushed her mouth to his.

His expression stayed mostly blank. Mostly. Definitely no smile. "I wanted to give you time to grieve for Royce."

She nodded. "I just had a talk with Royce, and I worked out everything with him." Millie paused. "I wanted to give you time to grieve Ella."

"I worked out everything with Ella, too. Thank you," he added, "for what you said about her in the research report."

Millie gave another nod, and the silence stretched out between them. Not a bad silence but one where their gazes stayed connected. Finally, Joe reached under the seat and took out a tablet.

"I figured since we're at the drive-in, we should watch a movie with our dinner date," he said.

Millie definitely didn't nod that time, and she was reasonably sure some horror crept into her eyes. "Please tell me that's not Laurie Jean and Asher's sex tape."

He laughed, and she hadn't known how much she wanted that laugh until she heard it. "Uh, no. But you might not approve of my viewing choice."

Joe set the tablet on the dash, turned it on, and the opening scene from *Jaws* started. Now Millie laughed, and she was still in mid-chuckle when Joe slid his hand around the back of her neck, pulled her closer and kissed her.

This wasn't a mere brushing of lips. Nope. It was the real deal. French, long and hot. When he pulled back, he met her eyes again.

"We can eat, watch the movie or have sex," he said. Millie was about to blurt out she wanted door number three, but Joe kept on talking. "Or I can tell you—without any post-sex haze interfering—that I've fallen in love with you."

That robbed her of her breath. "The last option," she managed. "I want to hear that part."

He kissed her again and murmured the words against her mouth. "I've fallen in love with you, Millie."

Her breath returned with a vengeance. One huge gust of air into her lungs, followed by an even larger gust of happiness. It filled her from head to toe.

"Good," she said. "Because I'm in love with you, too." She caught on to fistfuls of his hair and yanked him back for another kiss.

She felt him smiling against her mouth. Then, they were both laughing. *Giddy* was the right word. They were giddy and squishing the food, but she was positive neither of them cared about that.

However, Joe must have been concerned that they might catch themselves on fire, literally, because he blew out the candle. He also shoved the tray onto the back ledge of the seat and turned so he could haul Millie into his lap. She had already started in that direction so it didn't take much of an effort.

"I love you," she said, wanting to hear the words again.

Joe gave them right back to her with his own murmured, "I love you."

That spurred another round of scalding hot kisses. Then again, it was never less than scalding when Joe and she kissed.

"I want more," he insisted, but he held her off when she started to peel off his shirt. "I want to stop sneaking around to see you. I want us to go on dates. I want us to have sex, often, both in and out of bed."

She grinned. "I don't object to a single bit of that. Dates. Sex. Beds. Porn, optional."

With the scene from *Jaws* playing out from the dash, Joe kept his eyes on Millie. Just her. And she kept her eyes on him. Just Joe.

"I can promise you a lot more than this moment," he said. "More than tomorrow. More than a week."

Millie wanted to both smile and cry a whole bunch of happy tears, but she decided to save the tears for later. For now, she wanted to kiss her man and get something straight.

"I want more than a week, too," she assured him. "More than a month," she added.

Smiling, he moved in for another scorching round with his mouth. "I can do better than that. How about I promise you forever?"

Oh, the blasted happy tears came, anyway, blending with the smile and even a very giddy giggle. Millie tightened the grip she had on his hair and pulled him to her.

"Joe Cooper McCann, I'll take forever with you any day."

* * * * *

Look for the next book in USA TODAY
bestselling author Delores Fossen's
Last Ride, Texas series when
Christmas at Colts Creek *goes on sale*
in November 2021, only from HQN Books!

"The crime scene unit is out at your house," Daniel went on after glancing through his texts. "They've found two sets of footprints outside your office window. There are some drag marks, too. So maybe the guy had drugged Mandy before he got there, revived her enough so she could walk at least part of the way and then gave her a second dose of the drug once he got her inside."

Of course, the killer could have incapacitated the woman in other ways, smothering or a blow to the head, but it didn't really matter. He'd gotten Mandy into Kara's house, murdered her and staged the body. Maybe as a threat to Kara to tell her to back off her investigation into the missing and dead surrogates, maybe just to torment her.

The tormenting was definitely working.

She shook her head. "I didn't hear anything to let me know someone was in my house."

At the moment, he considered that a good thing. "If you had, you might have gone inside to check things out and been killed."

Daniel hoped that was a warning she'd take to heart. He didn't want Kara setting up any more traps for this snake. She certainly didn't jump to defend what she'd done. Nope. Her emotions went in the other direction. Her eyes filled with tears.

"Oh, God. Daniel, I'm so sorry."

Hell. He'd hoped she would be able to keep the aftermath of all of this at bay. Apparently not. Those tears didn't spill down her cheeks, but she was blinking hard to keep them from falling.

Daniel figured this was a mistake the size of Texas, but he went to her and pulled her into his arms. Kara practically sagged against him, her head landing on his shoulder. He didn't want to notice how well she fit. Didn't want to notice her scent, which he immediately took in. Or the soft, breathy sigh she made.

But he noticed.

Don't miss
Safeguarding the Surrogate *by Delores Fossen,*
available July 2021 wherever
Harlequin Intrigue books and ebooks are sold.

Harlequin.com

Get 4 FREE REWARDS!

We'll send you 2 FREE Books plus 2 FREE Mystery Gifts.

FREE Value Over $20

Both the **Romance** and **Suspense** collections feature compelling novels written by many of today's bestselling authors.